THE [...] Ravens Space
Marine[...] with a barbaric
ork invas[...] close and bloody, and
orks never [...] om a fight.

However, [...] Blood Ravens Brother-Captain
Gabriel Angelos prepares to throw his men forward in a last ditch defence of Tartarus, the
mysterious eldar and the traitorous legions of
Chaos are observed in the thick of battle. Angelos
must guide his brother Marines through a web of
deceit, intrigue and secrets that could threaten the
entire Blood Ravens Chapter.

*Pulse-pounding action and adventure, based on the
smash hit game from THQ, this is destruction on a
planetary scale!*

More Warhammer 40,000 from the Black Library

THE GAUNT'S GHOSTS SERIES
by Dan Abnett

The Founding
FIRST AND ONLY
GHOSTMAKER
NECROPOLIS

The Saint
HONOUR GUARD
THE GUNS OF TANITH
STRAIGHT SILVER
SABBAT MARTYR

The Lost
TRAITOR GENERAL

THE SPACE WOLF SERIES
by William King

SPACE WOLF
RAGNAR'S CLAW
GREY HUNTER
WOLFBLADE

A WARHAMMER 40,000 NOVEL

DAWN OF WAR

C S Goto

For Katrn – evil is always worse in real life

Original story by: Lucien Soulban, Jay Wilson,
Raphael van Lierop, Josh Mosquiera.

A BLACK LIBRARY PUBLICATION

First published in Great Britain in 2004 by
BL Publishing,
Games Workshop Ltd.,
Willow Road, Nottingham, NG7 2WS, UK.

10 9 8 7 6 5 4 3 2 1

Cover illustration by Creative Domain.

With thanks to Relic.

A CIP record for this book is available from the British Library.

ISBN 1-84416-152-8

Distributed in the US by Simon & Schuster
1230 Avenue of the Americas, New York, NY 10020, US.

Printed and bound in Great Britain by
Bookmarque, Surrey, UK.

See the Black Library on the Internet at
www.blacklibrary.com

Find out more about Games Workshop
and the world of Warhammer 40,000 at
www.games-workshop.com

It is the 41st millennium. For more than a hundred centuries the Emperor has sat immobile on the Golden Throne of Earth. He is the master of mankind by the will of the gods, and master of a million worlds by the might of his inexhaustible armies. He is a rotting carcass writhing invisibly with power from the Dark Age of Technology. He is the Carrion Lord of the Imperium for whom a thousand souls are sacrificed every day, so that he may never truly die.

Yet even in his deathless state, the Emperor continues his eternal vigilance. Mighty battlefleets cross the daemon-infested miasma of the warp, the only route between distant stars, their way lit by the Astronomican, the psychic manifestation of the Emperor's will. Vast armies give battle in his name on uncounted worlds. Greatest amongst his soldiers are the Adeptus Astartes, the Space Marines, bio-engineered super-warriors. Their comrades in arms are legion: the Imperial Guard and countless planetary defence forces, the ever-vigilant Inquisition and the tech-priests of the Adeptus Mechanicus to name only a few. But for all their multitudes, they are barely enough to hold off the ever-present threat from aliens, heretics, mutants – and worse.

To be a man in such times is to be one amongst untold billions. It is to live in the cruellest and most bloody regime imaginable. These are the tales of those times. Forget the power of technology and science, for so much has been forgotten, never to be re-learned. Forget the promise of progress and understanding, for in the grim dark future there is only war. There is no peace amongst the stars, only an eternity of carnage and slaughter, and the laughter of thirsting gods.

PROLOGUE

Tartarus: 999.M38

SHEETS OF WARP energy cracked through the night, bathing the mountain top in dark, purpling light. Clouds roiled and rolled across the sky, spiralling around the peak as though being drawn into an immense tornado. Lightning flashed through the barrage of rain, silhouetting monstrous forms against the heavens. The discharge of force weapons crackled brightly, sending sparks of blue spraying through the rain. In the strobes of visibility, blades shimmered and combat was joined in an odd, staccato rhythm.

The sky was weeping with energy, spilling oceans of unearthly fluid from one dimension into another, ripping the fabric of the atmosphere into serrations through which the immaterium could drip, ooze, and flow. The unclean energies sizzled and hissed as they broke through into the air, as though celebrating their liberty. Unaccustomed to the viscosity of air and the strictures of gravity, the sickly flows congealed quickly into pods and droplets, falling from the sky like mutant rain, lashing into the mountain top with toxic ferocity.

Macha stood on the second summit of the mountain, just lower than the main peak. Her arms were outstretched, as though trying to embrace the rage of the storm, her head held high, her eyes closed delicately in concentration. The wind whipped her long hair into a torrent behind her and, in the sudden flashes of lightning, she was deathly beautiful. Power radiated from her body, glowing with a faint blue like a holy aura. The intensity grew, focussed on a point just in front of her chest, where the light condensed into a brilliant ball of blue fire.

With a sudden flick, Macha's eyes were open and the ball of energy erupted into life, blasting through the air towards the eye of the storm. The light hissed and crackled as it scorched through the hellish rain, before it was finally swallowed whole by the spiralling clouds. It was gone. Vanished. And, for a moment, it seemed that it was lost.

A tremendous explosion shook the mountain top, sending avalanches of rock and slides of blood-drenched earth cascading down its crumbling sides. The sky was lit with blast-rings of blue fire, rippling out from the eye of the storm and incinerating the droplets of warp rain, which sparked with moments of death in the concentric bands of flame.

In the sudden flood of light, Macha could see the scene around her and she shivered. Looking back towards the base of the mountain, there was a bed of corpses, like rocks in the river of bloody soil that gushed down towards the valley. Some of her eldar warriors were still on their feet, battling desperately against foes that seemed to flicker in and out of existence. Towards the peak of the mountain were even more corpses, piles of them where entire squads had been annihilated with single blasts from the daemon. But there was Macha's avatar, towering over his brethren and locked in combat with the daemon on the crest of the mountain. His ancient weapon, the Wailing Doom, flashed in his hands with incredible speed, smashing great chunks out of the daemon's form while the rest of the dwindling eldar forces struggled to keep the daemon host at bay.

Then the light died and the scene was plunged into darkness once again.

Something shifted in her mind, and the eldar farseer strained her eyes into the night, struggling to fit images to the gyring confusion of thoughts that jostled for her attention. There was something else out there on the mountain, something moving with a hidden purpose. Macha could see flickering pictures in her head, a collage of past, present and future all blurred into one curdling image-pool. There were dark figures in those pictures – giant, pseudo-human warriors – and her heart shuddered each time her thoughts lingered on them. These clumsy humans were more fearsome than any daemon, in their own way, and Macha's soul was filled with dread by their sudden addition to the mix.

She could feel their presence on the mountain, but there was no sign of them. Even her perfect eldar eyes could not pierce the enveloping shroud of warp energy and driving darkness, and the constant discharge of weapons riddled the mountainside with squirming shadows and pushed the unknown deeper into invisibility.

Kaerial, we are not alone on this planet. Look to the blind-side of the ascent. Macha's thoughts wove their way through the tortuous eddies of psychic energy that swirled around the mountain, and she guided them home – into the soul of Kaerial, the wraith-guard commander who was holding the rear line of defences at the bottom of the slope.

Understood, farseer, came the simple reply, and the wraithguard loped off in search of prey. Towering over the battlefield in their psycho-plastic armour, the wraithguard were un-living warriors: artificial constructs housing the spirit stone of once mighty eldar warriors, giving their eternal souls the chance to wreak vengeance on those who slew them.

THE SHAFT OF las-fire lanced through the air and Jaerielle slid to his knees just in time, skidding a trough into the blood-slicked earth as the blast seared over his head. Without a moment of hesitation, he clicked the trigger of his shuriken catapult, loosing a hail of tiny projectiles into the bank of advancing Chaos cultists, felling four or five at once. As he sprang back to his feet, the rest of the Guardian Storm squad were already around him, braced into firing positions to protect their commander.

But the cultists kept coming, undaunted by the efficiency of the eldar defence, pressing on with sheer weight of numbers, even as hundreds fell and were trampled under foot. Their weapons were crude and increasingly scarce, but a spear will kill as well as a lasgun from close range, and the cultists were closing in on the eldar from all sides. The intervening air was alive with shuriken, flicking and flashing through the night with unerring precision, each one burying its monomolecular shock deep into the mutated flesh of the advancing hordes. Line upon line of cultists fell, but the crowd was edging gradually closer.

Jaerielle checked behind him. Nothing had yet breached his defensive line, and the farseer stood on the crest of the rise behind them, haloed in a glorious phosphorescence, untouched by the dirty business of close-range combat. Sizzling jets of blue flame burst from her body at regular intervals, plunging into the eye of the storm that raged above them. She needed more time to seal the tear in the immaterium, and the Storm squad would make sure that she got it. And beyond her, on the very summit of the mountain, Jaerielle could see the avatar of Biel-Tan locked into combat with the daemon prince; lightning and warp-tears flashed around the two figures, framing their magnificence for all the world to see. As he watched, a fire grew in the soul of Jaerielle and a thirst for blood doused his thoughts.

Snapping his head back round to the advancing cultists, Jaerielle licked his lips and leapt forward into the fray.

'For Khaine, the Bloody-Handed God!' he cried as he drew his long power sword and pushed its impossibly sharp blade through the abdomens of three humanoid cultists.

The call was returned by the rest of the Storm squad, but it was no dissonant cacophony of battle-cries. The

Guardian eldar summoned their call from the depths of their souls, chanting it out in tones both too high and too low for human ears to make out. In an exquisite and rumbling harmony, the name of their god of war flooded out across the battlefield, energising each of the eldar warriors who heard it, rallying them into a renewed quest: blood for the blood god. Soon, the call was reverberating around the whole mountain, pulsing through the rock itself, making the earth move with its sonorous power. On the peak of the mountain, acting like a conduit for the chants of the Biel-Tan eldar, Khaine's avatar threw back its head and let out a scream of power, repulsing the warp clouds above it as though they were feathers in the wind, staggering the daemon prince in a moment of awe. The name was thrown up to the shrouded stars: *'Kaela Mensha Khaine!'*

And the eldar god smiled back at his precious children.

The power sword swung and arced with grace and accuracy, defining a spiral of death around the spinning and dancing figure of Jaerielle. He had discarded his shuriken weapon and now clutched his blade in both hands as he flittered his way through the crowd of Chaos cultists, separating limbs from bodies as though it were an art. From around the perimeter of his elongated helmet spat tiny toxic shards, peppering the faces and necks of cultists who strayed too close, melting them from within – the mandiblaster helmet, still edged in a deep red, was all that Jaerielle had kept from his time as an Aspect Warrior of the Striking Scorpions, but he was glad of it now.

All of the Guardians of the Storm squad had served their warrior cycle in one of the close combat temples, making them perfectly suited for this kind of battle. Jaerielle could see his sister, Skrekrea, slipping elegantly through the forest of primitive blades and random smatterings of fire, dispatching cultists with splendorous ease. She had been a Howling Banshee once, and her elaborate mask was still fitted with the sonic amplifiers employed by Aspect Warriors of that temple. The terrible, shrill howl, from which the aspect drew its name, was beginning to rise in volume, emanating from the lithe form of Skrekrea as she swooped and lashed with her sword. The cultists nearest to her were beginning to feel the effects of the sound: their movements were slowing into confusion. Some had already come to a halt, shaking their heads in pathetic attempts to rid their ears of the invasive noise.

Suddenly, Skrekrea spun to a halt, raising her sword before her face, pointing into the stars. The screech from her helmet reached its crescendo and all around her the cultists fell to the ground clutching at their heads, blood coursing from their ears and oozing over their desperate fingers.

Jaerielle did not even pause to watch the impressive sight – he had seen Skrekrea in battle hundreds of times before and well knew what she was capable of. In truth, she was not an exceptional warrior. Frqual was a different story. A former Fire Dragon, he was a blur of motion, spilling great jets of fire from his flamer and incinerating swathes of cultists with rapid bursts from his fusion gun. Melta bombs sprayed out from unseen holsters around his legs, scattering into the oncoming horde and blasting great craters out of the mountain itself.

Frqual was an eldar Guardian on the edge. He lived to fight and relished the blood that soaked his long memory. He teetered on the edge of damnation, constantly questing for battles and contests. Jaerielle was sure that he would become an exarch one day, completely lost to himself but honed as the perfect embodiment of eldar warcraft. In general, the eldar could not afford such recklessness – they were once the dominant force in the galaxy, but now they were a dwindling race. They had to pick their battles carefully.

Tartarus was not a battle that they could avoid – the farseer had been preparing for it for centuries. The ancient tomes in the Black Library told of the return of the daemon prince, and it fell to the eldar to vanquish him every three thousand years. They could trust nobody else with this task, especially not the short-sighted humans who had bungled into space so very recently.

A spear thrust straight at Jaerielle's stomach, and he rolled easily outside it, drawing his own blade almost casually back along its path, slicing the cultist neatly in two at the waist. These humans are quite pathetic, thought Jaerielle, as he thwarted their futile attacks as though they were in slow motion. Their minds are weak, he added in a haughty internal narrative, for they have fallen to the paltry temptations of this daemon prince. And their bodies are weaker, he noted as another head was parted from its shoulders. The comparison with his Storm squad spoke for itself. Humans – if only there weren't so many of them.

* * *

'HOLD,' WHISPERED TRYTHOS, as he held up a giant, armoured fist, signalling to his kill team in case the vox beads in their helmets had failed. 'There is movement ahead.' He pointed sharply at two of the massive Space Marines, enshrined in ancient black power armour, indicating that they should go on ahead to scout. The auto-reactive shoulder plates of the Space Marines glinted against the distant lightning, and the insignia of the Undying Emperor shimmered in the darkness.

'You'd better be right about this, inquisitor. This planet is crawling with filthy xenos creatures, and the forces of Chaos are strong here. The local population have lost their minds to this daemon–'

'–not to mention their souls, captain,' interrupted Inquisitor Jhordine as a noise behind them made her turn. 'I *am* right about this, captain, as we are about to see.' The inquisitor was dwarfed by the huge Space Marine, who stood over two metres in height, and she did not wear the impressive power armour of the Space Marines, but the Deathwatch kill team were the militant arm of the Ordo Xenos, the branch of the Imperial Inquisition charged with combating the alien, and her authority over these Marines was unquestioned.

A stutter of fire erupted from behind the team, further down the slope towards the valley floor. Out of the mists and the darkness emerged a group of loping figures. Tall and slender, with massively elongated heads, they appeared to have no faces, but bright jewels inset into their armoured forms seemed to glow with life. Taking giant strides in smooth, soundless movements, they were rapidly closing the gap between them and the Space Marines.

'Eldar wraithguard!' called Trythos, turning to face the new threat as his team brought their weapons to bear in instantaneous reflex.

A volley of bolter fire punched out of the line of Deathwatch Space Marines, smashing into the advancing line of wraithguard. Great chunks of psycho-plastic splintered away into the darkness, but the strange creatures just kept coming, as though they couldn't feel the impacts. Their weapons flared with life, returning fire with a hail of projectiles that hissed smoothly through the air, ricocheting off the power amour of the Marines.

'Go for the jewels,' called Jhordine, drawing her own plasma gun and taking aim. 'The jewels are their heart stones.'

The inquisitor squeezed off a pulse of plasma that burst against the glowing gem stone on the chest of the leading wraithguard. The creature stopped short and a keening cry erupted from its mouthless head, before it suddenly broke into a run, spraying projectiles from its weapon as it charged towards the team.

Trythos matched the giant creature stride for stride, pounding out into the space that separated the two groups and intercepting the charge. As he ran, Trythos swung his power axe above his head, circling it in crescents of coruscating power. From behind him came the chatter of bolter fire and shells flashed past his head, peppering the charging wraithguard with impacts.

Then they were upon each other, but the wraithguard was not equipped for combat at this range. It was an uneven match. Trythos turned his charge into a dive, swinging his axe into an arc as he cleared the last few metres that separated him from the creature. The wraithguard tried to turn the Deathwatch captain aside with his long elegant limbs, but Trythos smashed through them with the servo-assisted power of his armour, shattering the psycho-plastics like wax, driving his power axe towards the gem stone on the wraithguard's chest.

The axe cracked into the jewel with a metallic ring that echoed with an incredible volume. The force weapon sputtered and sparked with power as the pressure against the gem increased, but the stone would not break. Trythos drove the head of the axe forward with all of his strength until a huge explosion threw him back from the shattered wraithguard.

As he hit the ground, Trythos saw another blast of energy smash into his kill team, this time coming from further up the mountain. His squad had split, with half of it continuing the assault against the wraithguard, and the other half turning to face the new threat.

A heavy foot crunched into the ground next to his head, bringing Trythos back to the present with a start. He rolled to his feet and shouldered the shaft of his axe, preparing for a strike against another of the wraithguard. But something was wrong – the shaft was light and unbalanced. The axe head was ruined and broken, shattered and rent by the force of the impact against the eldar stone. A burst of bolter fire from his battle-brothers gave him a split second of cover; he snatched his boltgun from its holster and loosed a tirade of shells against the wraithguard as they closed around him.

* * *

THE AVATAR SWEPT his immense sword with incredible ferocity, hacking it into the gradually solidifying form of the daemon prince, who winced slightly under the impact. The sword seemed to hum and glow with a life of its own, crying out for blood, wailing with doom. Its impacts resounded simultaneously in multiple dimensions, slicing into the substance of the prince on both sides of the breach in the immaterium.

The daemon roared in frustration as the rivers of blood cascaded freely down the mountainside. It was being violated even as it was being born into the material world, but the avatar was relentless in its assault. The daemon's cultists rushed at the towering Avatar of Khaine, but the ancient warrior hardly even noticed them, swatting them away in droves with the back swing of his blade or treading them into the ground under his feet.

The storm was spiralling in and out of the material realm, sucked into focus by the ungodly presence of the daemon prince. The clouds of warp energy just poured into the daemon's growing form, filling it with power and chaos. The prince lashed out in frustration, raking claws and talons across the body of the avatar, ripping into the warrior's metallic skin and sending spurts of molten blood jetting into the night. The avatar screamed his defiance to the gods, stepping inside the wildly flailing limbs of the daemon and driving his sword home where the monstrosity's heart should be.

Standing on the lower summit, her arms outstretched and open to heaven, Macha unleashed another blast of blue fire into the storm, desperate to seal the breach before the daemon could fully materialise. If the prince were permitted to take solid form, not even the Avatar of Khaine would be able to confront it.

Something clawed at her mind, breaking her concentration for a fraction of a second. For a moment she thought that the daemon was whispering into her soul, trying to lure her away from her purpose, but the voice was too weak, plaintive, and familiar. It was weeping into her thoughts and tears started to roll down her face as she realised what it was. Kaerial was gone. His spirit stone, which had been housed in wraithbone armour for centuries after his physical death, permitting the great warrior to go on living for the sake of the Biel-Tan eldar, had been destroyed. His death knell rang through the warp like a beacon of lost hope.

The farseer's pain was transformed into anger almost immediately, and she focussed her rage into a searing ball of energy that rocketed up towards the main summit of the mountain as she screamed her fury into the darkness. This time it smashed directly into the form of the daemon itself, sending it staggering back towards the precipice at the edge of the peak, pursued at each step by the frenzy of the avatar's wailing blade.

Tendrils of energy darted out of the daemon's limbs, questing for purchase to prevent its fall from the summit, from the epicentre of the warp storm that fed its manifestation. They lashed and whipped around the mountain top, vaporising clutches of cultists and lapping at the warp-shields that burned around a group of eldar warlocks, who returned fire with jabs of their own lightning,

riddling the daemonic form with javelins of blue
flame.

Macha smiled to herself: this was it. She threw
back her head and screamed into the sky, chan-
nelling the energies of her gods into her chest for a
final killing blow. The coruscating ball of energy
pulsed in the air before her, eager to be loosed
against the forces of damnation.

Then a blast of las-fire punched into the back of
Macha's shoulder, pushing her forward, stumbling
to regain her balance. The ball of flame hissed and
then blinked into nothingness, as Macha turned to
locate the origins of the blast.

A group of Chaos cultists had burst through the
defensive line of the Storm squad. The grossly
mutated humans bore Chaos brands on their skin,
which seemed to be the wrong size for their bones.
Two of them brandished primitive lasguns, which
whined with energy and heat as they discharged
them frantically in the direction of the farseer.

With a cursory brush of her hand, Macha sent a
torrent of lightning crashing into the pathetic
humanoids. She watched in curiosity as they
turned themselves inside out and then imploded
into tiny tears in the material fabric of the world,
sucked through into the immaterium where their
daemon lords waited to consume their souls.

The Storm squad were in some disarray. There
were new enemies emerging from the darkness,
popping directly out of the warp as the storm drew
the fabric of reality perilously thin. But Macha had
no time for these bloodletter daemons.

Kaerial… she began before she remembered. *Vre-
qur, you are needed.*

Turning back to the battle on the crest of the mountain, she could see that the daemon prince had found his footing once again.

THE CREATURE SEEMED to slip and slide around his blade, as though it were not wholly solid. Jaerielle spun with his sword, taking clutches of clumsy cultists with each turn, but the dancing, devilish form seemed to evade his every move. It glowed with a dark light, making it shimmer in the rain-drenched night. Its finger tips leaked energy, as though it flowed through its body like blood or cascaded down its arms with the rain. With sharp flicks of its wrists, the bloodletter splattered sizzling droplets of warp energy against the eldar warriors and cut into their armour with its scything finger nails.

Great plumes of flame jetted out from Frqual, engulfing the slippery form in chemical fire. But it just laughed, bathing in the flames and licking at them with its forked tongue. With a sudden movement it spat something back in the direction of Frqual. The old Fire Dragon's reflexes were the sharpest of any of the eldar in the squad, but the viscous liquid splashed into the face of his helmet before he could even flinch. A fraction of a second later, and Frqual was lying prone in the bloody mud, a yawing hole cut straight through his helmet where his head should have been.

'Frqual!' cried Jaerielle and Skrekrea in unison, each working their blades into intricate ritual patterns through the thick, humid air. Their elaborate movements came to rest in the pincer stance of the Striking Scorpions, with their blades held over their heads, pointing directly at the foe caught between them.

A flurry of gunfire told Jaerielle that the wraith-guard had arrived to reinforce the Storm squad. They could deal with the cultists, leaving him and his sister to deal with this bloodletter before it found its way to the farseer.

Jaerielle moved first, lunging at the figure's naked legs with his sword, sweeping his blade in a lateral arc. But the bloodletter was too fast, springing into the air in a breathtaking pirouette, kicking its tiny weight off Jaerielle's blade itself. But the eldar was ready for this, and the mandiblasters around his helmet fired instantly as the daemon-form flashed past his face.

At the same time, Skrekrea brought her blade across in an opposing arc, slicing in front of Jaerielle at about head height, catching the bloodletter full in its stomach. For a moment, Skrekrea's blade cut deeply into the white flesh of the bloodletter's gut, but then it caught as the flesh seemed to regenerate around it, leaving it stuck as a protrusion from the daemon itself. A blast of warp energy fed back along the blade and into the hilt, throwing Skrekrea from her feet and sending her sliding into the swampy earth.

Again Jaerielle was ready. He let the natural arc of his sword turn him into a spin and he came round again with his blade held high, slicing perfectly through the neck of the bloodletter. For a horrible moment, nothing happened. But Skrekrea pulled herself up onto her elbows, dripping with blood and soil, and let out a banshee howl that smashed into the frozen form of the daemon-creature, blowing its severed head from its rapidly disintegrating shoulders and casting it into the ravening hordes of cultists who snatched at it like a prize.

SUDDENLY THE WRAITHGUARD just stopped attacking and turned away, leaving Trythos clutching the shaft of his axe. He fired a volley of bolter shells into the retreating squad, then turned to rejoin his kill team, who were already in the midst of a new battle further up the mountainside.

Inquisitor Jhordine was standing forward of the team with her staff of office held proudly aloft. Next to her stood the Librarian, Prothius, who was spinning his force-staff in a frenzy of spluttering power, sending spears of fire lancing through the darkness ahead of them. The Librarian stood out from his brother-Marines as psychic power played around his form, and he muttered the forbidden words of an ancient mantra – only the Librarians of the Space Marines were sanctioned to use such ungodly forces. But Prothius and Jhordine suddenly stopped fighting, their adversary apparently gone.

'What's going on?' asked Tyrthos as he drew up to Jhordine.

'I'm not sure,' she said, scanning the darkness for signs of a trap. 'The eldar are cunning creatures, and it is not like them to abandon a fight.'

'Perhaps they knew that they were outclassed,' offered Trythos.

'No. They were not outclassed,' put in Prothius.

'And they would never admit it, even if they were,' concluded Jhordine.

'So, we proceed with caution,' said Trythos, waving the Deathwatch kill team into formation for an ascent of the south side of the mountain.

'Yes, extreme caution. There are greater powers at play on this mountain than even the Deathwatch can handle,' added Jhordine with a note of foreboding.

PROTHIUS WAS THE first to crest the rise and, perhaps, the only one of the Space Marines to understand what he saw. The others just stopped and stared. Jhordine, the last to complete the climb, without the advantage of the Marines' augmented physiologies, broke the silence immediately.

'So, I was right. There it is.' Her voice was barely more than a whisper, but they all heard her.

'Yes, inquisitor, you were right,' responded Prothius. 'Now, what do you intend to do to it?'

The avatar had lost his footing and was pinned to the rock at the summit, with the daemon prince's tendrils lashing him down. He thrashed and twisted to get free, but the other-worldly strength of the daemon held him fast. The magnificent sword of the avatar lay on the ground where it had fallen, a great crack ripping through the rock from its point of impact. From a lower summit to the east came blasts of blue power, emanating from an eldar sorcerer of some kind, who stood alone on a rocky outcrop, held clear of the turmoil of battle around her.

The whole side of the mountain was a death scene, lit by the eerie light from the storm and from the flashes of energy that darted through the combat, all reflected into ugly reds by the blood-slicked earth. As far as the Space Marines could see, from peak to valley, there were corpses of eldar warriors and strange misshapen humans. The remnants of each force still fought in pockets over the face of the mountain – fighting was particularly fierce just below the sorcerer and around the summit itself.

'Why are they fighting?' asked Trythos.

'I don't know, captain, but the eldar must have their reasons to fight this daemonic foe. They are an ancient race, and their ways are mysteries to us, even in the Ordo Xenos of the Inquisition. But they are a dwindling race, and they do not fight without reason, no matter how unfathomable that reason might be.'

'If they are dwindling, should we not help bring them to extinction: suffer not the alien to live,' said Trythos with some bravado.

'Not today, captain. We are not here for annihilation, but for knowledge. We are here because of that,' explained Jhordine, pointing towards the fallen weapon of the avatar. 'Over many millennia, the eldar have created a weapon to slay daemons and banish the forces of Chaos from this world – that is the Wailing Doom of Biel-Tan. That is why we are here. Even the smallest fragment could be wrought into a great weapon for the Emperor's Inquisition.'

A BOLT OF blue lightning smashed into the daemon prince, shifting its weight slightly as it turned to stare at the farseer, and triggering a terrible keening. This was all the opportunity that the avatar needed, as he bucked the daemonic form and reached for his fallen weapon. As the daemon returned his fathomless eyes to the avatar beneath it, the Wailing Doom slashed across its unholy face with a tremendous explosion of power.

The daemon screamed as the blade sliced into its head, shattering its skull in hundreds of dimensions at once. As it reared up in agony, a second great blast from Macha smashed into its face, lifting the contorted form into the air. Then the avatar was on its feet, molten blood cascading down its metal skin, spraying out of the terrible wounds that threatened to tear him apart.

With one last supernatural effort of will, the avatar brought the sword round in a magnificent arc. The weapon wailed into the eye of the storm that spiralled above it, promising doom, and the avatar let out a cry to Khaine. The sound brought silence to the mountain, as all eyes turned to watch the terrible blow. The eldar warriors had stopped fighting and a painfully beautiful chant rose from the remnants of their force – *Kaela Mensha Khaine.*

The Wailing Doom, the ancient weapon of the avatar of Khaine, seemed to fall into slow motion, sweeping up in a vertical crescent from the avatar's feet, leaving a stream of sparkling energy in its wake. Its tip ripped into the body of the daemon prince with the sound of reality being torn asunder, and the avatar pushed it on with the very last of his ageless strength. The blade ploughed through the abdomen of the shrieking daemon, spraying warp energy and toxic liquids across the mountain, and then sliced up through its neck, smashing into the base of its skull. The daemon's head was shattered in an immense explosion, sending the collapsing skull rocketing up into the gyring storm above.

The head of the daemon prince detonated like a mine, blasting rings of ugly, purple light and splatters of filthy ichor across the mountain top. The blast seemed to consume the storm, and the roiling clouds were a sudden blaze of red fire.

Macha raised her arms to the heavens, holding a small, shimmering stone of maledictum between her hands. She was whispering and chanting into the blaze that engulfed the sky. Then suddenly, as if on command, the fiery clouds spiralled into a whirlpool and vanished down into the farseer's stone, leaving the scene in stillness and silence.

The avatar of Khaine pushed his sword into the air and a last fork of lightning ruptured the sky, striking the ancient blade as though it were a conductor. The sword flashed momentarily and then shattered with a crack of thunder, sending a shard splintering off against the rocks, as the avatar slumped to the ground with the rest of the blade still clasped in its hand. He lay prone on the mountain top as the clouds parted, leaving him bathed in starlight. His magma-like blood oozed slowly from his stricken body, forming little streams of lava that trickled down the mountainside, as though it were a volcano.

On the lower summit, Macha the farseer collapsed in exhaustion, but she knew that this was not over. She struggled against her exhaustion, trying to warn the warlocks that were rushing to the aid of the avatar, but she could manage nothing more. *A curse on the naïve humans.*

'Now. Now's our chance,' said Jhordine, but Prothius was already on his way.

The Librarian vaulted across the lava flows that radiated out from the fallen avatar and rolled beneath the fire that seared out from the line of eldar warlocks who had already gathered to honour him. Streaks of blue power jetted through the

air, sending up explosions around the charging
Librarian. But the eldar were tired and spent, and
Prothius was easily their match. His spinning force
staff deflected the bursts of alien power, and sent
back flares of its own, smashing into the line of
stationary warlocks.

Stooping, Prothius scooped up the abandoned
shard of the avatar's blade, feeling its writhing
energies repulse at his touch. Voices started to
whisper into his mind, but he shut them out and
turned. The whispers persisted, pressing at his soul
and driving up the pressure in his head to bursting
point.

He leapt the last of the magma streams and slid
down a short cliff, crashing into the middle of a
ring of his battle-brothers who awaited him at its
base.

'Let's get out of here,' recommended Jhordine, as
streams of warlock fire crested the cliff top, raining
energy down onto the team.

The Deathwatch Marines returned fire instantly,
sending salvoes of bolter fire streaking back up the
cliff, breaking away chunks of rock and sending a
few eldar flipping over the edge to their deaths.

'Agreed. The Thunderhawk is already on its way.
Extraction point is less than five hundred metres,'
barked Trythos over the din.

PROTHIUS COULD NOT let go of the sword fragment.
It was as though it was fused into his grip. He felt
weak and drained, and the shard had grown heavier with every hard fought step. Heavier still after
they had climbed into the Thunderhawk and
blasted away from Tartarus. It was as though it

wanted to be back with the eldar. And the whispering wouldn't stop. His mind was peppered with thoughts that were not his own, chattering and debating all around him. But one voice was clear, and its pain was exquisite: *Human, you know not what you have done.*

PART ONE

CHAPTER ONE

Tartarus system, 999.M41

THE VOICES SOARED into an angelic chorus, filling the furthest reaches of space with silver light. It was a divine sound, ineffable in its beauty and valorous in purpose. The Astronomican pulsed with life, riddling the Imperium with the light of the Emperor, filling it with the perfect sounds of his psychic choir.

Gabriel held the voices in his head for an instant, thrilling at the touch of this sacred beacon. They filled him with cool light, flooding his soul with the promise of salvation. It was like looking into the eyes of the Emperor himself and seeing him gaze back with implacable calm.

But the sound seemed to shift. The harmony faltered and then collapsed. Soaring sopranos screeched into shrill screams, and the unblemished light was suddenly awash with tortured faces. Deep reds bled into the stream of silver, curdling his thoughts into a sickly blend of bloody images. The screams grew louder, threatening to overcome his mind with their potency. And voices started to emerge from the forest of sound – voices that called his name – *Gabriel Angelos, this was your doing.* They were accusing him, hating him, reaching for his soul with the ice-cold fingers of the dead.

'Gabriel!'

He fired out his hand, grasping the nearest neck in his iron-grip. The immense muscles of his shoulder and arm bunched in tension.

'Gabriel.' The voice was firm and gentle, but it was accompanied by a palm that slapped across his face.

The Blood Ravens' captain prised open his eyes and stared into the face of his friend. 'Thank you, Isador.'

Isador Akios gazed back at his captain with the tenderness of decades of familiarity. 'You look terrible.'

Gabriel's skin was glistening with sweat and a single bloody tear had streaked down his face, leaving a scar-like mark over his already scarred cheek. His lip was split and bleeding where Isador had struck him. The plain tunic that he wore was soaked with sweat, and it clung to his muscular form as he rose from he posture of supplication before the altar.

'Again, thank you, Isador,' he replied as he got to his feet, meeting the Librarian's eyes levelly with his own, and wiping the blood from his mouth. 'I was praying,' he explained.

'Yes, I can see that.' Isador had seen Grabriel pray at each of the designated times of every day for over a century. He had always been devout, as you would expect from one of the Emperor's Space Marines. But something had changed since the Cyrene campaign. There was not much room in their daily routine for personal space, but Gabriel now spent every spare moment in the temple, and Isador was concerned for his old friend.

'Are we closing on Tartarus?' asked Gabriel, reasoning that this would be why his meditations had been interrupted.

'Imminently, captain,' replied Isador, still studying Gabriel's face carefully. 'We have entered the Tartarus system and are preparing a trajectory for optimum orbit around the fourth planet – Tartarus itself.'

'Any more news from the regiment on the ground, Isador?'

'No, Gabriel, none. I pray that we are not too late,' said the Librarian with concern. The Blood Ravens' Third Company had received the distress call from the Tartarus Planetary Defence Force – a regiment of the Imperial Guard affectionately known as the Tartarans – a couple of days earlier. The report was broken and intermittent, but the Tartarans appeared to be under attack by a large force of orks. Gabriel had immediately directed the company's battle barge, the *Litany of Fury*, to make for Tartarus to offer assistance. The Blood Ravens had fought orks many times before, and they knew how to confront this foe.

'What do we know of the planet?' asked Gabriel as he brushed his way past Isador, heading for the command deck.

'It is a civilized world and semi-urbanised. There are a series of cities and one spaceport. Most of the indigenous population are focussed in the cities.'

'And what is the population, Librarian?' asked Gabriel, keen to know the details of the battle to come before throwing himself into it.

'Nearly four billion,' replied Isador, wincing slightly at the thought of the probable casualties.

'Any idea why the orks would be interested in this place?' asked the captain, wondering whether there might be some strategic targets that he ought to know about.

'No, Gabriel. But then, the orks know nothing of reason. They appear solely concerned with war for its own sake. Our librarium on the *Omnis Arcanum* holds many records on ork battle tactics, but little on their psychology.' Isador had spent long years studying in the legendary librarium sanatorium, housed in the Blood Ravens' Chapter Fortress, the *Omnis Arcanum*. It was justly famed as one of the most extensive archives in the Imperium, and the Librarians of the Blood Ravens were amongst the most knowledgeable servants of the Emperor anywhere in His realm.

'War for its own sake?' Gabriel stopped and turned to face Isador. He smiled. 'We can do that.'

THE APPROACH TO Tartarus was littered with space debris and junk. Great hunks of ruined space ships floated freely in the outer reaches of the system, as though they had just fallen off larger vessels and then been abandoned. They formed the ugly wake of the ork invasion fleet, polluting the Imperium with their crude technologies and their callous disregard for anything except war.

The massive bulk of the *Litany of Fury* eased its way through the detritus, destroying any of the wreckages large enough to cause any harm. The gun-servitors played casually with the debris field, as though they were on a training run, preparing themselves for the battle to come.

'Good of them to leave us a trail, Isador,' commented Gabriel dryly.

'Yes, subtlety is not their strongest asset, captain,' replied the Librarian. 'Orks are certainly not at their best in space. On the ground, it is a very different story, as you well know.'

As they spoke, the planet of Tartarus slipped onto their view screen, emerging out from behind the exploded remains of an old Onslaught attack ship that the ork fleet must have jettisoned as useless. Its jagged hull simply collapsed under the brief strafe of fire from one of the prow batteries of the *Litany of Fury*, leaving the field of vision clear for the first time since they entered the system.

The blue-green planet was shrouded in debris – ruined relay stations spiralled around abandoned junks, intermixed with what must have been the ork fleet. For a few moments, the Space Marines could not distinguish between the space trash and the ork vessels – nothing looked like it could sustain a orbital battle. Occasional bursts of flame from engines picked out some of the smaller craft, perhaps more Onslaughts or a Savage gunship, but there was no sign of the huge bulk of a kill krozer command ship. It was all very chaotic, but deathly quiet.

'What a mess,' muttered Gabriel under his breath, shaking his head with revulsion. The vulgar clumsiness of the orks never ceased to amaze him. They had no right to be a space faring race: their fleets were almost entirely salvaged from Imperial or even

Chaos vessels that were immobilised or weakened in the glorious Imperial crusades. They were vultures. The orks would steal the remains of an honourable space ship, ignoring the pleadings and death-throes of its machine spirit, bolt on a bristling array of heavy guns and prow batteries then plunge the hapless craft into battle. When the vessel died, they would simply abandon it unceremoniously, leaving it to float through space like junk.

Tartarus itself was no longer the pristine blue and green for which it was famed. It was not a heavily populated world, and there was a lot of agriculture. The atmosphere was usually clear and crisp, providing a perfect view of the verdant surface from orbit. No longer. Even from space the fires that engulfed the cities could be seen burning with a dirty orange. Great sheets of flames stretched across the arable lands and the wide prairies that rolled between the settlements. Plumes of thick, black smoke billowed into the atmosphere, shutting in the heat and moisture and changing the planet's temperate climate into a stiflingly humid monsoon.

A click of heels made Gabriel turn. A nervous curator stood before him, clutching a large, heavily bound book. The man was struggling slightly under its weight, as though he were not used to carrying anything heavier than a pen. Little beads of sweat trickled down his shaven head, leaving shiny traces over the cursive lexiographs etched into his skin. The writing marked him as a curator of the Blood Ravens' librarium but, instead of the usual grey robes of an Administratum curator, this man was bedecked in a smock of deep red.

Gabriel nodded at the man, indicating that he should give the tome to Isador. The prospect seemed to fill the small man with dread and his eyes bulged slightly as he turned to approach the Librarian.

'Thank you,' said Isador smoothly, taking the book in one hand and dismissing the trembling curator, who turned quickly and shuffled away, breathing hard.

It was one of the quirks of the Blood Ravens that each of their battlebarges contained its own librarium, and hence each required a team of curators to facilitate its smooth operation. The curators would also record details of each and every event that took place on the vessel, although they would rely on the testimony of the company Librarian for details of missions that took place off ship. Hence, every barge contained the history of the company that operated it, in addition to copies of more general Imperial tomes. Whenever the battle barges rendezvoused with the Chapter fortress, copies of every file would be transferred into the central librarium sanatorium, where only the most senior Librarians and the Chapter Master himself would have access to every detail concerning every company.

Gabriel had often reflected that his brother-librarians were rather fanatical about documentation, as though knowledge and experience were not real unless they were committed to paper. He knew that the Blood Ravens were unique amongst all the Chapters of the Emperor's Space Marines in being so studiously conscientious, and he was not sure why this was the case. He had asked Isador more than once, but had not received a satisfactory response, as though the Librarian was worried that he was not entirely trustworthy. He would mutter something about the appropriate designations of knowledge, and then would intone the Chapter's maxim: knowledge is power – guard it well.

'This is the recorded history of Tartarus,' said Isador, carefully laying the heavy book onto an intricately carved podium next to the view-screen.

'Anything we need to know?' asked Gabriel, his attention already turned back to the jumbled ork fleet around the planet. He trusted that Isador would find anything that needed to be found. He had a gift for these things.

The two Marines stood in silence for a short while; Gabriel gazing out into space, considering the ork formation, Isador leafing through the pages of the book with intense concentration, his blue eyes burning with focus. It was Gabriel who spoke first.

'The bulk of the ork fleet has already descended on the planet's surface. Those Onslaughts and Savages are running a patrol pattern, policing the inner orbit to protect the land forces from bombardments.' He had reached a conclusion and was simply sharing it with the command crew. He didn't turn to face the deck, but spoke into the view-screen. 'Take us in to a low orbit. Execute covering fire to keep those gunships off our backs. We will deploy in Thunderhawks and drop-pods onto the co-ordinates of the last message from the Tartarans.'

There was a flurry of activity on the command deck as servitors rushed to make the necessary arrangements and to notify the assault squads that they should start their purification rites and prepare their armour for battle.

'Inform Chaplain Prathios that he will join the party,' said Gabriel as he finally turned away from the viewer to oversee the bustling bridge.

Librarian Isador looked up from the pulpit at his captain's last order, and raised a single eyebrow. The old Chaplain had been a fearsome warrior in his time, but he was now the oldest serving Marine in the Third Company, and he would be the first to admit that he was past his best, even if he wouldn't admit it out loud.

'Is everything well?' asked Isador with genuine concern, closing the great book on the stand in front of him and walking back to the view-screen.

'I'm not sure. Something doesn't feel right about this,' said Gabriel, conscious that his words sounded rather too much like those of a Librarian. In the darkest recesses of his mind, he could still hear the silvery tones of a psychic choir singing to him. These were not sounds that a Space Marine captain was used to hearing, and certainly not something that he could discuss with a sanctioned psyker like Isador.

'No matter. The Emperor will guide our hands,' he said, rallying a smile for his old friend.

'Yes, indeed, Gabriel. The Emperor will guide us.' Isador held Gabriel's hesitant eyes for a moment, watching them for shadows.

'And what of Tartarus, Isador?' asked Gabriel, changing the subject with a characteristic inquiry.

Isador did not look away. 'For the most part, it seems an unremarkable planet, captain. It was settled in the thirty-eighth millennia by a colonising mission, who subsequently established it as an agricultural centre. More recently it has seen some affluence as a trading centre, and the population has grown. The Tartarus Planetary Defence Force has stood guardian over the planet since its foundation – successfully seeing off various incursions by the orks. Most of the Tartarans' activity, however, has been the suppression of civil wars and uprisings, of which there have been many. Some minor Khornate cults have been recorded amongst the population at various times, but they have been efficiently suppressed. Considering the relatively small size of the population on Tartarus, a great deal of blood has been shed here over the centuries.'

'That will make the soil fertile,' said Gabriel with a faint smile.

'So it seems, captain. There is one strange thing in the historical record, however: there are a number of references to events on the planet *before* the thirty-eighth millennia.' Isador loaded his observation with a significance that was lost on Gabriel.

'And why is this strange?'

'Because, captain, the planet was not officially colonised until 102.M39, and the records show that the planet was completely uninhabited at the time of colonisation. There should not have been any humans on this planet in the thirty-eighth millennia, and certainly none recording an official Imperial history.' Isador furrowed his brow and stared out of the view-screen at the burning planet. 'As you know, it is most vexing when Imperial records are incomplete or ambiguous.'

The two Blood Ravens shared a moment of thoughtful silence as they reflected on the history of their own proud Chapter. 'Yes,' said Gabriel eventually, 'most vexing.'

* * *

Planet Tartarus: Magna Bonum Spaceport

THE ROCKETS PUNCHED into the side of the Leman Russ, rolling the tank onto its side with the force of the impacts. The turret of the battle cannon swung round under gravity, smashing into the ground and rupturing instantly. Meanwhile, the hull-mounted lascannon spat impotently into the air, as though sending up flares. Colonel Brom could see the hatch flip open, and a tumble of tank-crew spill out onto the rockcrete. They were on their feet and running before another hail of rockets punctured the exposed underbelly of the tank. The explosion was massive as the rockets detonated in the fuel reserves and triggered the remaining cannon shells. A mushroom cloud plumed into the air as a fiery rain of shattered tank hailed down into the line of Imperial infantry that had been sheltering in its shadow. The fleeing tank crew were blown off their feet, skidding along the hard-deck on their faces.

The orks raised a loud, incoherent cheer, brandishing their weapons in the air and then charging forwards towards the breach. There were hundreds of them. Huge, hulking masses of green muscle bearing down on the Tartaran infantry, their massive axes and cleavers glinting viciously, already wet with Imperial blood. The weight of their charge made the deck rumble and roll, and their cacophonous war cries filled the air with aural terror.

The Tartaran infantry hastened to form a defensive line, troops from the rear rushing to fill the gap left by the ruined tank. From his vantage point behind the lines, Brom could see the fear plastered all over their faces, but they opened fire just as the colonel thought that they might turn and run.

Streaks of las-fire lashed across the closing gap between them and the rampage of orks. Volleys of fire from heavy stubbers and plasma guns strafed through the advancing pack of greenskins. Even as one or two of the slugga boyz and gretchin collapsed to the ground, the thundering gaggle of teeth and muscles stormed over their prone bodies, trampling them into pulped death.

A barrage of grenades hissed out of the Tartaran line, arcing in tight parabolas before plunging into the throng of orks. Pockets of explosions ripped through the crowd of wailing greenskins, shredding them in clusters, sending sprays of ichor and green flesh raining down over their brethren. But the charge continued unbroken.

At the head of the charge was a knot of massive creatures, each covered in crudely riveted plates of armour. They brandished evil-looking power claws in one hand and clunky guns in the other. Attached to the back of one of them was a towering bosspole, crested with three impaled, severed heads. Even from this distance, Brom could recognise one of the heads as Sergeant Waine, and he flinched involuntarily at the barbarism of these creatures. The other two heads seemed barely human at all.

Erratic splutterings of gun-fire spat out from the charging orks, smashing into the Tartaran line with crude power, lifting Guardsmen off their feet as shells punched into them. Stikkbombz flipped and spiralled through the air, detonating into blasts of shrapnel as they hit the infantry formation. Guardsmen fell in dozens, clutching at puncture wounds and lacerations. And all the time the charge was getting closer, full of the promise of gleaming choppas and ravenous teeth.

The Tartaran line was beginning to crack, and Brom could see the terror induced hesitation from his gunners. They were beginning to freeze. The colonel drew his sword from its scabbard and flourished it in the air, pulling his pistol from its holster with his other hand, and charged towards his men.

'For Tartarus and the Emperor!' he yelled, barely audible over the screeches and cries of the incoming orks. A few of the Tartarans turned to see what the noise was, and a faint cheer came from the line as they saw their colonel plunging into the fray with them. But most of the men were staring fixedly forward, watching the orks steamroller their way through the barricades around the edge of the spaceport's decks.

A couple of the orks in the front of the charge pumped their burnas experimentally, checking the range. Plumes of flame jetted towards the Imperial line, engulfing clutches of men, who fell screaming to the ground, thrashing in the fire. The orks screamed out in delight as they realised that they were now close enough for some serious fun. Burnas erupted throughout the charging rabble, dousing other orks and Imperial Guardsmen indiscriminately. Some of the shoota boyz cast their guns to the ground as they cleared the last few metres that separated them from the Tartarans, preferring to grasp their massive axes in both hands for the melee.

As THE ORKS closed, Guardsman Larius could see the hungry saliva dripping between the monstrous teeth of the orks. He could see their tiny, beady red eyes burning with a deep, thirsty malice. And he could smell the gallons of toxic sweat and fresh blood that poured off the huge beasts as they rumbled unstoppably forward.

Larius looked down at the rifle in his hands and then along the line of his fellow Guardsmen, each with their lasguns at their waists sending delicate javelins of fire into the rampaging advance. He looked back up at the thundering figures of the orks, as they snarled and wailed towards him.

'Hold the line!' came Brom's voice from behind him. 'In the name of the Emperor, you will not falter!'

Another weak cheer arose from the line of Guardsmen and an autocannon team opened up with a volley of heavy fire, shredding a knot of orks as they leapt the final few metres that separated them from their prey.

Larius turned away from the orks and ran. He ran like he had never run before, driven on by abject terror. He threw his rifle aside and pumped frantically with his arms, trying to drive himself faster and faster through sheer will power.

A faint piercing pain brought him up sharply, skidding to a halt on the rockcrete deck. His hand clutched at his chest in a reflex action and he looked down. Blood seeped out from around his fingers, trickling down over the blues and blacks of his uniform. He carefully lifted his hand away and looked at the gaping wound with something approaching puzzlement. As his legs gave way, he slumped down onto his knees, noticing the polished boots that stood in front of him for the first time. With the last of his strength, he looked up at the hardened face of

Colonel Brom whose pistol was still smoking. The last words that Guardsmen Larius heard in this world were spat at him by his commanding officer.

'Coward.'

'COWARDS!' YELLED CARUS Brom as a series of Guardsmen peeled away from the front line and ran. He fired some carefully placed rounds into the backs of the traitors as they fled. They flung up their arms and crashed into the hard-deck, skidding into death on their knees like the grovelling worms that they were.

'You will fight and die, or you will just die. It's up to you,' he shouted at a group of men who had turned away from the fighting just in front of him. Wild panic danced across their faces as they struggled to understand their options. They twitched and hesitated, terrified of the horrors behind them but deeply shamed by the man before them.

'You are Tartarans, damn you! Turn and fight!'

One of the men, Guardsmen Ckrius, suddenly snapped to attention and threw a crisp salute to Brom. Then he racked his shotgun and turned, screaming and firing madly into the fray. The rest of the group followed suit, inspired by the reckless bravery of their comrade and the steely gaze of their colonel.

But Brom couldn't hold the line together by himself and he was not willing to spend all of his ammunition killing Guardsmen when there were orks to slay. Clutches of Tartarans turned and fled back into the relative safety of the spaceport, which was now spotted with mortar fire from hastily erected ork emplacements in the combat line.

Stepping up along side Ckrius, Brom threw his officer's pistol to the ground and snatched up a fallen hellgun.

'For Tartarus and the Emperor!' he yelled as he sprayed las-blasts out into the wave of snarling green that roared straight towards him.

'WAAAAAAGH!' BELLOWED Orkamungus from the rear of the attack, slapping Gruntz across the jaw and knocking him clear of the wartrukk. The warboss pointed up at the sky over the spaceport and roared again, reaching down from his command post and grabbing Gruntz around the neck. The kommando thrashed in resistance, scraping at the warboss with his claws and hissing into his face. But Orkamungus shook him violently by the neck, beating him against the side of the wartrukk until he stopped kicking. Then he lifted Gruntz into the air with one immense arm, stuffing his snarling face towards the sky above the battle for the spaceport.

Crumpling to the ground with a resounding crash, Gruntz muttered under his breath, spitting globules of saliva and blood from his jagged mouth. 'You'ze da boss,' he spluttered, pulling himself to his feet and thudding off to join the rest of his kommandos.

SERGEANT KATRN WAS sprinting across the spaceport, flanked on both sides by members of his Armoured Fists squad – a Tartarans weapons team usually based in a Chimera transport. They had broken away from the fighting line when an ork had smashed down through their mortar emplacement with its axe and then ripped the weapon's crew into pieces with its power claw. Colonel Brom had been nowhere to be seen, and so Katrn had bolted, bring the remnants of his squad with him.

The Armoured Fists ducked and wove their way through the hail of ork bombs and mortar shells, striving to reach the flimsy cover of the spaceport's buildings. Ordnance pounded into the ground all around them, blasting craters into the hard-deck and spraying lethal shards of rockcrete through the fleeing troopers. As one, they dived for the temporary cover of a gaping crater, rolling into a false sense of relief and security. Impacts rained down all around them, shaking the ground itself.

Katrn peered over the edge of the crater, back towards the chaotic scenes on the front line. The Tartarans were holding their ground, fighting with frantic desperation against the pressing, green muscle of the ork rampage. The greenskins were on top of the infantry now, hacking indiscriminately with their brute choppas, slashing in every direction and pounding the wounded under foot. The infantry were struggling with their bayonetes and swords, thrusting at the immense creatures without much hope but with insane determination. Banks of hardened veterans had formed disciplined firing lines, sending salvoes of las-fire punching into knots of orks.

A squad of deformed, overly-muscled ogryns were pouring out of a Chimera transport and laying into the orks with their ripper guns and then using them as clubs to smash the greenskins when the range closed.

Striding out of one of the hangars on the far side of the spaceport came Mavo's Sentinel squadron. Sergeant Mavo took the lead, stamping down with

the huge legs of the armoured bipedal walker,
squashing an ork instantly, and then opening up
with the nose-mounted autocannon. He was supported on both sides by Catachan-pattern Sentinels
that spewed chemical fire from their heavy flamers as
they stalked into the mist of the battle.

TUCKED AWAY IN relative safety at the rear of the ork
rampage, Orkamungus cackled an inchoate noise to
Fartzek and the stormboyz. He was jumping up and
down and pointing towards the three large metal
stomping machines that were laying into the orks at
the front of the crowd. Under his immense feet, the
wartrukk was gradually crumpling, and one of the
axles snapped. Two stompers were spilling fire over
groups of shoota boyz, and one of them was rattling
cannon shells across the battle field, shredding the
stikk bommas in the heart of the gaggle.

A glut of activity surrounded Fartzek as his mob
responded to the cries from their warboss. Four of
them held him down while another strapped a large
rocket to his back. They snarled and slapped at him
as a mekboy riveted the fixings into his leathery skin.

When they were done, Fartzek climbed clumsily to
his feet, threw a thunderous punch into the face of
the mekboy, and then fired the rocket. The ignition
incinerated a gretchin that was creeping away from
the mob under cover of the flight preparations. It
squealed briefly and then collapsed into a pile of
ashes.

As the rocket flared and propelled the Fartzek into
the air, he let out a gurgling cry and the stormboyz
stamped their feet into the trampled earth in
response. The huge ork arced through a shallow

curve, rattling his slugga as he flew over the heads of
his brethren. After a couple of seconds he slammed
into the side of one of the metal stompers, smashing
his choppa into an armoured plate to ensure purchase. The human inside the machine leaned out of
the cockpit, eyes wide with horror, and Fartzek cackled into his face with a malicious and mirth-filled
snarl. Then, without even the slightest hesitation, he
detonated the warhead on the rocket.

SERGEANT KATRN WATCHED Mavo's Sentinel explode,
ducking back into the crater to avoid the waves of
concussion that radiated out from the destruction.
Mavo had only been in the field for a few seconds.

Most of the Armoured Fists were already scrambling out of the other side of the crater, tripping and
crawling their way though the rain of debris towards
the port buildings. Katrn scampered after them,
hunched over in the crazy belief that he would be
safer that way.

A series of tremendous impacts smacked into the
ground between the Armoured Fists and their objec-
tive. They all fell flat to the ground and waited for the
explosions to shred them, but the detonations never
came.

Lying prostrate on the rumble-strewn deck, Katrn
stole a glance towards the point of impact. A group
of three steaming drop-pods sat imperviously on the
rockcrete in front of him, errant ork fire ricocheting
harmlessly off their armoured plates. With a deep
metallic clunk and then a hiss of decompression,
hatches began to open on each of the pods.

Striding confidently from the steam-shrouded
doors nearest to Katrn came a huge warrior, fully two

metres tall, bedecked in shining red power armour.
As he cleared the cloud of steam, the massive warrior
turned his head calmly from side to side, taking in
the scene, his green eyes flickering with calculation
and thought. The figure made no attempt to take
cover from the hail of fire that rattled through the
spaceport towards him.

Katrn's jaw dropped in awe as he realised what
these monstrous warriors were. They were the Adeptus Astartes – the Emperor's Space Marines. These
soldiers were hand-picked from the elite of the
galaxy's fighting men and then surgically augmented
for years until they were finally implanted with a
black carapace that ran under their entire skin, permitting them to interface completely with the
ancient power armour that enwrapped them like a
second skin. Katrn had heard the legends, but he
never thought that he would live to actually see one.

Similar figures emerged from each of the other
pods, and several more followed from the first pod,
behind the eerily calm soldier. They deployed immediately into a wide fan around the first figure, the
green eye-visors of their helmets scanning the spaceport and the battle on its edge, their boltguns already
primed and trained on possible targets.

'Space Marines…' muttered Katrn to himself,
unsure whether to celebrate their arrival or to hide
back in the crater behind him.

The first Marine was the only one without a helmet, and Katrn couldn't help but cringe away from
his eyes as they caught sight of him lying in the rubble, clearly attempting to flee the battle. The Space
Marine looked him up and down in undisguised disgust then waved an order to his squad.

Without a word, the crimson-armoured Space Marines broke into a run and pounded across the space port towards the thickest and most ferocious point of the front line. They vaulted over the mortar craters with single strides, spraying precision bolter shells from their guns with each step. Already the Tartarans who had held their positions were cheering with renewed energy as the bolter fire streaked over their heads and punched into the orks, driving them back for the first time.

Sergeant Katrn watched the Marines bound over his head and then launch themselves into the fray with selfless abandon, and he slid back down into the crater, struggling to catch his breath. He could still see those piercing green eyes accusing him of treachery and cowardice. He could see the disgust and the revilement, and he shared it. He was a coward, unworthy of the proud uniform of the Tartarans. He had presented the Blood Ravens with their first sight of his regiment: crawling, snivelling cowards sneaking away from their deaths like traitors.

But he was not dead yet, and he would show them what a Tartaran could really do. Katrn sprang to his feet and jumped clear of the crater. Pumping his rifle from side to side as he ran, building his momentum, he sprinted back across the deck in the wake of the Space Marines, screaming the air out of his lungs.

'For Tartarus and the Emperor!'

STILL LURKING AT the rear of the battlefield, Orka-mungus beckoned to one of the nobz in his bodyguard, Brutuz, who slunk over to his warboss with justified trepidation. The giant ork was casually staring into the sky above the spaceport, watching the rain of drop-pods as they flashed down through the atmosphere like meteorites.

Brutuz presented himself to the warboss, already flinching in anticipation of the strike. For a moment, he was saved as something caught Orkamungus's eye. Gruntz and the kommandos had skirted the edge of the battlefield and the warboss could see them slipping around the perimeter of the spaceport towards the city of Magna Bonum beyond.

Orkamungus cackled deeply, baubles of phlegm bubbling in his massive oesophagus. He stomped forwards to the edge of the wartrukk and leant down to Brutuz, slapping him firmly on the back, causing the nob to spit in relieved shock.

The warboss pulled himself back up to his full height and roared his war-cry across the battlefield, 'Waaaaaaaaagh!' Hundreds of orks turned their eyes to him as they stumbled and lumbered away from the Space Marines. For a moment they were caught between fear of the Emperor's sword at their heels and terror at the wrath of their warboss. But it was only for a moment, and then they kept running.

Brutuz turned quietly and started to walk away from the wartrukk, hoping that Orkamungus had finished with him. He had taken only two steps when the warboss leapt from the side of his trukk and smashed down onto Brutuz, squashing him flat against the earth under his awesome weight. Then, sitting on the nob's back, pinning him against the ground, Orkamungus beat the hapless ork repeatedly in the head until he was sure that he had made his point.

* * *

IN THE THICK of the fighting on the front line, an axe flashed down a fraction too late as Brom rocked onto his back foot, unleashing a spray from his hellgun at close range. As the ork smashed its weapon into the deck the blade caught in the rockcrete and the creature roared with frustration. Brom's hail of fire strafed up the ork's bulging abdomen, riddling it with holes.

The colonel sighed slightly, propping himself up on the barrel of his gun for a moment, before hefting it once again and opening up at yet another of the greenskinned beasts.

All around him was the constant roar of battle. He could hear the cries of his sergeants rallying the troopers against wave after wave of ork assaults, and he could hear the screams of men as they fell beneath the monstrous blows from the inhuman creatures. Explosions filled the air with concussions and the ground shook under the constant impacts of mortars, grenades and rockets.

'Colonel!' cried Ckrius, staring in horror at Brom as his hellgun coughed savagely into the gut of a charging ork, dropping it to the ground amidst squeals of frustration.

Brom stole a glance at Ckrius, but he couldn't tell what the trooper was trying to tell him.

A projectile zipped over the colonel's head – Brom could feel the heated air sizzle as it shrieked past him, singeing his closely cropped white hair. He turned his head, following the flight of the bolter shell as it punched into the face of the ork behind him. The creature was already riddled with gunshot wounds all the way down its chest, but it had freed its axe from the rockcrete and was holding it high in the air, ready to hack down into Brom's back. The bolter shell buried itself into the beast's skull and then exploded into tiny lacerating fragments that shredded the thick bone instantly.

Before Brom had chance to react, a huge red-armoured warrior pounded up to his side, loosing showers of bolter shells into the frenzied mobs of orks that charged and lumbered towards the line. And the stranger was not alone, squads of similar figures deployed themselves into position in the heart of the defensive formation, towering head and shoulders above the Imperial Guardsmen around them.

In only a few moments the ork charge collapsed, and the chaotic assault seemed to fall into a frenzied retreat. The Space Marines pressed their advantage, striding forward of the Tartaran line and pressing the defensive action into an assault of their own.

By now the orks were in even more disarray: charging shoota boyz skidded to a halt and others ploughed into the back of them, unable to stop in time. The cleaver wielding slugga boyz had already turned tail and were lumbering back into the midst of the mobs of orks in the mid-field and the snivelling gretchin were diving for whatever cover they could find as the Space Marines' barrage continued relentlessly.

For the first time, the Imperial forces started to make ground against the orks. Blood Ravens strode forward at the head of the counter-offensive, scything their way through the disorganised greenskins with sputtering chainswords and disciplined volleys of bolter fire. The retreat rapidly collapsed into a rout, as the orks abandoned their positions and ran in erratic, wailing mobs.

Brom watched the fleeing orks with something approaching amazement, but was overcome with relief. He turned to the Space Marine who had saved his life and bowed deeply.

'I am Colonel Carus Brom, and you are most welcome here, captain.'

The Space Marine eyed him sceptically. 'Captain Gabriel Angelos of the Blood Ravens' Third Company. What is your status?'

'The Tartarans have suffered terrible losses, captain, but they have fought bravely and with honour... in the main,' said Brom, trying to draw himself up to a more respectable height before this giant figure.

Gabriel surveyed the ruins of the spaceport. It was spotted with ordnance craters and speckled with the corpses of Guardsmen – some of whom were facing back towards the centre of the compound with gunshot wounds in their backs. But he couldn't see a single greenskin corpse inside the defensive perimeter.

Nodding slowly, he turned back to Brom. 'You stood your ground in the face of the Emperor's foes. You have done your duty, colonel.'

Brom nodded and let out a brief sigh of relief as he realised what the Blood Raven was looking at. 'Thank you, captain.'

'I am not here for thanks, colonel. This spaceport must be held if we are to maintain troops and supply lines to planet's surface. It is only by the provenance of the Emperor that we arrived in time,' replied Gabriel, already scanning the scene for signs of supplies in the compound itself. 'And what of the wounded and the civilians?' he asked.

'They are stranded, captain. The Tartarans have few ships, and most were destroyed by the orks during the initial stages of the invasion,' explained Brom, feeling rather too much on the defensive.

'Then you shall have more ships,' said Gabriel simply, turning to Brother-Sergeant Corallis. 'Sergeant, contact the *Litany of Fury* and order that Thunder-hawks are deployed to evacuate the wounded. Meanwhile,' he added, turning back to Brom with the hint of a smile, 'we will dispatch the ground forces.'

'But captain,' replied Brom, slightly confused. 'The orks have retreated. The ground forces are already broken.'

The Blood Ravens' captain turned away from Brom and watched the greenskins scrambling away into the mountains on the horizon. His Marines had driven them out of the combat theatre, but then had broken off the pursuit, firing volleys at the heels of the scampering vermin just to keep them moving.

'If you are to defeat your enemies, colonel, you must first understand them. The orks have a saying: never be beaten in battle. Do you know what this means?' Gabriel returned his searching gaze back to the colonel, who shook his head nervously. Its meaning seemed obvious to him.

'It means, Colonel Brom, that orks never retreat, they only regroup. If they die in battle, then they do not think that they have not been beaten – they are only beaten if the battle itself defeats them. War for its own sake, colonel. The orks will be back, and they will keep coming until you or they are all dead.'

CHAPTER TWO

IN THE DISTANCE there was a constant rumble of thunder as artillery fire and pockets of fighting continued. But the spaceport was secure and, tucked into the cliffs behind, the city of Magna Bonum remained relatively unscathed by the ravages of war. Its gleaming white buildings shimmered with bursts of red as the setting sun turned to orange and bounced the dying light off the bloody battlefield. Nothing moved in the streets, and an eerie calm had descended on the city.

The Blood Ravens were making preparations for their pursuit of the orks, overseeing the fortification of the spaceport in case the greenskins returned while they were away. Gabriel had already dispatched a squad of scouts into the wilderness to locate the rallying point of the foul aliens, and he was awaiting the return of Sergeant Corallis with impatience. He was certain that the warboss would be regrouping his forces for another assault, and was eager to thwart it before it began. The best way to beat orks was to prevent them from forming their forces in the first place.

'Prathios, my old friend,' said Gabriel as the Chaplain walked into the spaceport's Imperial shrine. 'It is good to see you.' The two Marines bowed slightly to each other, showing a respect suitable to a holy place.

'It is good to be here, Gabriel. It has been a long time since I saw planet-fall. How can I serve you, captain?' The huge, old Marine looked down at Gabriel with compassionate eyes. 'Why are you so troubled?' he asked.

Gabriel turned away from the Chaplain to face the altar, dropping to his knees before the image of the Emperor's Golden Throne. It was encircled by a ring of silver angels, their wings tipped with blood. Facing away from the throne in the middle, their mouths were open and their heads thrown back, as though they were singing to the whole galaxy.

'I just need to be calm before the battle. I am impatient to deal with these orks, and impatience does not become me. I would not like to err in my judgment,' said Gabriel, admitting more than he would to anyone else.

'Your concern does you credit, captain,' answered Prathios, kneeling into prayer beside Gabriel, gazing at the images on the altar. 'It is a beautiful sight, is it not?'

For a moment or two Gabriel said nothing; he just stared straight ahead, as though his gaze was trapped in the icon. 'Yes, indeed it is. But tell me, Brother

Prathios, haven't you ever wondered what it might sound like?'

The Chaplain continued to look at the image, considering the question. 'I wonder every day, Gabriel, but I will hear it soon enough, when the Emperor finally calls my soul to him.'

COLONEL BROM LOOKED over his men in the remains of the spaceport. They were tired. Exhausted. The ork invasion had taken them by surprise and it had been more severe than any of the previous incursions into the Tartarus system. The Tartarans' small space-bound force had been virtually annihilated in the orks' attack run, and then the giant, clumsy kill kroozer had plunged into the planet's atmosphere, spewing an invasion force of orks onto the surface. The greenskins had no need for the spaceport, which the Tartarans had defended so desperately. They had just attacked Magna Bonum because that was where the Tartarans' Fifth Regiment had dug in – so that was where the good fighting was to be found. Brom shook his head at the irony: if they hadn't tried to defend the city, perhaps the orks would have just ignored it.

'Colonel Brom,' said Trooper Ckrius, flicking a sharp salute as he snapped to attention.

'Yes, trooper. What can I do for you?' Brom was getting a little tired of Ckrius's enthusiasm. The young Guardsman had fought bravely against the orks, standing his ground with Brom himself, albeit after attempting to desert the battle. This was as much as Brom could ask of any of his men, but Ckrius seemed to think that he owed more than any of the others. As though his moment of hesitation had condemned him to a lifetime of penitence and of service to the officer who had made him see the light.

'I have brought you some recaff, colonel,' said Ckrius, thrusting a battered, tin cup towards his commanding officer.

Despite himself, Brom was grateful. It had been a long day and, although the sun was setting in a dazzling array of golds and reds, he knew that there would be no sleep for them tonight. Perhaps never again.

'Thank you, Trooper Ckrius,' he replied wearily, reaching out and taking the hot cup from the young man, who was still saluting. 'You can relax, soldier.'

'We can sleep when we're dead, right colonel?' said Ckrius eagerly, excited that Brom had remembered his name. He nodded his head energetically towards the recaff cup as though it contained the elixir of life.

Brom glanced down at the steaming liquid and raised it to his lips. It was so hot that it burnt his throat as he swallowed a large mouthful. He didn't care. If that was the worst pain he would feel today, he would have no complaints.

'Let's hope that we don't have to wait that long,' replied the colonel, wiping his mouth with the back of his hand and looking levelly at the young trooper. The young man looked terrible, running on hysteria and nervous energy. 'You fought well today, son. Get some sleep, and you will also fight well tomorrow.'

'But there is no time for sleep,' protested Ckrius, twitching his head excitedly from side to side, taking in the flurry of activity around the spaceport. 'There is so much to do.'

'The orks will not be back for a while yet. Captain Gabriel tells me that they will have to regroup at a safe distance and then reorganise before they will return to face the Tartarans again. Evidently, the reorganisation of a mob of orks can take a long time. We will be ready for them,' said Brom, hoping that the Blood Raven was right.

'Captain Gabriel?' asked Ckrius, as though he had heard a secret password. 'Is that the Space Marine captain?'

'Yes, Captain Gabriel is the Space Marine commander. He is here to help us with the ork problem,' explained Brom carefully, conscious of the excitement in the young trooper's face.

'The boys... that is, we were wondering who they were, colonel,' said Ckrius self-consciously. He looked back over his shoulder to a group of troopers who sat around a small fire on the hard-deck, sipping recaff from mangled tins. They all pretended to be chatting casually or looking elsewhere when Brom followed his gaze.

'I see,' said Brom as the real motivation for bringing him the recaff dawned on him. He smiled – these troopers had probably never even seen a Space Marine before. 'They are Blood Ravens, trooper. The Blood Ravens' Third Company.'

Ckrius's eyes lit up. 'I've heard of them,' he blurted excitedly. Then he paused for a moment and a shadow fell over his face as his thoughts caught up with him. 'Aren't they–'

'Yes, I dare say you have, trooper. Their reputation precedes them wherever they go, I'm sure. The Adeptus Astartes are justly exalted throughout the Imperium. As I say, they are here to help us with the orks, and we should thank the Emperor for that.' Brom cut Ckrius off, aware of the rumours about the

Cyrene affair but unsure of the facts himself. 'Now I suggest that you get some sleep, trooper. Tomorrow will be a long day, and you will need all of your strength if you are to show the Blood Ravens the worth of the Tartaran Fifth.'

'Yes, colonel,' replied Ckrius, saluting weakly and turning away. Brom watched him walk back to his friends around the fire, and smiled to himself as they crowded around the trooper, pestering him with questions.

THE BLOOD RAVENS' scouts swept back into the space-port on their bikes, engines roaring with power. Against the setting red sun, the ruby bikes seemed to fluoresce with energy, and the heat haze from the exhaust vents blurred into the fading daylight. Brom watched them slide the huge machines to a halt, and shook his head in faint disbelief. Those assault bikes were faster than a Sentinel walker and probably packed more firepower than a Chimera transport. And just one Marine sat stride each of the awesome machines, throwing it around as though it were nothing.

The Marines climbed off their bikes and pulled off their helmets, apparently enjoying the last rays of sunlight on their faces. The air was cooling rapidly as the night drew in, and Brom could only imagine how hot the Marines must have been inside that heavy armour all day. But the faces of the scouts were even and unbothered. Their hair was not matted to their heads, and they looked perfectly comfortable. The colonel shook his head again, wondering what he could achieve with a squad of such soldiers.

There were mutterings and faint whistles from some of the Guardsmen as they saw the bikes roll onto the hard-deck. At the end of a day like this one, the sight of nine Blood Raven assault bikes riding out of the sunset was more than any of them could have expected, and they didn't try too hard to hide their awe.

Brom cast his eyes over his men once again, still shaking his head. They certainly needed this kind of inspiration. It had been a bad day for the Tartarans. Hundreds of men had fallen – good men who had stood their ground in the face of the alien onslaught. Many bad men had fallen too; he had dispatched them himself with own pistol as they had tried to run from their duty.

He had not known that the Tartaran Fifth boasted so many cowards. His men had stood defiantly in the face of many foes before today. They had confronted insurrections and rebellions. They had cleansed cities of perverted and mutated cultists. They had even met orks before, when greenskin raiders had tried to plunder the resources of Tartarus. And always his men had stood firm – fighting for their honour, for the Emperor, and for their homes.

Something was different about this invasion. Although the arrival of the Blood Ravens was welcome, and their timely intervention had been decisive, the Tartarans had dealt with orks before, even without the help of the Adeptus Astartes. This glut of greenskins was no bigger than any they had faced before. But something *was* different. The men were whispering amongst themselves, casting furtive glances at each other, muttering quiet suspicions around the camp fires. Brom couldn't help

but wonder whether the presence of the Space
Marines actually made the men more suspicious: if
the Adeptus Astartes are here, this must be some
serious shit.

And Captain Angelos didn't help – his haughty
attitude was almost insulting. He hadn't even
included the Tartarans in his plans for the fortification of the spaceport; the Blood Ravens were doing
everything. In truth, most of Brom's men were grateful for the chance to rest, but he had heard some of
them grumbling about not being good enough for
the Space Marines.

A shiver ran down his back as Brom realised what
Angelos's first impression of the Tartarans must have
been. In his mind's eye, he could still see those men
laying face down on the ground with his pistol
wounds in their backs.

Then a realisation struck him. Something had been
different even before the Space Marines had arrived.
Some of his men had been defeated even before the
battle had started. He had heard them talking about
the voices in the wind. Some of them had heard
warnings whispered in the breeze ahead of the ork
assault – whispering songs and choruses that echoed
into their ears from everywhere at once. Even Brom
had convinced himself that he had heard something.

The scouts were striding over to the Blood Ravens'
encampment around the spaceport's shrine, while a
team of other Marines walked back towards their
bikes, presumably to make the necessary offerings to
their machine spirits before they would be ready to
go out again.

Watching the scouts, Brom noticed a group of
Blood Ravens emerge from the shrine to greet them.

One of them caught his eye immediately – slightly taller than the others, his armour was the colour of a clear blue sky. He bore the insignia of the Blood Ravens on his auto-reactive shoulder guard, and his gleaming armour was studded with purity seals. In place of the grey raven that adorned the chests of his battle-brothers, the figure had a starburst of gold and, although he had no helmet, his face was obscured by an ornate hood that was somehow integrated into his armour. In his hand he held a long staff, crested with the wings of a raven with a glowing red droplet in its heart.

BROM MADE HIS way over to the Blood Ravens' compound and presented himself to the unusual Marine. 'I am Colonel Carus Brom of the Tartarus Planetary Defence Force. It is an honour to be in the presence of a Librarian of the Adeptus Astartes,' said Brom formally, after a short cough.

Isador turned. 'Wait,' he said sharply, then turned back to the scouts that were about to enter the shrine to make their report to the captain. 'Corallis – Captain Angelos should not be disturbed at the moment. He will be finished soon.'

The sergeant nodded his understanding to the Librarian and stood to the side of the doorway, as though on sentry duty, and Isador turned back to face Brom. 'Yes?'

'I am Col–' began Brom.

'Yes, I know who you are Colonel Brom. What do you want?'

In the rapidly fading light, Brom could not see Isador's face under the psychic hood, and the reddening sunset had transformed his pale blue armour into a disturbing purple. Brom swallowed hard, more cowed by this Librarian even than by the rampage of orks that he had encountered that afternoon.

He collected himself. 'I wish to know how the Tartaran Fifth can be of service to you.'

Isador watched the man closely, noting how the fear in his voice competed with the fierce pride in his eyes. There was something unspoken in that stare – something both hopeful and desperate at the same time.

'I saw you fight today, colonel. You are a brave man.' Isador's voice was calm and matter-of-fact.

'Thank you, my lord,' said Brom, genuinely proud.

'I am not your lord, colonel. We must all be watchful for false idols. I am a servant of the Emperor, just like you,' said Isador, watching Brom's response with interest.

A voice seemed to be whispering into Brom's mind and tugging at his consciousness. Without thinking about it, he flicked his eyes from side to side, looking for the source of the noise.

'Colonel?' inquired Isador, and Brom's gaze snapped back to Isador's shrouded face, where his eyes seemed to be glowing with a distant light. 'Is there something else?'

'No. No, there is nothing else, Brother-Librarian,' replied Brom, picking his words carefully.

'You are a brave man, Colonel Brom, but it seems that your men are merely shadows of your resolve. Brother-Captain Angelos is doubtful about their efficacy in this theatre,' said Isador frankly.

Brom smarted. 'I shall strengthen their resolve. You may rely on that.'

'See that you do, or we shall be forced to do it for you.'

Brom took a breath. 'I should like to offer my assurances and the Tartarans' services to Captain Angelos himself.'

The Librarian nodded slowly. 'As you wish. But you will wait until the captain has finished his prayers.'

For a few moments the two men stood in silence, but then Isador spoke again. 'You have something else that you wish to say. Say it, colonel.'

'I have no gift for words, Brother-Librarian,' said Brom, a little taken aback by Isador's astute question, 'so I will be blunt. Some of the men are talking about the fate of planet Cyrene, and I was hoping that you could set the rumours straight before they get out of hand.'

'What are the men saying?' asked Isador, checking that Gabriel had not yet emerged from the shrine behind them.

'They have heard that your company cleansed the planet of a terrible heresy,' explained Brom, hoping that the Librarian would finish the story for him. But there was silence, so he continued. 'They have heard that you performed an exterminatus, down to the last man, woman and child.'

'Rumours are dangerous things, colonel,' said Isador, leaning down towards Brom. 'Colonel Brom, your company and even your precious Tartarans are welcome, but such questions are not. You would do well not to ask the captain about Cyrene if you wish to retain what little good will he currently has towards you.'

The door to the shrine creaked open behind Isador, and Gabriel stepped out into the night air, stooping slightly as he passed under the mantel. He nodded a quick greeting to Isador and glanced down at Brom before turning swiftly to Sergeant Corallis, who stood crisply at the side of the doorway. Isador took a couple of steps towards Gabriel to join the briefing, leaving Brom standing on his own in the gathering dark.

'Sergeant, what news?' asked Gabriel.

'We found the trail of two mobs of retreating orks, captain. They appear to be heading on intersecting trajectories, presumably towards a rallying point deeper in the forest. If we leave now, we should be able to catch one of the mobs before it reaches that point.' reported Corallis.

'Understood,' said Gabriel. 'But what of the other mob?'

Corallis looked slightly uneasy. 'We caught up with it on our bikes, captain, or what was left of it.'

'Explain.'

'Something had already taken care of the bulk of the mob, and we had no problems cleaning up the remnants, captain,' explained the sergeant.

'"Something," sergeant? What? Who? The Tartarans?' asked Gabriel.

'With all due respect,' said Corallis, flicking a glance towards the dim figure of Brom, 'that is most unlikely. The attack was incredibly precise and the attackers left no trail at all. It is as though they just vanished after the battle. Not that there was much of a battle, it seems. More like a slaughter.'

'Marines?' asked Gabriel with some concern.

'No, captain. The wounds on the orks were too delicate to have been caused by bolter fire. It was as though they had been shredded by thousands of tiny projectiles. I've never seen anything like it. When we caught up with the stragglers, they were so dazed and confused that it was hardly worth wasting ammunition on them.' The report clearly disturbed Corallis as much as it did his captain.

'Very good, Corallis, thank you,' said Gabriel turning to face Isador. 'Isador, what does the good colonel want?'

'Brother-Captain, the colonel wishes an audience with you,' replied Isador, stepping back and sweeping his arm to indicate that Brom should approach.

'Captain Angelos. I wish to place the Tartarans at the disposal of the Blood Ravens. As you know, we have suffered many casualties, but between the fifth and seventh we can offer an entire regiment. They stand ready to serve you in the protection of the city. I realise what you may have seen, but my men wish to make amends for–'

'The Tartarans will have many opportunities to prove themselves warriors worthy to serve the Emperor, colonel. The Blood Ravens are leaving the city, and we are leaving its protection in your hands,' said Gabriel, already on his way to organise the departure.

'Very good, captain,' said Brom with a slight bow. 'I will ready my men. May I ask what your next course of action might be?'

Gabriel stopped walking and turned to face Brom directly. 'Orks respect only strength,' he said deliberately, 'and I intend to show them that we have it in ample supply. The Blood Ravens are going hunting.'

HIDDEN IN THE depths of the forest, a safe distance down the valley away from Magna Bonum, the orks had stopped their retreat. The clearing was already cluttered with spluttering machines and slicks of oil. A terrible stench filled the air and wafted up into the sky, forming dark, pungent clouds that obscured the moonlight. Groups of mekboyz pushed each other around, smashing their wrenches into wartrukks and warbikes, punching rivets through their armoured plates to keep them in place. Snivelling gretchin sat in packs, chained into little circles so that they couldn't run off into the forest. Some of the storm-boyz poked about at their jump packs experimentally, pretending that they were testing their components, while the flashgitz spat saliva onto their shootas and buffed them with the hair from decapitated heads.

In the centre of the clearing, Orkamungus was standing beside his crumpled trukk, yelling at the mekboyz who fussed around it nervously, trying to winch up the back wheels in order to fix a broken axle. The wartrukk was so huge and so badly damaged that it seemed an almost impossible task, and the mekboyz kept recruiting more and more orks into service – partly to help them lift the immense machine, and partly to share the blame when they failed to fix it.

The warboss himself was stomping up and down alongside his trukk, screeching and hollering, slapping the back of his hand across the heads of any boyz who looked like they weren't trying hard enough.

Suddenly he sprang into the air and crashed down onto the back of the wartrukk, thinking to use its elevation to help him see where the rest of the mobs had gone. The thicket of mekboyz working on the rear axle were instantly squashed into the ground as the orks that were already struggling to support the weight of the massive truck collapsed under the additional weight of the monstrous warboss. The trukk jolted back down into the earth with a crash that made Orkamungus stumble. He roared in displeasure and spun the rickety shoota turret to face the cowering orks at the side of the vehicle. They looked up at him with a mixture of resignation and terror, but then Orkamungus merely cackled his throat, pretending to riddle them with shot, sputtering and whooping with the imaginary report from the gun.

The clearing was not even nearly full, although Orkamungus could see more and more of his orks spilling out of the forest around the perimeter, barging their way through the thinning trees as their noses caught the scent of cooking meat. Fires were blazing all around, and the orks were roasting various creatures in the flames. The burning flesh sent thick clouds of black smoke billowing into the sky, and the gretchin strained to breathe it in, as though it was the only food they would get that night.

The warboss scanned the scene with his tiny red eyes. Still not enough. Wait more. He spun the shoota turret round to face the growing crowd and angled the barrel up into the sky, spraying slugs in a barrage of fire and crying out into the night.

'Waaaaaaaaagh!'

ONLY HALF AN hour after leaving the spaceport, the Blood Ravens caught the scent of the orks. In the distance was the echo of gunfire, and Corallis could make out the faint haze of fires on the horizon. But that was not their target tonight. The sergeant was at the head of the hunting squad, guiding them along the path that he had taken with the scouts earlier that evening.

The dark forest was littered with mutilated human corpses and the burnt out remains of woodsmen's huts. Not even these wilds had been spared the ravages of the ork invasion – although Gabriel could not imagine that the greenskins had found much satisfaction in the slaughter of these defenceless farmers. They were probably just venting their frustration and hatred after being repelled by the Blood Ravens at the spaceport. Orks in retreat were just as destructive as orks on the advance – they are always on the rampage. War for its own sake, thought Gabriel with a heavy heart.

The Marines moved swiftly and quietly through the shadows, pausing occasionally for Corallis to pick up the trail. It was not hard to follow. Scattered along the ground were discarded plates of armour, broken machine parts that must have fallen from rumbling wartrukks, pools of blood and slicks of oil. The Marines could have followed the stench even in perfect darkness – even without their enhanced night-vision.

With an abrupt motion, Corallis brought the group to a halt, raising his fist into the air as he stooped to the ground. The moonlight dappled his armour through the canopy, making his image swim and shift before Gabriel's eyes.

There was silence as the Marines waited for the sergeant to draw his conclusions. He was tracing a pattern on the ground with his hand and staring out into the darkness of the thick forest off to the side of the vulgar trail of debris and destruction. It seemed pretty obvious where the orks had gone, so Gabriel was concerned. He made his way up along side Corallis and rested his hand on the sergeant's shoulder. 'Corallis. What is it?'

'I'm not sure, captain,' whispered Corallis in response. 'There are some faint markings here, running along side the ork trail. They are hardly here at all, as though made by feet that barely touch the ground. But there is definitely something – something swifter and stealthier than we are.'

'Were they following the orks?' asked Gabriel, as the significance of Corallis's last words sunk in. 'Or are they following us?'

'I'm not sure, captain. The marks are too vague to render much information about when they were made.' But the sergeant was staring out into the forest again, making it clear that he suspected that whatever had made the marks was still out there. Gabriel followed his gaze, scanning the moon-dappled foliage for signs of movement.

'The moonlight and shadows would hide anything tonight – even an ork,' said Corallis, shaking his head.

'Yes, sergeant – or even us,' replied Gabriel with half a smile, pressing down on Corallis's shoulder as he stood and waved a signal to the hunting party. He clicked the vox-channel in his armour and whispered his directions to the squad. 'Let's take it off road. Keep to the thick foliage and trace this ork trail in a parallel motion. Silence, understood.'

Without a word, the squad of Blood Ravens dispersed into the trees, slipping into the shadows and the natural camouflage provided by the broken pools of moonlight.

HIDDEN IN THE shadows and the foliage, the Blood Ravens pressed on through the forest. 'There is something else in these woods, Gabriel,' said Isador, leaning closely to the captain's ear as they slipped through the undergrowth. 'Something unpleasant.'

'Besides us, you mean?' asked Gabriel with a faint smile, as he dropped to one knee and levelled his bolter. The rest of the Blood Ravens followed suit, each bracing their weapons and falling into motionlessness. There was a fire burning in a small clearing about one hundred metres ahead of them, and the smell of burning flesh was beginning to become overpowering. Gabriel signalled to Corallis to go and check it out, and then turned back to Isador.

'What do you mean, brother?'

'I'm not sure, captain. But there are voices in these woods. Silent voices that press in at my mind so sweetly…' The Librarian tailed off, as though remembering something beautiful. 'They are evil and heretical voices, Gabriel. But I do not know where they are from.'

Gabriel looked at his friend with concern, not knowing what to say. He simply nodded. 'We will be careful.'

'I do not care for all this sneaking about,' continued Isador, as though that might explain everything.

'I know, old friend. You have always preferred the direct approach,' replied Gabriel, trying to lift the mood.

'What about the Tartarans? Why not send them after the orks, instead of treating them like glorified baby-sitters? Better still, why not take the entire regiment and meet the main ork force head-on? It could not possibly stand before us.' Isador's voice was full of sudden venom.

'We have fought the orks a hundred times, Isador. And you told me yourself, they thrive on war. Nothing would please them more than a direct assault on their warboss. They would fight with greater passion than we have yet seen. Our casualties would be unacceptably high,' said Gabriel, explaining what Isador already knew.

'But what are the Imperial Guard for, if not to die for the Emperor?' He almost spat the words into the dirt. 'At the very least, we should have brought a few squads with us on this hunt – we would not want to be remembered for our carelessness, would we?'

The words were laced with disgust, and Gabriel was momentarily stunned by Isador's speech. There was more to this than a revulsion towards the cowardliness of some of the Tartarans. The Librarian was holding something back about Gabriel himself, as though not quite daring to challenge the judgement of his old friend.

'We, Isador? We, or me?' Gabriel was staring straight into the eyes of the Librarian, fierce with repressed pain. Isador stared back, meeting the captain's bright eyes and immediately seeing his mistake. With a quiet sigh, he responded.

'I am sorry, Gabriel. I am not quite myself today,' said Isador, looking around into the forest as if expecting to see someone watching them. 'I am not accusing you of anything, captain. And when I said "we," I meant it – we are the Blood Ravens, battle-brothers until the end.'

'Perhaps you are right, old friend. Perhaps I have grown careless. We are battle-brothers, Isador, but I am the captain. Responsibility is mine,' said Gabriel, dropping his gaze from Isador's face and shaking his head faintly. 'I also have not been myself lately.'

'I have seen how you have changed since Cyrene, Gabriel. But there was nothing that you could have done to save it. You did what had to be done.' Isador's tone was gentle again.

'Do not mention that place again, Isador!' One or two of the other squad members turned their heads as Gabriel raised his voice. He brought himself under control quickly and continued. 'Cyrene was my homeworld… it was my responsibility,' he said, his voice dropping to a barely audible whisper.

'Captain.' It was Corallis, stooped under the cover of giant fern fronds just in front of them. Gabriel looked up and wondered how long the sergeant had been there. By his side, Isador was doing the same thing. They shared a quick glance and then Gabriel answered.

'What news, sergeant?'

'The orks have established a camp at an old pumping station in the forest. There is good cover around the perimeter, and they are unprepared for our assault.'

'Excellent,' said Gabriel, relieved and enthusiastic at the thought of combat at last. Nothing cleared his mind better than a righteous cleansing. 'Then let us show these orks how Blood Ravens bring death to the enemies of the Emperor.'

THE SPACEPORT WAS shrouded in darkness as the thick black clouds rolled across the sky, obscuring the stars

and filtering the moonlight into a dirty grey. A thin
drizzle of rain fell continuously, coating everything
in a slick, oily ichor as the smoky clouds spat their
residue to the ground. Camp fires were scattered reas-
suringly over the deck, with groups of Guardsmen
huddled around them for warmth and companion-
ship. Others were hard at work on the port's
fortifications, tugging the ruins of Sentinels and
Leman Russ tanks into banks around the perimeter
that faced out into the wilderness. Autocannon,
heavy bolter and lascannon emplacements were
being dug into the barricades at regular intervals, facing out across the plain. That is where the orks would
come from, if Captain Angelos had been right about
their renewed offensive.

Colonel Brom stood on the tracks of a Leman
Russ that had been slid into the barricade on its
side. He was scanning the horizon for signs of
movement, but there was nothing except the faint
orange glow of distant fires. That's where the warboss must be, he thought. Captain Angelos was
right after all. They're regrouping, out of range of
our gun emplacements. But somehow the hazy
glow was reassuring; if the orks were playing by
their camp fires, then they were not about to launch
their second attack tonight.

The dull, misted moonlight bathed the afternoon's
battlefield in monochrome, and Brom slouched
down onto the side of the tank to sit and consider it.
He sighed deeply and shook his head, patting each of
his pockets in turn in a quest for a lho-stick. Finding
one in his left breast pocket, he tapped it methodically against the armour of the Leman Russ and then
flicked it into life.

Taking a long draw and letting the smoke blossom into his lungs, Brom tried to get the events of the day into some kind of perspective.

Behind him, he could hear the industry of his Tartarans. Most of them had recovered from the shocks of the day already, and they were struggling to prepare for tomorrow. There were whispers of excitement about the arrival of the Space Marines and occasional shouts of awe as stories were shared about the incredible feats they had accomplished on the battlefields of a thousand planets. Rumours and legends flooded the camp like a contagious disease, inflecting everyone with a new vigour and a thrill of excitement.

Not everyone. Brom sat on his own, staring out across the silvering corpses of his Guardsmen as they lay unrecovered where they fell, intermingled with the ork-dead, their blood mixing in the soaked earth. Hundreds of them. Almost half the Fifth and more than half the Seventh had been killed in one afternoon. And these were his men. Good men with whom he had fought on numberless occasions in the past.

And the Blood Ravens had called them cowards.

Taking another draw on his lho-stick, Brom blew a wispy thread of cloud out into the night air. It was a good weed – locally grown in the rich, fertile soil of Tartarus. For a moment, he thought that he could taste the blood-drenched soil seeping into the smoke, but he shut out the thought in a wave of nausea.

Cowards. The word stuck in his mind and cycled through his thoughts like a hot coal, scorching at his soul. Something had happened. Some of his men had turned and run. He had dealt with many of them himself – executing men who had saved his own life countless times. The guilt gnawed at his conscience, making his head hurt from within.

Glancing up and down the line of the barricade, Brom could see little pockets of men sitting in silence. They had obviously moved away from their comrades to be alone with their thoughts, gazing out over the carnage of the day. Not for them the naïve excitement about the Space Marines. Tiny little embers of fire marked them out as smokers, speckling the imposing weight of the barricade with the touches of fireflies.

Brom didn't have the heart to bust them for skipping work. The fortifications were going up quickly, as the most enthusiastic of the men laboured under a haze of optimism. He was happy to let his men deal with the events of the day in their own ways – the last thing they needed now was their commanding officer to yell at them about treachery and cowardice. Everyone knew what had happened. Some were trying to forget, to make the approaching battle less horrifying. Others had fallen into themselves, searching for their last scraps of resolve. But some, suspected Brom, would simply find the terrible truth – they were cowards after all.

Anger and confusion curdled together in Brom's head. The Blood Ravens had treated him like a lackey, and they had cast a slur on the honour of the Tartarans. He was a colonel of the Emperor's Imperial Guard, and should be treated as such. And it wasn't as if the Blood Ravens were beyond reproach themselves: mighty though they may be in battle, inside those giant suits of power amour there was the heart and soul of a man. They could make mistakes too, just like the Tartarans. And they had. He knew that they had.

Brom was hissing and muttering to himself as his anger seethed inside him. A voice called out from behind the barricade.

'Colonel Brom? Is everything alright, sir?' It was Ckrius, again, probably carrying another cup of recaff and grinning inanely.

'Fine, trooper,' said Brom dismissively, suddenly aware that he had been mumbling and spitting with quiet rage. 'Fine.'

'You need any more recaff, colonel?' asked the trooper hopefully.

Brom laughed. He knew it. 'No, thank you Trooper Ckrius. I'm fine.'

As Ckrius climbed back down the barricade to rejoin his friends, Brom shook his head again. Where had all that anger come from? He threw his lho-stick to the ground and stamped it out with his boot. The Space Marines were a blessing from the Emperor himself. They were the finest warriors in the Imperium, selected from the most able hopefuls from thousands of different worlds and then cultivated for decades. Their honour and judgement was beyond reproach. Who was he to question them? And Captain Angelos was right – the Tartarans had collapsed, some troopers had turned in fear. Without the Blood Ravens, the spaceport would have fallen. Perhaps Angelos had been right to assign them construction duty while the Blood Ravens hunted the orks.

* * *

IN THE SHADOWY depths of the forest, the Blood Ravens were deployed in an arc around the perimeter of a compound. The old buildings around the pumping station were decrepit and barely stable, but they still seemed to be in use. Certainly they would not provide any significant cover for the mob of orks that lumbered and snorted their way between them.

The makeshift ork camp was a jumble of debris and filth. The greenskins had pulled down a couple of the old buildings and were using the wooden frames for their fires. Some of them bore deep flesh wounds on their limbs, but they still jostled and pushed each other about, trying to find their place in the food chain around the roasting meat. They snorted and snarled, spitting phlegm onto the ground as saliva ran between their jagged teeth.

In the centre of the compound was the largest of the mob, one of the so-called 'nobz.' Gabriel was watching it carefully as it smashed its fist into the smaller greenskins that fussed around it. They cowered under the blows but then set about their business with renewed vigour, as though the violence were itself a kind of language between the savage creatures. The nob was inspecting the pumping station with a small team of mekboyz, who prodded and poked at the end of a pipeline with their clumsy tools.

'Corallis. Where do those pipes go?' asked Gabriel in a barely audible whisper.

'They carry the water supply into Magna Bonum, captain,' answered the sergeant, realising at once how important this pumping station was to the people of Tartarus.

Gabriel nodded, clicking open a vox-channel to the rest of the squad. 'Focus on the largest of the creatures first – if we break their strongest warriors, then the others will flee. We can mop up the stragglers later.'

After a brief pause, the forest erupted into a blaze of bolter fire as the Blood Ravens opened up from their positions around the perimeter of the compound. The fire flashed into the centre of the offensive arc, defining a lethal killing zone in which the orks were instantly cut down. The Blood Ravens loosed another hail of fire, and then Gabriel was on his feet and charging into the chaotic mess of the ork camp, his chainsword whirring with serrated death.

The surviving orks scattered around the compound, diving for their weapons and colliding with each other with horrendous thumps. In the disarray, Gabriel hacked into the nearest knot of fumbling greenskins, thrusting his spluttering blade through bone and flesh, while his boltgun coughed shells from his other hand. In the heart of the mob, he could see the nob screaming commands at its bodyguard, sending the surrounding orks into a frenzy. The giant beast itself had tugged on a gleaming power claw, which still dripped with blood, and had drawn a huge gun into its other hand.

Gabriel ducked a viciously curving cleaver, using his own momentum to cut down with his chainsword, taking the legs off the offending greenskin next to him. Firing a rattle of bolter shells into a couple of shoota boyz that were fumbling with their guns in front of him, the Blood Ravens' captain strode forward towards the nob. This kill was going to be his.

On the other side of the camp, Isador was a blaze of blue energy. He brought his force staff sweeping round in great crescents, smashing its power into gaggles of orks that shrieked and sizzled under the tirade. From his left hand pulsed javelins of blue lightning, which chased after the fleeing greenskins and incinerated them as they tried to dive for cover.

All around the compound, the Blood Ravens were laying into the broken camp of orks, capitalising on the confusion of the greenskins as the creatures struggled to mount a defence. Sergeant Corallis had lost his boltgun and was wrestling one of the beasts with his hands, pitting his power armour against the bunched musculature and the barbed teeth of the ork. In one smooth movement, Corallis rolled backwards onto the ground, carrying the greenskin with him and flipping it over his shoulder. As he rolled back up onto his feet, he snatched up a fallen cleaver from the dirt and smashed it down into the skull of the stunned ork before it could regain its feet. The cleaver dug deeply into the thick skull and the ork's eyes bulged in surprise before the handle snapped clean away and the creature fell onto its face in the mud.

Meanwhile, Gabriel was striding through the camp towards the ork leader, dispatching the smaller orks with almost casual abandon as they charged at him with axes and clubs. Nothing would draw him off course now. The ork boss could see him coming, and it was blasting out rounds from its crude gun, cackling into the air with insanity burning in its tiny red eyes. The shots bounced off Gabriel's armour, denting it and scratching away the brilliant red paintwork. One or two of the slugs buried themselves in the joints between the armoured plates, punching into his flesh and sending shafts of pain darting through his limbs. But the Space Marine's augmented nervous system quickly shut down the pain receptors and his enhanced blood clotted the wounds almost as soon as they were made.

He cleared the last few strides with a running leap, throwing himself through the air towards the huge ork with his chainsword spluttering greenskin blood in an ichorous arc. The creature met Gabriel's attack with a swipe from its power claw, dragging a clutch of deep gashes across the captain's chest plate and throwing him aside, his boltgun falling into the dirt.

Gabriel hit the ground in a roll, flipping back up onto his feet and spinning his chainsword with a flourish. In an instant he was upon the ork again, his blade flashing and coughing in a relentless tirade of hacks and swipes. But the greenskin was just as fast, parrying the Blood Ravens' weapon with flicks of his power claw and countering with a series of vicious kicks and scratches.

In the depths of his mind, Gabriel could hear the silver choir flooding his soul with light once again, and he pressed his attack with righteous desperation, throwing all of his strength into each strike. The ork seemed to be lapsing into slow-motion, and Gabriel blocked its attacks with increasing ease.

The opening seemed to gape and beg for him to slaughter the vile greenskin. Gabriel watched the ork flail and thrash with its power claw, but it all seemed pathetically slow. And there, in the centre of the frenzy of claws was a gap which the ork had left completely unprotected – Gabriel could see it as clear as day, as though the light of the Astronomican itself was piercing it for him. But, as he stepped forward to run his chainsword through the enemy, the choir in his head started to wail and scream, and the beautiful silver light started to run with blood.

Gabriel screamed as he thrust his blade into the beast's chest, and then he ground the whirring teeth of the chainsword deeper into the creature's abdomen before ripping it free with a vicious upward swing. The nob was rent in two as it fell back under the strike, already dead before it hit the ground.

All around the camp, the remnants of the ork mob started to wail and shriek. They turned and tried to run, but were easily cut down by volleys of fire from the other Blood Ravens.

'GABRIEL?' ISADOR WAS at his shoulder, his hand resting gently on his punctured and torn armour. 'Gabriel, are you alright?'

'Yes. Yes, I'm fine,' answered Gabriel, wondering why Isador was making such a fuss. He had fallen to the ground after the battle with the ork boss, but now pulled himself to his feet to face the Librarian. 'I'm fine, Isador.'

'Your scream had me worried, brother,' said Isador looking around the camp. 'And I wasn't the only one to notice it.' The rest of the squad were stalking around the compound, kicking each ork corpse in turn to make sure that the creatures were really dead, and firing a single shot into the heads of any that groaned.

'I'll be fine, thank you Isador. Where is Prathios? I must give my praise to the Emperor for this victory,' said Gabriel, searching the scene for the company Chaplain.

'Prathios fought well, captain. He is over there with Corallis, who was injured in the fight,' replied Isador, pointing with his staff to one of the ruined buildings. 'After you have seen Prathios, you should visit the Apothecarion to see about those wounds, Gabriel.'

Gabriel looked down at his armour and saw for the first time how much damage it had suffered. The paint was scratched and the plates were riddled with dents, gashes and holes. He couldn't really remember suffering such an attack.

'Yes, Isador. I will do that. Thank you again,' he said as he turned and made his way over to Prathios and Corallis.

Standing alone in the centre of the compound, Isador surveyed the scene. Not a single Blood Raven had fallen in the attack, although Corallis had lost his left arm. All of the orks had been slain. It had been a good night for hunting after all.

From out of the darkness something cold tapped at the inside of Isador's mind, and he snapped his head round to stare into the forest at the edge of the compound. There was something in the shadows, something that was not quite there. A wave of whispers seemed to emanate from the darkness, questing for a space in the Librarian's head.

Isador slammed shut the doors to his soul and sent a sharp, noiseless blast into the trees: *I will suffer no trespass.* At that, the voices seemed to die into silence. After concentrating his gaze on the forest for a few more moments, Isador turned his attention back to the camp. Squinting slightly at the sudden pain in his head, he made his way back towards Gabriel and Prathios, the sound of his captain's scream resounding in his mind once again.

CHAPTER THREE

TERROR GRIPPED AT his soul, releasing the one thought that the struggling man should have suppressed for all time. He couldn't hang on to his consciousness as it swam and curdled, as though stirred by the piercing force of a primeval spear. Voices were seducing him from all sides, licking at the inside of his head like exquisite flames, weakening his resolve and drawing him into hell. He could see the sorcerer towering over him, and could sense the muttering voices of his perverted priesthood ringed around him, but there was nothing he could do to fight them. Finally, without a word or even a breath, he cried out with his mind in desperate longing, *Choose me!*

Chaos Sorcerer Sindri looked down at the ruined husk that was once a Marine of the accursed Alpha Legion, but there was no pity in his stare. His fist was clasped around his Bedlam Staff, clenching and unclenching in impatient anticipation, and, buried deep in the visor sockets of his bladed helmet, Sindri's eyes glowered a thirsty red.

'He is ready, my lord,' hissed the sorcerer, clearly pained by the requirement of deference. Nonetheless, his tone was soft and sibilant.

'Then proceed, sorcerer, but proceed carefully. If you fail me, this will not be the only sacrifice tonight,' said Chaos Lord Bale bluntly, leaning his impressive weight against the great Manreaper scythe, which seemed to writhe hungrily in his grasp.

The sorcerer did not reply. Instead he pointed with his staff and, without a word, the chosen Chaos Marine slouched towards the edge of the crater, as though held in a trance.

At the bottom of the freshly excavated pit lay an altar. It was little more than a slab of rough hewn stone, but it pulsed with ancient promises. Its sides had been carved with snaking designs and icons depicting sacrifice and slaughter, and dark prayers had been etched into the rock with teeth and bones. Each inscription had drawn the blood of its artisan, and had been made in a frenzy of agony and love. The surface of the altar, stained with the life blood of countless sacrifices, ran with deep grooves and runnels.

The Chaos Marine climbed carefully down the sides of the crater towards the altar, more and more horrified with each step, not able to understand what he was doing. But the voices whispered into his soul, drawing him onwards and dissolving his resistance. He required no escort – despite himself he knew what he had to do. Stealing a glance back up to the rim of the pit, he could see a ring of his battle-brothers from the Alpha Legion, each shimmering in the dark, acid-green of their ancient armour. They stared down at him in silence, filling the humid night with their heavy malignancy.

As he approached the altar, he realised that Sindri and Lord Bale were there already with retinues of armed Marines fanned out behind them. Just in case. Even in the night and in the heavy shadow of the crater, he could see the steady evil throbbing in their eyes. Lord Bale himself was a monster of man – hugely tall and draped with corpse-like flesh that paled into a sickly white in the thin moonlight. Only his bladed teeth seemed to reflect any light at all, and that was vicious beyond the imaginings of men. A terrible stench wafted through the night air, and the Chaos Marine noticed for the last time how Bale's green and burnished gold armour was coated in a thick, ichorous film of ruined flesh. It was the last residue of the countless men who had fallen beneath the Chaos Lord's war-scythe in his millennia of bloody rampage across worlds and galaxies.

Without any prompting, the nameless Marine climbed up onto the altar and lay down, throwing his arms up over his head and pushing his feet across into the corners of the stone. He closed his eyes and felt the tablet's almost imperceptible vibrations beneath him. So, this is where it would all begin.

Sindri's voice was hissing and muttering at the head of the altar, drawing more and more movement from the rock itself, which began to emanate heat. Bale could see the runes and the prayers start to glow around the sides of the tablet, and blood started to ooze out of the eyes of the daemons etched into the stone. In the sky, dark clouds started to congeal and swirl, condensing a sleet of rain and filling the night with sheets of lightning.

The prostrate Marine could feel the rain falling onto his face and splashing off the altar. Droplets began to seep into his mouth, and his tongue licked at them automatically. The familiar irony taste rippled through his body, sending a thrill into his soul as he realised that it was a rain of blood, and that it was all for him.

Suddenly Sindri stopped his chant and silence filled the pit, broken only by the persistent spatter of heavy rain. Then the Marine screamed. A great gash had opened up across his chest, spilling blood and organs out across the altar. Another tore into his stomach, and then smaller cuts started to criss-cross his legs and arms. After a couple of seconds, his face was ripped to shreds by the invisible force and a torrent of blood was cascading down the sides of the altar, spewing out of every inch of the screaming Marine.

Lord Bale ran his tongue along his razor-sharp teeth, watching the Chaotic powers rack the body of the victim, dreaming that such power would one day be his. But his reverie was broken as Sindri raised his staff into the sky and drew down a sizzling bolt of purple lightning, wailing a prayer as the energy coursed through his body and bounced back into the dual-pronged blade at the crest of his Bedlam Staff. With a dramatic flourish, Sindri spun the blade and brought it down in a sudden, single sweep, cleaving the Marine's head from his shoulders.

'And so it begins,' hissed the sorcerer, as a raucous cheer arose from the Chaos Marines around the rim of the crater.

THE FIRST HINTS of daylight dusted the ornate stonework of the cathedral, but dawn brought with it the promise of war on the horizon. The city of Magna Bonum was still resting, its streets filled with the half-baked shelters of refugees who had flooded in through the great gates, thinking that the high city wall would bring them some measure of protection. It had never been breached before, but never before had it faced such a colossal onslaught of ork power. Despite the glorious sunrise, the horizon was heavy with a dark ocean of greenskin warriors, rumbling their way towards the city.

The Blood Ravens had returned from their hunt only a few hours before dawn, and Gabriel had appropriated the cathedral as the most suitable location for their base in the city. They had swept past the spaceport with barely a nod to the cheering troopers of the Tartarans. Sergeant Matiel had paused for a moment, and presented one of the Guardsmen with the severed head of an ork, as a memento and as inspiration for them in the battle to come.

The young trooper had stared at the huge, heavy skull in disbelief, and for a moment Matiel had thought that the man would drop it in horror. But as the Blood Ravens pressed on past the spaceport they could see the head lifted onto the barricades, skewered on the point of a lance. They would leave the defence of the spaceport to Brom and his men – it would fall anyway, and Gabriel was not about to lose any of his Space Marines in a futile fight.

The cathedral itself was a towering testimony to the
Emperor-fearing architects of Tartarus. Its main spire
thrust proudly into the sky like a giant sword, laced
with threads of gargoyles and inscribed with hymns
of duty over every stone. The immense adamantium
doors shimmered with etchings of saints and their
litanies of repentance, inspiring the people who
passed through them into passions of vengeance
against the vile forces that would challenge the glory
of the Imperium.

Inside, the massive, vaulted ceilings defined a cav-
ernous space of soaring columns and deepest
contemplation. Around the walls were frescos showing the heroism of the Tartarans in the face of
heretics, cultists and aliens. The stained-glass windows depicted the Golden Throne itself, surrounded
by the silver choir of the Astronomican, and the
morning sun streamed through them, flooding the
cathedral with the grace of the Emperor himself.

In the small chapel behind the altar, Gabriel knelt
in silent prayer. After a few moments, the glorious
rapture of the Astronomican washed into his mind
once again. It began with a single voice, silver and
pure. It was a solitary note, unwavering, struck and
held beyond all sense and perception, playing
directly into the soul. One voice became two, and
then two shattered into a miracle of harmonies, filling every last vestige of his soul with an aria of purity
and light.

Hidden in the depths of his conscious mind, part
of Gabriel resisted the magnificent vision, as the last
healthy cells in a body might fight an enveloping
cancer. Part of him knew that this was not a vision
for an untrained mind. Gabriel was no astropath,

and he had not spent decades of psychic torment in the secret halls of the librarium sanatorium, learning to control and shape the deceptive energies of the immaterium, like Isador. His soul simply knew not what to do with this rapturous vision.

It was no secret that the Blood Ravens boasted an unusual number of psykers, particularly in the upper echelons of their structure. There were even rumours of an elite cadre of Librarians who formed a combat squad on their own, for especially sensitive or secretive missions. But even Gabriel had heard only rumours about this, and he had never found the right moment to ask Isador; too much curiosity about the constitution of the librarium sanatorium from non-psykers was not encouraged, and he was not sure how his old friend would react.

Gabriel also knew that many of the most powerful psykers in the Chapter had been recruited from Cyrene, Isador included. Indeed, the Blood Ravens had recruited heavily from that planet before... before it had been cleansed. Even the great Father Librarian, Azariah Vidya, may the Emperor preserve his soul, was originally from Cyrene. In the years of the Blood Ravens' infancy, Azariah had been the first to hold the dual mantle of Chapter Master and Master of the Librarium, but with him had started the long tradition that marked out the Blood Ravens from other, more puritanical, Chapters of the Adeptus Astartes.

Nonetheless, the Blood Ravens had never adopted Cyrene as their homeworld, preferring to base their fortress monastery in the mighty battle barge, *Omnis Arcanum*. The Chapter returned to the planet periodically and conducted the Blood Trials, at which aspirant warriors would compete for the chance to become a Blood Raven acolyte. Gabriel himself had once fought in those trials, besting hundreds of his fellow Cyreneans before being whisked into orbit for further, agonising tests in a Blood Ravens' cruiser.

And then, one day, Gabriel had returned to Cyrene. By then he was an honoured captain of the Blood Ravens, returning to his homeworld with Brother Chaplain Prathios to conduct the Blood Trials himself and to sweep for new recruits. What he found on Cyrene on that trip was to change his life forever.

There had always been an uncommonly large incidence of mutant births on the planet, and relatively large numbers of nascent psykers amongst the populace. In fact, although such abominations were swiftly cleansed and burned by the local authorities, it had been suggested more than once that this demographic quirk could be linked to the unusual potency and number of Blood Ravens psykers.

Within only a few days of making planet-fall, Gabriel had cut short the trials and returned to his strike cruiser, *Ravenous Spirit*, from which he had transmitted an encrypted astropathic communiqué. Shortly afterwards, a flotilla of Naval and Inquisition vessels had joined the *Ravenous Spirit* in orbit and had proceeded to launch a unrelenting barrage of lance strikes, mass drivers and cyclone torpedoes, reducing the once green world to a primeval, molten state.

It had been his duty, and a Space Marine is nothing without his sense of duty. It had been his decision, which made it his responsibility. Billions of people. More people than were struggling for their survival here on Tartarus, and Gabriel could still hear their screams in his soul – they blamed him, and they were right. He was one of them.

Again, the crystal clear tones of the Astronomican started to slip and scrape, like claws dragging desperately for purchase as they fell from an elevated promontory. Gabriel could see his own fall in the screams of the desperate, melting faces that seemed to reach out for him, dragging him down into hell. But he did not try to hide from the accusations of the dead – they knew what he had done as well as he did. In some ways, their hideous taunts were more apposite and honest than the soaring magnificence of the Astronomican itself.

'FARSEER. IT APPEARS that the humans may deal with the greenskins for us,' said the ranger, stooped into submission before the unmoving figure of the farseer. 'I have seen them fight, and they are strong, if clumsy.'

'Yes, Flaetriu, the new humans will be able to see off the orks, but they are not entirely our allies,' said Macha, her gaze focussed in some unseen place elsewhere. 'We should not forget that they are treacherous creatures.'

The shade of the trees played in eddying patterns across the green and white armour of the Biel-Tan eldar. Their temporary camp was buried deep in the forest, at the end of pathways that seemed to lead nowhere. The camp itself hardly broke the rhythm of the trees, as the eldar structures flaunted a perfect match in colour and structure with the local foliage. A number of orks had already passed through the camp, utterly oblivious to its existence, until a rain of fire from shuriken catapults shredded them into mush.

The rangers had been roaming the woods for days now, monitoring the movements of the vile greenskins and plotting ways for the small Biel-Tan force to eradicate the space-vermin. Flaetriu could not even bare the smell of the creatures – their very existence seemed to offend his sense of reality. He and his fellow rangers had already dispatched large numbers of the disgusting creatures, and part of him was loathe to let the stupid humans enjoy the rest. Then again, pest control was not really a profession appropriate for an eldar – such mundane matters could be left to the more mundane races.

'Their arrival was well timed, farseer,' said Flaetriu.

'They were bound to come,' replied Macha, still gazing into the invisible distance. 'Their fates are inextricably bound to this place, although they have forgotten this already. The humans have such pathetically short memories. It is this, rather than the darkness in their souls, that makes them so dangerous.'

'When does the Swordwind arrive?' asked Flaetriu, looking into the sky, as though searching for signs of the rest of the Biel-Tan's army.

'They will be here in time, now that the orks are no longer our concern. For now, Flaetriu, go and see whether the humans require any assistance with the greenskin vermin.'

'Yes, farseer,' said the ranger, bowing his head with something like eagerness. Then, with a couple of long, bounding strides, he had vanished into the trees, keen to add some more kills to his day's tally.

THE FIRST SHELL exploded against the walls of the city with a screeching boom, sending a rain of rubble

tumbling to the ground. The sound brought everyone in Magna Bonum to a standstill, as they realised
that the dawn of war had finally come.

The first shell was followed by a second, this time
clearing the great walls and smashing into the smattering of hab-units that sheltered in their shadow.
The explosion sent groups of civilians running from
their homes and sparked fires across three blocks.

But these were just ranging shots, and the real barrage was yet to come. A spasm of artillery fire erupted
from the wilds in front of the city walls, raining shells
down into the buildings and the crowded streets of
Magna Bonum. Pandemonium was loosed on the
city, as civilians recovered from their shock and
started to run in all directions at once, seeking the
flimsy shelter of buildings and make-shift bunkers.
Guardsmen ran through the crowds, trying to calm
the people as they dashed towards the gun emplacements built into the walls.

Outside the cathedral a great mass of people had
gathered, hoping that the immense building would
provide them with shelter. But a squad of Blood
Ravens stood across the towering doors and blocked
their path, their red armour glinting gloriously in the
morning sun. Guardsmen and Space Marines darted
in and out of the cathedral, slipping between the
huge sentries with nods and salutes. Two Whirlwind
tanks had rolled into the plaza in front of the cathedral, emblazoned with the insignia of the Blood
Ravens and carrying clutches of Marines on their
roofs. The missile batteries of the tanks rotated
slowly to face out over the city to the south, ready for
the orks to come into range as they approached the
city walls.

A Rhino transport roared into the plaza, sending civilians scattering out of its path as it skidded to a halt at the bottom of the steps to the cathedral. As it stopped, a hatch folded out of its stern and a squad of Blood Ravens came pounding down the stairs to leap inside. Just as the last Marine cleared the hatch, the doors slammed shut and the vehicle's tracks spun into life once again, thrusting the Rhino back out across the plaza and off towards the squad's defensive assignment.

Inside the cathedral was a throng of activity. Gabriel was receiving a short line of sergeants, dispatching them with well-rehearsed protocols and precise orders. Pushing his way to the front of the crowd, with a small knot of Guardsmen around him, came Colonel Brom.

'Captain Angelos. Librarian Akios,' said Brom, nodding his greetings to Gabriel and Isador. 'I have taken the liberty of stationing Tartaran squads around key facilities in the city, especially the power plant. We are also standing guard over the spaceport.' Brom was standing crisply to attention and trying to communicate an efficient air of confidence.

'Ah, Colonel Brom, good of you to join us,' said Gabriel, deflating Brom immediately. 'Your initiative is admirable, colonel, but I need you to pull your men out of the spaceport and to man the defences of the city walls.'

'But, captain, if we abandon the spaceport–' started Brom, visibly exasperated.

'–the spaceport cannot be held by the Tartarans, colonel, and the Blood Ravens cannot spare any Marines for the defence of suboptimal positions at this time. Our priority has to be to maximise our defences in one location to assure victory. You should not mistake the orks' simple manner for stupidity, Colonel Brom. They are more cunning than they might seem, and splitting our defences would play straight into their hands.'

'I'm sure that you know best,' said Brom, biting down on his lower lip.

'Thank you, colonel. Now go. I have much to attend to,' replied Gabriel, turning sharply to address one of the waiting Space Marines. 'Brother Matiel, take your assault squad to cover the set of buildings opposite the market sector. And Brother Tanthius, take the Terminators down to the east gate.' Gabriel looked around. 'Corallis? Send word to the *Litany* that we may need aerial support before the day is over.'

Colonel Brom paused for a moment and pulled his cape more securely over his shoulders. Then he straightened his tunic and turned with affected dignity, making his way out of the cathedral with his subordinates in tow.

'I am not sure that I agree with this course of action, Gabriel,' said Isador, watching Brom disappear into the crowd. 'Why should we sit here within the city walls and wait for the orks to attack? Why not carry the fight to them?'

'Brother Isador, would you have us go out and meet the orks on open ground as they roll forward in full strength? That would be madness. You and I both know better than to try and engage the orks on their terms. Far better to let their charge break against the walls of Magna Bonum, and then to meet them on our terms. The Codex calls for a defensive action in these circumstances, Isador, and a defensive action is what we shall launch, no matter what the preferences of Colonel Brom.'

'Perhaps you are too harsh on him, Gabriel. This is his homeworld, after all, and he will fight for it harder than anyone,' said Isador, feeling the frustration in the captain's voice.

'I am well aware of the importance of one's homeworld, Isador,' retorted Gabriel, slightly stung. 'But I am a servant of the Emperor and an agent of the Codex Astartes. I will do my duty here, and I trust that the rest of you will do the same.'

'Of course... you are right, captain,' answered Isador smoothly, as though placating him. 'Perhaps patience is the better virtue here.'

THE TARTARAN GUN emplacements in the wall blazed with energy, lighting their positions like torches against the rockcrete. Lascannons, autocannons and heavy bolters lashed viciously into the charging mass of green muscle that thundered across the plains to the south of Magna Bonum. The orks had already overrun the spaceport, and its smoldering remains could be seen under clouds of black smoke to the south-west. But the defence of the spaceport had been half-hearted at best, despite all the effort expended on the construction of barricades. At the last minute, Colonel Brom had rushed round the site and ordered his men to rig the place for a special welcome for the orks, and then to get out.

The greenskins had crashed into the makeshift defences and overrun them almost instantly, hardly even noticing that the defensive guns were firing automatically and that there were no troopers to hack and dice. By the time that it dawned on the mob, it was too late. Brom flicked the switch with a satisfaction that he hadn't felt in years, and watched the spaceport evaporate in a furnace of flames and orks.

The bulk of the greenskin horde pounded on towards the city, hardly even flinching when hundreds of their number were incinerated by the crude trick. Most of them could already see the Imperial forces that lay in wait for them, resplendent in the morning sun, and the prospect of imminent combat drew them on even faster. The salivating and panting mob rolled onwards in huge numbers, filling the air with smoke, stench and the sound of thunder.

From their emplacements on the city wall, the Guardsmen of the Tartarans stared in awe at the scale of the army that was descending upon them. The plains of Bonum were thick with greenskins and their crude vehicles of war. Countless buggies swept along in the vanguard, flanked by huge ork warbikes. Behind them came a storm of infantry: shoota boyz and slugga boyz in incredible numbers. And in the heart of the mass were some bristling wartrukks, with enormous orks standing proudly on their roofs, howling into the air as though driving their forces onwards.

As the first of the speeding buggies bounced into range, the city's walls became a blaze of gunfire, shedding hails of las-fire and bolter shells in a constant barrage. Some of the buggies flipped and burst into flames, others crashed straight into the back of them, but most of them ploughed on towards the armoured forces waiting at the base of the wall.

Leaning hard against his autocannon, trooper Ckrius was jolted around by the powerful recoil, but he could see a stream of Blood Ravens' assault bikes heading out from the city, seeking to intercept the ork warbikes before they could draw in from the flanks. Huge, red Predator tanks rolled out away from the walls, their gun-turrets blazing with lascannon fire as they laid into the advancing tide of ork buggies, splintering the advancing mass before rolling over the top of anything that got in their way.

The Tartarans in the wall's launcher-emplacements were lobbing mortars and grenades, plotting the parabolas so that the explosions would clear the Imperial forces. But shells were also coming back from the greenskins, smashing into the wall and sending avalanches of rockcrete crashing to the ground. Guardsman Katrn ducked back away from the team of the heavy bolter, covering his head with his hands and muttering something inaudible amongst the din. The gunner crew turned and yelled at him to get back into position, but he just ignored them, shaking his head violently and crying out. The crew could see tears in the Guardsman's eyes, and they shook their heads in disgust, turning back to the weapon as dust and debris rained down on their position.

In his mind, from somewhere beyond the noise of battle, Katrn could hear the gun-crew taunting him. *Coward… coward… you are a disgrace to your family… the Emperor will spit on your soul…* In a moment of resolution, Katrn drew his hellpistol and levelled it towards the gun-crew. *Yes, that's it… the false Emperor doesn't understand you…* He clenched the trigger in a frenzy of violence, riddling the backs of his crewmen with bullet holes until they slumped forward, falling out of the emplacement and tumbling down to the ground outside the wall. With a flash of a smile, Katrn vaulted over the fallen masonry to man the heavy bolter.

A SMALL GAGGLE of greenskins had stopped in the middle of the field, just out of range of the city's ordnance, and Ckrius was watching them carefully from his position in the wall. They were running in circles and punching each other, but grabbing at tools and machine parts from inside one the wartrukks that had clunked to a halt beside them. There were pieces of piping and huge rivet-guns being thrown around, and seemingly random metal plates were being bolted together, but gradually a recognisable structure began to take shape. Guardsman Ckrius realised what was going on just in time, and he dived for cover at the back of the gunning alcove just as the immense bombardment shell smashed into the wall only a few metres above his emplacement. A rain of rockcrete tumbled down from the ceiling, burying the autocannon beneath a heavy pile of debris.

Crawling back to the edge of the wall and peering out over the battlefield, Ckrius could see a formation of Blood Ravens' Tornados changing direction to launch an assault against the huge bombardment cannon. The land speeders sped over the pounding infantry of greenskins, spraying bolter fire and plumes of chemical flame from their heavy flamers as they went. The Tartarans' very own Sentinels were stalking through the orks in the wake of the Tornados, scorching out spurts of las-fire to support their speeding allies.

A rattle of fire caught one of the Tornados in the rear, and Ckrius watched in horror as its engines started to smoke and splutter. Suddenly, they ignited and the Tornado was transformed into a cannoning ball of flame, skidding down into the sea of orks beneath it and scything to a stop. Ckrius could vaguely see a Blood Raven tumble from the wreckage and struggle to his feet as dozens of greenskins launched themselves at him. At least ten orks were thrown screaming into the air before the Space Marine was finally swamped.

A sudden realisation struck Ckrius: that burst of fire had not come from the battlefield, it had come from one of the emplacements in the wall. Leaning out of the gun alcove, the trooper craned his neck to the side, looking over the face of the wall. He was shocked to see that it was already badly pitted with shell marks, especially around the gates on the south and east. However, the gunners seemed to be holding their positions, and their positions were defined by bright bursts of fire as the cannons flared with life.

As he surveyed the scene, Ckrius could hear the whine of incoming ordnance and he actually saw the tumbling, gyrating shell punch clumsily into the south gate. The explosion was immense, rocking the wall and almost throwing Ckrius out towards the raging battlefield below. When he looked again, the gate was a ragged mess of ripped and shredded adamantium, and hundreds of orks were pouring towards the breach in the city's defences.

Another mighty blast made Ckrius spin, casting his eyes to the left where the east gate used to be. Now there was just a pile of rubble, some scraps of twisted metal, and a rampage of greenskins clambering over the ruins into the market sector of the city.

* * *

'THE TORNADOES HAVE taken out the bombardment cannon, captain, but the orks are already through the city walls,' reported Corallis sharply. 'We are making good progress against the orks' heavy weaponry, but there is only so much that the Predators outside the city can do to stem the tide of foot soldiers that are overrunning the breaches in the wall. Our assault bikes have their work cut out with the ork warbikes and can offer little support to the wall's anti-personnel guns.'

'Pull the bikes back into the city, sergeant. They will be more useful in the streets than running around in wild ork chases in the open country,' said Gabriel, trying to keep the defences focussed around the city itself. 'And get some Devastator Marines down to those breaches to support the Vindicator tanks.'

'There is something else, captain,' said Corallis uneasily.

'Yes? Time is precious, sergeant,' replied Gabriel, coaxing and impatient.

'There are reports from the wall, captain... Reports suggesting that some of the Tartarans have turned their guns against us.'

There was a pause while the significance of this intelligence sank in.

'I see,' said Gabriel, as though unsurprised. 'Tell Brom to get his men back in line before we deal with them ourselves. And where is Brother-Librarian Isador?'

Sergeant Corallis was not entirely comfortable with his new role as the command squad sergeant, acting as the ears and eyes of his captain. He would have preferred to be out there in the fray, bringing the Emperor's righteous justice to the foul aliens, but his injury had not healed properly and his body had rejected the bionics of his replacement arm. 'He's already on his way to the south gate, captain.'

'Excellent.' With that, Gabriel strode down the cathedral steps and vaulted onto the saddle of his assault bike, leaving Corallis to co-ordinate the battle from the cathedral. 'I'll be at the east gate,' he said as he kicked the bike into life, spinning its rear wheel in a crescent across the flagstones until it was pointing towards the east. 'For the Great Father and the Emperor!' he cried, as he released the front brakes and the bike lurched forward, sending him roaring out of the plaza.

Sergeant Corallis stood on the top of the cathedral steps and watched his captain plough through the crowds of civilians and weave between the hulking masses of Blood Ravens' tanks and gun emplacements, raising cheers from the Marines that saw him pass. His men loved him, and Corallis felt a sudden rush of pride that Captain Angelos had entrusted him with custody of the command post. One arm or two, Corallis would not let him down.

GRUNTZ KICKED ONE of his kommandos square in the jaw as the hapless creature scrabbled desperately to keep its grip on the roof top. Far below, the pathetic humans had bunched into a crowd in the plaza to watch. A group of the big, red-armoured soldiers had noticed all the fuss and were already training their guns on the orks. Bolter shells started to punch into the masonry around the dangling kommando, and Gruntz kicked him again.

'You'ze da prob, Ugrin!' he yelled, kicking Ugrin repeatedly in the face and stamping down on his hands. 'Dem'ze shootin at you!'

A final heavy stomp crunched into Ugrin's face, and he could hold on no longer. His fingers slipped from their hold on the roof, and he fell shrieking down the side of the building, all the way staring back up at Gruntz and trying to spit at him. Gruntz watched his kommando fall and then leant over the ledge and spat a huge globule of phlegm down after him, hoping that it would reach him before he splattered into the flagstones and died. A rattle of bolter fire pushed him back away from the ledge, and he stamped in frustration as he realised that he would never know.

The remnants of the ork kommandos were busying themselves on the roof. Two of them were supporting the weight of a rokkit launcha and one was scurrying around them with a rivet gun, anchoring the machine into the rockcrete of the ledge. Orkamungus had been very clear about their function, and Gruntz was not about to return to the warboss with anything other than good news. None of these runts could screw it up now, even after that clumsy oath Ugrin had slipped off the ledge and alerted all the humans.

Peering back over the edge of the roof, Gruntz could see the two great, red tanks positioned in the heart of the city, in front of the cathedral. Somehow, Orkamungus had known where they would be, even yesterday. Their missile turrets were twitching slightly, as they tracked distant targets outside the city. Then in a great roar of energy, a flurry of missiles burst out of their chambers, searing into the sky and vanishing from view. A couple of seconds later, Gruntz could hear the distant explosions as the warheads punched down into the ork positions.

'Waaaaagh!' he cried, with defiance and rage spluttering from his mouth. He turned to face his gunners and stamped his feet, pointing back over his shoulder into the open square below. Stamping and screeching, he slapped one of the orks hard across the face, and the stunned kommando yelled back, pulling the mechanical trigger-lever on the side of the rokkit launcha. The machine lurched and bucked, ripping itself free of its fixings in the roof, but the huge rokkit shell burst out of it and roared up into the sky, spewing a trail of thick smoke in a tight spiral.

As the rest of the kommandos struggled to keep hold of the launcha, Gruntz watched the rokkit vanish into the clouds. It was gone. Gruntz turned round to face his kommandos with his gun drawn. The crew struggled and jostled, trying to stand behind each other, but Gruntz just sprayed a barrage of slugs into the nearest of the inept bunch as they all stood, wideeyed, waiting for punishment. A moment later and a spluttering whine made Gruntz look up.

The rokkit coughed and rolled as it fell back out of the cloud line, its fuel clearly exhausted as it plummeted back down to earth. The red soldiers in the plaza had also noticed it, and salvoes of fire streaked up from their gunners to try and take out the warhead before it fell. But the rokkit plunged straight down, flipping end over end and spluttering with smoke.

As the red soldiers finally scattered out of the way, the falling rokkit smashed straight into the roof of one of their tanks, exploding with tremendous force. The shell pierced the armoured plating of the tank and the flames detonated the reserves of missiles inside. An instant later and missiles were jetting around the plaza, most of them flying off into the distance but some smashing into the surrounding buildings and reducing them to rubble.

Gruntz leapt into the air, punching his fist into the sky with a victorious cry. Turning to congratulate his kommandos, he was riddled with a silent spray of tiny projectiles, which killed him instantly.

Flaetriu, the eldar ranger, tugged his elegant blade out of the throats of two of the vile greenskins, and re-holstered his shuriken catapult as another collapsed to the ground. The final ork had panicked and fallen off the rooftop as it had fumbled with its cleaver.

'That counts as four more,' muttered the ranger to himself as he nodded a swift signal to the other members of his squad on a rooftop across the plaza.

GABRIEL SLID HIS bike around the next corner and powered on towards the gate. He could hear the cacophony of battle rumbling and blasting ahead of him, beckoning him with its chorus of glory.

As he dropped his knee and banked the bike into a tight bend, he saw the crude shredders strewn across the road. But it was too late, and the bike's front tyres ran into the spikes on the apex of the curve. The tyre exploded in a burst of decompression and the bike scraped into a vicious skid along the road, shedding sparks and parts before smashing into a building at the side of the street. Gabriel was dragged along with his machine, his leg trapped under its weight when he crashed out of the turn.

The bike crunched to a standstill, and Gabriel struggled to lift the weight of the machine off his leg. Spasmodic slugga fire zipped across the street from the other side, speckling the bike's armour with darts of ricocheting bullets. Glancing back over his shoulder, Gabriel could see a ragtag mob of orks scrambling out of the buildings, stomping their feet in anticipation of a kill and firing their guns erratically in his direction. He kicked at the bike and twisted his own weight, but he was stuck under the machine. Grabbing his bolt pistol from its holster along his other leg, Grabriel wrenched his body into an awkward firing position and opened up at the gaggle of orks.

The first shots punched straight into the face of the mob's leader, the biggest of the bunch, dropping him to his knees in a bloody cascade of his own brain tissue. His henchmen wailed in anger and brought their weapons into sharper focus, as a hail of slugs crunched into the bike on all sides of Gabriel and bit into his armour.

Gabriel gritted his teeth as the onslaught started to penetrate his armour and the ork slugs began to dig into his flesh. He struggled against the weight of the mangled bike, trying to shift his body to minimise the orks' firing line and to maximise his own freedom of movement. He had managed to yank his chainsword free of the wreck in preparation for the close combat, and his bolter was spitting with venom. Voices in his mind spiralled into focus. *Not like this.*

A sudden roar filled the air and a powerful volley of fire pulsed across the street from above his head.

Blasting up from behind the buildings into which Gabriel had crashed, a squad of Assault Marines roared into the sky with their jump packs a blaze of afterburners. As the squad sprayed the street with bolter shells and gouts of flame, two Marines dropped to the road next to Gabriel and prised the bike off their captain.

With just a nod to the Sergeant Matiel, Gabriel was on his feet at once, and pounding across the street to engage the orks. The squad of Assault Marines was descending into the melee with their chainswords whirring as Gabriel charged into the fray with two Blood Ravens storming in behind him.

WITHOUT BREAKING THE rhythm of his fire into the mob that was pouring through the south gate, Tanthius slammed his power fist down onto the head of an ork that was charging towards the Terminators from the side, brandishing its huge cleaver threateningly. The blow crushed the greenskin's spine and cracked its thick skull instantly, and the creature slumped into a motionless heap.

Hundreds of orks were stamping and pushing their way through the breach in the city walls, and even the squad of Terminator Marines could not hold back the tide. Tanthius and his battle-brothers were standing against the pressure of an ocean of green muscles and a continuous barrage of fire. Their storm bolters were smoking with discharge as hellfire shells filled the breach with shrapnel and shattered fragments of death. The orks fell in wave after wave, ripped to pieces by the tirade launched from the Blood Ravens who were defending the breach, but still they came, spilling out into the outskirts of the city and running off into the interior.

Isador was in the breach itself, standing on top of a pile of fallen masonry and lashing out with his force staff in a blur of unspeakable energies. Pulses of lightning jousted out from his fingertips, frying orks as they dived for him or incinerating them as they struggled to make clear shots in the densely packed muddle of greenskins. His staff flashed and spun, cracking across skulls and slicing through abdomens as rivers of blue power flooded from the raven-wings at its tip. He was a burst of blue rock against which the green ocean was breaking.

A strafe of explosions ripped through the masonry on the ground, sending chunks of rockcrete flying into the air, defining a line straight for the blazing Librarian. The shells exploded as they hit Isador's coruscating power field, throwing him backwards into the city. He rolled back over his shoulder and up onto his feet, levelling his staff as he came up and letting out a terrible javelin of blue flame that roasted the knot of orks who tumbled after him. But deep, resounding footsteps told him that something bigger than an ork was headed for the breach.

Tanthius saw it first and turned all of his guns onto the monstrosity as it lumbered into the southern gateway. 'Dreadnought!' he yelled into the vox-unit in his helmet. The hulking, stomping machine almost filled the breach all by itself, with its clumsy mechanical arms thrashing into the masonry to help it keep its balance. Two weapons turrets protruded from the side of its stomach on either side of an armoured porthole, through which Tanthius could see the ugly face of its ork pilot.

The rest of the Terminators turned their guns in unison, abandoning the flood of smaller targets that burst over the banks of their own dead and gushed into the city. Lashes of hellfire shells blasted against the huge, hulking ork machine as it stomped clumsily through the ruins of the wall, knocking great chunks of masonry flying with its flailing arms as it fought for balance.

The hellfire shells rattled the loping machine, but it eventually planted its feet and turned its own guns on the Terminators, sending out blasts of flames and a fleet of rokkits that smashed into the Blood Ravens' formation. Tanthius felt the flames douse his armour as the skorcha bathed the Terminators in fire, but it would take more than a few flames to arrest the might of a Blood Ravens' Terminator. He took a couple of steps forward into the flames, stomping down on the slowly roasting greenskins by his feet, splattering them into the rough masonry, and spraying insistent hails of hellfire shells against the armoured can.

Three rokkits slid out of the flames in front of him and shot past his head. Even without turning, Tanthius knew that the huge explosion behind him was Brother Hurios, and he punched his humming power fist into the chest of another ork in rage. Lifting the struggling creature by its leg, Tanthius swung the beast around his head and used it to batter a gaggle of its greenskin brethren as he pounded forward towards the dreadnought.

Pulses of cackling energy sizzled against the sides of the ork dreadnought, destabilising it just enough to throw its aim, and Isador hacked at the machine's legs with his staff as sheets of lightning lashed out of his fingers. Just as Tanthius erupted out of the inferno inside the city, charging towards the breach, Isador jammed his staff into the crude, exposed knee joint of the dreadnought. The huge machine stumbled as its weapons tracked across to trace the motion of the charging Terminator and, as its weight shifted, Isador threw a javelin of power up into its undercarriage. As the machine lifted fractionally into the air, Tanthius took a flying leap and rammed into the side of it, plunging his power fist straight through the crudely riveted armour into the head of the ork inside. The dreadnought swayed under the assault and then its legs buckled from beneath it, sending it crashing to the ground, leaving Tanthius standing proudly on its fallen shell, ork blood and ichor dripping from his power fist.

The victory was short lived as row of explosions signalled the arrival of another dreadnought. Turning with determination, Isador and Tanthius saw a pair of ork dreadnoughts step into the breach, flanked on both sides by knots of smaller killer kans, each bristling with power claws and heavy weapons.

'We must hold this gate!' cried Isador into the vox-unit.

Another voice crackled onto the hissing channel. It was Corallis, from the command post. 'Brother Librarian. Pull the Terminators back away from the wall and into the city. We will make our stand around the cathedral. Captain Angelos has called for orbital support, and the bombardment is imminent.'

Tanthius shared a glance with Isador before signalling the orderly retreat to the remaining Terminators. Isador ducked an axe blade that cut into the side of a building next to his head, and then reached out with his hand and unleashed a fountain of pain directly into the flesh of the salivating ork that had struck at him. The Librarian's thoughts were riddled with doubts. *Another bombardment, Gabriel? This is not the captain that I have come to admire.*

THE CONCUSSION OF a huge explosion rippled up the street, knocking the remaining orks from their feet as the assault Marines continued to cut them down. A line of Blood Ravens appeared at the end of the road, marching backwards in an orderly fashion and firing continuously into the crowd of orks that were threatening to overrun them.

'The Devastators from the east gate, captain,' said Sergeant Matiel, nodding in the direction of the retreating Marines, as the last of the ork gang was dispatched at the blade of Gabriel's chainsword.

'Yes, sergeant. So it seems. The explosion must have been the Vindicator,' answered Gabriel as he started to run towards the retreating line, keen to get back into the action and to rally his Marines.

The vox channel hissed with static. 'Captain, the *Litany of Fury* reports that its bombardment arrays are now ready for firing.' It was Corallis, back at the cathedral. 'Reports from the wall defences suggest that the orks have breached the city limits, captain. If we are going to use the bombardment cannons, we have to use them now.'

Gabriel shivered as he heard the words, and he tried to ignore them. He was still running when he burst through the line of Devastator Marines and plunged into the wave of orks that hounded them. His chainsword was already spluttering with ichor, but he was roaring with energy himself. 'For the Great Father and the Emperor!' he yelled, and the Devastators stopped retreating. They planted their feet and braced against the onslaught of ork bodies, chainfists whirring thirstily, mutli-melta's whining with heat, and heavy bolters rattling off shells.

The Assault Marines had kicked their jump packs into life and were hovering above the Devastators, adding their rain of bolter shells to the fury of heavy weapons blasting out from their battle-brothers on the ground.

'Captain,' crackled an inconstant signal into the vox in his amour. 'There are too many of them. They are spilling around the edges of our position, flanking us on both sides and penetrating further into the city. We cannot hold them here,' reported Matiel from his vantage point above the skyline.

'Understood,' said Gabriel with frustration, as he dragged the teeth of his chainsword across the neck of one ork and jammed his boltgun into the mouth of another. 'Sergeant Matiel, take your assault squad back into the cathedral precincts. And Brother Furio,' he said, nodding a greeting to the sergeant of the Devastator squad who was fighting at his shoulder. 'We must pull back towards the cathedral – we can make our stand there. It is senseless to spend our lives so cheaply in these streets.'

Switching the vox-channel, Gabriel reluctantly made the call to Corallis. 'Sergeant. Recall the Marines from the wall and tell that idiot Brom to get his men into the cathedral precinct. Tell the *Litany of Fury* to give us five minutes.'

* * *

STANDING AT THE top of the steps in front of the cathedral, Gabriel and Isador watched the bombardment shells sear through the sky like falling stars. They thudded into the plain outside the city and exploded into sheets of white light. Mushrooms of dust and dirt billowed up from the impacts, and ripples of concussion throbbed across the skyline of the city.

A second flurry of meteoric strikes flashed down into the outskirts of Magna Bonum, just inside the ruins of the once defiant city wall. The immense explosions pounded the rockcrete and tore buildings apart, sending waves of fire rushing through the streets. Huge fountains of rubble and broken masonry were thrown high into the air, only to rain down again like cannonballs into those structures that had survived the initial blasts.

The edges of the city and the plains of Bonum beyond were submerged under a blanket of brilliant white as the superheated charges from the bombardment shells fried the air itself. The orks at the gates and those that had just broken through into the city were instantly incinerated, leaving nothing but faint thermal shadows scorched into the crumbling rockcrete.

'Did everyone make it back?' asked Isador, looking past Gabriel and addressing the question to Sergeant Corallis.

'Nearly everyone,' answered the sergeant without turning. He couldn't take his eyes from the awesome scene before him. 'All functional Marines are within the limits of the cathedral compound. Some squads of Tartarans were cut off in their wall emplacements.'

Gabriel was just staring at the ruined remains of the city. The bombardment had prevented the loss of

Magna Bonum, but it had levelled most of the city in the process. He was speechless as he struggled to reconcile himself with the wisdom of his decision.

'It had to be done,' said Corallis, turning at last and bowing slightly to his captain. 'The walls were breached and the orks were simply too numerous for us. The city was lost, captain.'

'And now it is won?' muttered Gabriel in self-recrimination.

Without saying a word, Isador walked slowly down the steps into the crowded plaza. The rattle of gunfire had started again, and the Librarian paused to look out into the streets nearby. Some of the orks had clearly penetrated more deeply into the city than the blast radius. He signalled to Colonel Brom, who was standing at the bottom of the steps with a group of subordinates, summoning him.

'Yes, Brother-Librarian Akios?' said Brom without ceremony as he walked over to Isador. 'I think that the Tartarans could have let the orks destroy Magna Bonum themselves, without the help of the Blood Ravens,' he added, as though unable to keep his rage bottled up.

'Quite possibly,' replied Isador. 'But the captain's purpose was to eradicate the orks, not to preserve your precious city, colonel. He has done Tartarus a service, even if you are too short-sighted to notice it.'

Brom smarted at the personal slight. 'Is this the same service he did for Cyrene?'

Isador's hand slapped across the colonel's face in a blur, knocking the man from his feet. 'You will not speak that way, colonel. Captain Angelos is an honourable man and a fine strategist. He does not take his responsibilities lightly.' Isador paused for a moment, conscious that he should not react too much to this provocation. 'Besides, colonel,' he continued, 'it seems that the Tartarans did quite a fine job of destroying their own forces, even before the bombardment.'

Climbing back to his feet and wiping the blood away from his lip, Brom replied. 'I am sure that the Blood Ravens know better than most not to listen to rumours, Librarian Akios.'

'Colonel Brom,' said Isador, ignoring the last slight, 'I expect that the Tartarans will want the honour of cleansing the remaining streets.'

Brom brushed the dust from his tunic and turned back to his subordinates. 'Sergeant Katrn, take your Armoured Fists squadron and sweep the ruins in the south of the city. Trooper Ckrius – you are now a squadron sergeant – form your own squad from whatever men you like and sweep the east.'

CHAPTER FOUR

'KNOCK IT OFF, all of you'z! We'ze movin' out!' bellowed Berzek, clattering the gretchin round their heads with a sweep of his huge arm. The grots snivelled and whined, flicking recriminating glances up at their massive keeper.

'We'ze not gonna stay an' fight?' asked one of them, scowling.

Berzek smashed the rotten little creature across its face with the mechanical claw that was bolted onto his forearm. The gretchin stumbled backwards and smacked into a wall, before it slumped to the ground whimpering.

'I'ze da biggest ork 'ere, which meanz I'ze da leada an' you'z a lousy bunch a gitz. We been waitin' an waitin' a fight deze marine-boyz, an' we'ze gonna stomp dem but good. To do dat, we need da strength of all da boyz, not a small weak mob ov runtz like

you'z boyz.' As he splattered his words, Berzek
reached out and gripped his power claw over the face
of the fallen gretchin, lifting it up by its head and
shaking it around for the others to see.

'We'ze orks! An' we'ze made for fightin'. Fightin'
and winnin! So uze you'z skulls fa sumtin.' With
that, Berzek clenched his fist and crushed the
gretchin's head into a dripping, bloody pulp.

'We'ze gonna go get Big Boss Orkamungus. He got
sumtin' special planned for deze humies,' explained
Berzek with a cackle of phlegm building up in his
throat. He spat it into the street, where it splattered
over the dusty, red helmet of a fallen Marine.

THE GREAT VAULTED space in the cathedral was strung
with ropes, from which swung artificial floors. The
cathedral was one of the only large structures left
undamaged by the bombardment, and it had been
rapidly transformed into a medicae-station for the
Imperial Guard and civilians of Magna Bonum. Each
of the four temporary floors was already strewn with
injured bodies, and servitors rushed between the
makeshift beds administering pain-killers. There was
little else they could do for the wounded until fresh
supplies arrived.

'The remaining greenskins seem to be fleeing the
city, captain,' said Colonel Brom. 'I sent out two
squads and neither of them has reported any serious
resistance. Sergeant Ckrius has indicated that a number of ork groups actually refused to engage with his
troops. They fled when he approached. I assume that
they have had enough of fighting for today.'

'You should never assume anything about the orks,
colonel,' countered Gabriel, looking up from a large

map that was spread over the altar of the cathedral. 'And you should certainly not think that they will ever have had enough of fighting. They live to fight, colonel. If they are fleeing, you may rest assured that it is not because your squad of Guardsmen scared them away. It is more likely because they have more important battles to fight later.'

'Colonel,' interjected Isador from the side of the altar, looking from Gabriel to Brom as though trying to build a bridge. 'Perhaps you can help us with this map? Orbital imaging from the *Litany of Fury* suggests that there is an even larger ork force massing in this area here,' said the Librarian pointing to a spot about fifty kilometres away from Magna Bonum. 'Can you tell us anything about that site, colonel?'

Colonel Brom hesitated for a moment, waiting for Gabriel to look up from the map again, but the captain didn't move. So Brom approached the altar with a nod to Isador, and inspected the map.

'That is the river basin that feeds the reservoirs for the city of Lloovre Marr,' said Brom, tracing his gloved finger along the valley floor towards the capital city. 'If they cut off the water, the city will not be able to stand against them for long. Our problem, however, is that the valley is the easiest approach to the city.' Brom traced his finger back across the site of the ork encampment towards Magna Bonum. 'And it is the only route along which we can transport heavy weaponry. The valley walls are sheer, and the plains on either side are thickly forested. We will not be able to reinforce the regiment in Lloovre Marr without passing the ork forces in the valley.'

'If you are right, colonel, then this is an unusually well planned assault by the greenskins. Their attack on Magna Bonum served merely to pull our forces into this city, while their real target was the capital. And they have cut us off from that quite effectively,' said Gabriel, looking up at last.

'It would confirm reports that the main warboss was not actually part of the assault on Magna Bonum,' offered Corallis. 'The boss would stay with the bulk of his force, would he not?'

'You're right, sergeant. Dispatch a scout squad up into the forest on the rim of the valley, and let's see what these orks are planning. In the meantime, the Blood Ravens will move out in force and try to catch the ork army before it reaches the city. Colonel Brom, we may yet have need for your Tartarans.'

'EVERYTIN' IZ READY, boss!' spurted Berzek as he threw himself face-down into the swampy ground with his arms spread out wide in supplication.

'Dem humies is in fa a good stompin'!' replied Orkamungus, chuckling with colic. 'Dis is gonna be da best fight o' dere miserable lives!' The warboss stepped forward and trod affectionately on the back on Berzek's head, squashing his face further into the sodden ground until he started to thrash with suffocation. But a slippery voice oozed into Orkamungus's ear and disturbed his show of appreciation.

'Just make sure that it is the last fight of their lives,' hissed Sindri, as he walked out from the shadows of the forest.

Orkamungus turned in surprise, and pulled himself up to his full height when he saw Sindri and Bale standing before him. The Chaos Marines were imposing figures, resplendent in their shimmering power armour, but they were dwarfed by the immense physical presence of the ork warboss, who towered over them.

'I don't takes ordaz from you, humie,' bellowed Orkamungus, showering the Chaos sorcerer with globules of spittle and slimy ichor.

'We've kept our side of the bargain, ork,' said Bale, stepping forward past his sorcerer and spitting the words back at the huge creature. Bale was not about to be cowed by this brainless beast. 'You wanted a new planet on which to wage war, and we have given it to you.'

Sindri eased back into the conversation. 'You wanted to face the Imperium's finest warriors, remember? You wanted to face the Space Marines, Orkamungus. And they are here. We have given you the Blood Ravens.'

'We have even provided you with weapons to use against them,' rumbled Bale, bluntly insinuating that the ork force would have crumbled without the aid of the Alpha Legion.

Orkamungus howled at the slight and raised his immense hand, ready to level a blow against the Chaos Lord. 'We'ze don't need need yor fancy weaponz!' As he did so, a clatter from the shadows of the trees revealed a squad of Alpha Legionaries with their boltguns trained on the huge warboss. Bale himself had moved faster than everyone, having already stepped inside the range of the ork's strike with his manreaper scythe poised.

'All we ask in return,' said Sindri, filling the awkward moment with velvety tones, 'is that you keep your end of the bargain. We simply want you to keep the Imperials distracted from our operations here. I'm sure that you'll enjoy that.'

'You'ze kept your word, humie. Dat's da truth. But dat don't mean you'ze can orda da orks around,' said Orkamungus, eying Bale warily whilst talking to Sindri.

'My apologies. We've delivered the last of the weaponry,' continued Sindri, indicating the pile of crates on the edge of the tree-line. A group of orks were already prising open the containers and prodding about at the devices inside. 'I'm sure that you'll make sure they find their way into capable hands.' As he spoke, one of the orks yelped in pain as a plume of flame jetted out of one of the weapons it was holding, bathing his own head in fire.

'Now, if you will excuse us, we will take our leave. I... respectfully request that you keep the Blood Ravens busy for as long as you can,' said Sindri, bowing slightly in mock grandeur.

'Bah! We'ze keep dem more dan buzy. We'ze keep dem dead!' spat Orkamungus, stomping his foot down into the wet ground with a tremendous splash, missing Berzek's still-gasping head by fractions.

DISAPPEARING INTO THE shadows of the forest, the Alpha Legion squad moved rapidly towards their extraction point. The legionaries were fanned out around Sindri and Bale, defining a perimeter that bristled with barrels and blades. They were alert and focussed, just like their delusional brothers in the Adeptus Astartes, but they were also liberated from the pathetic constraints of the Imperial creed. The orks may have been their allies, but they knew better than to underestimate the greenskins' hatred towards humans. All humans. The legionaries scanned the forest for signs of an ambush.

'The thought of kowtowing to these filthy creatures disgusts me,' said Bale, his voice rich with anger. 'I hope you know what you're doing, sorcerer. Otherwise, I will throw you to them as a personal gift.' The Chaos lord was storming through the foliage, lost in the intensity of his own repulsion.

'The orks are a tool, my lord, nothing more,' said Sindri smoothly, keeping pace with Bale. 'And quite an effective one, I might add.'

'Perhaps,' coughed Bale, stopping abruptly and turning suddenly to grasp Sindri by the neck. 'But I dislike providing such unpredictable aliens with our own weaponry.'

'Lord Bale,' managed Sindri between gulps of air. 'Orks are not unpredictable. Quite the contrary.' The grip around his neck loosened and he dropped to the ground. Bale snorted roughly and started back towards the waiting drop-ship. Sindri rushed after him, abject, humiliated and fuming inside. 'You can rely on them to turn against you. But they will honour their agreement for as long as we can provide them with enemies to satisfy their lust for battle.'

'There are other ways to make people do as you please,' answered Bale with off-handed ferocity. 'Ways more appropriate to warriors of the Alpha Legion. If we intimidated them with our strength, then they would take pause before betraying us.'

'But my lord, you cannot intimidate something that knows nothing of fear.'

'I can teach them to fear the Alpha Legion, sorcerer,' countered Bale with calm certainty. 'Just as I have taught hundreds of worlds to tremble at our name.'

'My lord, trouble yourself no longer with these orks. They will serve their purpose. Already the pathetic Imperials will be heading for Lloovre Marr, in pursuit of the mob. We will have what we came for and be gone before the orks finish off the Imperials and turn on us.'

'The Blood Ravens are not fools, Sindri. The Alpha Legion have had dealings with them before. You risk underestimating our allies and our enemies, sorcerer, and that is not the kind of wisdom I need from you,' said Bale as he climbed up into the hatch of the drop-ship.

BERZEK SPAT A fountain of mud and blood out of his gaping mouth as he lay imprinted into the fecund earth. He looked up at the huge form of his warboss, and watched him foaming at the mouth. The immense ork was on the verge of catatonia, and Berzek didn't know whether to speak or to attempt to slither away. If he said the wrong thing, he would be stomped. If he said nothing, he could be stomped anyway. Orkamungus was one massively stompy ork.

'Why'ze we talkin' wit dem humies, boss? Why'ze we no fight wit dem good?' said Berzek from amidst a mouthful of swamp. His decision was made.

Orkamungus looked down at him in surprise, as thought he'd forgotten all about him, or perhaps the boss simply assumed that the grunt had died.

'Dem smelly Chaos-boyz iz weak. Not nearly enuff of a challenge for orkz boyz. If dey were strong like orkz, dey no need us ta fight for dem. We'ze takin' dere guns and dere help and, when we'ze done choppin' up all the otha humies, we'ze comin' back here to chop dem up az well,' said Orkamungus with surprising composure.

'Dat plan'z a good'un, boss,' offered Berzek in relief, as he realised that he was still alive.

THROUGH THE SHIFTING shadows of the foliage, Flaetriu flashed a signal to Kreusaur on the other side of the clearing. The rangers had been keeping their eyes on the ork camp when the Chaos Marines had dropped in, making sure that the stinking greenskins were not about to stray into the farseer's plans, and they had quickly melted further back into the forest to observe the events that unfolded. Now, with half of the Alpha Legion squad already in the drop-ship, the rangers could contain their disgust no longer.

As one, the rangers opened up with their shuriken catapults, transforming the clearing into a mist of tiny, hissing projectiles. The air was perforated by the rattles of rapid impacts against the power armour of a clutch of Chaos Marines, who dived for cover behind the hatch of the drop-ship. But there was no cover, because the eldar had the clearing surrounded.

'Orks?' bellowed a rumbling voice from inside the drop-ship, and thunderous footfalls could be heard storming back down the ramp.

'No, my lord,' hissed Sindri, who was still on the ground. He turned his head slowly, taking in every shadow in the tree-line, apparently oblivious to the hail of lethal molecules that were hurtling about the glade.

'How many?' asked Bale as he leapt from the top of the ramp and thumped into the ground next to the sorcerer, his huge scythe glowing with thirst.

'Two, I think,' replied Sindri as his eyes settled on those of the invisible Flaetriu. 'Two eldar.'

The sorcerer stabbed his force staff into the turf and sent an arc of purple energy sizzling through the canopy. It smashed into a tree, which burst into incandescence instantly. But the ranger was already gone.

'Two? Where are they?' asked Bale, his head snapping from side to side as the incessant shuriken bounced and ricocheted off the armoured plating on the drop-ship, giving the impression that the eldar were everywhere at once. He couldn't see them.

Sindri ignored Lord Bale and lashed out with another bolt of lightning that incinerated another tree and brought a scream of frustration from the mouth of the sorcerer.

A wail of pain made them turn, just in time to see one of their Marines shredded by a focussed barrage of shuriken projectiles. He was riddled with tiny holes all across his abdomen, as though each of his major organs and both of his hearts had been shot through. He had fallen forwards onto his knees and blood was pouring out of the joints in his armour, from around the edges of his shattered helmet, and from the hundreds of tiny wounds all over his body.

Bale took a step towards him and swung his scythe cleanly through the Marine's neck, taking his head off with a single strike. 'Silence!' he yelled, still searching the tree-line for signs of movement.

A series of heavier impacts suddenly strafed across the ground towards Bale's feet, coughing up little divots with each strike. They weren't shuriken hits, it was bolter fire. Bale spun to face the other side of the clearing and saw a squad of Blood Ravens scouts burst through the thicket with their boltguns blazing.

The Alpha Legionaries responded instantly, turning their guns onto these new targets and rolling for positions of cover behind rocks and the ramp of the drop-ship. Bale howled with relief – at last he had enemies that he could see – enemies he could kill. Without any regard for the torrent of bolter shells that whistled and streaked past him in both directions, Bale broke into a run, charging through the crossfire at the Blood Ravens' scouts with his scythe whirling round his head.

Sergeant Mikaelus rallied his men with a battle cry, knowing full well that his scout squadron, formidable though it was, was no match for a full battle squad of Chaos Marines. 'For the Great Father and the Emperor!' he yelled, receiving an echo from his men. The scouts were relatively new initiates into the Chapter, but even they knew of the Alpha Legion and the particular hatred felt towards them by the Blood Ravens. None of them would have thought twice about launching this attack, despite the probability of death.

Lord Bale was on top of the line of Blood Ravens in an instant, his scythe flashing with vile energies as he brayed bestially. The scouts fought valiantly, sending disciplined salvoes of bolter fire sleeting across the glade and punching into the cover of the Alpha Legionaries. But their cover held, and the scouts had only trees and foliage to protect their armour from the onslaught that burst back across the clearing.

Two scouts were already pierced with fatal wounds when Bale hacked through their necks with a majestic sweep of his blade, and three more had been brought down in a hail of fire as they had charged towards to the drop-ship with their own guns blazing with honour.

Mikaelus placed a careful shot straight into the eye-socket of a Chaos Marine who poked his head over the ship's ramp to make his own shot. The Blood Ravens would take some of these traitors with them. As he drew his combat knife and charged towards the Chaos Lord who was scything through his squad Mikaelus sprayed a spread of automatic fire towards the muttering sorcerer in the centre of the glade.

He was only a couple of strides away when the burst of power smashed into his back, sending Mikaelus sprawling to the ground at the Chaos lord's feet, his combat knife falling just out of reach. Something was forcing its way through his armour and infusing into his blood. He could feel fire pulsing through his veins, as though his body had been injected with raw warp taint. The scream of another scout brought sudden silence to the forest, and Mikaelus felt the burning certainty that he was the last of his squadron.

'That was pathetic, Marine,' spat Bale, rolling Mikaelus onto his back with a prod from his barbed boots. 'I have come to expect better from the Blood Ravens over the years. But I suppose that you are not what you once were.' Bale stooped down and picked up Mikaelus's knife, fipping it playfully in his hand. 'I had heard, in fact, that some of you might show enough promise for me to welcome you into the Alpha Legion.'

The sorcerous energies pulsing in his blood racked Mikaelus with agonies of paralysis, depriving him of his last wish – to spit his hatred into the face of this Chaos lord.

'I suppose that I must have heard wrongly,' said Bale, catching the combat knife and plunging it down through the chest of the Blood Raven at his feet.

'THE FORCES OF Chaos have revealed their hand, farseer,' reported Flaetriu, bowing deeply to the seated figure in the trees.

'Yes, Flaetriu. They too have a role to play in this affair, although the presence of the Alpha Legion changes the balance of power here. You were right to attack them, ranger, even if you were too hasty.' A look of deep concern glided across Macha's beautiful face. 'How did the other humans fare against their dark brethren?'

'Not well, farseer. Not well at all.'

THE CONVOY RUMBLED on through the valley, with the wide treads of Rhinos, Razorbacks and Predator tanks flattening everything before them. The Whirlwind missile launchers had already ground to a halt as they came into range, and the sky above the convoy was streaked with vapour trails from the flurry of rockets that were being loosed over the horizon.

At the head of the column were a spread of assault bikes and the hovering forms of land speeders, which darted ahead and then dropped back into line on reconnaissance sorties. The bulk of the Blood Ravens' force, however, was led by the massive weight of the Predators and Vindicators. Flanking them were the remnants of the Tartarans' heavy weaponry: some spluttering Leman Russ tanks, a squadron of Hellhounds, and a couple of Basilisks, both of which were starting to pull off to the side to start their barrage of earthshaker artillery from long range.

The impacts of the ranged ordnance could already be felt on the ground. As the distant thuds drew nearer, rockslides started to cascade down the steep valley walls and the water in the river jumped with kinetic energy. In their hearts, many of the Tartarans hoped that the bombardment would be enough, and that the ork army would already be shattered by the time they arrived. But, as they rounded a bend in the meandering valley, the thunderous wailing of orks ready for battle rolled over the convoy, squashing any thoughts of an easy victory.

The valley was overflowing with ugly, snarling jaws, huge jagged teeth and massive green muscles. The greenskins were erratically spread across the river basin, randomly bunched into growling mobs, each ork jostling for position at the front of their groups. There were craters in the valley floor where the Whirlwind rockets had done their damage, each carpeted with broken green bodies. But for every ork that had fallen under the rain of rocket-fire, twenty more snarled with defiant thirst as the Blood Ravens swept around the meander in the valley. And when they caught sight of the humans, every greenskin throat was opened into a terrible keening for war: 'Waaagh!'

Ordnance started to fall onto the Imperium's forces as the range closed and the ork mortars began to hurl stikkbombz. By the time the Rhinos and Chimeras screeched to a halt, spewing Marines and Tartarans onto the valley floor, the Imperial column was caught in the eye of a pungent, smoky storm.

As battle was joined across the whole valley floor, with rockets and artillery shells pounding the ork position and a flood of troops firing hails of bullets into their disorganised lines, a Thunderhawk roared through the sky over the Imperial forces, its guns ablaze in salute to the Emperor and His Blood Ravens. The soldiers on the ground raised their weapons and cheered as they saw Captain Angelos's personal heraldry fluttering from the roof of the vessel.

The lascannons on the gunship flared and pulsed, sending streams of las-fire slicing into the orks as it descended onto the valley floor, burning gaggles of orks as it came down straight on top of them. The vessel dove into the middle of the ocean of green, cut off from the Imperial troops, but providing them with a rallying point in the heart of the enemy lines. With a clunk and a hiss, the hatch popped open and Gabriel leapt clear of the ramp with a single bound, his chainsword already a blur of motion and his bolter coughing. Close behind him was Isador, dropping to the ground below the Thunderhawk and calmly surveying his surroundings before lashing out with his force staff, sending a ring of energy pulsing out into the pressing perimeter of orks that encircled the gunship.

Then came Tanthius, crunching into the rocky ground with the full weight of his Terminator armour, his squad thudding down around him. A huge eruption of firepower burst out of the vanguard group, with the Terminators towering over the orks and unleashing waves of autocannon fire and sleets of bolter shells from their storm bolters. Jets of chemical flame doused the charging orks, sending them wailing and screaming into the river for relief, only to be cut down by the Thunderhawk's gun-servitors.

The unexpected penetration into the heart of the orks' position took the greenskins by surprise, and some of the forces that were charging towards the Imperial convoy broke off in confusion. Turning, they started charging back through their own brethren, knocking each other aside in the frantic scramble to engage their enemies. For a while, it looked as though they would start fighting amongst themselves, and the Imperial column took advantage of the confusion to press forward into the sea of green, pushing an incursion through it like a lance into the heart of the ork infantry.

Meanwhile, the Thunderhawk was back in the sky, hovering over the battlefield and employing its las-cannons to great effect in the confined space of the valley floor. Beneath it, the Terminators stood immovably against the tide of orks that rushed, dived, and charged at them, ploughing through their number with a combination of continuous bursts of heavy fire and simple, brute force from their power fists. In amongst the throng, standing back to back in their own pocket of resistance, Gabriel and Isador fought off the mob with incredible ferocity and skill. Gabriel's bolter had jammed, leaving him with only his chainsword and his combat knife to dispense the Emperor's benevolence. And Isador was alight with divine grace, slicing and searing with his staff as though guided by the hand of the Emperor himself.

Gabriel felt more alive than he had felt in years. It was almost like dancing, as he parried a cleaver chop with one hand and spun his combat knife in the other, plunging it up to its hilt into the ear of the offending ork. The screams and inhuman shrieks of combat gradually faded out of his hearing, only to be replaced by a single searing note of unbelievable beauty. The voice multiplied into a choir, filling his soul with light and washing over the action around him, making it seem clumsy and slow in comparison. Gabriel ducked and swirled with unprecedented grace, slicing cleanly through limbs with his chainsword and pushing his short combat knife into all the soft, vulnerable places of ork anatomy.

The explosions of ordnance fire boomed in the background, and Gabriel was vaguely aware of it as his knife stuck in the neck of a greenskin. He kicked the beast clear of his blade before turning and throwing it into the snarling, open mouth of another. With only his chainsword left, he clasped it in both hands and swung it powerfully around in an arc, slicing through the guts of six orks as they tried to close him down from three sides. Behind him, Gabriel could feel the motion of Isador as the Librarian flared with power, dispatching orks three at a time with blasts from his staff or fingertips. The pair were gradually cutting a path further and further into the ork forces, moving away from the Terminators on their own.

Whispering voices quested for their ears as they fought onwards into the orks. *Kill. Kill. Bleed them dry. It is your responsibility. We all look to you. Drench the soil with their blood. Kill. Kill.* Suddenly the silvery voices of the heavenly choir were shattered again by the screams of tortured souls, and Gabriel shrieked with pain as Isador's staff scraped across his chest before cracking into the ork that was about to plant its cleaver in his head.

As GABRIEL WALKED through the forest, he could still hear pockets of fighting continuing amongst the trees. The bulk of the ork army had been broken, and most lay dead in the valley, with their pungent blood running red in the river. The thump of dreadnought footfalls and the rattles of their autocannons could still be heard as the last of the fleeing orks were mopped up by the Blood Ravens. Small groups of the greenskins were mustering for their last stands, desperate to make one more kill before they died.

Gabriel had been slightly concerned that they had not found any orks large enough to be the warboss of such a significant force, but he had other things to attend to and he let a squad of scouts disappear into the forest to hunt down the ork leader. He had also noticed that a number of the larger orks appeared to have Imperial weaponry, including the boltguns such as Space Marines used. It was not uncommon for a few of these scavenger creatures to have weapons from other races, but the numbers here were noticeably larger than he expected. He was increasingly suspicious that there was more to this ork invasion than a typical greenskin jaunt.

'Captain Angelos,' said Sergeant Corallis, hastening from a clearing in the trees ahead. Corallis's face was crestfallen and he was obviously distraught. As he approached, Gabriel noticed that he was carrying something roughly hemispherical in his hands.

'It's Kuros,' breathed the sergeant, pushing the object towards his captain.

Gabriel reached out and took the shoulder plate, nodding in understanding. The underside of the armoured panel was covered in a thick layer of carbon, as though it had been used as a bowl in which to overcook some meat. 'What happened to this?' asked Gabriel, handing the shoulder guard over to Isador but addressing his question to Corallis.

'It was still attached to his body, captain,' explained Corallis, tremulous with anger and disgust. 'He is burnt beyond recovery of his gene-seed. Something seems to have reached into his soul and burnt him from the inside out.'

'What about the others?' asked Isador.

Gabriel placed his hand on Corallis's shoulder. 'It's not your fault, Brother Corallis.'

'They were my squad, captain. I should have been with them.' Corallis punched his right fist against his left shoulder, where his left arm should have been. 'This is a pathetic excuse.'

'Corallis, this is not your fault. Sergeant Mikaelus was leading the squad. He is a fine Marine and a devoted servant of the Emperor. You could not have left your squad in better hands,' said Gabriel.

'Mikaelus is also dead, captain, along with the rest of the squad. Their bodies are up there in the clearing.' Corallis would not be consoled.

'Are they all burnt like this?' asked Isador with concerned tone.

'No, Librarian Akios. Only Kuros is like this. Mikaelus is worse. Most of the others died like warriors, and we will be able to recover their gene-seed,' answered Corallis, turning to lead them back to the clearing.

The little glade was a scene of carnage. The bodies of the scout squad were strewn over the rocks and grass, lying in ruined poses, in pools of blood that matched the deep reds of their armour. The trees around the edge of the clearing were battered and shredded with bolter holes, and patches of the ground were scorched into dry browns.

Mikaelus was lying on his back across a large rock in the centre of the glade. His face was contorted with pain and his skin was blistered, as though burnt on the inside. Protruding from his chest was the handle of his own combat knife, and the earth around the rock was sodden with blood, as though he had been slowly drained of his life.

'He was still alive when we found him, captain. But his mind had gone. His soul had already left this realm, and he was rambling like a conduit to hell itself,' said Corallis numbly.

Scratched into Mikaelus's armour was a crude mark. It looked like it had been carved with the tip of a dagger, or gnawed with a claw. In a vulgar way, it resembled an eight-pointed star.

'This is not the work of orks, Gabriel,' said Isador, giving voice to the feelings of everyone. 'This is a mark of the ruinous powers. It is a mark of Chaos.'

'He is right, captain,' added Corallis. 'The others were killed by bolter fire, not by slugs or cleavers. Boltguns are the weapons of Marines, not aliens.'

'Perhaps, Corallis,' said Gabriel.

'And the burns, Gabriel. They are warp burns, of the kind unleashed by sorcerers of Chaos. This looks like the work of a squad of traitor Marines,' concluded Isador reluctantly.

'The documents you found about Tartarus, Isador, did they say anything about what happened to it during the Black Crusades? Is there any history of Champions of Chaos bringing war to this planet?' asked Gabriel, still unwilling to make the logical leap.

'The great book does not mention these things, Gabriel, but I suspect that the tome is incomplete. I have a number of curators investigating the archives already,' replied Isador.

'Isador, can you sense anything unusual in this place?' asked Gabriel without daring to look the Librarian in the eyes, but willing to trust the senses of his old friend.

The Librarian concentrated for a moment, opening his mind to the eddies and energy flows of the glade. Instantly a flood of voices crashed into his head, screaming and shouting of pain and death. But there, hidden behind the shockwaves of the slaughter, was a careful, delicate whisper, trying to slip unnoticed into his soul. He had heard that voice before, and he hesitated slightly before replying.

'No. No, Gabriel, I have sensed nothing since we arrived. But if there is a sorcerer of Chaos with the enemy, he may be able to mask their presence, especially with all the background static caused by the battles and the uncouth aliens.' Isador looked away into the trees, as though looking for someone.

'There is something else you should see, captain,' said Corallis, leading Gabriel to a point on the other side of the glade, pointing out the burns left by the thrusters of a drop-ship.

'This,' said Corallis, picking up a fragment of ceramite from the grass. 'This is not Blood Raven armour, and it was not shot by a bolter.'

The shard of ceramite looked as if it had been punched out of the armour of a Space Marine, but it was a dull, acid green. Moreover, it was perforated by a series of tiny holes, barely a couple of centimetres across.

'It looks to me, Corallis,' said Gabriel, 'like our friends the Alpha Legion are on Tartarus, and that we are not the only ones who are not pleased to see them. These are shuriken marks, are they not? It seems that the orks are just a distraction from the main game.'

PART TWO

CHAPTER FIVE

THE FOREST SHUDDERED and rippled, sending shock-waves of green pulsing across the canopy. A couple of seconds later and the Thunderhawk dropped slowly down through the trees, its engines roaring and whining as they fought for a soft landing. The gunship came down just outside the busy clearing, crushing trees and plants like blades of grass.

Gabriel and Isador watched the vessel descend in silence. They already knew who was waiting for them inside, but they were not sure why he had come to Tartarus. The *Litany of Fury* had not been sent any warning of his arrival, but the crew had managed to get a message down to surface before the inquisitor could requisition one of the Chapter's Thunderhawks and make planetfall himself.

The two Blood Ravens cast their eyes around the scene of carnage in the glade, and shook their heads.

There were dead Marines strewn over the ground, and one that had apparently been ritually sacrificed across a rock in the centre of the clearing. It didn't look good.

'What do you think he wants?' asked Isador, voicing the worry of everyone. 'Do you suppose that he suspects one of us of heresy?'

'He is an inquisitor, Isador, protector of the Emperor's divine word and will. He suspects everyone of heresy,' answered Gabriel flatly. 'That is his job.'

'Perhaps he has sensed the taint of Chaos on this world?' offered Corallis, looking back towards the ruined figure of Mikaelus.

'Yes, perhaps,' replied Gabriel, as the hatch hissed open on the Thunderhawk and its boarding ramp lowered slowly.

Isador took half a step back as Inquisitor Mordecai Toth strode down the ramp towards the group of Marines, and Gabriel stood forward to greet him. Despite the absence of a Space Marine's suit of power armour, Mordecai was an imposing man. He was tall and well muscled, and his dark skin glistened under the dappled light of the forest. His armour was elaborately etched with runes and sprinkled with purity seals. Emblazoned on his chest was the Imperial 'I,' marking out the inquisitor's almost limitless authority in the realm of the Emperor. A great book of law, sealed with locks and runes of binding, was chained around his waist, and an ornate warhammer swung casually from his right hand as he strode down the ramp.

'Inquisitor Toth,' said Gabriel, drawing himself up to his full height in front of the newcomer. 'Welcome to Tartarus.' The captain spared a quick nod for each of the two Blood Ravens who had accompanied the inquisitor from the *Litany of Fury,* and he noticed that a nervous-looking curator from the librarium was still hovering in the hatchway behind them clutching a package of papers.

For a moment, Mordecai looked Gabriel up and down, the movements of his one human eye not quite matched by those of his augmented bio-monocle, which seemed to take in the rest of the glade. 'Thank you, captain, but we have no time for welcomes or courtesies. The Blood Ravens must leave Tartarus immediately.'

THE GUARDSMAN PRODDED the stonework gingerly, pressing his gloves up against the intricate carvings, tracing the forms of the runes. They seemed to slip and slide under his touch, as though striving to avoid his fingers. But the man's eyes gleamed with a long forgotten magic, as though something primal were gradually seeping out of his pupils. The runes on the stone were reaching into his soul, even as they danced and swam around his fingertips.

Behind him, he could hear the voices of his comrades, each barely a whisper as they jostled for better positions. One or two of them were getting impatient, and he was certain that they were complaining about how long it was taking him to decipher the symbols. Up on the rim of the crater, a row of men stood guard, keeping their eyes peeled for any sign of movement in the surrounding wilds.

The stone was roughly cut, but slick with recently let blood. It was stained a rich, deep brown where countless trails of blood had caressed the sides of the altar, streaming their way into the fertile earth below. Tavett could almost feel the energy pulsing along the stains, as though they were themselves veins. Even through his gloves, the rock altar seemed to throb with inorganic life.

Firing a quick glance over his shoulder to check on his comrades, Tavett sprung from his kneeling position, launching himself onto the surface of the stone altar. He could hear his companions shriek as they saw him jump, and their rapid footfalls filled his ears as he spread himself across the cold stone tablet. They are so pathetically slow, thought Tavett. That's why I was chosen, because I'm better than they are. My blood burns, and they are nothing more than cold husks.

By the time Sergeant Katrn had reached the altar it was already too late. Tavett lay on his stomach with his arms and legs outstretched to the corners of the tablet, as though struggling to embrace its huge form. His uniform was ripped to shreds, and his back was a web of lacerations and carved symbols. Blood poured out of him, coasting over his skin and gushing down the wriggling runes on the sides of the altar. His head was pushed round, so that he was looking awkwardly to the side, as though his neck was broken. And he was chattering incoherently as trickles of blood seeped out of his open mouth, a grotesque smile etched into his emaciated cheeks.

Katrn watched the ruined trooper with a fixed expression, staring with a mixture of hatred, anger, revulsion and jealousy. Why had that wretch Tavett been gifted with this glorious end? The little runt wouldn't even have been here if it wasn't for Katrn's leadership. He had shown no understanding of the true nature of combat and war until Katrn had skewered him with his own bayonet on the walls of Magna Bonum. Only then, as Katrn had stared down into his streaming face, had a flash of realisation seared into Tavett's stricken mind: blood for the Blood God – that's what war was for.

The sergeant looked down at the bloodied form of Tavett and saw the last flickers of ecstasy dying in his eyes. There was still blood in him, still some life left to be bled before his soul would be sucked from him and cast into the unspeakable realms of the immaterium, where it would be enveloped in the ichorous embrace of the daemons of Khorne. Katrn shook his head in disgust and drew his pistol, firing directly into Tavett's temple. This wretch was not a fit sacrifice for the Blood God, and he was certainly not deserving of such a glorious end.

As the shot passed straight through Tavett's head and ricocheted off the stone beneath, something else stabbed into Katrn's shoulder. He spun on his heels just in time to see the rest of the Guardsmen rack their weapons, some of them already diving for cover behind the altar and others wailing into shredded deaths as hails of shuriken rained down from the rim of the crater. A lance of pleasure fired through his shoulder as a trickle of blood started to soak into his tunic. Instinctively, he pressed a finger into the tiny wound and drew out more blood, letting it drip to the ground in great globules.

Thrilled, Katrn levelled his pistol as he ducked behind the stone of the altar and fired off a couple of rounds, but the figures around the pit were constantly moving and he could not target them. They flicked and fluttered with incredible speed, almost dancing around the crater, but constantly loosing hails of fire into the pit. Despite himself, Katrn found himself marvelling at the grace of his assailants. Compared to the orks and even to the Blood Ravens, these were enchantingly elegant warriors.

'Bancs! Let's have some grenades up there,' called Katrn, as the trooper came flying over the altar into the pocket of cover behind.

'Yes, sergeant,' replied Bancs, instantly rummaging into his pack for frag-grenade ammunition for his shoulder launcher. 'What are they, sergeant?'

'I'm not sure, Bancs. I've never seen anything like them. Could be eldar,' answered Katrn, still gazing in wonder at the attackers as they ducked and bobbed their way around volleys of las-fire from Katrn's Armoured Fist squad.

'I'm sure that they'll bleed just like the rest of us,' answered Bancs enthusiastically, ramming the ammunition stock into his weapon and bracing it against the edge of the altar.

'Yes,' said Katrn. 'I'm sure they will. All the same, I think that it's time to leave this place. We will be missed. We have to get back to camp.'

The clunk and hiss of the grenade launcher was followed by a series of explosions around the rim of the crater, which sent mud and rubble sliding down into the pit in miniature avalanches. The eldar seemed to vanish, and it was impossible to tell whether any had been hit by the blasts. After a few seconds, another rain of grenades shot over the lip of the crater, detonating over the open ground beyond. There was still no sign or sound of the eldar.

'Let's move out,' said Katrn, waving his bloody arm like a banner for the rest of the squad.

The Armoured Fists squad and the ramshackle assortment of other troopers that Katrn had recruited from the regiment during the battle for Magna Bonum scrambled up the walls of the crater on their hands and knees. Peering over the rim, Katrn could see the pockmarks left in the ground by the grenades, but there were no bodies and no blood had been spilt. Scanning his eyes quickly through the tree-line, he waved a signal to his men, and they all pulled themselves clear of the pit, readying their weapons as they ascended onto the level ground. But no shots came.

'I don't like this,' said Bancs, his head twitching nervously from side to side. 'Maybe they don't bleed like us... I think I preferred fighting the orks.'

'Shut it, Bancs,' hissed Katrn, silencing the anxious trooper with a powerful authority that even surprised himself.

'S... sergeant–' started Bancs, unable to control himself.

'–I said shut it, Bancs. What are you...' Katrn followed the trooper's horrified gaze and saw his own blood seeping out of his wounded shoulder and wrapping itself around his right arm. The blood was congealing and solidifying, as though sculpting muscles out of blood on the outside of his body. A rush of power flooded into his mind as he watched the awful mutation of his arm. A mark of Khorne, thrilled Katrn, turning to gaze back down on the altar, still bedecked with the tattered remains of Tavett.

'Bancs, give me your cloak. Now, let's get back to the camp.'

* * *

THE GRENADES EXPLODED around the rim of the crater, but Flaetriu's rangers had already withdrawn into the trees. The farseer had told them to prevent any bloodshed in the pit, not to slaughter the humans, and Flaetriu was as good as his word. How was he supposed to know that the weak-willed mon-keigh would butcher themselves, even without the help of the Biel-Tan?

From the shadows of the forest, Flaetriu watched the second rain of grenades and scoffed quietly. A blind ordnance barrage was no way to fight eldar rangers, and he laughed inwardly as the scrambling, crawling mon-keigh flopped over the lip of the crater, confident that they had dealt a deadly blow to their foes. The fools.

'Flaetriu,' said Kreusaur, appearing at his shoulder and pointing a long slender arm. 'What is happening to that one?' The eldar's keen eyes could make out the grotesquery that was squirming around the mon-keigh's shoulder and enveloping his arm. 'Should we kill him?'

'No, Kreusaur. The farseer was very explicit – there is to be no bloodshed here. We must let them leave,' answered Flaetriu, fighting against his nature. 'We should fetch her now, before this commotion attracts the attention of the orks.'

The two rangers took one last look at the group of humans, who were making ready to leave. Then they flashed a quick signal to the rest of their party, turned, and vanished back into the forest.

'YOU MUST LEAVE, and that is final,' said Mordecai without raising his voice. His manner was infuriatingly calm, as though he was asking Gabriel to do the most natural thing in the world.

The men had retired into the Thunderhawk in order to conduct their conversation in privacy. Gabriel and Mordecai were on opposing sides of the uncomfortable drop-bay, sitting into harness fixings usually used by Marines in rough descents. The Thunderhawk was not designed with conferences in mind, and neither man was happy with the inappropriate surroundings for their important discussion. Standing in the hatchway that led into the cockpit was Carus Brom, who had insisted that he should be included in any decisions that might effect the defence of Tartarus.

'You will need to give me a better reason than that, inquisitor,' replied Gabriel, teetering on the edge of composure.

'I need give you nothing of the sort, captain,' countered Mordecai, leaning back in mock relaxation, hiding his face in the shadows, and letting the light reflect off the insignia on his breast plate.

'I am well aware of the powers and function of the Emperor's Inquisition, inquisitor. You may well have the authority to evacuate every last civilian and Guardsman off this planet,' said Gabriel with a casual nod towards Brom. 'But you are very much mistaken if you think that I will cede command of the Blood Ravens to you. The Adeptus Astartes are not common soldiers, inquisitor, and I will thank you to show us the appropriate respect.'

The inquisitor leaned forward again, bringing his face back into the light, and gazing levelly into Gabriel's keen green eyes. He nodded slowly and then leant back into the shadows. 'Very well, captain, I realise that you have had experience of the Inquisition before.' He watched Gabriel smart slightly, and then continued. 'If you must have a reason, then I shall give you one: a giant warp storm is sweeping through this sector of the galaxy, wreaking turmoil and havoc on each world that it touches. It is pregnant with the forces of Chaos and it is unclear what fate might befall any life-forms touched by its wrath. It will arrive imminently, and it could trap us here on Tartarus for more than a century, raining the terrors of warp energy into our souls each moment. We must evacuate the planet, and we must do it now. Would you like me to explain that again, so that we can waste some more time, captain?'

'The Imperial Guard can attend to the evacuation, inquisitor. We have already given them the use of some of our transport vessels to assist with the wounded civilians. The matter is already in hand, and I am sure that Colonel Brom here is more than capable of ensuring the success of such a logistical exercise. The Blood Ravens, however, are not logisticians, inquisitor. We are Space Marines, and we have more pressing issues to attend to,' replied Gabriel, conscious of Brom's eyes from the cockpit.

'More pressing issues?' asked Mordecai, raising an inquiring eyebrow.

'Yes, inquisitor. I have reason to believe that there are forces of Chaos working on this planet,' answered Gabriel simply.

The inquisitor said nothing for a few moments, and Gabriel could only vaguely see his face in the shadows. Then Mordecai leant forward, pushing his face towards Gabriel, his eyes dancing in the sudden light.

'Strange that I sense no taint here, captain,' he said, almost whispering. 'In any case,' he continued in a more casual tone, 'if there were a Chaos presence on Tartarus, it would be better for us to leave it here with the orks, rather than wasting any more lives trying to combat it. Believe me, captain, we could not dispense any fate worse than that which will be dealt out by the storm itself – these forces of Chaos and the orks will not be able to stand against each other and the storm.'

'What if they do not need to stand against each other? I suspect that the orks and the Chaos powers are in cahoots on Tartarus, inquisitor. Could they not stand together against the storm?' asked Gabriel, his voice earnest and firm.

'They are welcome to try, captain. But we must leave here, and we must leave now,' said Mordecai, leaning back into the harness once again and letting out a quiet sigh of exasperation.

'You may leave whenever you like, inquisitor, and the Blood Ravens will gladly donate the use of our transport facilities for your purpose. We, on the other hand, will stay long enough to satisfy our suspicions and settle our affairs. How long until the storm arrives?' asked Gabriel, his mind made up.

'Three days, captain. Perhaps less.' The inquisitor turned to Brom for the first time and waved his hand dismissively. 'Colonel Brom, would you be kind enough to leave us alone for a moment? The captain and I have some matters of faith to discuss.'

The Imperial Guard colonel stared back at Mordecai and then shifted his gaze to Gabriel, searching for an unlikely ally. 'With all due respect, Inquisitor Toth, this affair involves me and the Tartarans as much as it does any of you. Tartarus is our home, and we know it better than anyone. I have heard stories of this warp storm before – legends speak of it visiting this planet once every three thousand years, bringing with it–'

'–that's all very interesting, colonel,' said Mordecai, cutting him off and rising to his feet. 'But perhaps I did not make myself clear? When I asked you to leave us, I expected that you would leave the Thunderhawk now.'

Brom's mouth snapped shut and his eyes narrowed as he met the inquisitor's gaze. 'As you wish, Inquisitor Toth,' he said, forcing the words out through gritted teeth. He turned to face Gabriel and bowed very slightly. 'Captain Angelos, I take my leave.'

Gabriel did not stand, but he nodded an acknowledgement to Brom as the latter turned and strode rigidly down the boarding ramp. 'Thank you, Colonel Brom,' he said softly, unsure whether Brom could hear him or not.

'This does involve him, inquisitor. He may well have some knowledge that could be of use to us – and knowledge is power, as you well know. You could have shown him more respect,' said Gabriel as Mordecai retook his seat.

'Captain Angelos,' began Mordecai, ignoring Gabriel's protests on the behalf of Brom. 'I understand that you uncovered deep-rooted heresy and the taint of Chaos on the planet Cyrene. That was your homeworld, was it not?'

Startled by this sudden shift in the conversation, Gabriel recoiled. 'I fail to see how that is relevant to the present situation, inquisitor, even if I were disposed to discuss it, which I am not.'

'You should feel free to discuss such things with me, Gabriel,' said Mordecai ingratiatingly. 'I may not be your precious Chaplain Prathios, but I am an agent of the Emperor's Inquisition and nothing needs to be hidden from me.'

'Even so, Inquisitor Toth,' replied Gabriel formally, 'I cannot see what Cyrene has to do with this situation on Tartarus.'

'That is why you are not an inquisitor, Gabriel,' said Mordecai, smoothly persisting with his familiar tone. 'As I recall, you were the one who requested the assistance of the Inquisition in the performance of an exterminatus on Cyrene – the systematic annihilation of all life on the planet – genocide by another name.'

'Toth, I'm not sure what you're trying to do here, but you are succeeding in trying my patience,' said Gabriel, anger tingeing his voice.

'I am not questioning your loyalty, captain. But I am concerned that your actions on Cyrene may have affected you in ways that even you do not fully understand.' Mordecai paused to take in Gabriel's response, but the Blood Raven's face was simply knitted in anger. 'In particular,' he continued, 'I must wonder whether your actions there might have effected your judgement here.'

With a sudden crack, the harness behind Gabriel whipped out of its fixings in the wall, sending a little shower of adamantium raining down over the two men. Gabriel released his grip on the straps as he realised that he had been pulling them unconsciously. He said nothing, but just stared at the inquisitor with burning green eyes. Mordecai held up his hands, as though signalling that he didn't mean to be confrontational. He knew that he had gone too far, and he made a mental note of Gabriel's limits.

'Perhaps that was a... poor choice of words, Captain Angelos,' said Mordecai, retreating into formality once again. 'My fear, captain, is simply that you may have become oversensitive to the appearance of taints of Chaos following the ordeal on Cyrene. It would be quite understandable.'

'Are you suggesting that I am making this up? Have you seen the Marines in the clearing outside!?' asked Gabriel, his voice grating with volume and indignance.

'No, captain. I am merely asking that, as a loyal subject of the Emperor, you keep the interests of the Imperium in mind before your own... agenda.' The inquisitor was choosing his words carefully now, intending to make Gabriel think without being overly inflammatory.

'I suggest that you leave my Thunderhawk, inquisitor,' said Gabriel, rising to his feet and indicating the boarding ramp, 'for the good of the Imperium.' Inquisitor Toth may have commandeered the vessel from the *Litany of Fury*, but it was still a Blood Ravens' gunship.

Toth rose and stood directly in front of Gabriel, staring him in the face with deep brown, almost black eyes. He was shorter than the captain, and lighter. Gabriel's power armour transformed him into a giant, superhuman warrior, but Toth faced him calmly. He had confronted Space Marines before and was not about to be intimidated by this captain. 'Thank you for your time, Captain Angelos. We will talk again soon,' he said, before turning and making his way out into the forest.

* * *

ISADOR AND CORALLIS found Gabriel still in the Thunderhawk. He was kneeling quietly, as though in mediation, and Isador could hear faint whispers questing through the air. The captain's face was calm and his eyebrows were slightly raised, as though he were listening to a majestic symphony. A tear ran down his rough cheek, vanishing into the depths of an old scar, and a trace of light danced along its tail. In the shadows at the far end of the chamber sat Prathios, half hidden and perfectly silent. He nodded to the two Marines as they entered the chamber.

With a sudden gasp, Gabriel flicked open his eyes and stared directly ahead. His eyes were wide and burning, as though gazing on some distant horror. Then it was over and he seemed to return to himself; turning his head to face Isador he smiled faintly.

'Isador, it is good to see you. We have much to discuss,' he said, rising to his feet and gesturing for the Marines to join him.

'Are you alright, Gabriel?' asked his old friend, momentarily looking around the chamber for the source of the whispers, which seemed to persist even after Gabriel's mediations ended.

'Yes, Isador. I'm fine. The good inquisitor gave me much food for thought, that is all,' replied Gabriel, still smiling weakly.

'Captain,' interjected Corallis. 'The inquisitor had no right to speak to you in such a manner. And he has no reason to doubt you.' Corallis and Isador had already spoken to Brom, and they had a good idea what Toth would have said to Gabriel.

'On the contrary, sergeant,' answered Gabriel frankly. 'The inquisitor has every right to speak in whatever manner he chooses. That is his prerogative.

And he has his reasons to doubt me. He is wrong, but he has his reasons, and I cannot blame him for that. We must each serve the Emperor in our own ways, Corallis.'

'So, are we going to leave?' asked the sergeant hesitantly.

'Do you trust that the storm will deal with our enemies for us?' asked Isador, as though anticipating that Gabriel would have succumbed to Toth's pressure.

'No, my brothers, we are not going to leave. We will not use this storm as an excuse to avoid our enemies or our responsibilities. The forces of Chaos are here for a reason, and I suspect that this fortuitous storm has some part to play in their plans. Coincidence is not the ally of fortune, only knowledge can overcome ignorance. We must stay and discover the truth.'

Isador and Corallis nodded and then bowed slightly. 'We are with you, brother-captain. As always,' said Corallis, his voice full of relief.

'Sergeant Corallis, organise the remaining scouts into two squads and dispatch them to sweep the areas flanking the valley. We need to see why the Alpha Legion chose this spot to engage the Blood Ravens, if indeed it is they who are here on Tartarus.'

Corallis nodded and then strode off down the ramp to organise the scouts, leaving Isador and Gabriel together in the belly of the Thunderhawk, with Prathios still silently observing his younger battle-brothers.

'What news from the librarium, Isador?' asked Gabriel, recalling the sight of the curator who had accompanied Mordecai.

'Interesting news,' replied Isador, checking back over his shoulder to make sure that they were not being overheard. 'It seems that there are records of Imperial settlements on Tartarus dating from before the thirty-eighth millennia. However, the records themselves have been expunged from the Chapter archives. So, whilst there are references to them, the references lead nowhere – simply to empty shelf space.'

'I assume that your curators have pursued these missing files,' said Gabriel, encouraging Isador to continue.

'Of course, Gabriel,' replied Isador. 'But their inquiries have been met with silence and the seals of the Inquisition. It seems that there is more to the history of Tartarus than we are supposed to know, captain.'

Gabriel nodded, unsurprised. 'I agree, Isador. And what about this storm? Do the records say anything about a warp storm?'

'There are a few references to various legends about a warp storm that is supposed to visit the planet every couple of thousand years. Folk stories, Gabriel, nothing more. No mention is made of any verification,' said Isador hesitantly.

'Is there something else, Isador?' asked Gabriel, taking note of his friend's tone.

'I'm not sure. However, when we tried to discover the details of the legends, we discovered that they had also gone missing from the archives. It does seem as though somebody has tried to eliminate all accounts of the pre-Imperial past on Tartarus – but that this person did not do a very good job of covering his tracks,' conceded Isador.

'They did not anticipate an investigation by a Blood Ravens' Librarian, clearly,' said Gabriel affectionately. 'Have you spoken to Brom about this? He mentioned something about a legend when Toth started to talk about the warp storm. Perhaps the colonel will be of use to us after all, Isador.'

'I did see him,' said Isador, shaking his head slowly. 'He came storming out of his meeting with you in an evil mood. I left him alone, and he went off with some of his men.'

'We need to find him. They may be only folk stories, Isador, but even fairy stories can reveal something of the truth, if you know how to read them. And I am confident in your skills in this regard, my friend,' said Gabriel with a faint smile. 'If we can find out anything at all, it may give us the advantage we need. Make sure that your inquiries are discrete, Isador. It would not do for the honourable inquisitor to think that we did not trust him.'

THE BROKEN BODY of a mon-keigh soldier lay across the altar, and Farseer Macha inspected it with a mixture of disgust and despair. The human's blood was still warm, dripping into little, vanishing pools on the earth. She shook her head in disbelief and prodded her finger into the cauterised hole in the man's temple. The wound was clean and crisp, as though the las-shot had carefully parted each molecule of tissue as it had passed through. With a wave of relief, Macha realised that the mon-keigh had been killed before the sacrifice had been completed. Apparently, the pathetic humans couldn't concentrate long enough to conduct a proper sacrifice. She praised

Khaine for the stupidity of the mon-keigh – blood for the Blood God, indeed.

However, the mon-keigh's blood was not pure. As Macha withdrew her finger from the man's head, she noticed that something was growing up through its skull from the underside, as though rooted in the stone of the altar itself. She clasped the human's hair in her hand and quickly tore its head away from its shoulders, pulling the head into the air. A rainbow of blood swept out of the body, dappling droplets into the already sodden soil. Sure enough, writhing in ungodly ecstasies under the man's body was a bunch of snaking capillaries, growing directly out of the stone, drinking the man dry. They were discoloured and brown, hardly matching the man's blood at all. Beneath them, as though trapped deep within the material of the altar itself, Macha could see the suggestion of a face, contorted in agony. It was just the ghost of a once human face – an immaterial representation trapped in the material realm, taunted and tortured by the gyrating sea of souls that made up the fabric of the altar.

'Flaetriu? Was this the first sacrifice that the humans made?' asked Macha, standing back from the altar in revulsion.

'We saw no others, farseer,' answered Flaetriu.

Casting her eyes around the crater, Macha realised that the little group of mon-keigh encountered by her rangers could not possibly have excavated the site. It would have taken them days, especially if their attention spans were really as short as suggested by the botched sacrifice.

'Something else has been here, Flaetriu. Something more powerful than the mon-keigh that you saw off.'

She had returned to the altar and was running her delicate fingers through the wriggling capillaries, almost caressing them. 'Something got here before the humans and before us.'

'The orks?' offered Flaetriu half-heartedly, casting his hand up towards the rim of the crater where a mob of the greenskins had been slaughtered by the eldar, as both had come to investigate the pit.

'No, ranger, not orks. Orks care little for such things, and they have not the wit for an archaeological dig. This is the work of the minions of Chaos. I sense the hand of the Alpha Legion in this, Flaetriu, and that is most troubling. It seems that the Chaos Marines are not here merely to war against the other humans.' She paused for a moment, letting the tiny tendrils tickle around her fingertips. 'But their hand is dark and the future is confused. I cannot see their intentions. We must move quickly.'

'Farseer!' The call came from Kreusaur, standing dramatically on the lip of the crater, shuriken catapult held vertically into the sky. 'The mon-keigh, they are coming. Do you wish us to execute them?'

No, Kreusaur, replied Macha, her voiceless words slipping directly into the ranger's mind. *The time for conflict with the red soldiers will come. But this is not the time, and this is certainly not the place. Distract them, ranger. We must press on before the other humans do something that we will all regret.*

THE THIN BREATH of smoke eased its way into the air in front of Brom, its calm tranquillity belying the turmoil in his head. He stuffed the little roll back in his mouth, his hands trembling with agitation, and sucked a series of shallow draws. The smoke caught in his tense throat, making him cough and splutter, and he threw the little stick down into the grass and ground it into the mud with his boot.

The smoke seemed to hang in the air in front of him for a long time, keeping its coherence in the form of a small cloud. As he breathed, the cloud gently washed away from his face, only to be drawn back again when he inhaled. In annoyance, Brom lashed out with his hand, swiping his glove straight through the smoke, muttering to himself about the audacity of the inquisitor and the arrogance of the Space Marine. One day they would need his help, and then they'd see what their lack of respect had cost them.

Down on the valley floor, Brom could still see the carnage that the battle had wrought. He was sitting on a small rock promontory that stuck clear out of the tree-line about half way up the valley wall, and even from there he could see the piles of ork corpses and the streaks of blood that ran across the river basin. The green, verdant land of Tartarus was slowly being transformed into a blood-soaked offering to the glory of the Emperor – and the Tartarans were celebrating his majesty with their own blood, mixing it with that of these filthy xenos.

How much blood had been spilt today? Enough to make the Lloovre River run red. For a moment he wondered whether the people in the capital city would see the red in the water before they raised it to their lips to drink. But the planet was soaked with blood in any case – it wasn't as though the people hadn't already consumed their fair share of produce from the tainted soil, thought Brom sourly, tugging out another smoke.

'People are so hypocritical when it comes to blood,' he hissed to himself, without really thinking.

The little cloud of smoke in front of his face had still not dissipated, and it seemed to be curdling into vague eddies as he tried to wave it away. It slipped and flowed around his hands, presenting no obstacle against which he could strike, almost enwrapping his limb with its weightless form. For an instant, Brom thought that he could see a face crystallise in the smoke, but it was just a fleeting moment and then it was gone.

A gentle breath of wind whipped through the valley and dispersed the smoke in a reverie of whispers, making Brom check quickly from side to side to ensure that he was alone. He was not.

'Colonel Brom. There is something that I would like to ask you.'

'Librarian Akios,' said Brom, standing awkwardly to his feet and turning to greet the Blood Raven. 'How may I be of service?'

'Captain Angelos has asked me to question you about the local legends concerning the warp storm,' began Isador, realising his own clumsiness as soon as he spoke. He did his best to recover. 'And I would be most interested to hear what you have to say on the matter, colonel.'

'There is not much to tell, Librarian. Mostly just folk stories, I'm sure. Nothing that would interest the Adeptus Astartes or the good Captain Angelos. Certainly, Inquisitor Toth showed no interest in what I had to say,' said Brom, almost poisonously.

Isador watched Brom closely as he spoke and noticed the particular way in which the colonel emphasised the inquisitor's name. He paused momentarily, unsure about the meaning of Brom's tone. Just then, Sergeant Corallis's voice hissed into the vox unit in Isador's amour.

'Librarian Akios, the scouts are back from their sweep, and Captain Angelos requests your company,' said the sergeant simply.

'I will be right there,' replied Isador, turning away from Brom immediately.

'WHERE IS BROM?' asked Gabriel curtly, as Isador came up the ramp of the Thunderhawk. 'This concerns him also.'

'He is smoking, captain, out in the forest,' answered Isador.

'I would have thought that he would have better things to do,' replied Gabriel. 'His men need discipline and courage drilling into them, Isador. After the fiasco on the walls of Magna Bonum, there is worse to tell.'

'What has happened?'

'The scouts returned with news of a excavated crater about ten kilometres from here,' began Corallis. 'They were ambushed by a group of eldar rangers as they closed on its location, but successfully repelled the xenos. Strewn around the rim of the crater they found the bodies of a mob of orks – evidently they had also been interested in the crater for some reason–'

'–and evidently the eldar did not want them to see it, for some reason,' interjected Gabriel.

'Indeed. The scouts proceeded down into the crater, where they found a disturbing artefact. Some kind of altar, marked all over in runes that they could not decipher. They hastened to bring this news back to us, so that Librarian Akios might have the chance to see the writing,' finished Corallis, turning to Isador.

'The involvement of the eldar on Tartarus is certainly unexpected. It bespeaks something terrible – the eldar do not concern themselves in the affairs of others without a reason, even if their reasons are often incomprehensible to us,' said Isador, distracted by the casual mention of the ancient, alien race. Then he realised why the eldar had been glossed over in the story – there was something more pressing between the lines. 'What does this have to do with Brom?' asked Isador quickly.

'Stretched over the altar, gashed and torn with sacrificial markings, was one of Brom's Guardsmen, Isador,' explained Gabriel.

'One of Brom's men was sacrificed? We should inform him, of course,' said Isador, still not quite understanding what all the fuss was about.

'There's something else,' continued Gabriel. 'The man was executed by a single shot to the head. A shot from an Imperial Guard officer's laspistol.' Gabriel could see the Librarian's mind racing with the significance of these facts. 'He was sacrificed and executed by other Tartarans, Isador.'

CHAPTER SIX

STANDING ON THE edge of the crater, Gabriel stared down at the altar, a spread of Blood Ravens lining the rim of the pit with their weapons trained. Gabriel had selected a small detachment to check out the reports about the altar – just the command squad, some scouts, and Matiel's squad of Assault Marines. In the end, he had decided against telling Brom about his scouts' reports, and the team had slipped out of the makeshift camp in the valley before Toth could ask any questions. No doubt it would not take long for the inquisitor to realise that they were missing, but, hopefully, by then Gabriel would understand what was going on.

'So, the good inquisitor senses no taint of Chaos here. How fortunate for the Imperium that such keen-eyed eagles stand vigil over her gates,' said

Gabriel, shaking his head and laying his hand onto Isador's shoulder.

The decapitated body of an Imperial Guardsman still lay across the face of the altar, with his head visible in the swampy ground a stone's throw away. As Matiel surveyed the territory surrounding the crater, casting his intricate and suspicious gaze over the mess of dead greenskins, Isador made his way down into the pit, letting the force of gravity ease his weight down the crater walls in a smooth landslide.

Satisfied that the pit was secure, the Assault Marines broke away from their vigil around its lip and followed Matiel's lead, stalking between the corpses of the orks and prodding them with blades and gun barrels. The orks might not be the smartest race in the galaxy, but even animals could play dead when it suited them. But these orks really were dead. Some of the them had been shredded by thousands of tiny projectiles, others had been felled by a single, precise shot through the soft tissue just below their jawline, and some had simply been sliced into pieces.

Stooping to pick up a fallen weapon, Matiel gasped audibly. It was a boltgun – the distinctive weapon of the Space Marines. But the designs etched into the material of the gun were not very clear – the ork had obviously tried to scratch them away in an attempt to make the weapon his. Deep grooves and scars were dug into the metalwork, wrought by claws or teeth, but they could not fully obscure the markings that were set into the weapon when it was first made. Wriggling out from under the clumsy marks of the ork were the points of a star, each at the end of an axis that bisected a smaller circle. The eight-pointed star, thought Matiel: the mark of the Traitor Legions and the forces of Chaos.

He turned the weapon in his hands; he was repulsed slightly by the touch of a weapon that had been twice damned: once by the unspeakable evils of the heretic Marines that had turned their backs on the Emperor himself during the galaxy-shattering horrors of the Horus Heresy, and once by the taint of grotesque xenos savagery.

The metal was cold, and it lay just out of reach of the ork that had fallen next to it. Inspecting it more closely, Matiel realised that the gun had not been fired. The trigger-happy orks had been slain almost instantaneously, and it looked like most of them had not managed to get off a single shot. Not even the Blood Ravens would hope to kill a pack of orks so efficiently, reflected Matiel, his opinion of the eldar teetering perilously close to admiration.

Meanwhile, Gabriel was watching Isador climb down into the pit and approach the altar. He turned as Matiel approached him from behind, and took the weapon held out in the sergeant's hand.

'A boltgun,' said Gabriel with mild surprise. 'So we were right about the presence of a Traitor Legion here on Tartarus,' he added, pressing his thumb against the markings on the weapon's hilt, as though trying to divine their origin.

'It has not been fired, captain,' explained Matiel. 'The eldar must have laid an ambush for the orks, and then slaughtered them like animals before they even had chance to react.' A mix of repulsion and admiration were evident in his voice.

'They are animals, sergeant, so that is only fitting. We would do the same,' said Gabriel, drawing an un-self-conscious comparison between the Blood Ravens and the eldar, 'if we could.'

Matiel nodded, acknowledging Gabriel's shared admiration for the mysterious aliens, realising that respecting the skills of another warrior, even an alien warrior, did not necessarily make you a heretic. 'Perhaps there is something that we can learn from them,' ruminated the sergeant, almost to himself.

'Yes indeed,' replied Gabriel confidently. 'Knowledge is power – we must seek it out. From this,' he said, casting his hand around the remains of the ork mob, 'we learn not to underestimate the potency of an eldar ambush.' There was a smile on the captain's face as he turned back to watch Isador in the crater.

'What dark crafts have these eldar invoked?' asked Matiel, following Gabriel's line of sight.

'I DO NOT think that this is the work of the eldar, Gabriel,' said Isador, looking up from the remains of Guardsman Tavett. 'I am reasonably sure that it was the eldar who removed the man's head, but he had already been dead for some time by then. For one thing,' he added, 'this man had already been shot through the brain with an Imperial issue laspistol.'

'So, did the Tartarans sacrifice this man themselves?' asked Gabriel, walking around the altar and inspecting Tavett's remains for himself. Despite the evidence, Gabriel could not quite bring himself to believe so little of the Imperial Guardsmen of Tartarus. Most of them had fought valiantly at the side of the Blood Ravens, and some had died as heroes of the Imperium. In the main, the Tartarans were a credit to the spirit of the Undying Emperor, and this was such an epic betrayal that Gabriel refused to make the logical leap. Whatever his personal feelings about Brom and the smattering of cowards in his regiment, he should not prejudge them.

'No, I'm not sure that they did,' replied Isador thoughtfully. 'It looks as though the shot was designed to kill this man before the sacrifice was complete. Perhaps the Guardsmen interrupted the ritual.'

Chaplain Prathios was stooped over the altar, staring into the stone where the Guardsman's head should have been. He seemed transfixed, and almost motionless, as though watching something complicated and partially hidden.

'This man was not the first sacrifice on this altar today,' said Prathios, lifting his head and looking at Isador. 'You should take a look at this.'

The Librarian stepped over to the position indicated by Prathios and looked down into the slick pool of blood. Tiny little stalagmites of red poked up through the blood and, for a moment, Isador thought that they were merely small spikes designed to prevent the victim from slipping off the tablet during its agonies. But then he saw them move. They vibrated and pulsed microscopically, swaying like a miniscule forest.

Looking back along the stricken figure of the Guardsman, he could see that these tiny tendrils had worked their way into his flesh. They appeared to be dragging him down into the stone itself, drawing him bodily into the material of the altar. In a sudden moment of understanding, Isador realised why the Guardsman looked so odd – he was not all there. Crouching down to look at the side elevation, Isador could see that the prostrate trooper, lying on his stomach, was half absorbed into the altar – his chest had already been assimilated, as had his thighs and feet.

In horror, Isador drove his staff under the body of the man and levered him off the tablet, ripping the tendrils free of his body as it slipped from the altar and squelched to the ground in a bloody heap. The man's body looked as though it had been sliced roughly in two, parted lengthways to separate front from back. All that was left was the bloody pulp of his headless back.

The tendrils on the altar shot out after the falling body, questing blindly for the source of their sustenance before shrinking and slurping back into the surface of the tablet. Where the threads of blood touched it, Isador's staff flared with power, spitting sparks of blue fire into the coagulating pool on the altar. The pool hissed and steamed as the righteous energy spilled into it, but Isador pulled his staff clear and peered into the fizzing surface.

Beneath the sheen of slick rock, Isador could see the suggestion of a face wracked with agony, a flock of swirling daemonic forms tearing at it from all sides. A number of the curdling images seemed to be reaching for the surface with immaterial claws, scraping at the substance of the altar from within, as though swimming through an impossibly dense medium. The face pulsed and oscillated, thrashing from side to side in death pains, or birth pains. Then it stopped abruptly, spinning round and resolving into focus in an instant, staring straight into Isador's soul.

With an audible gasp, the Librarian drew back from the altar, pushing his staff into the ground to support himself. Prathios and Gabriel reached for their battle-brother, steadying him with their powerful arms, and watching the colour gradually return to his face.

'Brother Isador, you have one hour to study the altar. Document everything – let us see whether we can fill in some of the gaps in the history of this planet for ourselves.' With concern amounting to worry, Gabriel was watching the pale expression on his old friend's face. 'Then we will destroy it, lest its vile taint infect us all.'

The Librarian's face was still white and his blue eyes were wide and icy. 'Gabriel, we must not destroy this artefact. We are Blood Ravens, and we must not turn our backs on the search for knowledge, no matter how distasteful it may seem.'

'You had better not let Toth hear you saying such things, Isador. He views our Chapter with suspicion enough already, without you giving him the idea that we covet the knowledge of heretics.' Gabriel's voice was only half mocking, for his point was serious. 'Learn what you can, brother, but then we will destroy it. There are boundaries between research and complicity, and we must be careful to stay on the right side of them.'

With that, Gabriel turned and started to climb back up the earthworks towards Matiel and the Assault Marines that stood sentry over the distasteful scene, leaving Isador and Prathios with the altar. 'One hour, then we move on,' he called over his shoulder, as though worried that Isador might have already forgotten.

* * *

THE CARVINGS AND etchings were buried beneath a thick treacle of congealed blood, and Isador struggled to make out the runes. He pulled his gauntlet off and pushed his fingers into the cracks in the stone, scooping out gobbets of viscous ichor and tracing the unfamiliar lines. His fingers scraped against the rough surface of the stone, catching on the pointed nicks and grooves, drawing tiny beads of his own blood into the mix. But he worked methodically, struggling to uncover the ancient engravings in time to give them the attention that they deserved.

The runes seemed dead under his touch, cold and hard like inanimate stone, and Isador lamented that he had been so hasty to rip the Guardsman from its diabolical embrace. Without the flow of new, rich blood, the altar was nothing more than a monument, albeit a monument covered with ancient, runic script.

Here and there, Isador could just about make out some of the words, but the language of the runes was old and unfamiliar to him, and many of the symbols were still obscured under a thick coating of blood. The characters seemed to tell a story about a quest, a heroic mission to uncover the key to salvation for Tartarus and the surrounding worlds. There was an icon representing a mountain and then the phonetic symbols for Korath. There was some mention of the Blood God and the appearance of his messengers, but Isador had seen enough of these artefacts before to know that all of them contained such slogans. He was unimpressed.

One rune struck his eyes and drew his attention, pulling him in with its own gravity. *Treraum* – storm. It was an ancient rune, and for a moment Isador did not recognise it. Not since his years in the Blood Ravens' great librarium sanatorium had he seen this style of rune – ornate and twisted, as though it strove to hide its own meaning from the prying eyes of men. The characters next to it were even more obscure and intricate. They sounded little bells in Isador's memory, but he could not quite place them. He had seen them before, he thought.

'Isador!' called Gabriel from the top of the earthworks. 'Time to leave. Do you have what you need?'

The Librarian looked from the altar to his captain and then back again, thinking of what he could say to waylay their departure. But Gabriel saw his movements and assumed that he was shaking his head.

'Isador – I said one hour, and I meant it,' he said, waving his arm to Matiel. 'Sergeant, rig that monstrosity for destruction, and then let's get out of this Emperor-forsaken place.'

Matiel kicked in the burner on his jump pack and rose noisily, if gracefully, into the air. Behind him, two other members of his squad of Assault Marines did the same, each carrying clusters of mines. And the three of them descended rapidly into the pit, like red angels carrying the promise of redemption.

Isador turned back to the altar, a wave of desperation spilling into his mind. Those idiots were about to destroy one of the most valuable artefacts found in this sector in centuries. Gabriel was just too narrow-minded to see what he was doing. Cyrene had made him weak and paranoid. The path of the Blood Ravens was not supposed to be easy – the pursuit of knowledge required certain sacrifices, but its use could transform a Space Marine into a god. Who else but a god could command the lives of a planet's entire population? Gabriel was too short-sighted, and his guilt threatened to wreck his judgment.

When Matiel touched down behind Isador, he found the Librarian muttering to himself, as though reading from a foreign text. He hardly seemed to notice the arrival of three Assault Marines roaring down with their jump packs blazing.

'Librarian Akios, time's up. The captain wants us to blow this place right now. And good riddance to it, I say,' said Matiel, gesturing for his men to fix their charges to the other side of the altar. 'The stench of the xenos and the heretic is almost overpowering. It is an offence to the Emperor.'

'Just give me another minute,' hissed Isador, snapping his head round to face the sergeant and fixing him with narrowed, blue eyes. 'I need just one more minute. Alone,' he added, as Matiel nodded but showed no signs of moving.

The sergeant nodded again and then turned smartly, walking round to the other side of the altar to check on the progress of his team. Turning his attention back to the runes, Isador produced a small combat knife from a holster on his belt. He muttered something inaudible as he ran his finger along its blade, and the sheen of the metal seemed to burst into effervescence. When he pressed the blade into the side of the altar, a trickle of blood seeped out of the stone, as though he were inflicting a wound. The blade hissed and vibrated under his touch as he cut through the altar, defining a neat rectangle around the constellation of runes that surrounded *Treraum*.

As Matiel came back round to set his mine on Isador's side, the Librarian was tucking something into his belt and wiping blood off the blade of his knife on the grass.

'Matiel! Let's blow this thing and get out of here,' yelled Gabriel, standing on the rim of the crater.

'Yes, captain,' replied Matiel. Then he dropped his voice and turned to Isador. 'Time's up, Librarian.' Isador was already on his feet. He nodded a quick acknowledgment, strode away from the altar, and started to climb up towards Gabriel.

What are you doing, Librarian? For a moment, Isador thought that the words were his own, swimming around inside his head as though they had always been there. But there was an unusual quality to them – something slippery and immaterial. Whenever he tried to grasp one of the thoughts, it eased clear of his mind, vacillating in and out of his memory like a ghost.

I know that you can hear me, Blood Raven, came the voiceless words again. *What are you doing, hiding arte-facts from the heroic captain… acting against his orders?*

Isador did not break his stride as he climbed the banks of the crater. *He doesn't appreciate the value of this find, and I had no time to convince him. He will thank me for my vigilance, when the time comes.*

I understand, Isador, just like you, said the voice, finding his name for the first time. *And I am also able to thank you for your conscientiousness.*

I do not want your thanks, sorcerer, replied Isador, real-ising the nature of the voice at last. *And I will use the powers I glean from this ancient knowledge to destroy you.*

Oh, Isador, you poor, misguided fool. I will be waiting for you on Mount Korath, and then we will see who will do the destroying… whispered the voice, tailing off into silence.

I'll be there, sorcerer, thought Isador as he crested the rise. He nodded a greeting to Gabriel, without meeting his eyes, and turned back to the crater in time to see the three Assault Marines blast into the air, flames pouring out of their jump packs as they distanced themselves from the altar. A sudden explosion shook the ground, sending a plume of smoke and sodden earth mushrooming into the sky, chasing the trails left by Matiel and his Marines. After a slight delay, a second explosion sounded with a tremendous crack – flames and fragments of rock blew diagonally out of the crater, and the sides of the pit started to collapse. Isador and Gabriel took a step back as the ground subsided beneath their feet, and waves of earth slid down the banks to drown the shattered remains of the altar.

'JAERIELLE'S STORM SQUAD have caught the tail end of the Chaos Marines' column near the summit of the mountain, farseer. He has engaged them, but he is badly outnumbered. A ranger detachment is with him, but they are no match for the heavy firepower of the Marines,' reported Flaetriu as he swept into an elegant bow.

Seated in meditation upon a large, smooth rock which held her clear of the foliage in the forest, Macha opened her eyes and looked at the ranger. 'Yes, Flaetriu, the Storm squadron will not be able to hold the Chaos forces on their own. They will need help, but it is not clear that we will be able to provide it.'

'Are you saying that all is lost, farseer?' asked Flaetriu, raising his head and staring at her, his eyes flashing with stung passion.

'Calm yourself, ranger. I am saying no such thing; we do not have it all to lose,' replied Macha cryptically. 'And what of the other humans? The soldiers in red?'

'They have found the altar, farseer. One of them, a psyker I think, studied it briefly, but then they destroyed it. Those mon-keigh have no idea what they are doing, farseer. They just stumble on blindly, destroying everything that they do not understand,' said Flaetriu, his voice dripping with disgust.

'And yet they are coming this way.' Macha was talking to herself as much as to Flaetriu – pondering the role of the Space Marines in the larger picture. 'Perhaps they are not as stupid as you think. This psyker, did he know that you were watching him?'

'No farseer, we were cloaked in the edge of the forest. There is no way that he could have seen us. And we made no contact with our minds. There was something...' Flaetriu trailed off, unsure of the words.

'Something else, ranger?' prompted Macha.

'I'm not sure. But it did seem that there was more than one psychic presence in the area,' replied Flaetriu, unconvincingly.

'Perhaps one of the other humans is also a psyker. It is of no concern to us,' dismissed Macha, her mind already on other things. 'Let us set an ambush for these red Space Marines. Flaetriu, take a detachment of Falcon grav-tanks and a wraithguard squadron back down to the Korath Pass – that is the perfect location for an ambush, especially if the mon-keigh are on their way to the summit of Mount Korath.'

'Excellent, farseer. The humans will walk straight into our trap,' replied Flaetriu, the passion of battle already beginning to flow into his temperamental soul.

'Yes, they will walk into the trap, Flaetriu, but they will not be unprepared; you can never ambush a Space Marine, for they expect treachery and war around every corner. However, we should be happy to validate their paranoia…' said Macha, already sliding off into meditation as she spoke.

'We will destroy the Space Marines, and then concentrate our wrath on the forces of Chaos,' said Flaetriu, flourishing his cloak into an ostentatious show of deference for the farseer.

'Perhaps, young ranger, perhaps,' said Macha, her eyes closed and her voice barely a whisper. 'But just as we have locked the mon-keigh into their path, so they have surely locked us into ours. As we lay traps for the humans at our heels, they trap us between their own forces and the forces of Chaos that we chase. I do not trust the mon-keigh to understand their importance on Tartarus – they have already failed us once. But the future is hazy and confused, and I am not sure that we can do this on our own. Only time will reveal the full character of our respective paths. For now, we must fight everyone: war is not an end in itself, ranger, but it is the most powerful tool we have.'

HALF WAY UP the sparsely forested side of Mount Korath, two eldar Vypers skimmed out to the flanks of the Alpha Legion column, hissing through the evening air as their anti-gravitic engines propelled them up the mountain slope. Each skimmer was supported by a pack of jetbikes that spread out in wakes behind them. They were racing against the armoured column of Chaos assault bikes that roared with brutal power as they bounced and tore their way over the ground behind them.

The Vypers wove and slid gracefully between rocks, trees and the hail of fire that spasmed out of the horde of Chaos bikes. Their weapons-turrets spun smoothly, and their gunners released a constant tirade of shuriken fire from the heavy cannon fixtures. Behind them, the jetbikes bobbed and swerved with incredible manoeuvrability, darting between obstacles and cutting through the crossfire as they flew past the Vypers and pushed on towards the summit.

At the head of the Alpha Legion bikers, Krool screamed into the reddening dusk as the engines of his bike roared with passion and hunger. A splattering of shuriken projectiles clinked into the armour of his left leg, sending pins of pain darting through his nervous system as they penetrated his skin, parting his armour at the molecular level. His bike responded to his rage as though it were an extension of his body; it snarled and spat energy as the Chaos Marine struggled to direct the twin-linked bolters mounted on either side of the front wheel. He clicked the thumb-triggers, and parallel streams of bolter fire seared out of his bike, tracing the wake of a fluttering Vyper but finding no target.

Roaring in frustration, Krool demanded more speed from his bike and it let out a high pitched shriek as it strove to satisfy his bidding. He banked abruptly to one side, throwing his weight towards the ground to tighten his turn as he peeled off to the left of his comrades. Then, flipping the bike back over to the right and almost laying it on its side, Krool brought himself into the slipstream of the offending eldar vehicle. Nobody was going to flank a squadron of Alpha Legion bikers, and certainly not a delicate bunch of effete aliens.

Krool could see the gun-turret on the back of the Vyper spin round to face him, and he laughed out loud at the idea that the eldar would have time to get off·even a single shot. Again he clicked the thumb-triggers, and a stuttering burst of fire flashed out of the twin boltguns. This time he found his target, and the bolter shells punched into the rear of the Vyper, shattering one of the stabiliser-fins and spinning the Vyper laterally. Its gun-turret spun wildly as it tried to compensate for the erratic motion of the vehicle, and a gout of shuriken sprayed out towards the rest of the Alpha Legion bikers.

As his bike closed on the hobbled Vyper, Krool drew his bolt pistol and placed the reticule directly onto the head of the rear gunner, clicking off a single round that cracked the eldar's helmet and lifted him out of the turret. Before he hit the ground, Krool had riddled him with fire from his bike's guns.

But the Vyper was not finished yet, and the pilot spun the destabilised vehicle around to face the charging figure of Krool. The nose-mounted shuriken catapults sputtered a sheet of projectiles into the path of the roaring biker, but Krool yelled his defiance into the storm and pushed his bike even harder.

The shuriken clinked, thudded and ricocheted off the front of the bike, shredding the tyre and ruining the huge suspension coils. The front of the bike dropped as the wheel rim ground into the dirt, and the boltguns dipped their fire short of the Vyper, strafing back through the earth.

Krool let out another yell, screaming into the onslaught of alien projectiles as they sliced and punched into his armour. His bike snarled with power and then bucked, pulling the front wheel out of the soil and pushing it into the air, presenting the undercarriage to the tirade of eldar fury.

In another second the bike smashed into the grounded Vyper, crunching into its thin armour with the full weight and force of the assault bike. The long spikes that adorned the frontal plates of the bike punched straight through the walls of the Vyper's cockpit as the front of the bike crashed back down to earth. The pilot was killed instantly as a spike pushed unstoppably through his face. As the momentum of the bike was suddenly arrested, Krool was bucked over the wreckage of the two vehicles, landing in a crumpled heap on the other side of the Vyper.

Struggling to his feet, Krool turned to look at the ruin that he had wrought, and let out a howl of victory as the two vehicles convulsed and then exploded. He threw up his arms and yelled, watching the Alpha Legion bikers press on towards the summit of the mountain, now flanked on only one side by an eldar Vyper. He screamed after them, punching the air to will them on.

A burst of fire punched into his back, shredding his organs, and the bladed prow of a Wave Serpent transport sliced him neatly in two. The armoured panels on the sleek, green and white sides bore the runic symbols of the Guardian Storm squad, and Jaerielle stood dramatically on the roof, directing the anti-gravitic transport after the speeding column of Chaos

Marines, determined to prevent them from reaching the marker on the summit.

STANDING ON TOP of a majestic Blood Ravens' Rhino transport, his red armour resplendent in the reddening light of the dusk, Gabriel peered through a set of image-enhancers, studying the narrow mountain path before them. Purpling in the sunset, Isador stood stoutly next to his captain, his blue power armour shimmering in the dying light.

The mountain rose from the edge of the river valley, sheer and imposing, bursting out of the tree-line and casting a deep shadow across the oranging landscape. Deep in the valley below, a rough circle of burnt out forest marked the location of the altar, and gentle wisps of smoke still floated into the air from the smouldering remnants of the forest fire caused by the explosions.

Gabriel took the binocs away from his eyes and shook his head. 'Are you certain, Isador?'

'Yes. The Pass of Korath – the only traversable route to the summit of Mount Korath. This is where the inscriptions on the altar said that we must go,' said Isador firmly, as a gust of dusty wind brushed across their faces, whispering inaudibly. 'Do you question my findings?' he added, as though giving voice to another's doubts.

Yyessisador, hedoubtsssyou. The wind blew stronger, whipping up the sand from the ground and blowing it into clouds.

'I do not question your abilities, brother, but I wonder about the tactical sense of this move. That mountain pass is the perfect location for an ambush – see how the crags reach over the path at its narrowest point? There are too many enemies of the Emperor on Tartarus for us to be complacent,' replied Gabriel, surprised that Isador required an explanation.

Ssseeisador, sseee how he doubtss you, the whispers in the wind were beginning to resolve themselves more clearly. *He fearss your powerss, Librarian. He calls you mutant behind your back. You must placate the child for now. Lead him, but let him lead.*

'I do not deny that this is likely to be a trap, Gabriel,' responded Isador, narrowing his eyes as though disturbed. 'But a trap would at least be proof that we are going in the right direction. If the Blood Ravens were being pursued, you would take them through this pass, would you not?'

'You are right, old friend,' said Gabriel warmly, with a faint, weary smile. 'We will follow this path. Stay alert, and follow my lead. I want no mistakes here.'

'Agreed,' replied Isador, nodding his confirmation.

'Corallis!' called Gabriel, crouching down to talk to the sergeant as he approached the side of the Rhino. 'Send a scout squadron ahead into the pass. Tell them to be careful, and to keep off the main path – I suspect that we are expected. We will follow in force with Brother Tanthius's Terminators and Matiel's Assault squad. The tanks will be too slow and may clog the pass, so the assault bikes and a squadron of Typhoon land speeders will provide support.'

'Understood,' nodded Corallis as he turned to distribute the captain's orders.

'What about the Tartarans?' asked Isador. 'Shouldn't we send word back to the camp to summon Brom and a detachment of Guardsmen? We should make use of their numbers – and we could push them through the pass first, to spring whatever trap might be waiting for us.'

'There is no time to send for the Tartarans,' said Gabriel, regarding his friend closely, 'and no need. The pass is narrow, and greater numbers would not help. In any case, their numbers are dwindling, Isador. Besides, the Blood Ravens do not require anyone else to do their fighting for them. We will take swift death to the enemies of the Emperor, as we have done for millennia. Brom and Inquisitor Toth can relax in the soft comfort of the camp for a little while longer – their times to fight will come soon enough.'

THE COLUMN OF warbikes split in two as it hit the eldar defences, peeling left and right to encircle the Wave Serpents and warriors that had ringed the strange menhir on the summit of Mount Korath. The eldar had got there first, as their anti-gravitic vehicles had skimmed over the rough terrain as though it were a perfectly surfaced road. The Chaos bikes had bounced and powered their way across the rubble, skidding over the loose sand and smashing through the increasingly sparse foliage.

Eldar jetbikes seared around the ring, their engines whining as they pursued the circling Chaos bikes in a lethal spiral. Bursts of bolter fire and sleets of shuriken sizzled through the air, gyroscoping around the menhir and the eldar emplacements that surrounded it. Jaerielle watched the dogfights impatiently, taking the occasional pot-shot at a warbike as it roared by, waiting for the melee to begin when the rest of the Chaos Marines arrived. He waved his Storm squad into a fan formation, facing down the mountain side towards the rumble of the Alpha Legion's Rhino transports, shielding the menhir behind them.

A screeching sound made him look round to the left, and he saw one of the Biel-Tan jetbikes burst into flames, spinning on its axis as its stabilisers failed. A hulking warbike ploughed after it, its boltguns flaring with firepower as it continued to pound the spluttering eldar. The jetbike could no longer hold the curve around the menhir and it broke away from the circle, rolling and spinning like a drill, whistling down the slope towards the advancing forces of Chaos.

Just as the first Chaos Rhino crested the rise at the summit of the mountain, its fore-guns blazing with fire and with two horned Chaos Marines dousing the field with flamers from the hatch in its roof, the jetbike reached the ridge from the top, drilling straight into the front of it. A huge explosion shook the ground as the jetbike detonated like a warhead, blowing open the front of the Rhino and enveloping its occupants in superheated chemicals.

A squad of Chaos Marines spilt out of the rupture in the front, thrown by the force of the impact and the arrested momentum of the Rhino. They tumbled through the flames, diving and rolling to control their falls. And then they were on their feet, their bolters braced and coughing at once, spraying the first salvo of fire directly into the eldar defences, clipping at the circling jetbikes and riddling Jaerielle's line with venom.

The Storm squad reacted instantly, moving into new formations like a fluid organism and releasing disciplined volleys of shuriken fire back into the face of the advancing Chaos Marines. Jaerielle watched as two giant warriors strode out of the blazing remains of the Rhino, stepping through the chemical fire as though it were a cool river. One of them must have been over two metres tall. He was bare-headed and carried a huge scythe, its blade easily the length of a human. The other was slightly shorter, but the ornate blades on his helmet thrust viciously into the sky, making him seem even bigger. In his hand he carried a long, dual-pronged force staff, which sizzled and hissed with purple energy, repelling the flames effortlessly.

Behind the two huge warriors, two more Rhinos crested the summit of the mountain, skidding to a halt and spilling two more squadrons of Alpha Legionaries into the fight. As they did so, the circling warbikes broke off from their ring and arced back round to provide flanks for their battle-brothers – forming a single, wide line of fire that advanced steadily towards Jaerielle's small unit.

The eldar may have made it to the menhir before the Chaos Marines, but they had sacrificed power for speed. Jaerielle's Storm squadron contained ten eldar warriors. He had one Vyper left at his disposal, and three jetbikes. Looking down the slope from the menhir, with the last red rays of the sun flooding down the mountain face from behind him, casting his own deep shadow right up to the feet of the enemy, Jaerielle could count five bristling bikes, two hulking armoured transports, and nearly twenty-five mammoth Chaos Marines. For the first time in his long life, even the supreme arrogance of the eldar could not convince him that victory was certain.

* * *

THE PASS OF Korath was little more than a narrow path cut through the cliffs, providing a hazardous route from the Lloovre Valley to the summit of the ancient mountain. On both sides of the rough path were steep cliffs, sheer and unforgiving, and in the half light of dusk the pass was cast into near darkness by their shadows.

Up ahead, already at the narrowest point of the pathway, barely wide enough for a Rhino to pass through, Gabriel could see his scouts. They had paused momentarily, and he could see them looking from side to side, scanning the rock faces for signs of trigger mechanisms or mines. So far, there had been nothing, and Gabriel was beginning to feel uneasy.

The makeshift road had been chewed up by the passage of a number of heavy vehicles. The scouts had noted the wide tracks of Rhinos and the bouncing intermittent marks of assault bikes in the dust. But the eldar seemed to have left no trail at all, if indeed they had even passed this way.

Corallis raised his arm, indicating that the pass was secure. The sergeant had insisted that he should lead the scouting party despite the loss of his arm. He was determined that no other Marine should suffer the fate of Mikaelus in his place, and Gabriel had not the heart to argue with him. Besides, Corallis was the best scout in the entire Third Company, and Gabriel was pleased to have his eyes to survey the pass.

With a sudden cutting motion, Corallis changed his signal, pulling his arm down in a swipe across his body and drawing his bolt pistol. The other scouts dived for cover at the edges of the path, rolling behind boulders and bracing their weapons against them. Gabriel could see the movement from

his vantage point on top of the command Rhino further back down the pathway, but it took a fraction of
a second for the sound to reach him, echoing back
and forth through the sheer crevice.

All at once, he could see flickers of green catching
the last rays of sunlight, high in the cliff face; and
there, through the eye of the narrowest point of the
pass, he could see a group of sleek, green grav-tanks
slide into place. So this was the trap, thought Gabriel
calmly. This we can deal with.

'Corallis,' he hissed into his armour's vox-unit.
'Keep in the cover at the edges of the pass – the
Typhoons are coming through. Tanthius – get the
Terminators into the breach behind the Typhoons.
And Matiel – see what you can do about those
snipers up on the cliff face.'

As he finished talking, everything happened at
once. The Typhoon land speeders roared into life,
accelerating to attack speed almost instantaneously
and flashing through the pass amidst a hail of fire,
engaging the Falcon tanks on the other side. The
jump packs of the Assault Marines erupted, pushing
the squadron into the air as they traced their bolter
fire against the cliff faces, splintering the stone and
sending avalanches of rock tumbling down into the
pass.

Sergeant Tanthius broke into a loping run, waving
his arm to the rest of the Terminators to follow him
into the breach. As he passed the scouts, who were
stabbing out rapid volleys of fire and then ducking
back into cover, Tanthius saw that the pass opened
up into a wider valley on the other side. There were
three Falcon tanks arrayed across the space and at
least two squadrons of wraithguard lying in wait. The

Blood Ravens' Typhoons were skidding and darting under heavy fire, trailing threads of smoke from their engines.

The Terminators fanned out into a firing line and braced their feet into the rocky ground. As one, they opened up with storm bolters and assault cannons, strafing a line of fire across the wraithguard squadrons as they started to run towards the Marines. Tanthius levelled a careful shot into the elongated headpiece of one of the alien warriors, cracking the helmet but not stopping its charge. Another three shots smashed into its head, shattering the strange carapace completely, but still it ran, as though its head had been mere ornamentation.

One of the Typhoons banked sharply to avoid overshooting the Falcon tanks, but as it turned it presented its thin undercarriage to the eldar line and they punished it with a volley of las-fire that blew it immediately into a tumbling fireball. A second Typhoon burst through the burning wreckage of the first, its heavy bolter sputtering, spitting a typhoon missile directly into the sloping prow of the offending tank. The missile skidded across the sleek armoured panels and slid off into the air, spiralling harmlessly into an explosion against the cliff face beyond.

The Typhoon flashed in between the tanks, clearing the eldar line and then banking into a tight turn to attack it again from the rear. Another missile jetted out of the land speeder. This time it punched into the thinner, oblique armour at the back of the tank, ripping through into the Falcon's interior where it detonated ferociously. The tank bucked and spasmed before exploding outwards from within,

scattering fragments of the chassis across the valley
floor.

Meanwhile, Gabriel's Rhino rolled through the
narrow point of the pass with its storm bolters strip-
ping a constant line of fire. It came to a halt in the
midst of the line of Terminators, emptying the command squad onto the deck behind it. Gabriel drew
his chainsword into his right hand and his bolter
into his left and called out to his men. 'For the Great
Father and the Emperor!'

A great chorus of voices echoed back through the
narrow crevice. 'For the Great Father and the
Emperor!' And the small Blood Ravens' strike force
was now fully deployed, as gouts of flame, bolter fire
and coruscating blue energy lanced out of the command squad towards the advancing wraithguard.

Above the fray, hovering on bursts of flame from
their jump packs, Matiel's Assault Marines were
spraying bolter shells against the rock faces as the
eldar snipers leaped and danced from ledge to ledge,
evading the lethal barrage but unable to return fire.

'FARSEER,' SAID FLAETRIU, hastening into a bow.
'Jaerielle requests support. He fears that the Chaos
Marines will soon overrun his position and occupy
the site of the menhir.'

Macha nodded slowly. She knew that this would
happen, and she was prepared for it. 'Send a squad of
Warp Spiders to assist Jaerielle. Instruct them to rig
the menhir for detonation. If the defences fail, the
forces of Chaos cannot be permitted to possess the
knowledge hidden in that marker.'

The ranger nodded quickly. Warp Spiders carried
warp jump generators in their armoured carapaces,

enabling them to slip in and out of even the most secure locations, flitting in and out of the warp at will. A squadron could jump through the webway straight to the site of the menhir without having to penetrate the line of Chaos Marines assaulting it. But there were not many of them, and certainly not enough to turn the tide of the battle on the summit of Mount Korath.

'The Blood Ravens are being held down at the Pass of Korath, farseer, but the conflict is a bloody one on both sides. You were right that it would be hard to ambush these mon-keigh,' reported Flaetriu, as Macha turned her gaze away from the flashes of fire just visible up at the summit, and he stared down the mountain side where an explosion had just mushroomed into the air. The Biel-Tan were engaged on two fronts, and they could not win them both.

'Our priority must be the menhir, ranger. Withdraw the wraithguard through the webway portals and tell the Falcons to blow the pass. We need only delay the Blood Ravens long enough to ensure that the Chaos Marines cannot triumph,' ordered the farseer. 'Our battle with the soldiers in red can wait for another time.'

LORD BALE SWEPT his scythe in a powerful arc, but Skrekrea was faster than the Chaos Marine. She leapt clear of the swing, spinning into a pirouette as she kicked out at the ugly, misshapen face of the Chaos Lord. The kick made firm contact with his jaw, turning his head in a fountain of blood from his mouth. But he did not even stagger under the blow. Instead, he brought the scythe back round in a rapid backswing as he yelled in fury. The butt of the scythe struck Skrekrea in the side of the head just as she landed, knocking her off her feet, and Bale roared with rage.

As the scythe fell for the death blow, Bale let out a scream. A bright flash flared next to him and a rush of warp power poured out onto the mountain side. A heavily armoured eldar warrior leapt out of the warp-tear with a death-spinner gatling gun churning out projectiles that rattled into Bale's armour. The Chaos Lord stepped back under the onslaught, swinging his blade wildly in the direction of the Warp Spider, Skrekrea momentarily forgotten.

Sindri was at his shoulder, stabbing out with a spike of purple energy from his force staff. The blast sizzled and cracked against the eldar's armour, which was warded against the forces of the warp to permit travel through it. Nonetheless, the Warp Spider was thrown back by the energy, flying off his feet and crashing to the ground in front of the menhir.

The Chaos Marines were pressing in now, closing their grip around the dwindling forces of the eldar defenders, and Sindri could taste the power of the menhir in the air as he spun and stabbed with his staff. Bale was a roaring monster of fury, scything and slicing with his manreaper, defining a frenetic sphere of death around him as he strode forward. The air around him was thick with bolter shells, clouds of shuriken, and flashes of las-fire, but he ignored it, focussed exclusively on his blade and the menhir. It was almost in reach now.

A blue fireball exploded into the back of one of the Chaos Marines in front of Bale, opening up a hole in reality and punching the screaming Marine through it into the immaterium. He just vanished into the heart of the explosion.

Bale and Sindri turned together, tracing the path of the fireball. Behind them, advancing up the mountain side, just clearing the crest of the summit, was a line of eldar soldiers. They were different from the ones defending the menhir – taller and more mechanical-looking: wraithguard. Interspersed in the line were three warlocks, each with crackling staffs of power that flared and jousted with energy, firing strips of blue lightning into the rear of the Alpha Legion's forces. In the centre of the line was a female figure, bathed in an aura of light that seemed to hold her hovering above the ground. Her arms were outstretched to the heavens, and great balls of blue energy kept forming in front of her, then searing through the air into the Legionaries, picking off a different Marine with each blast.

'The farseer!' gasped Sindri, his voice cold with surprise as Bale's Marines struggled to reorganise their deployment, striving to fight front and rear actions simultaneously.

'I thought you had arranged for her to be tied up elsewhere, sorcerer,' hissed Bale as his blade swept through the legs of a charging eldar warrior, sending his two halves tumbling to the ground in twitching heaps. The Chaos Lord was in the thick of the close-range melee, and he was enjoying himself. The eldar were suitable opponents, and the ground was slick with the blood of his Marines and eldar both. Blood for the Blood God, he thought with satisfaction. But he had no intention of dying on this mountain, and he was not fool enough to believe that even he could survive the crossfire of these deadly aliens.

Sindri planted his staff into the rock and started to mutter indistinctly to himself, letting a field of energy build around him, shielding him from the blasts of the eldar warlocks. 'It is of no consequence, Lord Bale. We should retire from this theatre and let the Blood Ravens deal with the eldar. They will lead us to our goal in the end, and in the meantime they will bleed in our place.'

'You'd better be right about this, sorcerer,' said Bale, shooting a hate-filled glance at Sindri, as a pulse of las-fire flashed past his shoulder, singeing the acid-green paint from his armour. 'I grow tired of your faltering schemes. These are not orks, and they will not be so easily manipulated.'

Bale took another look around and realised that he had no choice. The eldar defending the menhir had received reinforcements from somewhere, and they were all fighting with renewed spirit now that the farseer had come into view. And the wraithguard were advancing relentlessly from the rear, rapidly closing down Bale's scope for movement. If they were going to get out of here, they had to go now.

With a tremendous leap, Jaerielle vaulted over the head of a Chaos Marine, dragging his blade across his throat under the helmet seal and slicing the head free. He landed lightly, pulling his sword clear and spinning it in a low arc towards the feet of another. His blade was met by a great curved scythe that shattered his sword with one sweep. But as Jaerielle discarded his blade and rolled for his gun, the giant Marine turned his back on him and strode away, shuriken ricocheting off his massive armour. Looking around, Jaerielle could see that the other Chaos Marines were also disengaging – their remaining assault bikes were already streaking off down the other side of the mountain.

Jaerielle, you will not pursue these forces. It was the farseer, speaking directly into his mind. *Let them go. We have more pressing objectives to achieve. Remember, Jaerielle, war is a means to an end, not an end in itself. Let them go.*

In his soul Jaerielle could feel the fire of combat burning, and he longed to pursue the disgusting mon-keigh – to cleanse the galaxy of their vile presence. The Biel-Tan may hate the bestial orks more than anything else in the galaxy, but the mon-keigh were a close second.

As you wish, farseer, he replied, fighting to control his urges, realising for the first time that he was thoroughly ensnared by the Path of the Warrior, unable to suppress his desire for combat and riddled with desperation to shed blood for Khaine, the Bloody-Handed God.

'Where did they go?' asked Matiel as he crunched to the ground at Gabriel's side, his jump pack spluttering into silence. The snipers had all been killed, or had vanished, and the rest of the eldar force seemed to have fled. They had suddenly disengaged and turned tail, as though conceding defeat. But they had not been beaten, reflected Gabriel uneasily.

'What were those portals?' asked Gabriel, turning to Isador. The fighting had simply ceased, and the Blood Ravens had been left unsure about how to proceed. Gabriel had ordered caution, and his Marines had taken up tactical positions but had held their fire. They had refrained from pursuing the eldar; Gabriel suspected that their real fight was not with these mysterious aliens. He was simply pleased to see them leave.

The Falcon tanks had turned their guns on the cliff walls of the pass itself, causing a huge avalanche that blocked the crevice completely, sealing the Blood Ravens on one side and most of the eldar force on the other. The wraithguard that had been trapped with the Space Marines had charged into a series of circular, stone portals and vanished – the portals exploding into fragments behind them. It had all happened in an instant.

'They are webway portals – temporary doorways from one point in space to another,' answered Isador. 'They are a unique eldar technology, captain, and incredibly unstable. Stepping through throws you instantaneously into the warp and then drags you out again into another place, where another portal is open. An unshielded soul would go insane,' he added, shaking his head at the apparent recklessness of the aliens.

The sudden silence in the valley was eerie, as the chatter of falling rocks and the dull echoes of foot-falls gradually ceased. Gabriel looked around carefully at the scattering of dead and wounded Marines on the valley floor, together with the remains of ruined equipment and the broken figures of wraithguard.

'Get a dreadnought up here to clear away this rock-fall,' said Gabriel as Corallis hastened to report to his captain. 'In the meantime, this is a good location to establish a field base. Get hold of Brom and tell him to bring a detachment of Tartarans to defend this pass. And make sure that those web-portals have really been destroyed – it would not do to have our eldar friends popping up in the middle of our base.'

'What about Toth?' asked Isador carefully.

'What about him? I'm sure that he will make his own way here in good time, but I am equally sure that I am not going to help him interfere with our purpose here,' replied Gabriel gruffly.

'And what exactly is our purpose here, Gabriel?' asked Isador.

'You were correct, Isador,' said Gabriel wryly. 'The fact that the eldar laid a trap for us does suggest that we are on the right path. We will follow the aliens to the summit of this mountain, and we will discover what they are so keen to hide from us. There is a bigger picture here, Isador, although we cannot yet see what it is. There are still two days before the warp storm arrives, and before then we will find out why Tartarus is so important to these aliens, and to our old foes, the Alpha Legion. And we will do it with or without the blessing of Inquisitor Toth,' said Gabriel firmly. 'Corallis. Where is Prathios? I must pray,' he added, turning away from the Librarian.

A whisper of wind gusted through the mountain pass as the red sun finally set, and Isador breathed it in like a breath of fresh air.

CHAPTER SEVEN

As THE FIRST rays of the dawn pierced the heavy shadows of the mountain pass, Brom walked away from the newly completed field-station. He kicked at the pebbles on the ground, frustrated and discontented. Before the arrival of the Blood Ravens he had been the ranking officer on Tartarus – a commissar in all but title. It was not that he was not thankful for the help of the Adeptus Astartes in the war against the orks, but he had not anticipated the way in which the Blood Ravens' captain would take control of all the military affairs of the planet after their victory.

The arrival of the inquisitor had not improved matters. Toth and Angelos had been at loggerheads from the start, squabbling over their powers and jurisdictions. They had even had the gall to argue about who would have control over the Tartarans in front of him. Brom shook his head in disbelief, kicking a stone so hard that it shattered against the rock-face at the side of the crevice. Who did they think he was? Treating him like a grunt. He was a colonel in the Emperor's own Imperial Guard, and he deserved some respect. He had stood his ground against the uprisings of cultists and the raids of ork pirates, fighting for the honour of the Emperor Himself, and for the safety of the people of his homeworld. What would Captain Angelos know about that, he scoffed, kicking another stone against the cliff face.

The colonel paused as he reached a large boulder. It had been rolled up against the edge of the pass after a Blood Ravens' dreadnought had blasted its way through the avalanche in the middle of the night, splintering the rockslide into smaller boulders that the Space Marines had pushed aside like pebbles.

He pulled himself up onto the rock and tugged a lho-stick out of his pocket, tapping it several times against the packet in a personal ritual. Flicking it into life, he gazed back over the new field-station, bathed in the fresh light of morning. Despite his resentment, he was proud of what his men had achieved here in such a short period. If Angelos persisted in assigning the Tartarans such menial and logistical functions, at least they could take pride in how well they performed.

In truth, some of his men were only too pleased to become support personnel – to let the Blood Ravens do the fighting for them. Brom shuddered slightly at the thought of those cowardly troopers, feeling the disdain pouring out of Angelos even from the other side of the camp. But there were some Guardsmen who knew the true value of war – they knew that combat was a goal in itself, that shedding blood was the highest form of offering to the God-Emperor, whether it was the blood of the enemy or your own. There was but one commandment for the loyal soldier: thou shalt kill. Sergeant Katrn knew, and Brom knew that he could rely on Tartarans like him to sustain the honour of his proud regiment.

He took a deep drag on his lho-stick, letting the local weed fill his lungs. He held it there for a few seconds, and for a moment he thought that he could feel the substance of Tartarus itself bleeding into his soul.

Yes, he thought, we will fight again. The Tartarans will show these Blood Ravens what it means to be Tartarus born and bred.

'I SEE THEIR faces every day, Prathios. They scream into my dreams and disturb my prayers. It is as though they haunt my mind, now that their planet is no more,' confessed Gabriel, kneeling in supplication before the company Chaplain. The two Marines were hidden in the heavy shadows of a temporary shrine, hastily constructed by the Tartarans in the heart of the new field-station.

'Their souls are at ease, brother-captain. It is yours that can find no peace. You call out into the warp, like a beacon for the pain of those who have passed before you,' said Prathios in a low voice.

'I am calling daemons into my mind?' asked Gabriel, his voice tinged with horror.

'No, Gabriel, the daemons come by themselves, drawn by the agonies of a soul at war with itself. Your anguish exposes you to their taunts, just as a ship at sea exposes itself to a storm.' Prathios's voice was deep and soothing. He had seen Gabriel change since the Cyrene affair, and he was concerned for his captain. Inside all the magnificent power armour, and behind the myths and legends, a Space Marine was just a man. Not quite a man like any other, but a man nevertheless.

The Apothecaries and Techmarines of the Adeptus Astartes could effect profound transformations on the body of an initiate – augmenting the internal organs, adding sensory implants and bolstering muscle strength, they could even insert a delicate carapace under the skin of the whole body, ready to interface with the power armour. However, there was only so much that could be done for a Marine's mind and soul.

The selection procedure for induction into the Blood Ravens – the Blood Trials – were rigorous in the extreme. Not only were aspirants required to demonstrate the physical prowess of a superior warrior, but their genetic code would also be tested for the smallest sign of mutation. But genetic mutation and a taint of the soul were not the same thing. For detection of the latter, the Blood Ravens would rely on the shadowy expertise of the librarium sanatorium – where all would-be Librarians were screened psychically, to the point of insanity, probing the depths of their souls to find the cracks and fissures for which the forces of Chaos would quest constantly.

The Chapter's Chaplains would oversee all of this, and Prathios had done so innumerable times in his long life. Over a century earlier, in his younger years, the Chaplain had even recruited Gabriel himself in one of the Cyrene trials.

Prathios could remember the trial clearly. He could still see the defiant face of the young Guardsman, burning with passion and smothered in the blood of his competitors, as the young Gabriel Angelos fought for his right for a place on the Blood Ravens' Thunderhawk. His brilliant green eyes had flared with resolution – certain that of the millions of Cyrenean warriors, he was the best. And he had been the best, reflected Prathios, without a doubt.

Even then, there had been something unusual about the young Angelos. His sparkling eyes burned a little too brightly, and his soul seemed to shine almost too purely, as though it were untouched by the horrors of the universe. His genetic tests had all come back perfectly – absolutely flawless, which was almost a mutation in itself, especially on Cyrene. Although he had a sensitive mind, the Chapter had decided not to push Gabriel through the horrors of the sanatorium – he was not a psyker and he would never be a Librarian.

Prathios himself had voiced some reservations about this decision. Part of him was concerned about how the prodigal young initiate would respond when the horrors of the galaxy finally breached the purity of his soul. He was concerned that the Blood Ravens should attempt to prepare his mind for the shock of the terrible responsibilities of the Adeptus Astartes. No matter how spectacular his physical and tactical capacities, Gabriel's soul shone with naïve clarity, and Prathios feared that this beauty belied fragility.

And then there had been the return to Cyrene, and Gabriel had looked upon his homeworld with the eyes of a Space Marine for the first time, charged with conducting the Blood Trials himself. What he had seen there had filled him with horror, and what he had done had shattered his naivety forever.

Prathios sighed deeply, reaching his hand down to Gabriel's shoulder, and he shivered at the thought of the storm raging in his captain's soul. No man, not even a captain of the Adeptus Astartes, should have to exterminate his own home planet – what effect had this duty had upon his unsullied mind?

'IT OFFENDS ME to flee from combat, sorcerer. The Alpha Legion has not won its reputation by turning its tail in the face of aliens. We may not have the pathetic paranoia about honour that is shown by the Adeptus Astartes, but we are still warriors, Sindri, and you would do well not to forget it.' Bale was breathing hard, struggling to keep his temper under control. The sorcerer's plans were not playing out in accord with his own, and he was being humiliated at every turn. If the sorcerer did not promise so much, Bale would have flayed him years ago.

From the entrance to a cave in the side of the Lloovre Valley, Bale could see the sun rising above the shimmering city of Lloovre Marr. The Alpha Legion had sped down into the valley during the night, taking cover in the dense forest. Sindri had spotted the cave, and the Chaos Marines had made their way up the opposing wall of the valley to set up a temporary camp in the cover that it afforded. From there they could monitor movements along the river basin and Sindri could attempt to divine the intent of the eldar. Meanwhile, Bale had sent out a rider to summon reinforcements; the next time he came across the eldar, he would not bow to their onslaught.

'My Lord Bale,' whispered Sindri, as the first light of the morning glinted menacingly off the blades that adorned his helmet. 'We work towards a common end. The honour and prowess of the Alpha Legion are under no threat. Rather, we stand on the brink of a great awakening – something infinitely more powerful than our pride is glittering just out of reach. Our rewards will justify our sacrifices a thousand times over.'

'You had better be right, sorcerer,' said Bale, almost spitting with distaste at his manipulative ways. 'Otherwise your sacrifice will follow quick on the heels of your failure. Your reassurances that the orks would keep the Blood Ravens busy have proved false, and your calculations appear to have underestimated the strength of these eldar. I will not tolerate another mistake, sorcerer, and you would not survive it.'

'My lord, I will not fail,' replied Sindri, without bowing. Inside his helmet, his jaw was clenched, and it required a real effort of will to smooth his tone. 'The eldar will guide us to our goal – they will underestimate our strength and our vision. Their arrogance will be their undoing. As we fled, we reinforced their prejudices, my lord. And, as for the Blood Ravens, they are of no consequence. They are… in hand.'

The Chaos Lord scoffed audibly and brushed past Sindri, pushing his way further into the cave, where his Marines were tending to their weapons in preparation for the combat to come.

Sindri, left alone in the mouth of the cave, walked out into the morning air and raised his arms to the sun, bathing himself in the red light of dawn as though it were a shower of blood. His mind was racing with resentment at the ingratitude of that near-sighted oaf, Bale. But he laughed quietly to himself, whispering his voice into the trees: at the end of the affair, nobody will be able to treat me with such disrespect.

THE RUNES ON the altar fragment were unusual, and Isador could still not decipher their precise meaning. He had retreated to the very edge of the camp, climbing into the shattered remains of the avalanche out of sight of the rest of his battle-brothers. The early morning sun was shedding a faint, reddening glow onto the inscription, coating each of the runes in the suggestion of ghostly blood. Isador sighed humourlessly, wondering how much actual blood had coursed across these etchings in their long history.

The character *Treraum* – storm – kept drawing his eye, and his memory ached as he tried to recall the meanings of the runes that appeared after it. He hated himself for being unable to remember, and his hate seeped through into resentment against Gabriel for making them abandon the site so quickly.

They were Blood Ravens, after all, was it not their Emperor-given nature to seek out new knowledge that might be of use to the Imperium? And who was Gabriel to judge whether this altar might be of use? He had not served his time in the librarium sanatorium, not like Isador, and had not spent long years exposing his soul to the torturous mantras of heretics and aliens. He had never read the forbidden books of Azariah Vidya, the Father Librarian of the Blood Ravens, may the Emperor guard his soul. Gabriel had never even heard the silver tones of the Astronomican;

never had his soul been seduced into the unspeakable symphony of that choir and left hanging in the deepest reaches of the immaterium, utterly alone with only his knowledge and discipline to bring him home again.

Home. Gabriel knew nothing of the value of homecoming. Cyrene had been Isador's home too.

In truth, Isador had never understood why the Blood Ravens did not require all of their senior officers to be Librarians. There were enough of them in the Chapter – far more than was typical in any other Chapter of Space Marines – and the Chapter Master himself was a powerful Librarian. It was ridiculous to expect that captains like Gabriel could really make sensible decisions about relics like this altar – only a Librarian could know the true value of the artefact. But Gabriel would not ask advice on command decisions, he was adamant that the responsibility was his.

In practice, however, only a handful of Librarians ever acceded to positions of command, except temporarily, in the absence of their captain. It was as though the Chapter had learnt nothing from the example of their Great Father, Azariah Vidya.

Once, during the early stages of his training, Isador had asked Chaplain Prathios about the politics of promotion within the Blood Ravens, but the Chaplain had just shaken his head sadly and said: there is no promotion, young Isador, there is only service – we all have our parts to play for the glory of the Great Father and the Emperor. At the time, Isador had nodded sagely, believing that he saw the sense in subsuming himself into the organic unity of the Chapter. But now, with the morning wind whispering down through the valley and whistling between the rocks, after two days of war against orks and eldar, on an alien planet that was about to be swallowed by a warp storm, he was not so sure. Different decisions could have been made – and he would have made them better.

But all was not lost, since he had saved this altar fragment, and he would work out a way of using the knowledge that it contained to save the Blood Ravens' Third Company from making any further mistakes.

'Knowledge is power,' he muttered to himself, reciting the Chapter's motto as though it were his own. 'Guard it well.'

'Librarian Akios. What a surprise to see you here.' The familiar voice came down from the top of one of the large rocks behind which Isador was sitting

'Colonel Brom. I had no idea that you were there,' said Isador, wondering exactly how long the Tartaran had been watching him. He had been so absorbed in his thoughts that he hadn't noticed, and he made a mental note that he should not let that happen again. For all of his faults, Gabriel was never complacent enough to be taken by surprise by a Guardsman.

Brom breathed a plume of smoke out of his lungs, enjoying being higher than the massive Marine for the first time. The smoke settled slowly down towards Isador, dissipating as it reached his immaculate, blue armour. Instead of speaking, Brom took another draw on his lho-stick and looked off into the sunrise, apparently enjoying the beauty of dawn on his homeworld.

'It is beautiful, is it not?' asked Brom openly.

Isador turned and looked at the sunrise for the first time and nodded. 'Yes, colonel. Tartarus is a beautiful planet.'

'It is my home, Librarian, and I will not give it up. Not to the orks, not to the eldar, and not even to the Blood Ravens.' As he spoke, Brom turned his head away from the sun, fixing Isador with a firm and determined stare.

'I can assure you that Captain Angelos has no designs on your planet, colonel... beautiful though it is,' said Isador, trying to diffuse the anger that seemed to bubble in the background of Brom's tone.

'Do you remember your homeworld, Librarian?' There was some acid in the question, and Isador flinched slightly as it stung him. Even if Brom had been watching him for a while, how could he know? A cold wisp of wind flickered between the rocks, making them both shiver.

'Yes, I remember it well,' he replied plainly.

'And did the good captain save it?' asked Brom. He knew. Somehow he knew.

'Gabriel did what had to be done,' snapped Isador, suddenly leaping to the defence of his old friend. 'I would have done the same thing had the decision been mine.' And I would have done, he realised as he spoke.

Brom let another thread of smoke ease out between his pursed lips, as though unconcerned by the Librarian's sudden emotion. His eyes were still burning into the radiant blue of Isador's, glowing with an inhuman taint of red. For a moment, Isador wondered whether it was really Brom that was staring down at him.

'And what of Tartarus?' he asked, changing the subject and watching the colonel carefully. 'You mentioned some legends about a storm, colonel. I would be most interested to hear more about it.'

'You can read it yourself, can't you?' hissed Brom, his voice dripping with venom as his eyes swam with red, as though riddled with burst capillaries.

Stung again, Isador vaulted up the side of the rock and grabbed Brom by the collar of his coat, lifting him clear off the ground. As they turned away from the dawn, the red faded from Brom's eyes and he began to cough violently, exhaling gouts of smoke into a sudden gust of wind.

'Librarian Akios!' The voice made Isador drop Brom into a heap on top of the rock, as he turned back towards the camp.

Standing just outside the fortifications was Sergeant Corallis, waving a summons to Isador. 'The captain wants to see you. You can bring the colonel.'

'CAPTAIN ANGELOS, I am here as you requested,' said Brom, pushing aside the curtains that hung across the entrance to the command post next to the shrine. Isador loomed behind him for a moment, before pushing past him into the hab-unit and nodding a greeting to Gabriel.

'Colonel Brom, thank you for coming. We need your Tartarans to cover this pass. The combat in this sector will be sure to attract the attention of the remnants of the ork forces, and we cannot afford their interference further up the mountain. If the Blood Ravens have to engage the eldar, we will need no other distractions,' explained Gabriel, watching the tension between Brom and Isador with unease.

'Understood, captain,' replied Brom professionally. 'You may count on the Imperial Guard to hold this pass. No ork will get through while a Tartaran still holds his weapon.'

'Very good, colonel. Keep me appraised of the situation and, if possible, I will send support if the orks do attack.' Gabriel hesitated for a moment, as though on the brink of adding something. But then he waved his hand dismissively. 'Thank you, colonel. Your assistance in this matter is much appreciated.'

Brom bowed sharply and then left, leaving Isador and Gabriel alone.

'What is wrong, old friend?' asked Gabriel – the angst on Isador's face was plain to see.

'I do not trust him, Gabriel,' said Isador, watching the curtains close behind Brom.

'He is a good man, Isador. A good soldier. His men love him, and they follow him without question, mostly. He may not be a Space Marine, and he may not even be the finest officer in the Imperial Guard, but he is a good man. I have been too harsh on him, and it is time for me to share some responsibility. This is his homeworld, after all,' said Gabriel frankly.

Isador observed his old friend for a few moments, a torrent of emotions flashing through his mind as the events of the last few minutes rehearsed themselves in his head. They had been through so much together – born and raised on the same planet, and then inducted into the Blood Ravens in the same Blood Trials. A wave of remorse and affection washed over him, and he felt like himself again.

'Forgive me, captain, I am still thinking about the altar,' confessed Isador.

'There is nothing to forgive, old friend. You are a Librarian of the Blood Ravens, and I would be disappointed if you stopped thinking about it before you

have solved the riddle,' replied Gabriel, laughing
faintly.

'I am frustrated that you decided to destroy it so
quickly, Gabriel. I think that we could have used it to
learn more about what we are facing here. Knowledge is power, and we sacrificed some of that power
today.'

Isador's honesty touched him, and Gabriel slapped
his friend heartily on his shoulder. 'You may be right,
Isador. My decision was made in haste. There is
much that I do not understand on Tartarus, and I fear
what I do not understand – such is the bane of our
Chapter. It is the other side of our nature, and that
part of us with which we must all struggle. Speed is
very important on this expedition, with the storm
only two days away, but I was wrong not to give you
more time. It will not happen again.'

Isador was overwhelmed by his captain's confession and he fell to his knees before him, bowing his
head. 'Thank you, my lord,' he said, adding the epi-
thet that he had never before used with Gabriel.

Captain Angelos of the Blood Ravens returned the
bow formally, and then dragged his friend back to
his feet. 'What is it, Isador? There is something else?'
he said, gazing directly into his blue eyes.

'Nothing. There's nothing, Gabriel,' replied Isador,
his fingers rubbing involuntarily against the altar
fragment in his belt as he spoke. 'When do we get to
kill some eldar?'

As THE MORNING sun broke the horizon, the summit
of Mount Korath was already speckled with light.
Torches adorned the great menhir and circled it in a
gradually expanding spiral. Strewn over the mountain

top were the dead bodies of Biel-Tan eldar and the Alpha Legionaries. The eldar dead stood out gloriously in the dawn, as a single, blue flame licked out of the heart of each, picking them out like candles in the faint morning light.

After the battle, Macha had moved through the eldar corpses one by one, kneeling silently at the side of each and muttering in an ancient tongue. She had carefully removed the waystone from the breastplate of each warrior, storing them in an elaborate crystalline matrix – a fragment of the infinity circuit of the Biel-Tan craftworld. The waystone contained the very soul of the warrior, sealed into an impenetrable gemstone that kept the eldar safe from the ravenous clutches of the daemon Slaanesh, that roamed the warp in a perpetual search for their souls.

If their waystones were lost, so too would be the precious soul of this ancient, dwindling race. When Macha returned to the Biel-Tan craftworld, their giant space-born home, she would return the crystalline fragment to the craft's own spirit pool – the infinity circuit in which the souls of deceased eldar could swim until they were called on again.

Having removed their waystone, Macha had reached out with her long forefinger and delicately touched the tiny crater left in their armour. As she had done so, a burst of blue fire had leapt from her fingertip and settled into a single, perfect flame on the fallen warrior's chest. The Chaos Marines she left as they lay.

By the time the morning light had pushed the darkness down into the valley below, the bodies of the slain eldar were a blaze of glory on the mountaintop. The surviving warriors knelt onto one knee and bowed their white and green elliptical helmets to the rising sun, welcoming the new day and giving thanks that Tartarus had not stolen the souls of their brethren.

As the eldar climbed to their feet and broke free of the observances of the ceremony, they set about readying themselves for the short journey to Lloovre Marr. The path down into the valley on the north side of the mountain was steep, and the valley floor itself was shrouded in tree cover. Macha was certain that the Alpha Legion was laying in wait to exact their vengeance on the Biel-Tan, and she wanted to ensure that her warriors were ready. The fate of Tartarus was in their hands – and it was a fate just as precarious as that of the souls of the eldar themselves. Macha had a responsibility, and she would be damned if she was going to fail to live up to it.

The farseer stood on the far side of menhir, gazing out across the valley below while her warriors busied themselves. It looked so peaceful in the gentle light of dawn, and the deep shadows seemed to languish sleepily.

'Farseer. May I speak with you?' asked Jaerielle, stopping a respectful distance from Macha and touching his left knee to the ground.

Macha turned and smiled weakly at the Storm Guardian. 'Of course, Jaerielle. I was expecting to see you this morning. You want to ask me about the eldar path, do you not?'

'Yes, farseer,' replied Jaerielle, unsurprised by the precise question. 'I fear that I may be straying from it.'

'You are a warrior, Jaerielle, and have been one for many centuries. I wonder whether you can even remember a time when you trod any of the other paths of our ancient culture,' said Macha, explaining how he was feeling, rather than asking. 'The Path of the Eldar was put in place to guard us against ourselves, Jaerielle. We are a passionate people, and easily fixated. The path allows us to cycle through various arts and explore all aspects of ourselves, not only the warrior within. It does sometimes happen,' she continued, 'that an eldar becomes trapped in one path or another. His soul becomes unable to make the transition into another part of itself, and the eldar becomes consumed by the art that has chosen him. In your case, Jaerielle, you have been chosen by the Path of the Warrior, and it seems that you may never leave it.'

'War for its own sake, farseer? You are talking about the Way of the Exarch?' asked Jaerielle in whispered tones, hardly daring to speak the name of the most feared of all eldar warrior castes. The exarch is completely lost to himself, enveloped by a passion for war, and utterly dedicated to the arts of one of the eldar aspect shrines. Over time, he will gradually be assimilated into his armour, which will never be taken off. And when he is finally slain, there will be nothing left but the armour itself, a testament to the dedication and sacrifice of this most lonely path.

'Yes, Jaerielle. You have felt it. I saw it in your soul as you battled the Chaos Marines last night. There was delight in your heart, and joy in your abilities. Your memory is already awash with images of blood, drowning out the dances and poetry of your youth. Soon there will be nothing but battle for you,' said Macha with solemnity.

'Then I am lost?' asked Jaerielle, a hint of panic sounding in his voice.

'You are lost to yourself, child, but not to Biel-Tan. Your path is a glorious one, and we will rejoice in your majesty. The blood you spill will be for the Biel-Tan and for Khaine, the Bloody-Handed God. You will be a hero amongst the eldar, but you will be utterly alone,' explained the farseer.

'I am not ready, farseer,' said Jaerielle, denying the shouts in his soul.

'You came to me, Jaerielle. You are ready. And we need you to be ready. I will talk with the Shrine of the Striking Scorpions, your old aspect temple, and the ritual of transition will be performed before the sun reaches its third quadrant,' concluded Macha, as though this were the most natural thing in the world. She looked down at the kneeling eldar at her feet and shivered slightly – he was about to step into a place where even she could not see.

THE COLUMN OF Blood Ravens roared up the mountain side, dazzling in shimmering reds in the morning sunshine. At the head of the line was the command Rhino, with Gabriel and Isador riding on its roof, shoulder to shoulder. The Rhino was flanked on both sides by the remaining Typhoons, and a squadron of assault bikes sat in behind, ready to be deployed when required. Following behind the bikes were two more Rhinos, one carrying Matiel's Assault Marines and the other a squad of Devastators. A Land Raider tank brought up the rear, stuffed full of Tanthius and his Terminators.

The route to the top of the mountain was littered with debris and bodies. Chunks of eldar jetbikes and the ruins of a Vyper still smoked vaguely, but there were also burnt-out assault bikes bearing the markings of the Alpha Legion, and smatterings of corpses, both eldar and Chaos Marine.

The Blood Ravens ploughed on undaunted. The roar of their engines and the sight of the detachment deployed in such formidable force filled their hearts with pride. At the head of the column, standing heroically against the red sun was Gabriel, his chainsword already drawn in readiness, and the image swelled the confidence of every Marine in the line, as they drew their weapons to honour their captain.

As the summit approached, the Marines could see bursts of blue flame jousting out of the mountain top towards the heavens, but the angle of the slope blocked their view of the ground up there.

Gabriel waved his chainsword, and two clutches of bikes peeled away from the convoy, drawing up along side the Typhoons on either side of his Rhino. He wanted to make sure that the eldar saw an imposing front line as they crested the summit. He gazed proudly across the line, and could think of few sights more splendid than a solid bank of Blood Ravens roaring over the crest of a mountain pass.

As the Rhino rolled up onto the mountain top, bringing the whole of the summit into view, Gabriel was surprised to see the extent of the killing field that unfolded before him. He raised his fist into the air, bringing the Blood Ravens to a halt, as he swept his gaze over the vista and tried to take it in.

There were dozens of Alpha Legionaries lying where they had died, riddled with holes and oozing with blood, their armour shattered beyond repair by the strange alien weapons. Their bodies gave the

rocky mountain top an aura of acidic green. Intermixed amongst them were the bodies of the fallen
eldar, each was a blaze of blue fire, with flames reaching seven metres into the air as the supernatural fire
consumed their bodies.

Beyond them, on the very peak of Mount Korath,
was an unusual-looking menhir, roughly elliptical in
shape and covered with an indescribable array of
blue torches. But, as far as Gabriel could see, there
was no eldar army lying in wait. The scene was eerily
silent.

Jumping down from the roof of the Rhino,
Gabriel strode off toward the menhir, picking his
way between the corpses. Isador leapt down after
him, and the Rhino door opened to let Prathios
and Corallis join them. The four Marines fanned
out and made their way towards the giant marker
stone.

Suddenly Corallis dropped down onto one knee,
inspecting the ground at his feet. The others stopped,
watching the sergeant carefully, trusting his eyes.
Isador planted his staff against the rock and Prathios
spun his crozius arcanum menacingly.

'Something was here only moments ago,' crackled
Corallis through the vox system. 'But the tracks are
strange. They just seem to appear and disappear,
without leading anywhere.'

Gabriel strode forward of the group, unwilling to
be intimidated by the unusual ways of the eldar. As
he approached the menhir, something flickered into
his path and then vanished. He paused, scanning the
scene for other signs of movement. Another flicker
made him turn. A heavy-looking eldar warrior
appeared suddenly to the side of the menhir. It

planted its feet and let loose with a spray of fire from some kind of gatling gun.

There were a series of cries from behind him, and Gabriel turned as he rolled clear of the gout of fire, and he saw three other eldar, similar to the first. They had appeared from nowhere, and were now arrayed against the rest of his team, cutting them off from him.

As he came out of his roll, Gabriel squeezed off a rattle of shots from his bolter back towards the alien in front of him, but the Warp Spider had already gone. It had simply vanished. Turning, he saw his battle-brothers snapping their weapons from side to side, impotently searching for their targets in the same way.

'Warp Spiders, Gabriel,' hissed Isador's voice through the vox. 'This could be another trap.' A great flash of lightning jousted out of Isador's staff, flashing towards the menhir. Just before the bolt reached the huge stone, there was a faint shimmer in its path and a Warp Spider chose that point to slip back into real space. Isador's bolt crashed into the eldar, catching it full in the chest and lifting it off its feet, throwing it backwards against the menhir with a crack.

Immediately, Gabriel and Prathios opened up with the bolters, riddling the alien with fire and shattering his thick armour, leaving nothing but splatters of blood against the marker stone behind it.

Meanwhile, Corallis had stalked off to the other side of the menhir, keeping low to the ground as though tracking something. He stopped suddenly and rubbed his hand over the loose topsoil. As he looked up, back towards Gabriel and the others, the

remaining Warp Spiders sprung into being before
him, their death-spinners releasing a tirade of projectiles from close range.

'Corallis!' cried Gabriel, pounding across the summit of the mountain toward the besieged Marine, his
boltgun spitting in his hand. Prathios was with him,
matching his run stride for stride, strafing his fire
back and forth across the backs of the Warp Spiders.
Without moving, Isador planted his staff and muttered something inaudible, sending sheets of blue
power coruscating through the ground, racing
against the storming Marines.

Isador's bolts seared under the feet of Gabriel and
Prathios as they ran, and then exploded into flames
as they crashed into the stances of the Warp Spiders.
The creatures shimmered slightly, trying to leap back
into the webway, but Isador's energy blast had done
something to their warp jump generators. Before
they could even turn to face the charging Marines,
Gabriel and Prathios were upon them, riddling them
with bolter shells.

In the last stride before he reached them, Gabriel
cast his bolter aside and drew his chainsword into
both hands. Out of the corner of his eye, he could see
Prathios dropping his own gun, and swinging the
crackling crozius into his fist. Gabriel launched himself at the Warp Spider in the middle, crashing into
its back and flattening it against the ground. In one
smooth movement, he flourished his chainsword
into the air and drove it down through the alien's
spine. The creature twitched momentarily, and then
fell still.

A shower of fire speckled his armour as he sprang
off the corpse and rounded on the last eldar, seeing

that Prathios had already incinerated the other one in an inferno of holy fire from his crozius.

Gabriel brought his sword down swiftly, but the Warp Spider was fast, dancing around his blow and punching a flurry of shots straight into the captain's chest plate. His chainsword missed its target but hacked into the alien's weapon, where it stuck, spluttering impotently. As one, Gabriel and the eldar discarded their chewed-up weapons and started to circle one another like animal predators, flexing their shoulders ready for the fight.

A javelin of power flashed over his shoulder from Isador. It seared past Gabriel's face, punching into the stomach of the eldar and blowing a hole clear through. The alien staggered for a few more steps and then sunk to its knees facing Gabriel – it seemed to be staring at him with the alien eyes hidden behind its elongated helmet. Then Prathios stepped up and swung at the Warp Spider with his hissing crozius, striking it cleanly and knocking the creature's head crisply off its shoulders as its body slumped to the ground at Gabriel's feet.

'Corallis?' asked Gabriel urgently. The sergeant was lying on his back in a pool of blood, his armour punctured by numberless holes, and Gabriel knelt swiftly by his side. 'Corallis?'

'The others have gone on ahead, captain,' replied Corallis, coughing as a trickle of blood seeped out of the corner of his mouth. 'They have rigged this marker to explode. It was a trap.' As he spoke, he lifted his hand from the ground, revealing what he had found before the battle started. A small, blinking device was buried just beneath the surface.

It was a mine.

CHAPTER EIGHT

'THERE ARE ELDAR explosives and demolition charges all around the menhir, captain,' reported Matiel. His squad of Assault Marines were working their way around the great stone marker, studying the ground and noting the relays clamped into the stone itself. 'We dare not move them – the trip mechanisms are unknown to us, and we would risk destroying the stone… and us.'

'I understand,' said Gabriel, his attention still distracted by the scouts who were carrying their sergeant into the back of one of the Rhinos. Corallis was not quite dead – it took more than a few bullet wounds to kill a Space Marine – but he was as near as it was possible to get.

'What about the triggers?' he asked, collecting himself again.

'I think that we can replace the triggering devices, but that is all I would care to do with this xeno-tech,' replied Matiel, somewhat reluctantly.

'See that it is done, Matiel. We would not want the eldar to pay us a surprise visit and blow us all into the warp,' said Gabriel, a characteristic smile drifting across his face, in an attempt to lift the mood.

'Was this a trap?' asked Isador, striding over from the Rhino, into which Sergeant Corallis had just been loaded. The Librarian looked resolute, as though the ruin of Corallis might have been the last straw.

'No, I don't think so,' replied Matiel, nodding a swift greeting to the Librarian as he joined the group. 'Judging by the placement of the charges, it seems likely that they planned to collapse this area of the summit – burying the menhir, and anyone else who happened to be nearby.'

'Corallis did say that the eldar left in a hurry, so perhaps we disturbed them before they could finish the job? Maybe the Warp Spiders were left to complete the demolition?' suggested Gabriel, looking to the others for their opinions.

'Or perhaps they left the summit to lure us in, leaving this stone as bait, planning to use the Warp Spiders to blow it when we arrived?' said Isador, more suspicious than his captain. 'We should not give these aliens the benefit of the doubt, Gabriel. Just because they are the enemy of our enemy doesn't mean that they are our friends. Look at what they did to Corallis.'

'Either way,' said Gabriel, nodding at the plausibility of Isador's version, 'the eldar clearly thought that we would want to take a look at this stone, and it also appears that they were keen to ensure that the Alpha Legion did not get the chance to look at it.' Gabriel flicked his head towards the killing field behind them.

'We should certainly see what is so special about it. Isador, please take a look at the stone... Take as much time as you need.'

Isador nodded and made his way over to the menhir, carefully stepping between the Assault Marines that ringed it. He raised his hand and touched the smooth, featureless surface of the stone, closing his eyes in concentration. Somewhere deep inside the rock, there was a faint, rhythmical pulse, as though it was breathing. He leant in closer, pressing his ear against the rock, straining with his mind to discern the hint of sound within. It was a whisper.

THE ROAR OF a Rhino engine starting up made Matiel and Gabriel turn away from the menhir. One of the Rhinos started to roll down the mountain side, heading back towards the field-station in the Pass of Korath. An escort of scout bikes ran alongside it, as Corallis's squadron refused to abandon their sergeant. The banner of the Blood Ravens was held by the company standard bearer, who stood solidly on the roof of the armoured transport, marking the passage of an honoured warrior. It fluttered in the strong winds that blew across the mountain top, beating the wings of the black raven and making the scarlet drop of blood in the centre of the emblem pulse like a heart.

'May the Emperor heal his wounds,' whispered Gabriel, staring after the Rhino. Matiel just bowed his head in respect.

As the Rhino dropped out of sight, the sound of another engine drifted through the breeze, and Gabriel watched the horizon intently. It didn't sound like another Rhino, but it was moving much faster than the slow procession that was taking Corallis down for medical care, whatever it was. After a couple of seconds, a red and black Tartaran Chimera crested the summit at high speed, lifting into the air as the angle of the ground flattened out and then crashing back down onto its tracks.

The transport skidded abruptly, sliding in an ugly arc as its momentum pushed it precariously close to the side of the summit, but then its tracks bit into the rocky ground and dragged it towards the Blood Ravens, sending sprinklings of soil and stones cascading over the edge of the peak.

The Chimera rumbled heavily over the corpses that were strewn over the mountain top, squashing them unceremoniously under its thick caterpillar tracks, apparently unconcerned about whether they were Chaos Marines or the smouldering remains of eldar. As the transport ground to a halt in front of Gabriel and Matiel, it left a path of mulched flesh and pools of blood in its wake.

Given the manner of the arrival, Gabriel already knew who to expect when the rear hatch lowered into a ramp and Inquisitor Toth stamped out into the mid-morning sun, dragging Colonel Brom behind him like a beaten dog.

'Captain Angelos, this is insupportable–' began Mordecai, striding straight up to Gabriel and breathing directly into his face.

'Inquisitor Toth,' interrupted Gabriel smoothly. 'How nice to see you. As you can see, we have been rather busy, and I should apologise for not finding the time to keep you informed.'

'It is too late for pleasantries,' replied Mordecai, unimpressed by Gabriel's transparency. 'Not only did you break from camp without informing the official representative of the Emperor's Inquisition, but I am given to understand that you also found and destroyed a potentially valuable alien artefact, before declaring war on an eldar force and then requisitioning a detachment of Brom's Imperial Guard to oversee your field-station. Needless to say, captain, the Inquisition will not look favourably on these actions.'

'And Colonel Brom, greetings,' said Gabriel, choosing to ignore the tirade from Mordecai – reminding everyone that the inquisitor had no power over the Adeptus Astartes. Brom nodded a brisk greeting and then shrugged his shoulders, perhaps indicating that he was as much a victim of Toth's umbrage as Gabriel.

'I will not be ignored, Captain Angelos, and you will answer to me. I may not have the power to commandeer your precious Blood Ravens, but I certainly do have the power to have you placed into custody for obstructing the affairs of the Inquisition,' said Mordecai, fuming.

'You overstep yourself, inquisitor,' replied Gabriel quietly, fixing Mordecai with his sparkling green eyes and narrowing them slightly. 'I am obstructing nobody. You made it perfectly clear that you had no interest in the events on Tartarus, having already condemned it to the ravages of the imminent warp storm. In this context, I fail to see why it would have been more than mere impoliteness not to inform you of our movements here. If you wish to dispute this matter in the company of the inquisitor lords, then I will be happy to entertain you. But not now – perhaps later. As you can see, there is rather a lot for me to attend to here first. You may notice, for example, the litter of dead Alpha Legionaries strewn over this very mountain top – the very forces of Chaos that you seemed certain did not exist on Tartarus,' finished Gabriel with something of a flourish.

'Yes, captain, it is an impressive sight,' responded Mordecai, recovering his composure and affecting a survey of the scene around him, 'but I did not claim that Chaos had never set foot on this planet. I said, rather, that if the forces of Chaos were present, then the impending warp storm would eliminate them for us – saving us from needless conflict, and saving the lives of many of your Blood Ravens and Brom's Tartarans. Sergeant Corallis, for example, would be alive and well,' he added, twisting the blade.

'Sergeant Corallis *is* alive,' replied Gabriel from between gritted teeth, 'and he will be well.'

'I hope you are right, captain, since his death would be entirely on your conscience. And I would think that your conscience is crowded enough already.' Mordecai did not flinch away from the Blood Ravens' captain, even as Gabriel's muscles bunched in his neck. Sergeant Matiel stepped up to his shoulder, but Mordecai was not sure whether he intended to support or restrain his captain's anger.

'As I have already explained, Inquisitor Toth, the Blood Ravens will remain until the very last minute – and, until then, we will pursue this unfolding riddle. There is still time – nearly two days,' managed Gabriel, his jaw still knotted in tension.

'Captain, I do not... presume to question your decisions concerning the Blood Ravens.' Mordecai's words were carefully chosen. 'But when it comes to employing the colonel's Imperial Guard in your quest–'

'*My* quest!' cried Gabriel, struggling to control his outrage. 'Yet again you accuse me of pursuing my own personal agenda, inquisitor. If you were not an agent of the Emperor, I would slay you where you stand for challenging my honour and that of the Blood Ravens. But the badge you hide behind also confers a duty on you, Toth,' said Gabriel, almost spitting the man's name into his face. 'It is your duty, as well as mine, to expunge any scent of heresy or taint of Chaos. My conscience is clear about my duty, is yours?'

'Now, it is you who overstep yourself, captain,' replied Mordecai, flinching inwardly against Gabriel's words. This captain was not like any he had encountered before: his mind was sharp, and he had turned the tables on one of the Emperor's inquisitors. The scholarly reputation of the Blood Ravens was not without merit, it seemed.

'Perhaps, but you have overstepped the mark and then marched off into the killing zone: they are not "the colonel's Imperial Guard". They have sworn their lives to the Emperor, not to Brom and certainly not to you, and it is by His mandate that I employ the Tartarans in this war against the forces of Chaos and the xenos here. Through the glory of this holy battle, I elevate them to a status worthy of their oaths of allegiance.' Better that than run away and hide like cowards, Gabriel added to himself.

'I can see now that coming here to Mount Korath
to reason with you was a mistake. If you are set on
this path that will lead nowhere except to the
destruction of you and your Blood Ravens, then I can
do nothing to stop you. But I will not allow you to
drag the rest of this planet down with you. By
Inquisitorial edict, I am taking control of planet Tartarus – all requests for planetary resources, including
its military resources, must be approved by me. Captain, from this point on, you and your Marines are
on your own,' concluded Mordecai dramatically,
turning immediately and striding back up the ramp
into the waiting Chimera.

For a moment, Colonel Brom stood at the foot of
the ramp, looking from Gabriel to Mordecai and
back again. The inquisitor's voice boomed down the
ramp, 'Brom!' and the colonel looked up at Gabriel,
apparently searching for a sign.

'Go,' said Gabriel quietly, releasing him. 'Make sure
that the spaceport at Magna Bonum is held against
the orks until the last of the civilians are evacuated.'

THE ELDAR FORCE, arrayed in all of its glory, swept
across the valley floor like a bristling dam of lethal
weaponry. The gates of Lloovre Marr had been
slammed shut hours before, and the remaining
defenders of the capital city had hastened to the gun
emplacements in the great wall. It was a testament to
the tumultuous history of Tartarus that all of its
major cities were walled – and Lloovre Marr was no
exception.

The sheer, white walls curved around the southern
perimeter of the city in a sweeping semi-circle. Each
end butted up against the high cliffs of the Lloovre

valley, and the northern sectors of the capital had been built in a great cave, scooped out the rock itself. This unusual defensive design had withstood the test of time, and Lloovre Marr had only ever fallen once in its whole history: a revolt had erupted within the city walls, and the governor had been unable to escape the bloodshed, trapped in the impregnable fortress. Since then, a complicated system of tunnels and caves had been dug into the cliffs, in case the rulers of Tartarus ever needed to escape again.

Looking out on the awesome might of the Biel-Tan craftworld – the Bahzhakhain, the Swordwind, the Tempest of Blades, a maelstrom of alien power, silent, beautiful, and breathtaking – the leaders of Tartarus could have been forgiven for taking to the caves at once.

However, the leaders had already fled the city. The governor had been on the first transport to Magna Bonum, and then on the first shuttle to the *Litany of Fury*, when he had received word from Inquisitor Toth that the warp storm was on its way. The ruling council had left a skeleton force of Imperial Guardsmen behind to defend the city against looters and pirates until the storm broke. Then they would be airlifted off the surface by a Blood Ravens' Thunderhawk.

Looters and pirates were one thing, the Swordwind army of the Biel-Tan was something else entirely. There were one hundred Guardsmen lining the walls of the city, and a smattering of others throughout the streets of the capital itself; not one of them had ever even seen an eldar before in their lives. Now they could see more of them than they had ever wanted to.

A single, impossibly elegant figure strode forward of the eldar line. Her slender and shapely body appeared to be female, but she was taller than most men. Her emerald green robes flowed out behind her like water, and the white detailing seemed to dance over the cloth, as though it was merely the echo of a life being lived in another dimension. A veil fluttered around her face, shedding the vaguest glimpses of an unearthly beauty beyond. In her hand she carried a long, simple staff. It was nearly two metres in length and perfectly smooth from one end to the other. It appeared to be completely without decoration. But it moved, or rather, it seemed to move. It was as though it was a tiny tear in the fabric of space, the merest crack in a window to another realm. The mid-afternoon light just seemed to fall into it, as though being sucked out of this world altogether. And something on the side moved, curdling and gyrating in a world of pure energy, pushing up against the tear, eager to break through.

The figure opened her arms to the city, holding them wide as though trying to take in the whole of Lloovre Mar. And then her voice was heard by everyone. Each of the Guardsmen stopped their preparations for war and listened, struck by the angelic lilt of the feminine voice. It was as though they didn't have to listen at all, as though the voice just slipped directly into their heads, delicately caressing their ears with the idea of sound.

People of Lloovre Marr, I bring you a choice, said Macha, letting her thoughts drift across the valley and into the city. *And choice is the greatest gift that you can receive from anyone.* For a moment, the farseer thought about her own life and that of Jaerielle.

Indeed, the whole of the Path of the Eldar was premised upon the annihilation of choice. Choice brought selfishness. And selfishness was the beginning of the end. But still, even a farseer had choices to make – the future was not an uncomplicated place. *Either you open the gates and leave the city… or you die where you stand. The choice is yours, but choose, and choose now.*

Macha lowered her arms and stood quietly between the Swordwind of Biel-Tan and the walls of Lloovre Marr. Nobody moved. Her army stood perfectly motionless behind her, only the banners of the Biel-Tan fluttered in the wind that swept through the valley: crisp white flags bearing a golden rune, *Treraum*, and a crimson heart.

In the main line, the Storm squad and Defender squads shone in pristine white psycho-plastic armour, with elongated green helmets glinting in the sun. Behind them were the wraithguard, towering over their living brethren in inverted colours: green, wraithbone armour and white helmets. And in front were the Aspect Warriors, resplendent in the brightly coloured uniforms of various shrines. At various points throughout the formation were the sleek, deep green Falcon tanks and a few Vyper weapons platforms, each flanked by a couple of jetbikes.

On the city wall, the Guardsmen gradually realised that something was expected of them. Shaking their heads to clear their minds of the sweet invasion, they glanced up and down the battlements, looking to each other for ideas. None dared be the first to move. All of the senior officers had already left the city, and the soldiers needed their leadership more than ever.

Then, simultaneously, two different decisions were made. One Guardsman, Bobryn, started to work the release mechanism for the gate, reasoning that Tartarus was already doomed and therefore not worth dying for at this late stage. And another, Hredel, opened fire from his autocannon platform.

As the first shots rang out through the valley, Macha turned and walked back into the midst of her army. She shook her head sadly: humans, she thought, both the hope and the bane of the galaxy.

FROM THEIR VANTAGE point, high in the walls of the Lloovre valley, Chaos Lord Bale and the sorcerer Sindri watched the eldar force assemble at the gates of the capital city. Their own force of Alpha Legionaries was collected into the deep cave in the cliffs, where the Chaos Marines fumed in frustrated silence. Great fires had been lit, and swirls of noxious smoke filled the close air of the cavern, smothering the oxygen with a blanket of burning flesh.

The broken remains of eldar warriors were strewn over the cave floor, their armour cracked open and their flesh scooped out like giant shellfish. The thin, slender bodies of the eldar were broken and cast into the fires; there was precious little meat on them and they tasted disgusting, but they made pungent firewood.

'The eldar will take the city quickly, sorcerer,' said Bale, emerging out of the smoky cave to join Sindri on the ledge outside. The smoke and the corpses in the cavern had put his soul at ease, but fury remained bubbling beneath the surface of his composure.

Sindri nodded without looking round. His eyes were fixed on the distant scene to the north. The white walls of the city shimmered slightly in the sunlight, but the Biel-Tan army was a blaze of reflections and starbursts before them. The rumble of cannon fire had already started, and Sindri was sure that he had caught the scent of a voice in the air before it had all begun. Tiny bursts of fire were visible in the walls as the heavy weapons platforms flared with activity, and the eldar lines had begun to swim with motion. And, unless his eyes were deceiving him, the great gates of Lloovre Marr were lying open in the centre of the wall.

'Yes, my lord. The eldar will take the city. But it is of no concern to us. We need not race against our guides, Lord Bale,' said Sindri smoothly.

'You'd better be right about this, sorcerer,' replied Bale, his voice tinged with his natural disgust for scheming and his frustration about watching combat without being able to reap the carnage himself.

'We do not need to be there yet. But when the time comes, we will move swiftly,' said Sindri calmly. 'Then you will have your bloodletting.'

Bale inspected the territory between their cave and the city walls. Even for Chaos Marines the distance was too large for a swift attack. It would take them several hours to traverse the valley, and they would be clearly visible to the guards on the city wall – especially if those guards were eldar rangers. Launching a rapid strike would not be possible from this position, and the Alpha Legion would be humiliated yet again by Sindri's meddling schemes.

'I do not like this, sorcerer. I do not place my faith in the hesitant or the probable – it is better to feel the certainty of my scythe than the inconsistency of your reassurances.' The effects of the smoke were wearing off, and Bale's temper was rising yet again.

'Patience, my lord,' soothed Sindri. 'We do not have to cross the valley.' He turned back towards the cave and pointed vaguely towards the entrance. A thick blanket of smoke hung across it like a curtain, but only the smallest wisps were escaping into the air outside.

'Where do you think all of that smoke is going?' asked Sindri coaxingly.

'I don't have time for your games, sorcerer. And neither do you,' menaced Bale, unamused by Sindri's rhetoric.

'The smoke is being drawn further into the cave, my lord, because there is a network of tunnels beyond. A network that leads right into the heart of Loovre Marr – I was given a map many years ago, by a… friend in the governor's office. When the time comes, the Alpha Legion will already be in the city. There will be no storming through the valley and no cumbersome siege of the city walls… At least not by us,' added Sindri cryptically.

Looking from Sindri to the battle and then back again, Bale snorted an agitated acknowledgment. It did sound like a good plan, but Bale would believe it when he saw it happen. Until then, the sorcerer lived on borrowed time. Turning suddenly, Bale strode back through the curtain of smoke and disappeared into the interior of the cave.

THE SCRIPT ON the menhir was different from that on the altar in the crater: it contained the characteristic angles and runic curves of an eldar tongue. Isador had searched the stone for a long time before he had found it, for it was not literally on the surface of the rock at all. Rather, the markings swam just underneath the surface, all but invisible to the eyes of men. They had been etched into the essence of the menhir itself, not hacked and carved into the mundane rock like the clumsy scribblings of cultists.

The Librarian had pressed himself against the rock and felt the residue of a soul oscillating deep within, as though the eldar artisan had left a fragment of herself to imbue the stone with meaning and life. As his mind tuned in to the gentle pulsing of the rock's rhythm, the script had begun to flicker into life, glowing with an unearthly blue somewhere inside. It was as though the material of the huge rock had gradually shifted into translucence, revealing a liquid heart in which an ancient message swam like the memory of stars.

The message itself was straightforward enough, belied by the breathtaking beauty of its form. There was something about a curved blade – some sort of key. And there was a string of co-ordinates, coded in an elaborate manner than made Isador's head spin; the figures spiralled and shifted until his mind discovered their secret, bringing them under control and settling them into a firm pattern.

When the eldar hid their secrets, they placed them in full view of all, knowing that only the rarest of individuals would be able to see them, let alone decipher them. The problem was not a linguistic one – the runes were simple enough for an educated Blood Raven to understand – rather, the problem was psychic. Only the most gifted of human psykers would taste even a hint of the presence of the runic script in the first place.

Stepping back from the menhir, Isador looked at it with fresh eyes. He could see now that it was a blaze of runes and twisting lines of script. The psychic etchings snaked and spiralled around the smooth form, flowing and coalescing like mountain streams, mixing their meanings together into transient poetry and garbled gibberish in equal measures. The tiny section on which his mind had focussed was merely the most miniscule fragment of a grand, sweeping narrative.

The rock itself seemed to shimmer with release, as the texts that it contained were freed to swim and shift before the eyes of a reader once again. It was as though the menhir wanted to be read. For the first time, Isador realised that the menhir was not a rock at all – it was a giant tear-drop of wraithbone, the mysterious material employed by eldar artists and engineers to construct their unfathomable technologies.

'What do you see, Isador?' asked Gabriel, approaching his friend from behind and placing a gentle hand on his shoulder.

Isador started at the touch, and his head snapped round to stare at his captain, his eyes wide and wild. 'Oh, Gabriel,' he managed, bringing his shock under control and turning back to the menhir. The lights and the script had vanished, leaving no sign of ever having been there at all. 'It was so beautiful…'

Gabriel looked at the rock for a moment, noting its graceful curves and its smooth lines. He shook his head vaguely. 'Your eyes are different from mine, old friend. What did you learn?'

'The menhir is a marker. It must have been left here by the eldar thousands of years ago. It speaks of a bladed-key, buried beneath the ground for all time,' said Isador, his mind drifting back to the images that he had seen in the wraithbone.

'A key to what?' asked Gabriel.

'I am not sure. It would take me months to decipher all of the text,' lamented Isador.

Again, Gabriel looked up at the menhir and gazed at its perfectly smooth, flawless surface. He raised his eyebrows. 'It is enough, I suppose, to know that the Alpha Legion and the eldar are both pursuing this key. Do you know where it is?'

'Yes. The runes are very clear. They were clearly intended to guide an eldar force to it at an important moment,' replied Isador, deep in thought.

Gabriel's thoughts were catching up with those of his Librarian. 'So, the eldar have been here before, and they anticipated the need for a return to Tartarus?'

'So it seems, Gabriel.'

'Did the historical records make any mention of an eldar invasion or presence on this planet in the past?' asked Gabriel, already sure that Isador would have mentioned such a thing.

'No, Gabriel. I can only assume that the eldar were here before the colonisation of Tartarus – before the Imperium's records began,' said Isador, his mind racing with the possible implications of this knowledge.

'Can this all be coincidental?' asked Gabriel, giving voice to their joint concerns. 'The return of the eldar, the presence of our old adversaries, the Alpha Legion, the invasion of the orks, and the imminent arrival of the warp storm?'

Isador shook his head. 'I do not believe in coincidences – they are the symptoms of ignorance. I fear that the Blood Ravens may be the only force on this planet who do not know what is going on.'

THE STRIKING SCORPION squad was first into the breach as the gate ground slowly open. Their new exarch – the eldar warrior that was once Jaerielle – was their spearhead, dancing and flipping through the hail of fire from the gunnery emplacements on the city wall. He was through the gate and into the courtyard on the other side before the mechanism had even wound open fully, flicking and darting between shots from the Imperial Guardsmen, as though they were moving too slowly to trouble him.

Inspired by their exarch, the emerald green figures of the rest of his squad stormed into the city behind him, flourishing their chainswords and dispatching sheets of shuriken fire from their pistols. Following in the wake of the Striking Scorpions came the reds and golds of the Fire Dragons, dousing the wall defences in chemical flames from their fire-lances and fusion guns. And then, bursting through the flames, hissed the Vypers and jetbikes, flashing through the open gate into the city streets under cover of heavy fire from the Falcon tanks outside.

The Falcons had slid to a halt in front of the walls, and were battering the gun platforms with barrages of fire from their shuriken cannons and lance arrays. The impacts strafed across the wall, blasting great chunks of rockcrete out of their structure and shaking the weapons emplacements.

The Imperial Guardsmen in the city defences found themselves in crumbling alcoves, with debris and rockcrete raining down onto them from great cracks in the superstructure. The fixings for their autocannons and multi-meltas were breaking free as the rockcrete splintered out from underneath them, denying them the stability needed for accurate fire.

Guardsman Hredel threw his weight against his weapon, hoping that his mass would keep the auto-cannon rooted while it fired a constant stream of shells down towards the breach in the open gates.

Down in the courtyard inside the gate, a smattering of Guardsmen, led by the hapless Bobryn, who had opened the gate and then regretted it instantly, staged a last ditch defence of the city. Eldar jetbikes zipped past them into the capital, not even bothering to engage the defenders. The Vypers slid to a halt in the courtyard, but did not open fire on the Guardsmen. Instead, their gun-turrets spun around and started to blast away at the rear of the wall, where the wall's gun platforms were unshielded. Hredel turned to look into the courtyard just in time to see the withering hail of shuriken crash into his gunnery platform, killing him instantly. Meanwhile, Jaerielle sprang into the line of defenders in the courtyard, flourishing his toothed blade in a dizzying display of virtuosity.

Bobryn's mouth dropped open as the eldar warrior spun through the air in a graceful arc, vaulting the impromptu barricade in a single bound, its blade whipped into a blur by the speed of its motion. He just had time to marvel at the skill of the alien, before the blade passed straight through his neck.

Jaerielle swooped and sliced with his chainsword, letting it dance all by itself, pulling him from one kill to the next in a frenzy of blood. The little stand of Guardsmen dwindled into nothing in a matter of seconds, and Jaerielle spun to a standstill in amongst the spread of dismembered corpses, striking the victory pose of the Striking Scorpions, with streams of mon-keigh blood coasting down his emerald armour.

As he struck the pose, Farseer Macha walked calmly through the gates into Lloovre Marr, flanked on both sides by a retinue of warlocks, claiming the city for Biel-Tan. She stood for a moment, motionless in the entrance to the courtyard. The barricades of the defenders were still in place, and the Striking Scorpions and Fire Dragons had fanned out around the perimeters – they showed little sign of having seen combat today. But there, standing on the far side of the barricades, was Jaerielle, surrounded by a litter of corpses and running with blood. His blade was held dramatically above his head, and his pistol was pointing at the ground, as he stretched his legs into a long, low stance.

The sound of a distant explosion made Macha turn and look back out of the open gates. In the distance, directly below the sun, was the imposing sight of Mount Korath. Its peak was a blaze of light, and a mushroom cloud of thick smoke and debris had plumed into the air above it, casting the valley into shadow as the cloud obstructed the sun for a moment. The Blood Ravens, thought Macha, hoping that her Warp Spiders had done their job.

In the foreground, the rest of the Biel-Tan army remained positioned for battle before the walls. The wraithguard trained their wraithcannons on the defensive gunnery positions, although most had already fallen silent. The Storm and Defender squads were starting to file through the gate, keeping the farseer in sight in case they were needed, but the battle for

Lloovre Marr was basically over. The Swordwind had swept the pathetic defence before it and, turning again to look at Jaerielle, Macha wondered whether he could have done it all by himself.

A line of ranger jetbikes hissed through the gates, and Flaetriu vaulted off the leading machine before it slid to a halt. He swept into a bow before the farseer.

'Farseer, the Chaos Marines are regrouping in a cave in the valley wall. They are several hours' march from here. We have time to refortify the city before they arrive,' reported the ranger, his concentration suddenly broken by the sight of Jaerielle further inside the courtyard.

'Thank you, Flaetriu. In the meantime, take your rangers through the city, and find those cowardly mon-keigh that fled their positions at the wall. We want no surprises today,' said Macha gravely. Even as she spoke, she could feel that surprises were on their way.

As the column of Blood Ravens thundered down the north side of Mount Korath, Gabriel clicked the detonator-trigger that Matiel had given to him. Behind them, the summit of the mountain erupted like a volcano as the eldar charges exploded. The mountain top was vaporised and a huge cloud of debris and smoke blasted into the air, obscuring the sun. The rocks around the summit were instantly rendered into flows of molten lava that sprayed outwards from the mountain in a superheated fountain. Great sheets of molten rock started to ooze down the mountain side, chasing the heels of the Blood Ravens as they roared down into the valley towards Lloovre Marr.

CHAPTER NINE

THE GRAND STREETS of Lloovre Marr were quiet and deserted. Vehicles and market stalls had been abandoned by the sides of the roads, and the doors to buildings had been left swinging in the breeze. The population had left in a hurry, and it looked as though they had not anticipated returning. Lights still burned behind some of the windows, but Macha was certain that these had simply been left burning when the occupants left – there were few signs that anyone remained in the capital.

The eldar convoy moved along the central boulevard with swift urgency, heading for the very heart of the city. Jetbikes flashed through the adjoining streets, running parallel to the convoy to ensure that it was left unchallenged. The boulevard itself was lined with tall, white statues. Each depicted a human figure, usually a warrior, presumably from the history of the city. Their heads were all turned towards the centre of the city, as though gazing up towards the great palace of the governor that dominated the administrative core of the capital.

To Macha's eldar eyes, the statues looked clumsy and ugly – not merely because they depicted the disproportionate features of the mon-keigh, but also because the artisans had been poor. In general, reflected the farseer, this was true of all human art – it all seemed so rushed and underdeveloped. It was almost as though art were a hobby, rather than the highest expression of the soul. It would be inconceivable that the Biel-Tan would grant a commission of the magnitude of a public statue to an artisan who had not been walking the Path of the Artist for many centuries, perhaps even millennia. The commission itself might take decades to fulfil. But these pathetic lumps of stone looked as though they had been turned out in a matter of months, by artisans barely old enough to hold the tools.

Shaking her head in disbelief and pity, Macha took a moment to consider what these statues said about the soul of the mon-keigh. Each of them represented a warrior, and each was gazing on the buildings of the Administratum, fierce with pride. It is not the art itself that these humans exalt, realised Macha, but power and war. Art is merely a means to praise the warriors – and combat is the highest expression of their souls. She nodded to herself in satisfaction, as she thought about the dedication of the mon-keigh's Space Marines, and compared their abilities to wreak destruction with the mon-keigh's pathetic attempts at the construction of art. For the eldar, war was embraced as a artistic path – the most feared of many equal paths to truth and glory. For the humans, it seemed, the whole society was subordinated to war – only in war did the human soul find itself. They were only slightly more civilised than orks.

Behind the statues, running along both sides of the boulevard, were grand stone buildings, each rendered in the same white stone. The structures grew larger and more imposing as the eldar moved further and further into the city – as though the heart of the city warranted the most glorious architecture. All of the structures showed signs of age and decay, giving the street the aura of an ancient capital of culture, resting on the strong arms of thousands of warriors that had died for its glory.

The last time Macha had been on Tartarus, Lloovre Marr did not even exist. This end of the valley had been nothing but thick forest, huddled in the basin of the valley's flood plain, where the soil was richest and most fertile. She had known, of course, even then, that the mon-keigh would recover their strength and rebuild their cities on Tartarus. She had even seen that they would build here – away from the sites of the destruction of their other cities, starting afresh, carving their new capital into the cliffs with their very hands.

That had been why she had picked this site, where her secrets would be buried beneath the cheap grandeur of the Imperium of Man. The mon-keigh would never think to look right under their noses. And, sure enough, the whole population had left at the first rumblings of a problem, never even pausing to see what they were leaving behind.

As the eldar convoy neared the end of the boulevard, Macha let a faint smile float across her lips: this

grand capital city was nothing more than a tiny blip
in a war that had begun countless millennia before
mankind had even made its first leap into space; for
the sake of Khaine, she had been a farseer for longer
than these buildings had stood against the elements
of Tartarus. And now she was being chased across the
planet by two bumbling platoons of children – one
carried with them the doom of Tartarus and its surrounding systems, and the other brought hope with
them, like a delicate, flickering candle. She had never
thought that the once mighty eldar would be reduced
to playing nanny for the younger races of the galaxy
– but here she was.

The end of the boulevard opened up into a wide
plaza, in the centre of which was the focus of the
gazes of the all the statues along the way. A huge figure rose out of the pristine white flagstones – a statue
taller and more magnificent than any of the others. It
was the figure of Lloovre Marr himself, the founder
of the city, acclaimed as the first governor general to
rule Tartarus in the Emperor's name. The official historical record recounted stories of his valour and
strategic genius, organising the planet's defences
against the incursions of ork raiders and the uprisings of cultists.

In one hand, Lloovre Marr was holding his sword,
pointing up into the heavens, as though redirecting
the admiration of his people towards the Emperor
himself. In the other, a great slab of white stone represented a scroll, on which Lloovre Marr was reputed
to have written the constitution of Tartarus, pledging
its future to the cult of the undying God-Emperor,
and vowing never to permit the seeds of heresy to
take hold in this fertile soil.

Macha smiled to herself at the constellation of ironies as she realised that the monument had been constructed directly upon the site that she was looking for.

JUST BEFORE THEY broke the tree-line, the Blood Ravens' convoy drew to a halt. The co-ordinates that Isador had deciphered from the eldar menhir on Mount Korath, before they had blown it up, seemed to refer to a point in the middle of Tartarus's capital city. On their way down into the valley, the Blood Ravens had seen hints of an eldar trail, as well as tracks of Chaos assault bikes, so Gabriel was certain that they were on the right track. All sign of the Alpha Legion had vanished half way through the valley, but Gabriel had pressed on after the eldar, fearing what might happen if they reached their goal. He disliked such games of cat and mouse, but he took some solace in the fact that he was the cat. At least, he hoped that he was the cat.

The convoy stopped in the fringe of the forest and Gabriel jumped down from his vantage point on the roof of his Rhino, making his way to the very last line of trees before the ground fell away into the plain in front of Lloovre Marr. With Isador at his shoulder, Gabriel dropped to the ground as the foliage thinned, and he crept further forward.

Lying flat against the earth, Gabriel took out his binocs, letting them whir and blip until they clicked into focus against the great wall of the city before him. The once shimmering rockcrete was now a pitted and stained mess where ordnance and flamer gouts had smashed into the formerly smooth surface. The wall's gun emplacements had been shattered and cracked with precision fire, but the great gates showed no sign of damage at all.

'Do you think the defenders repelled the attack?' asked Isador, trying to make sense of the unexpected scene.

'No. There was only a minimal force left to defend the city, thanks to Toth's alarmist pronouncements. There is no way that they could have confronted the eldar,' replied Gabriel, half-whispering.

'Then what happened?'

'It looks to me,' answered Gabriel, thinking as he spoke, 'as though somebody inside the city opened the gates and let the eldar in. There seems to be no damage to the material of the gates at all so I think that they were open before the first shots were fired.'

'Then why was there firing at all?' asked Isador, seeing the logic in Gabriel's train of thought, but still unsure.

'Perhaps not everyone was ready to surrender,' answered Gabriel. 'The Guardsmen were left here without any senior officers – each would have had to make their own choice, and bear the responsibility for it.'

'So, someone opened the gates, and somebody else started firing…' said Isador, incredulously shaking his head. 'These Tartarans are an inconsistent people – with cowards and heroes in equal measure,' he added, thinking back to the stand against the orks at Magna Bonum.

'I'm sure that the same could be said of any planet,' responded Gabriel thoughtfully. 'Even Cyrene,' he added without meeting Isador's eyes.

A rustle in the foliage made the Marines turn – Matiel was working his way through the undergrowth towards them, keeping as low as his power armour would let him, before sliding down onto the ground next to them.

'Are the eldar manning the gun emplacements?' asked the sergeant, staring forward at the walls and shielding his eyes. The red sun was setting behind them, and it bounced off the reflective surface of the walls before them.

'I don't know,' replied Gabriel, honestly. 'But it would not be characteristic of the eldar to appropriate the weapons of humans, so my guess would be that they would make their stand on the other side of the walls, making us waste our energies destroying the wall itself before we even engage the aliens.'

'What do you suggest, captain?' asked Matiel with a hint of impatience.

'I suggest that we do not disappoint them,' said Gabriel, standing up out of the foliage and making no attempt to conceal himself. 'The time for subtlety is over, my friends. This is a situation that calls for the exercise of power.'

As he rose to his feet, threads of blood trickled down the chest plate of his armour. Isador sprang up to inspect the wound on his friend, but found none. Instead, he noticed that his own armour was running with blood. As Matiel climbed to his feet to join them, his red armour was slick with streams of blood as well.

'What's going on?' asked Matiel, flicking his eyes from Gabriel to Isador and then back to his own chest.

Gabriel knelt back down to the ground and pressed his hand into the earth. It compressed like a sponge, and a little pool of blood oozed out over his fingers, filling the depression. He looked up at Isador. 'The ground is saturated with blood.'

'The historical records show that Lloovre Marr was constructed on the cusp of the water-table, Gabriel. All of those pumping stations that we saw near Magna Bonum were used to lower the water-level so that the city would not subside,' explained Isador, his voice tinged with disgust as he realised what was going on.

'So, all of the blood spilt here over the last few days has seeped down to this level, turning this place into a swamp?' asked Matiel, sharing Isador's disgust.

'There is more than a few days' worth of blood here, sergeant,' replied Gabriel standing once again, 'however bloody these days have been. This swamp must have been forming for years.'

'Surely the people of Lloovre Marr would have noticed this?' said Matiel, stubbornly entertaining his own disbelief.

'Yes, Matiel,' said Gabriel. 'I'm sure that they noticed it, and I would be very interested to know why this city was built here in the first place. The blood-drenched history of Tartarus is beginning to look rather more sinister, is it not, Isador?'

'Gabriel, the city was built by the founder of this planet, three thousand years ago,' replied Isador.

'Yes, but as we have just discovered, the eldar were here before then. Why should we not believe that humans were here before then as well?' asked Gabriel.

'But why would there be no records?' countered the Librarian.

'Why indeed?' replied Gabriel, nodding as though his question answered itself.

* * *

'YOUR CONNIVING WILL COST us this war, sorcerer,' bellowed Bale, his huge scythe swept out towards the raging battle before the walls of Lloovre Marr. The Blood Ravens had broken cover at the edge of the tree-line and were lashing out with their heavy weapons, bombarding the walls and the city beyond with cannons and rockets. 'The false-Emperor's lackeys... those Blood Ravens have beaten us to the city. While we hide in this cave like cowards, they fight like warriors against the aliens.'

'They are merely puppets, my lord,' responded Sindri smoothly, as though unperturbed by the Chaos Lord's anger, but watching the blade of his scythe carefully. 'You have been generous with your patience up until now, Lord Bale, and I beg only a little extra indulgence. Events are proceeding to my... to our benefit, according to my devices.'

'Are you blind, sorcerer? As you gaze into the patterns of the warp, are you rendered utterly oblivious to the events of reality?' Bale was in no mood for Sindri's empty assurances – the Alpha Legion had a proud history and it was not forged by shying away from combat.

Although the Alpha Legion was counted amongst the Space Marine Chapters of the First Founding, it had been the last of this most glorious group, and its primarch, Alpharius, had vowed that his Marines would prove themselves the finest of the Emperor's warriors. More than anything else, Alpharius despised weakness and cowardice. Long ago, it was his passion for strength and power that had drawn the primarch to the side of Warmaster Horus, welcoming the opportunity to test his Marines against the might of their brother Space Marines. Alpharius

had gloried in the war that engulfed the galaxy as
Horus turned against the Emperor in those fateful,
ancient days, bringing the Imperium to the point of
annihilation. And in the millennia since the end of
the Heresy, which saw Horus killed and his forces
driven from the heart of the galaxy, hunted constantly by the misguided fools who remained loyal to
the false-Emperor, the Alpha Legion had not once
shied away from battle. Indeed, they searched it out,
eager to test themselves against the self-righteous,
loyalist Space Marines, like the Blood Ravens.

'I see the battle, my lord, but it is of no concern to
us,' hissed Sindri, squirming slightly. 'The Blood
Ravens are but hapless fools before the might of the
Alpha Legion – they are no test of our strength. Far
better to let the eldar deal with them, preserving our
own forces for more worthy foes.'

'As I recall, sorcerer, you once told me that we
could leave these Marines to the orks – you were
wrong then. What makes you think that the eldar
will fare any better against these Blood Ravens?'
asked Bale, spinning his scythe with slow menace.

'The eldar are entirely a different matter,' answered
Sindri, shrinking slightly from the scythe and dismissing the question of the orks quickly. 'They are an
ancient and formidable force, my lord. And they
know why they are here. Their farseer will ensure their
effectiveness. They do not go to war for fun, my lord,
but with the determination of an ageless purpose.'

'It sounds as though they are a foe worthy of the
Alpha Legion, sorcerer. So why must we sit and watch
these Blood Ravens steal our glory?' said Bale, bringing the debate into a vicious circle that was echoed
by his spinning scythe.

'My lord, we will have our chance to fight – have no fear of that. We must merely seek to apply our force at the most advantageous moment. Alpharius himself taught that the enemy is humiliated most when they are defeated with the least effort. Let us humiliate these Blood Ravens completely,' responded Sindri, finding his escape route at last.

'If you fail me in this –' began Bale, a hint of acceptance in his voice.

'–yes, then I will suffer greatly… and gladly. I understand,' interrupted Sindri, recovering the initiative. 'Just be ready to move when I instruct.'

A ROCKET WHINED overhead, crashing into one of the once grand buildings at the back of the plaza. The formerly smooth masonry was already a ruin of pits and pock-marks, and tendrils of smoke had stained the once pristine white surfaces. The rocket punched through the outer wall of the building and detonated inside, blowing a section of the wall out into the plaza in a shower of debris.

Macha didn't even flinch as the ordnance flashed over the monument in the centre of the plaza. She stood calmly in its long shadow, watching the sun dip down towards the horizon as the daylight started to die. The Blood Ravens' rockets seemed to slip directly out of the red sun as they strafed across the city from the launchers outside the gates.

The city was crumbling all around her, and Macha shook her head in amazement as she watched the mon-keigh bring destruction to this monument of their own magnificence. How much more impressive is their ability to destroy than their ability to build, thought the farseer.

The Striking Scorpions were darting around the statue of Lloovre Marr, erecting a ring of barricades and defences in case the Space Marines broke through the city wall. The Scorpions were perfectly adapted for this kind of close-combat – their temple prided itself on a matchless reputation for proximal fighting. Their helmets integrated the notorious mandiblaster arrays – a pair of weapon pods positioned on either side of the warrior's face. This Sting of the Scorpion could fire bursts of laser-accelerated plasma into the body of a close-range opponent, lacerating their armour in advance of a strike from the Scorpion's chainsword.

In the midst of these Aspect Warriors stood Jaerielle, issuing directions and manoeuvring great lumps of masonry into position as though they were weightless. The Striking Scorpions obeyed their exarch without question, transforming piles of debris into elaborate barricades that rivalled the surrounding buildings in their elegance – giving off the sense that they had been there for as long as the city itself. For the exarch, war was the highest form of art.

Farseer Macha watched the symphony of preparation with a mixture of admiration and terror. She realised that she was in awe of this exarch – the eldar warrior, once known as Jaerielle, who had lost himself to the temptations of Khaine. And in that moment, she also realised that his transformation was not yet complete. He was destined to be both more and less than an exarch.

Flickering visions burned themselves into her mind, and Macha slumped towards the ground, unable to sustain the barrage of images that pummelled against her consciousness. The eruption was unbidden and powerful, shaking the farseer to her soul. The pictures flashed and spiralled through her mind, sizzling with potency and branding their images into the backs of her eye-lids.

Seeing the farseer waver and stumble, Jaerielle vaulted over the barricades and sped to her side, catching her falling form an instant before her head crashed into the flagstones. He scooped her up in his arms and carried her over the barriers, climbing up the steps at the foot of the grand statue, where he placed her gently onto the ground. She sat, propped up against the figure of Lloovre Marr, staring at Jaerielle with her eyes wide.

'What do you see, farseer?' asked the exarch, searching Macha's face for a sign.

'The past and the future coalesce in the present, exarch, and the dizzying confusions of temporal distance are focussed only momentarily,' said Macha, conscious that there was no time to explain properly. She started again. 'I see the past and the future as one, Jaerielle, and I see you in both. You are the same, and yet you are different, as though transfigured by some greater power. You are fighting everything, and overcoming all, and yet you are dead to yourself.'

Macha's head was jittering spasmodically from side to side, and her body seemed to have lost all of its strength. She slumped over to one side, and Jaerielle caught her again before she fell.

'They are calling for you, Jaerielle. Their voices run through my mind, like beams of light falling into a warp-hole. They are reaching for you, trying to pull your soul back to them. You have been chosen, Jaerielle – and now that you are chosen, you have always been so. The future loops back through itself, touching your soul and setting you apart from the beginning. You were here before, and now you are here again. This is your place – it is where you are, and where you cannot be otherwise. You were here on Tartarus three thousand years ago – and you watched yourself die then. Now you must be reborn.' Macha's voice was rasping and low, as though she was struggling for enough air to give sound to her words.

Jaerielle peered uncertainly into the farseer's fathomless eyes, uncomprehending but feeling the truth of her rambling words.

'Farseer, you cannot ask for anything that I do not willingly give,' he said, bowing his head even as he held Macha by her shoulders.

'It is already given, yet the souls of the Biel-Tan already sing with praise for the sacrifice that you are about to make. The blood of many foes stains our hands, and there will be more to come before this war is over. Your hands drip with the blood of the mon-keigh and the ancient daemons of this world, as though today's battles and those of long ago were one and the same. Your soul cries out to Khaine, the Bloody-Handed God, and demands union with his substance, just as the souls of all those who have gone before you call out to you.'

'Yes, farseer, I can feel the truth of it,' replied Jaerielle, his own eyes burning with certainty and excitement.

'The other exarchs and the seers of the Court of Biel-Tan are calling for you, Jaerielle. I can feel the touch of their voices, icy with the depths of space. The shrine of the avatar is aching for you. You must go to them – you, who are the best and the worst of us all. You must go to them now, so that you may return to us in our time of greatest need – returning as the very incarnation of Khaine himself.'

Macha drew herself up onto her feet, supporting herself against the statue behind her. She held out one arm, pointing into the flagstones on the ground nearby. As she muttered some inaudible sounds, a translucent haze jetted out of her fingertips, pouring onto the stone tiles, where it pooled and shimmered.

'You must go. You must go now,' she said, as rockets fizzed overhead, blasting concussive waves across the plaza as they punched into the buildings on all sides. She staggered under the effort of concentration, struggling to keep the portal open amidst the gathering turmoil of battle.

Jaerielle hesitated for a moment, staring at the farseer, desperate for a last sign of guidance. But Macha would no longer look upon him. It was as though he were suddenly repulsive to her, as though he were already the bloody hand of a war-god, bent solely on death and destruction, utterly without balance. Searching her face, Jaerielle also saw fear flashing over her features – there was nothing so terrifying to the eldar as the loss of balance in one's soul.

He walked slowly over the shimmering pool on the flagstones, following the stream of warp energy that poured out of the farseer's hand. Looking down into the pool, he could see the distant throne room of Biel-Tan as though it were a rippling reflection. Arrayed throughout the great chamber were the exarchs of the other shrines, and the seers of the grand council. They were waiting for him – the most lost soul of all the Biel-Tan. They waited to sacrifice him to Khaine, so that he might be reborn as the god's avatar.

'You are lost on the Path of the Warrior, Jaerielle of the Striking Scorpions – your soul is lost to you already. Now it belongs to all eldar. May Kaela Mensha Khaine find you worthy of becoming his avatar,' said Macha, sharing a brief, compassionate glance.

And with that, Jaerielle stepped onto the warp-pool, sinking into it as though it were water, and vanishing from the face of Tartarus.

CHAPTER TEN

THUNDERING THROUGH FROM the back of the Blood Ravens' column came the massive Vindicator tank, grinding to a halt in front of the gates to Lloovre Marr. The rest of the detachment from the Third Company was already arrayed before the walls, waiting for a breach to be opened in the city's perimeter. Not a single shot had yet been fired, despite the fact that the Space Marines were out in the open, with no appreciable cover. The eldar were clearly not stationed in the wall's gun emplacements. Either the Blood Ravens were not expected – which seemed unlikely – or the eldar had other plans for them

Standing beside the Vindicator, inspecting the Marines that were spread out around him, Gabriel nodded a signal to Matiel, whose Assault Marines were deployed in a single line, parallel to the curving wall. At once, a great gout of flame burst out of the sergeant's jump pack, launching him into the air and up the side of the wall. On both sides of him, his squad followed suit, and the Assault Marines rapidly crested the wall, stepping onto the battlements as they reached the correct level.

'Company!' hissed the voice of Matiel through the vox unit in Gabriel's armour. Simultaneous with the crackle of his voice, Gabriel could see the report of Matiel's bolter flare from the top of the wall. Suddenly, the Assault Marines were a blaze of fire as they stooped into the cover of the castellated fixtures – disciplined volleys of bolter fire flashing down into the city on the other side of the wall. Above the pitch of the rattling bolters, Gabriel could hear the faint whine of shuriken as the eldar returned fire, and then the dull booms of frag-grenades as the Marines tossed them down into the courtyard.

'How many?' asked Gabriel, his transmission whistling with feedback from the explosions.

'Too many, captain,' said Matiel simply. 'The eldar positions are trained on the gate. They are just waiting for you to blow them and step into their killing zone.'

'Understood, sergeant. Hold your position,' replied Gabriel, turning smartly towards the squad of Devastator Marines that was waiting impatiently for the gate to be opened. 'Let's have some supporting fire for the Assault Marines.'

The Devastators angled their grenade launchers into the sky, punching out salvoes of frag-grenades in tight parabolas. The grenades arced over the city walls and crashed down into the courtyard on the other side, setting off explosions that made the ground rumble.

Meanwhile, Gabriel had climbed up on top of the Vindicator and was muttering down through the top hatch, directing the pilot to a new target. The heavy tank jolted and its tracks spun, rotating the vehicle on the spot as the differentials worked. Then, with a sudden convulsion, the massive demolisher cannon roared with life, sending a huge blast of power punching into the rockcrete wall, about one hundred metres west of the city gates. Before the dust had time to settle, the cannon coughed again, smashing into exactly the same spot and collapsing a section of the wall.

As soon as the second blast struck, Tanthius and his squad of Terminators were storming towards the felled section of the wall, their storm bolters spluttering with fire, punching stones and chunks of rockcrete out of the edges of the ruined structure, widening the breach. Lumbering along behind them was the Third Company's massive dreadnought, piloted by the ancient form of a near-dead Blood Raven, held away from death by the sarcophagus in the heart of the great war-machine. Thousands of years before, Blood Ravens' Captain Trythos had been mortally wounded whilst on secondment to the Deathwatch. His soul had refused to die, and he had been enshrined in the Third Company's dreadnought so that he might continue to vanquish the foes of the Emperor beyond his natural years.

Dreadnought Trythos stomped into the breach, pushing ahead of the Terminators, its multi-melta hissing with power in one hand and great plumes of chemical flame jetting out of the other. It stood dramatically in the gap in the wall as debris rained down around it and dust hazed the crimson of its massive armour. Already, sprays of shuriken fire were bouncing off it, as the eldar started to reposition their forces to focus on the breach. But the small arms fire meant nothing to it; as it plunged forward into the city and out of Gabriel's sight, with Tanthius's Terminators close behind.

Gabriel and Isador were pounding across the level ground in front of the walls, sprinting for the breach. Behind them came the Devastator squad, still launching salvoes of grenades over the wall towards the eldar positions, even as they ran. The Typhoon land speeders zipped through the gap ahead of them, flashing over the piles of rubble as though the ground were a smooth road. They tore into the city in support of Trythos and the Terminators, heavy bolters strafing a line of fire before them.

By the time Gabriel reached the breach, the battle on the other side of the wall was already joined. The hole in the wall was just to the west of the main gates, and Gabriel could see that the eldar had been forced to abandon many of their fortifications as the Blood Ravens had blasted through the wall behind their positions. But some of the aliens remained dug in on the east side of the gate, although they were being pestered from above by volleys of fire from Matiel's Assault Marines.

At the north side of the wide courtyard, the bulk of the eldar defences were under attack by the Terminators and the dreadnought, which advanced relentlessly despite the torrent of fire that flooded out of the eldar lines. The two Blood Ravens' Typhoons had vanished into the streets of the city, searching out the location of other eldar emplacements.

A massive explosion shook the wall, sending great chunks of rockcrete tumbling down into the breach. As Gabriel turned back to the east, he saw the city gates blow inwards, cracking off their massive hinges and crashing down into the courtyard. Out of the cloud of fire and dust rolled the Vindicator tank, crumpling the remains of the gate under its heavy tracks and spitting huge gouts of power from its demolisher cannon towards the main eldar force, incinerating sections of barricades with each blast. Flanking the Vindicator on both sides, and squeezing past it to rush through into the city streets, streamed a line of assault bikes, making the most of the smoother ground. And rumbling in behind came two Predator tanks, one sending out jets of las-fire and the other chattering bursts from its auto-cannon turret.

By now the eldar seemed to be in disarray, swamped by the awesome firepower of the Blood Ravens that converged on their positions, pummelling them from a distance. But Gabriel was uneasy – the eldar didn't seem to be engaging. Whenever their positions came under fire, the alien warriors would abandon them and move further back into the city, sucking the Blood Ravens northwards, into the central avenue. Searching the battlefield with his eyes, Gabriel was also concerned to see relatively few eldar corpses.

And then it happened. As the Terminators pursued the gradual retreat up into the wide boulevard, a flurry of Falcon tanks skimmed out of the side streets, strafing the Terminators with lines of shuriken from their catapults and blasting javelins of lance fire into their midst. A tremendous blast of las-fire lashed out of one of the side streets, punching into Dreadnought Trythos as it doused the retreating eldar in flames; the thick pulse of energy virtually vaporised the dreadnought where it stood. Its giant limbs clattered to the ground as its body was utterly shattered by the incredible blast.

Tanthius let out a yell as Trythos collapsed to the ground, and he pounded off in the direction of the blast. As he rounded the street corner, he skidded to an abrupt halt as the huge, crystalline turret of an eldar Fire Prism tank flared with energy before him. He dived for the ground, crashing the immense weight of his Terminator armour into the flagstones as the powerful pulse of energy lanced over his head. He could hear the explosion behind him, and shuddered at the thought of what the Fire Prism had just hit. Climbing back to his feet, Tanthius rolled into the cover of the building on the corner of the street.

Meanwhile, back on the main street, the eldar had been reinforced by a squadron of war walkers that came striding out of cover behind the various statues and monuments that lined the avenue. The Blood Ravens' Terminators were now under heavy fire, drawn into a narrow column where their power was compromised.

As Gabriel broke into a run towards the beleaguered vanguard of the battle, one of the Typhoons burst back into the courtyard in front of the gate, and slid to a halt before the captain.

'Captain Angelos, we have found the co-ordinates that you gave us. There is a great statue in the centre of the city, and it is being guarded by a heavily armed group of eldar warriors. They appear to be engaged in some kind of ritual,' reported the pilot breathlessly.

'Very good, pilot,' replied Gabriel. 'Thank you.' He turned to Isador. 'This battle is a distraction, designed to keep us away from the key while the eldar take it for themselves. The aliens are drawing us into a stalemate in that avenue, to slow us down.'

'I thought that this was too easy, Gabriel. The eldar are cunning indeed,' replied Isador.

'How many aliens are defending that site, pilot?' asked Gabriel, his mind racing with a plan.

'No more than twenty, captain, but they look different from the warriors here,' said the Marine, indicating the forces defending the courtyard and those in the wide avenue up ahead. 'Their armour is different, and their weapons are more elaborate.'

'Twenty we can manage,' said Gabriel, clicking his vox channel into life and turning away from the Typhoon. 'This is Captain Angelos. Get me a squadron of assault bikes and a Rhino, and get me them now. Matiel? I'm going to need you down here in the courtyard in two minutes.'

'Brother,' said Gabriel, turning back to the pilot of the Typhoon, 'I am going to need your vehicle.'

'THEY ARE ALREADY inside the city, sorcerer. Perhaps, if you really have a plan, now would be a good time to act?' scoffed Bale, his face taught with anger and frustration.

'Yes, my lord. Now is the time to move,' replied Sindri, dismissively, turning away from the Chaos Lord and striding back into the cave, vanishing into the curtain of smoke before Bale even had chance to speak. Instead, the Chaos Lord stomped after him, cursing under his breath.

The sorcerer picked his way through the temporary camp inside the cavern, moving around the fires and the clutches of seated Chaos Marines, whispering into the darkness as he went. His words curdled and swam with the threads of smoke, easing themselves into the clouds that hung from the stalactites in the low ceiling. As each of the Marines breathed in gulps of the damp, smoky air, their lungs were inflated with his intent, and they stirred into motion as though commanded.

By the time Sindri reached the back of the cave, where a narrow tunnel bored down into the rock, the Alpha Legionaries were already arrayed behind him, their weapons braced and their dark eyes gleaming with anticipation. Lord Bale pushed his way through his men, shouldering them aside as he made his way to the front of the group.

'This had better work, sorcerer,' he hissed, pushing Sindri in the back with the pole of his scythe so that the sorcerer stumbled forward into the tunnel. 'You first,' he added, bearing his yellow teeth in the faint light.

The tunnel was narrow, only wide enough for one Marine to pass at a time. It had clearly not been built with such huge figures in mind, and the line of Alpha Legionaries grumbled and complained as they stooped and ducked their way deeper into the side of the valley. Sindri removed his high, bladed helmet, stowing it under his arm as he pushed his glowing staff out before him as a torch.

As the passageway plunged down into the cliffs of the valley, bringing the Alpha Legionaries closer to the level of Lloovre Marr, Sindri noticed that the rock walls were becoming moist. In the gentle glow of his staff-light, the rocks began to shimmer and shine, casting dull reflections through the tunnel, making the shadows flicker and dance. The ground underfoot was becoming slick and slippery, as the moisture ran down onto the rocky floor, but the Marines were sure-footed and alert.

Eventually, after the tunnel had dropped another few metres, the rock on the ground gave way to a soft earth. Lord Bale paused for a moment, watching the figure of Sindri stumble and stoop ahead of him. He knelt briefly, pressing his hand onto the ground to feel the new surface, wondering whether they had already passed through the cliff-level and down into the soil-strata of the river-basin itself. The ground was soft and saturated with water; it squelched under his hand like a swamp. He shook his head slightly, disliking the confined space and the prospect of a flooded tunnel if the passageway dropped any lower. This would not be a fitting place for the death of an Alpha Legionary, let alone a Chaos Lord.

'Sorcerer!' he bellowed, his voice bouncing and echoing through the tunnel. 'Sorcerer! Where does this tunnel lead? This had better not be some kind of trick,' he said menacingly, realising how vulnerable he was to the powers of the sorcerer in this narrow space, and how useless his scythe would be if it came to combat.

Up ahead, Sindri stopped walking. He stood upright, unfolding from his stooped position, with his back to the Chaos Lord. He did not turn around. 'It leads to power and glory, Lord Bale,' he said in a barely audible whisper that seemed not to echo at all. With that, the sorcerer pressed on into the darkness, and Bale, unsatisfied but trapped

before a line of impatient Marines, walked awkwardly after him.

After a while, Bale saw Sindri draw to a halt a little
way ahead of him. He stood upright and then vanished from view. The Chaos Lord roared his rage into
the tunnel, filling it with palpitations of anger as he
stormed forward in pursuit of his sorcerer. The cursed
sorcerer has tricked me after all, he thought, thrusting his great scythe in front of him and watching its
blade glint with thirst. Behind him, he could hear his
Marines breaking into a run to follow him – the
sound of weapons being readied for firing rattled
through the passageway.

Suddenly, Bale burst out of the confined tunnel
into a wide chamber. He lost his footing as he
charged into the subterranean cavern; the ground
dropped away from a ledge at the end of the tunnel,
and he fell a couple of metres into a pool of liquid.
Landing on his feet, Bale flourished his scythe in a
dramatic arc, ready for whatever lay in wait for him.
Splashes sounded all around as a squad of Marines
leapt down into the water to support their lord, and
behind him he could hear the clatter of footfalls as
the rest of the detachment fanned out around the
stone ledge.

The darkness was dense, and Bale opened his augmented eyes wide, straining to see the details of the
chamber. But there was hardly any light this far
under the ground, and he could make out very little. Then, far away, presumably on the other side of
a huge chamber, Bale saw the glimmer of Sindri's
staff.

'Sorcerer!' yelled Bale, formulating threats in his
mind as his deep voice resonated through the cavern.

The point of light stopped moving, and then rose into the air, growing brighter as it did so. Bale shot a signal to his squad to spread out and prepare to return fire. But the light continued to increase in intensity, and the radius of its reach started to seep out across the cavern, lighting Sindri himself like a target on the ledge against the far wall.

After a few seconds, the full extent of the massive chamber began to become evident. The ceiling was a giant rocky dome, vaulted and grand, as though carved out to approximate the interior of a cathedral. The stone walls above the ledge were curved in a huge circle, and they were covered in frescoes and images, painted crudely in a deep red ink. Below the ledge was a vast lake of liquid, big enough to submerge a small city. The ledge itself seemed to mark the intersection of the rock-layers of the valley walls from the soft soil-strata of the river basin on the valley floor.

Bale looked around the chamber in amazement as the orb of light from Sindri's staff flooded out to fill the whole space. As the light crept over the surface of the water, Bale noticed that it was not water at all. Scooping his hand down into the dark liquid, he lifted a fist full up to his mouth, tasting the rich iron as the thick liquid gushed down his throat.

It was blood.

This was a vast, underground reservoir of blood, cut into the river basin below Lloovre Marr and, from the look of it, it had been lovingly created and cared for over a long, long time.

'We are nearly there, my lord,' came Sindri's voice from the other side of the chamber, apparently unsurprised by the scene around him. 'But we must hurry. The path heads back up into the cliffs now, and it will take us up into the heart of Lloovre Marr itself. Come.'

THE FARSEER SLUMPED to the ground, exhausted and spent, as the pool of warp-energy on the flagstones faded out of existence. A couple of Striking Scorpions sprang forward from their places in the defensive emplacements around the monument, gathering the farseer into their arms and carrying her back behind the elegant barricades, leaving the figure that had just emerged from the pool crouched into a ball on its own. It looked as though it had just been born, fully formed and terrible. The figure was huge, much bigger than any other eldar, even in its crouched posture. As it gradually unfolded itself, drawing itself up to its full height and stretching its metal skin in the dying light of the red sun, even the Striking Scorpions shrank back from it.

The Avatar of Khaine threw back its head and let out a blood-curdling howl that could be heard for several kilometres in every direction. Macha narrowed her eyes in pain as the hideous sound scraped into her ears, grating against her finely tuned sensibilities like teeth down the blade of a sword. She knew that every eldar in the city would hear the cry, and that they would fight with renewed passion as the spirit of Khaine riddled their souls with the lust for blood.

Great bladed horns rose from the avatar's ornate wraithbone helmet, and a plume fluttered between them, displaying the colours of the Biel-Tan. Its armour burned with a fiery red, as though its molten blood radiated through the plates, and the intricate web of runes that laced its body glowed with ancient powers, forgotten even to the eldar themselves.

Its left hand was a dripping mess of blood and pulp, as though it had been melted in the wet heat of boiling oil. But this disfigurement was a mark of distinction and, more than anything else about the avatar, it was this bloody hand that would inspire the Biel-Tan to greater feats on the battlefield. It was the mark of Kaela Mensha Khaine himself – echoing the injury inflicted on him at the beginning of time, when the Great Enemy had destroyed him and scattered his substance across the material realm. This Avatar of Khaine was the embodiment of one such fragment – a fragment kept in the heart of the Biel-Tan craftworld until its moment of greatest need.

Jaerielle? asked Macha, speaking her words directly into the avatar's mind, searching for any spark of recognition. But there was nothing, just a cold blast of psychic energy that washed back into the farseer's mind, chilling her to her soul.

Pulling herself onto her feet, Macha drew her own ancient force sword from its holster on her back and walked gingerly forward towards the avatar. For the first time in the history of the Biel-Tan, the avatar had been incarnated without its Wailing Doom – the ancestral weapon of this god-eldar.

The Ceremony of Awakening had been performed too quickly, and shards of the avatar's energy were still missing. It was born incomplete. As Macha stumbled, too weak to support the weight of her own weapon, the two Striking Scorpions rushed to her aid once again, grasping her elbows and supporting her weight. Her blade was a pathetic shadow of the great Wailing Doom lost on this very planet three thousand years before, but it was the finest blade on the whole of Biel-Tan, and a weapon worthy of a great eldar warrior.

The farseer walked towards the avatar, and dropped to one knee before it, holding her long, two-handed force sword out in front of her. The avatar looked down at the small figure of the farseer and tilted its head slightly, as though confused by an inappropriate sight. Then it reached out its right hand and lifted Macha back onto her feet, before kneeling itself and bowing its head to the farseer who had brought it back from the fathomless depths of Biel-Tan's infinity circuit. Macha nodded with satisfaction and held out the sword. Without a word, the avatar took the great blade into one hand, and leapt backwards away from the farseer, flourishing the sword in a complicated and elegant pattern. Then, as it turned its back on her to set out into the city, a Typhoon missile blasted out of an adjoining street and smashed into its chest.

THE LAND SPEEDER banked around the building on the corner of the street, bursting out into the plaza. Gabriel hit the brakes hard and skidded the Typhoon, banking again to bleed some energy as Isador punched the trigger of the missile launcher. The rocket roared out of the turret and spiralled straight into the chest of the monstrous warrior in the centre of the plaza, where it exploded in a shower of flames.

Meanwhile, the Blood Ravens' assault bikes poured into the plaza out of the street behind them, each skidding to a standstill in a neat formation across the square, training their front guns on the green eldar figures that flickered with motion behind the structure around the statue of Lloovre Marr. As the bikes opened fire with their twin-linked bolters, battering the barricades with a tirade of explosive shells, the Rhino finally rolled into the plaza, spilling Matiel's Assault Marines out of the back before it had even stopped moving.

The flames from the missile impact had not abated, but the colossal eldar warrior sprang clear of the inferno that had erupted around its chest. There was hardly even a mark on it as it flipped across the plaza, closing the space between it and the Blood Ravens in a flurry of somersaults. Isador punched the missile launcher again, but the rocket flashed harmlessly over the gigantic eldar and smashed into the statue of Lloovre Marr, blowing it into a crumbled ruin.

With its last flip, the eldar creature reached the Typhoon and brought its flashing blade smoothly down on top of it. Gabriel and Isador dived out of the vehicle as the sword passed straight through it, rupturing its fuel lines and detonating the engine core. As the Blood Ravens rolled for cover at the edge of the plaza, the monstrous eldar creature stood bathing in the flames that ripped out of the wrecked Typhoon.

'In the Emperor's name,' said Matiel, tumbling into cover next to Isador. 'What is that thing?'

'It is a daemon conjured by the treacherous eldar, brother. It is called an avatar,' replied Isador, levelling his force staff at the creature and loosing a javelin of energy directly into its stomach. The blast was enough to attract the avatar's attention – it turned to face Isador and began to stride in his direction.

Meanwhile, Gabriel was back on his feet and charging at the gigantic creature, his chainsword sputtering in his hand and a chorus of silver voices singing in his ears. Once again, the world was rendered into slow motion as Gabriel pounded across the plaza, his every step apparently accompanied by the symphonic tones of the Astronomican.

The avatar bent its legs, ready to spring forward at Isador, just as Gabriel crashed into it from the side. The two warriors tumbled to the ground, and Isador leapt out of his cover to assist his friend. Sprinting towards Gabriel, he called back over his shoulder to Matiel: 'Deal with the barricades!'

Immediately, the Assault Marines powered up into the sky, their jump packs flaring and their bolters coughing shells down towards the eldar encampment in the centre of the square. But the green-armoured eldar were fast and nimble, evading much of the fire and returning it in stinging volleys. From his vantage point in the sky, Matiel could see the figure of a robed eldar woman lying down in the middle of the defensive ring, propped up against the ruins of the monument that they appeared to be defending. He pulled a chain of frag-grenades from his belt and lobbed them down towards her.

Meanwhile, Gabriel wrestled with the avatar, struggling to keep the huge creature from bringing his great blade into play. The Blood Raven pummelled his power fist against the avatar's burning armour, punching over and over again until the faintest of cracks began to appear. Sheets of blue lightning jousted out of Isador's staff, as the Librarian stood just clear of the two writhing warriors, launching javelins of power to assist his captain.

Lying on the ground with the Blood Raven on top of it, the avatar bucked and threw Gabriel over his shoulder, away from Isador. In the same movement, it reached for its fallen sword, but a blast from Isador sent the blade skidding out of its reach. As it sprang back up onto its feet, the avatar was pounded from both sides at once – Gabriel launched himself back into the creature's face while Isador ploughed into its legs with his force staff. A huge explosion shook the ground at the same time as a cluster of grenades exploded behind the barricades. With a shriek of frustration, the avatar crumpled to the ground once again.

Gabriel drove his power fist into the weakened crack in the avatar's armour, finally breaking through. A sizzling jet of molten blood spurted out of the hole, spraying Gabriel in the face, making him cry out and reel in pain. As the captain rolled backwards off the avatar, Isador leapt forward into his place, thrusting the tip of his force staff deep into the wound and leaning his entire weight onto it. As the staff sunk deeper into the creature's chest, Isador closed his eyes and released his rage into the weapon, letting its power cascade down the shaft and explode into a starburst of blue energy inside the eldar warrior.

The explosion threw Isador and Gabriel a hundred metres back through the air, until their flight was broken by the stone of a white building on the fringe of the plaza. They thumped into the wall, and then slid down into heaps at its base. When they looked up, the bloody remains of the avatar were fizzing and hissing all over the flagstones, but Matiel's Assault Marines were still raining fire on the barricades.

Gabriel was first on his feet. Pausing to offer Isador his hand, Gabriel pulled his friend onto his feet with a nod of admiration, and then sprinted off through the plaza towards the barricades. As he reached them, Matiel crunched to the ground next to him, and Isador skidded to halt at his other shoulder. The other Assault Marines had also returned to the ground, and there was no sign of movement on the other side of the barriers.

The three Marines clambered over the barricades and jumped down the other side, where they saw a solitary eldar woman standing before a large pit in the ground, where once the statue of Lloovre Marr had been. She appeared unarmed.

Kill me, if you must, humans, began the eldar in an odd tongue that spoke directly into their minds. *Cast my name to the winds, if it pleases you. But you must heed me. Bury again that which lies beneath my feet, for it will be the ruin of us all. I may have been your enemy in this – but we have a greater foe than each other.*

Gabriel stared into the farseer's eyes for a moment, and a torrent of images invaded his mind. Pictures of flames and blood, of the Astronomican itself lost in an inferno of chaos and darkness. Then the eldar looked away, fixing Isador with her stare.

'Do not listen to this alien, Gabriel. We must destroy it,' said Isador, apparently unable to tear his eyes away from those of Macha. His face was suddenly gaunt and pale.

Gabriel was silent for a brief moment. 'She knows much, much that we need to learn, old friend.' As he spoke, he peered past the eldar and down into the pit. Its sides were sheer, and at the bottom was a pool of blood, as though it had seeped in to reach its own natural level. Held proud of the blood on a stone plinth was a curved, bejewelled dagger. Was this the key of which Isador had spoken, wondered Gabriel?

Isador was struggling within himself, trying to find his own thoughts in amongst the confusion of images that invaded his head. A familiar voice was whispering into his mind: *It lies within your reach now, Librarian – reach out for it – it is yours – only this pathetic farseer can stop you – see how your captain doubts you still…*

'What could she offer, except lies and treachery? Do not trust her, Gabriel! Suffer not the alien to live,' added Isador, quoting the motto of the Ordo Xenos Deathwatch kill teams.

'Knowledge is power, Isador–' began Gabriel, but his voice was cut off by a rattle of bolter fire from the Assault Marines on the other side of the barricade. The three Blood Ravens turned to see what had drawn the fire, spying a squad of Alpha Legionaries emerging into the plaza from one of the side streets. But then a gasp of agony from the farseer made them all turn back again.

'The key!' cried Macha, pointing down into the pit.

Gabriel and Isador rushed to the side of the pit, flanking the farseer, and stared down. Isador let out a streak of fire from his staff as Gabriel snapped off a flurry of bolter shells, but the figure in the bottom of the pit was gone before the shots hit the pool of blood.

'Who was that, alien? And what did he steal?' hissed Gabriel, turning suddenly and gripping the farseer by the throat. The figure had worn the apparel of a Chaos Sorcerer, and the colour of his armour suggested that he was part of the Alpha Legion. He had taken the dagger and then vanished into one of the walls of the pit, as though there were a hidden tunnel under the plaza.

He took a key. The last step along a long, bloody path.

'A key? A key to what?' asked Gabriel, trying to meet the farseer's gaze, but it was still fixed on Isador.

To the undoing of us all, human.

'Stop speaking in riddles!' cried Gabriel, shaking her by the neck and lifting her slight form clear off the ground.

He stole a key, a key to the shadows of this world, to the evil horrors that lie within.

'Tell me what the key does, alien, or I will kill you,' said Gabriel, increasingly exasperated.

You do not know already? Your inquisitor keeps you on a very short lease. He knows. Ask him.

Gabriel was stunned into silence, unable to see how Toth could be involved in any of this, and yet intuitively sure that the eldar witch was telling the truth.

He has known since he arrived. Or, should I say, since long before he came to Tartarus. His kind have been before – they have never left. Did you not find it all too convenient that he appeared from nowhere and landed just on the cusp of a warp storm? Human, you are caught in events and machinations beyond your reckoning. But we can help one another – stop the forces of Chaos succeeding…

'Your people have fought well, alien,' said Gabriel, releasing his grip on the farseer's throat, his mind racing. 'And I can see that we may share some common goals here. But you cannot ask me for trust, and I cannot risk betrayal. I will not be responsible for the loss of any more unnecessary lives – and you have cost enough of those already. You should have asked for an alliance before you squandered your position of strength, then I may have taken you seriously. Now, you have wasted enough of my time.'

Gabriel drew his bolter and levelled it at the farseer's head. In that instant, she finally tore her eyes away from Isador and fixed them on Gabriel, a flood of compassion pouring out of them, touching his very soul. But a searing pain in his shoulder yanked him out of his reverie, and he spun to find the source of the shot, snatching his bolter around in a sudden movement. A Warp Spider blinked out of existence just as he caught sight of it.

Turning back to the farseer, Gabriel saw the Warp Spider standing beside her, with his death spinner gatling gun pointed straight at his face. Gabriel narrowed his eyes as Isador and Matiel hesitated about taking their shots – unwilling to risk their captain's life.

The farseer held up her hand, placing it onto the barrel cluster of the death spinner, apparently in a signal not to fire.

Your enemies have taken up a position in the Dannan sector of the city. They will not remain there long. We are too weak to fight them, and far too weak to confront that which they seek to unleash – you have seen to that, human.

With that, the Warp Spider and the farseer simply vanished, leaving Gabriel with doubts, questions and uncertainties spiralling in his head.

CHAPTER ELEVEN

A MAN STUMBLED up the steps of the Temple of Dannan, tripping and falling flat onto his face as he reached the top. His head crashed down against a massive, acid green boot, harder than the rockcrete on which it stood. As he lifted his face off the foot, a thin trickle of blood oozed from his temple, running unevenly over his already disfigured face. The man looked like a half-melted wax figurine, with the flesh on the right-hand side of his body distended into hideous folds. He was panting with excitement as he finally lifted his gaze to meet the eyes of the Chaos Lord, who stood magnificently at the top of the steps, surveying the throng of cultists that had gathered in the precinct since his arrival less than an hour earlier.

'M-my… my lord,' stuttered the cultist, still prostrated awkwardly on the ground, with blood bubbling out of his mouth. 'The Marines of the false-Emperor approach from the south.'

Lord Bale looked down at the cultist for a moment, almost acknowledging him, then turned away to address Sindri, who stood next to him in the door-way to the temple. Behind them, in the interior of the chapel, the faint sound of screams pulsed rhythmi-cally.

'Sorcerer, how long before the ceremony is completed? It would not do for the Blood Ravens to catch us before we are ready for them,' asked Bale, still unwilling to acknowledge that Sindri's plans appeared to be panning out exactly as he foresaw.

'Bale,' said Sindri, smoothly, using the Chaos Lord's name in a simple and unadorned way. 'These flies are but minor annoyances. We have the key, and we have ample bodies here,' he said, indicating the mass of cultists in the temple precinct. 'If necessary, we can imprison the Blood Ravens behind a wall of corpses while we finish the ceremony – and then, afterwards, we will not have to think about them at all.'

Bale looked at the sorcerer, and he could see the confidence flowing out of him. This was the first Marine in decades to speak his name so directly and not feel the icy pain of his scythe through their necks. The Chaos Lord could not bring himself to speak in response – he ground his teeth together in irritation, hating Sindri's success, but eager to reap the rewards of the ceremony.

'Events have proven my words true, have they not,' continued Sindri with a smug, rhetorical flourish. 'We are in no danger–'

'Events have proven you fortunate, sorcerer,' inter-jected Bale, unable to hold his tongue any longer.

'The Blood Ravens are not to be underestimated – they made short work of your precious orks, and they have already proven themselves against the cursed eldar. To what do we owe your most recent bout of nauseous optimism concerning our own safety?'

'I have reason to believe,' replied Sindri, his voice hissing with serpentine sibilance, 'that we have a new ally in their camp. An individual more than ready to betray the Blood Ravens.'

Again, Bale ground his bladed teeth together as Sindri appeared ready for his attack once more. One day, the sorcerer would slip up and Bale would make sure that he was there to enjoy it.

'Very well,' muttered the Chaos Lord, waving his hand dismissively. 'Prepare for what is to come... and dispose of this cretinous fool.' Bale kicked casually with his foot, cracking the cultist in the face and shattering his jaw.

'W...why? M... my lord,' spluttered the cultist, spitting blood and breathing roughly to suppress his screams. 'H-how have I failed you?'

But Bale was already deaf to his words, and instead Sindri stooped down and picked him up by his hair. 'You brought unwelcome news to his lordship. You will not make this mistake again,' said Sindri, himself an expert in never delivering bad news to Bale. He dropped the cultist back onto the flagstones, then grabbed a fistful of his hair again and dragged the hapless fool into the dark interior of the temple, the shrieks of sacrificial victims echoing louder as they entered the vaulted space.

THE BOLTER SHELL punched into Matiel's jump pack as he roared around the street corner in pursuit of the

squadron of Alpha Legionaries. The pack whined in
resistance as its power started to fail, and then sput-
terings of smoke started to cough out of the
puncture. Matiel lost altitude rapidly, and the stabilisers failed almost instantly, flipping the sergeant
onto his side and blasting him across the street
towards the buildings on the other side. The rest of
his squadron rocketed after him, fighting against the
centrifugal forces as they flew round the corner in his
wake.

The Chaos Marines had formed a temporary firing
line across the street, and a sheet of fire erupted from
them as the Assault Marines rounded the bend. The
volley of fire stripped through the Blood Ravens' formation, bolter shells punching into armour and
pinging past to impact against the buildings beyond.

Meanwhile, Matiel smashed into a building at the
side of the street, slumping down its face until he
crunched into the road at its base. His jump pack was
still spitting gouts of fire, throwing him off balance as
he struggled to his feet. He clicked the release, and
the pack leapt from his back, spiralling into the air at
the head of a whirling trail of black smoke. It pitched
suddenly, zig-zagging down the narrow street, and
then crashing into a building just ahead of the Alpha
Legionaries. The explosion shook the building, dis-
lodging a rain of masonry down onto the Chaos
Marines.

The rest of the Assault Marines thumped to the
ground, rolling into the cover of doorways and
behind abandoned vehicles. They had not expected
the Alpha Legionaries to end their retreat so abruptly,
and the firing line had taken them by surprise. Now
a disciplined bank of fire erupted out of the Chaos

line, strafing down the road towards the Blood Ravens. Matiel's Assault squadron was pinned.

The sound of heavy footfalls pounding through the adjoining streets made Matiel look round, checking behind his own squad in case he had been led into an ambush. But he was greeted with the magnificent sight of a squadron of Blood Ravens' Terminators storming into the street, with Tanthius in their heart, his storm bolter a blaze of firepower.

The line of Alpha Legionaries was broken almost immediately as the awesome power of a Terminator squadron bore down on it, pummelling it with hellfire shells and gouts of flame. Tanthius himself squeezed off a couple of cyclone rockets that zipped along the street ahead of his squad, exploding into the now disorganised clutch of Chaos Marines. Matiel waved a signal to his Assault squad, and the Marines were immediately up onto their feet, joining the charge of the Terminators, adding salvoes of fire from their bolters.

The Chaos Marines scattered into side streets, vanishing from the main road, leaving three smoking corpses laying on the flagstones. As they disappeared from view, a thunderous boom shook the street, sending a series of ripples along the surface of the road, toppling the Blood Ravens as the ground under their feet oscillated and convulsed.

The thunder grew louder as the Marines rolled towards the edges of the street, searching for patches of firm ground. Tanthius stood defiantly in the middle of the road, riding the waves of rockcrete as they rolled beneath him. His feet were planted, and behind his helmet his jaw was set – a Blood Ravens'

Terminator would not give ground to the trickery of
the Alpha Legion.

The waves of rockcrete grew higher and more powerful as gusts of wind started to rip down the street,
funnelled into gales by the high buildings on either
side. With an immense crack, the flagstones at the
end of the street were catapulted into the air in a
fountain of rockcrete. The line of the fountain accel-
erated down the street towards the Blood Ravens,
throwing the flagstones wildly in the air as it pushed
onwards. Tanthius twisted his feet, grinding them
into the rockcrete beneath him, planting himself
against the onslaught rather than diving for cover.

The immense wave of flagstones broke over the
defiant, crimson form of the Blood Raven, exploding
into a tremendous fountain of masonry and crumbling debris. The street was filled with a mist of dust
and steam, as flagstones crashed down all around,
shattering into fragments and throwing up plumes
into the air.

As the dust finally settled, Matiel wiped the debris
from his visor and surveyed the ruin of the street.
There, exactly where he had been before the storm
had hit, Tanthius stood proudly in the middle of the
road, his blood-red armour radiant in amongst the
speckling rain of debris. All around him was broken
masonry and the remains of ruined flagstones. And,
only a metre in front of his feet, the road had simply
vanished; it had dropped away completely, swallowed up in a colossal chasm that seemed to have
split the entire city in two along a line that bisected
the street just in front of Tanthius's feet.

On the far side of the chasm, about a hundred
metres away from Tanthius, Matiel could see the

Alpha Legionaries spilling back into the street, staring back over the destruction that had rent the road asunder. They looked as surprised as I feel, thought Matiel, watching them turn their backs and head off into the distance. Instinctively, he reached for the ignition switch for his jump pack, but then realised that he had jettisoned it already.

WHINING SLOWLY TO a halt at the edge of chasm, Gabriel peered over the lip. The bottom was about fifty metres down and, even in the fading light of the dusk, Gabriel could see that it was flooded with blood. For a brief moment, the Blood Ravens' captain wondered whether the entire city had been built atop a lake of blood – it seemed to seep through everywhere when a hole appeared. He shook his head, dismissing the thought and drawing the bike back away from the ledge.

'What happened here?' asked Gabriel, addressing his question to Matiel and Tanthius, as Isador clambered out of the Rhino that ground to halt before the group. 'I felt the earthquake from the plaza, but this is not quite what I expected to find here.'

'The chasm has split the entire city in two,' reported Isador, joining the group after peering down into the ravine. 'Early signs are that it has cut off the Dannan district completely, isolating the Temple of Dannan at the centre of a virtual island.'

Gabriel nodded his acknowledgment to Isador, but kept his gaze on the other two, waiting for their explanations.

'We were pursuing the Alpha Legionaries, captain. They set a trap for us in this street, forcing us down onto the ground and pinning us in defensive positions,' reported Matiel. 'When Brother Tanthius arrived, we drove the enemy back down the street together. They were on the point of breaking when the quake struck, ripping the street in two and cutting us off from the cursed Marines of Chaos.'

'Brother Tanthius, what happened to the eldar forces near the main gates?' asked Gabriel, keen to keep abreast of the situation throughout the city.

'There was a tremendous shrieking noise, like a scream, emanating from deeper in the city. When they heard it, they simply stopped fighting and disappeared, darting through those Emperor-forsaken warp-gates once again. The eldar are slippery creatures, captain,' replied Tanthius. 'Before they fled, we inflicted great damage on their forces – they will not be so keen to tackle Terminators of the Blood Ravens again,' he added with satisfaction.

'Isador, do you have any idea where the sorcerer will take the key?' asked Gabriel, furrowing his brow as he tried to keep track of the complicated events of the day.

'Not really, Gabriel,' replied the Librarian. 'I suspect that he will need consecrated ground and a controlled atmosphere to perform any rituals that he may have in mind.'

'Consecrated ground?' asked Gabriel. 'What would that entail in this case?'

'It would depend upon the nature of the artefact. Judging by the markings on the altar we found in the valley, I imagine that we are dealing with a Khornate artefact here – so the ground may have to be consecrated with blood,' said Isador.

'How much blood?' asked Gabriel, walking back towards the chasm and looking down into it again.

'Would you say that a lake the size of Lloovre Marr might be enough?'

'By the Throne, Gabriel!' said Isador, stepping onto the rim of the abyss. 'If this blood really stretches out under the entire city, then Lloovre Marr itself would constitute ground consecrated for the Blood God, Khorne. The power of a cultist ritual here would be immense.'

'It seems that there was some measure of truth hidden in the riddles of the eldar witch,' said Gabriel, thinking of Macha's warnings and the pool of blood that had gathered in the crater below the ruined monument. 'We must get to the Temple of Dannan and stop the foul ceremony of the heretics before it can begin.'

The others nodded in agreement, but Gabriel remained motionless for a moment. His mind was racing with the other words of the eldar woman – she had said that Inquisitor Toth knew more than he was revealing and, if he was honest with himself, Gabriel had known this from the start. Rather than putting his mind at ease, this insight made his soul shrink from his consciousness, hiding from the articulation of the idea that he may possess unsanctioned psychic abilities. This was not the time to confront his own daemons – there were real daemons to slay on Tartarus, and it was up to him to see it done.

'Get a bridge built over this chasm, and get it done now,' he barked to Matiel, delegating command of the logistics to the sergeant, and cursing inwardly that all of the Thunderhawks were in use in the evacuation at the spaceport. Matiel nodded sharply and hastened off to organise the emergency construction.

'And Isador, get a message to Toth – tell him… tell him that we respectfully request his presence in the capital city,' said Gabriel, considering how best to phrase it.

As Isador's face cracked into a faint smile, a gunshot pinged off his shoulder plate. A flurry of activity instantly erupted behind them, as the Blood Ravens organised themselves for battle, fanning out across the street to form a bristling barricade.

Turning, Isador saw crowds of people pouring out of the side streets into the main road. They were human – or had once been human. Their flesh was melted and disfigured, and they loped and staggered through the street in vulgar lurches. They each bore the touch of Khorne – mutating them into the minions of the Blood God – and there were hundreds of them. And they just kept coming, spilling out of the side streets and stumbling along from the other end of the main road, as though there was no end to their number. Perhaps there were thousands. They pressed down the road, trapping the Blood Ravens between that sea of cultists and the chasm of blood, hurling crude projectiles, and snapping off shots with shotguns and pistols.

'The people of Lloovre Marr?' asked Gabriel, a nauseating sickness dropping into his stomach as he braced his bolter. 'Living on the consecrated ground of a daemon can have unfortunate effects on people,' he added, his thoughts dizzy and spiralling with images of Cyrene.

'Brother-captain,' said Tanthius, stepping forward in his massive Terminator armour and placing a firm hand on Gabriel's shoulder. 'Allow your blessed Terminators to cleanse these aberrations in your place. Your attentions are needed elsewhere.'

Gabriel looked up into the visor of his long-serving sergeant and smiled weakly. 'Thank you, Tanthius,' he said, 'but this is not a responsibility that I can shirk.'

He appreciated his sergeant's concern and his unspoken understanding, but there was no way that Gabriel was going to hide from his responsibilities just because of events on his homeworld. If anything, he was buoyed by a violent sense of justice for all – if the heretics on Cyrene had to die, then so too did the vile mutants of Tartarus. There could be no exceptions.

Nonetheless, Gabriel's stomach churned with nausea as he drew his chainsword. But then, just faintly in the back of his mind, the gentle tones of the silver choir started to wash across his soul once again, reassuring him that his direction was correct and his purpose firm.

'We will fight together, Brother Tanthius,' he said, striding towards the Blood Ravens' barricades with his chainsword held high and his bolter braced in his hand.

THE THUNDERHAWK ROARED over the street, strafing fire through the throng of cultists, overshooting them and coasting over the Blood Ravens as they retreated across their makeshift bridge. The gunship pulled up dramatically, soaring vertically into the sky and arcing back on itself. It rolled to level out and then dived back down into the street, its guns pulsing with fire as its strafing run ripped through the cultists a second time. But the thinning crowd did not disperse, and the cultists pressed on towards the temporary bridge over the chasm, walking relentlessly into lashes of fire from the retreating line of Blood Ravens and falling in droves.

As his Marines filed over the narrow bridge, Gabriel stood shoulder to shoulder with Tanthius and Isador, blocking the path of the cultists and cutting them down with bursts of bolter fire and hacks from his chainsword. The three of them held the crowd at bay until the rest of the Blood Ravens reached the other side of the chasm, where they peeled left and right, lining the opposite ledge of the ravine. As one, the line erupted with fire, sending a hail of bolter shells flashing across the chasm, leaving glittering trails as the sun finally dropped below the horizon and the street was cast into darkness.

The disciplined volleys of fire punched into the cultists, dropping dozens at a time, driving them back through sheer pressure of fire.

'Isador. Tanthius. Time to go,' said Gabriel, as a shredded cultist fell at his feet. The supporting fire from the far bank had given them a little breathing space.

Loosing a couple of final blasts with his storm bolter, Tanthius turned and sprinted across the bridge, with Isador close behind. Gabriel hesitated for a moment, listening to the pristine chorus that still echoed in his head as he stepped forward into the throng, carving his blade through limbs and cracking skulls with the butt of his gun. Then, as though suddenly changing his mind, he turned and ran towards the bridge – the cultists being sucked into the fire-vacuum left by his departure.

From the far side, shots flashed through the night, picking off the cultists that tried to run after the sprinting captain, knocking them wailing into the depths of the chasm itself. Repeated splashes could be heard as the corpses dropped into the river of blood that filled the bottom of the ravine.

As Gabriel ran, the Thunderhawk swooped in for another run, dragging its fire through the crowd but then dumping a whistling projectile towards the bridge itself. Gabriel threw himself headlong as the bomb smashed into the apex of the bridge, detonating in a great ball of flame. The flimsy structure buckled and collapsed, free-falling into the chasm together with the cultists who had managed to evade the fire of the Blood Ravens.

A strong arm reached out and caught the grasping hand of Gabriel as the bridge fell away from under him. For a moment, the captain was held dangling precariously over the bloody chasm, but then he was pulled clear and deposited on the flagstones.

'Thank you, Isador,' said Gabriel, climbing to his feet. 'My apologies, Tanthius – thank you,' he corrected himself when he saw that it was the sergeant who had saved him.

Another explosion erupted behind him, and Gabriel turned to see the Thunderhawk dump more explosive charges into the cultists on the other side of the ravine. The brief fireballs shed sudden bursts of light in the darkness, highlighting the grotesque and contorted agonies of the cultists as they were blown apart. Then the Thunderhawk stopped its raids, and the remains of the road fell into abject darkness. Gabriel could only assume that the cultists were either all dead, or that they had finally fled.

PLUMES OF FIRE jetted against the flagstones as the Thunderhawk lowered itself gently onto the road.

The hatch opened, and a shaft of light flooded out, silhouetting the impressive figure of Inquisitor Toth in the drop chamber within. He stood for a moment, his ornate warhammer slung over his shoulder in the image of a barbarian warrior, and then strode down the ramp, his boots clanking solidly.

The dramatic gesture was wasted, as Gabriel and Isador were deep in conversation. The inquisitor made his way into the midst of the Blood Ravens, most of whom were busily securing the area.

'How could I not have seen this, Isador?' asked Gabriel. 'How is it that I am most blind when it matters most?'

Isador looked at the pain in his friend's green eyes, the faint light of torches dancing in them in the darkness. 'Your intuition was right about Tartarus, old friend – that is why we stayed on this planet... Or, are you not talking about Tartarus at all?'

'I should have seen the rot before it started to spread – I was blind for too long. I put my own world to the torch, Isador – our world. How many innocents died on Cyrene, so that the heretics would burn? And yet... here I am again, at somebody else's doorstep, flourishing the executioner's blade so righteously...' Gabriel trailed off, unable to finish his thought.

'Blessed is the mind too small for doubt, Gabriel,' said Isador, managing a faint smile for his friend.

'I have no doubts!' snapped Gabriel, a little too sharply. 'I still believe in the purity of the Imperium... in the sovereign might of the Golden Throne... even in the guidance of the Astronomican itself,' he added, almost as a confession. He looked around for a moment, wondering where Prathios was.

'It is in yourself that you have lost faith, my friend,' said Isador, finally giving voice to a concern that he had harboured ever since Cyrene.

'No, Isador. Not in myself, only in what I see,' replied Gabriel, his eyes still searching for the company Chaplain in the night.

'And what is it that you see, captain?' asked Inquisitor Toth as he strode in between the two friends, cutting off their conversation.

Gabriel twitched visibly, shaken a little by the sudden arrival of the inquisitor. But he recovered quickly and drew himself up to his full height as he addressed Mordecai.

'I see conspirators and liars more concerned with their own agenda than with the will of the Emperor, inquisitor,' he said, making no attempt to hide the venom in his voice.

'And you expect me to break down and confess to being such a heretic?' responded Mordecai with a snort and a brief laugh. 'I am not so easily cowed by your accusations, Marine, and I have nothing that I must confess to you.'

'You lied to me!' shouted Gabriel, stepping closer to the inquisitor and making Isador reach for his shoulder to restrain him. 'You lied to me, and many good Marines are dead because of it.'

'They are better off dead with pure hearts than caught in this warp storm, captain. If you really feel that accusations are an appropriate subject of conversation with an inquisitor, then I might accuse you: their deaths are all on your head, captain, for I warned you to leave this world and you ignored me. I told you about the storm, but you had to go looking for the taint of Chaos, as is your wont, it seems,' said Mordecai, calm and calculating as usual.

'Your words still ring untrue, inquisitor,' countered Gabriel, although he had to acknowledge the literal truth of them. 'I know that you are not new to Tartarus – I know that your masters at the Ordo Xenos have been here before.' Isador withdrew his hand, evidently shocked at the risk Gabriel was taking – confronting an inquisitor with the knowledge of an eldar witch.

For the first time in their acquaintance, Gabriel saw Mordecai flinch. 'I am not in the habit of explaining the affairs of the Emperor's Inquisition to Space Marines, captain. But yes, you are right, the Ordo Xenos has been watching Tartarus for longer than you might imagine.'

'What are they watching, Toth?' asked Gabriel, his contempt fired by Mordecai's confession.

'They are watching for signs of unspeakable horror, captain,' replied Mordecai, his tone softening even as Gabriel's hardened.

'Would these be the same horrors pursued by the Alpha Legion?' he asked, almost spitting as he recalled that the inquisitor had claimed to feel no taint of Chaos on Tartarus.

'There are no coincidences on Tartarus,' began Mordecai, almost to himself. 'There is only the storm that winnows the faithful from the heretic.'

'And are we faithful men, Toth? Are we good servants of the Emperor?' bit Gabriel, challenging the inquisitor.

Mordecai looked down at his feet for a moment, hefting his heavy warhammer from one hand to the other, swinging it like a metronome, as though trying to keep pace with his thoughts.

'This world is cursed, captain,' he began, as though he had reached an important decision. 'Three thousand years ago an artefact of ancient and evil power was lost here. The forces of Chaos seek this artefact – they have sought it for centuries, but they have never been in possession of all the pieces of the puzzle.'

'Until now,' offered Gabriel, encouraging Mordecai to continue.

'Secrets are hard things to keep, captain, as the Blood Ravens themselves know well. The events of that day three thousand years ago drew the attention of many eyes, some of which have not aged as rapidly as our own. For them, it has simply been a matter of waiting for the right time to return to this world. Not long ago, an Imperial excavation team accidentally uncovered a marker – the first of a series of coded markers. I'm afraid that the Inquisition was not quick enough to silence news of this find, and it quickly found its way into ears that should not have heard it. This marker indicated the location of the altar that you yourself discovered in the valley. From then on, it was a simple matter of following the trail.' Mordecai was on a roll now, evidently relieved to be getting this off his chest.

'And this artefact, what is it?' asked Gabriel, trying to cut through the irrelevant details – time was short.

'It is a stone – a small gem called the Maledictum. Inside is contained a daemon of great power – a daemon prince, born of the forces of Chaos itself,' replied Mordecai with sinister force.

Gabriel was shaking his head, trying to make all of the pieces fit together. It didn't make sense. 'How is it possible that the citizens of Tartarus did not know all of this? These markers... and the artefact itself must lie buried beneath their own cities. Why do their records contain no mention of any of this?'

'When the warp storm last visited Tartarus, three thousand years ago, it drove the local population into insanity. When the Imperium resettled the planet, it did so as though for the first time. Lloovre Marr himself cleansed the planet of all survivors of the storm – it is said that the rivers ran with blood. All traces of the previous colonists were eradicated. Lloovre Marr and his comrades built over the dark places without ever knowing what lay beneath,' explained Mordecai.

'That is why the history books begin so precisely in 102.M39?' asked Isador.

'Yes, the previous records were all expunged by the Inquisition,' replied Mordecai. 'And thus the people of Tartarus remained ignorant of what lay beneath them, even when they built a network of underground tunnels as escape routes from the capital city.'

'Knowledge is power, inquisitor,' said Gabriel, quoting the motto of his Chapter with a wry smile. 'The Inquisition's secrets may have hobbled the people of this world.'

'If this Maledictum stone is as powerful as you say, inquisitor,' said Isador, his interest piqued, 'would it not exert some kind of effect on the people even whilst it is buried?'

'A good question, Librarian,' replied Mordecai. 'The ancient text in the *Registratum Malfeas* suggests that the daemon within the stone may be imprisoned, but it is not without power, particularly if its thirst for blood is satiated. It is possible that the stone could affect the affairs of Tartarus – it is certainly affecting them now.'

'And what about the eldar?' asked Gabriel, as he realised that the words of the eldar witch had proven true. 'Do they seek this power for themselves?'

'No, captain. It was they who imprisoned the daemon in the first place, placing it behind a complicated combination-lock. Their farseer entrapped the daemon in the stone, and buried it. She rigged the burial chamber with a psychic lock that could only be breached by the residual power that she imbibed into a ritual dagger, which she also buried. Even if someone were to recover the stone itself, it could only be awoken in a final ceremony performed on ground consecrated by the blood of a devoted population,' explained Mordecai, pausing as the expression on Gabriel's face changed.

'Inquisitor, the whole of Lloovre Marr is constructed on top of a giant reservoir of blood – just look down into that chasm. It appears that large sections of the population must have been cultists for some time – perhaps influenced by the power of the stone, or perhaps mutated by the sea of blood that seeps through their soil. Even their lho-sticks must be saturated with the resonances of blood and death,' responded Gabriel. 'It seems that it was not only the people of Tartarus who were ignorant about the events here, it seems that the Inquisition was also kept in the dark.'

'How do you know this story, inquisitor?' asked Isador, his scholarly scepticism making him suspicious. 'Did you learn it from the eldar?'

'No, Librarian,' answered Mordecai. 'The eldar have fiercely safeguarded all knowledge of the stone – even going so far as to interfere with our efforts to retrieve it. As Chaos's most ancient enemy, they see themselves as the only capable defence against its influence. And we are all paying for their arrogance now.'

'I'm not sure that you have answered my question,' persisted Isador, his years of training in the librarium showing. 'How do you know all this?'

'Because we were here, Librarian Akios,' said Mordecai, pausing to let the statement sink in. 'The Inquisition was here three thousand years ago, when many Chapters of the Space Marines were still young. An inquisitor of the Ordo Xenos led a Deathwatch recovery team to Tartarus, drawn by the presence of the eldar and a particular eldar artefact. This team saw the eldar farseer imprison the daemon with its own eyes.'

'And what was the Deathwatch team here to "recover"?' asked Gabriel, one eyebrow raised incredulously.

Mordecai sighed audibly, as though he had not been willing for the conversation to reach this point. His warhammer was still swinging rhythmically from one hand to another, but he broke the rhythm and hefted it into the air, brandishing it above his head in both hands. 'This,' he said. 'The Deathwatch team came for the materials needed to construct this warhammer – a daemonhammer. It was forged from a shard broken from the sword of the avatar of the Biel-Tan – the fabled Wailing Doom of Khaine himself. That was the very weapon with which the avatar slew the daemon prince on that dark night – and this is a daemonhammer unlike any other. It is the God-Splitter.'

'And the Inquisition stole part of this glorious weapon,' said Gabriel, shaking his head in disappointment. 'What a mess.'

'You still do not know it all, Captain Angelos of the Blood Ravens. That Deathwatch team was led by a certain Captain Trythos, also of the Blood Ravens – the first Blood Raven ever to serve a secondment with the Ordo Xenos,' said Mordecai, revealing more than he should have done, but enjoying this last fragment of power.

Gabriel shook his head. The great Trythos had been here before – was it here that he had been mortally wounded whilst on a Deathwatch mission, before his body was returned to the Third Company and enshrined in the sarcophagus of a blessed dread-nought? The same dreadnought that was destroyed by the eldar this very morning.

'Yes, Gabriel – Brother Trythos, Captain of the Blood Ravens' Third Company lies at the start of this affair – the hidden history of your own company is also embroiled in the history of Tartarus.'

'I assume that there is still time to avert the disaster,' said Gabriel, resolution fixing itself across his face.

'This is already a disaster, Gabriel. The power of the Maledictum has grown – it is enough to turn the faithful and drive men mad. Many of the local pop-ulation have already turned, as you have seen, but some of the Imperial Guard also teeter on the edge of a precipice. It is affecting you and your Marines too, I can feel it.

'It is calling to the warp storm, drawing it in to eclipse the system when dusk falls tomorrow. It wants to trap us here with it, so it can force even the best of us to serve its twisted will. This is why I encouraged you to leave... and why I still encourage it,' explained Mordecai, appealing to Gabriel to see sense at last.

'You should have revealed this to me at the start, Toth. It would have made matters easier, although it would not have changed my decision. You know that I cannot leave this planet as it is. I will not shrink away in the face of such evil,' said Gabriel, full of resolve.

'I would not have it any other way,' said Mordecai, slinging his warhammer over his shoulder and thumping his other hand down on Gabriel's shoulder guard. 'Let us end this bickering and face our enemy together. United, we have a better chance of thwarting the Alpha Legion's plans for the Maledictum.'

Returning the gesture, Gabriel slammed his palm down onto Mordecai's shoulder. But when they turned to Isador, the Librarian was already walking away, muttering to himself, whispering silently.

They are weak, Isador. Terrified of the power that you alone amongst them can understand. It is yours... yours for the taking... before the small-minded cowards destroy it... think of the good you could do in the name of your Emperor... think of the power you could wield in your Chapter...

Isador shook the voice out of his head. *It is mine...*

PART THREE

CHAPTER TWELVE

IN THE VERY centre of the Temple of Dannan, the dark corridors gave way to a majestic courtyard. It was bounded on each side by the arches of stone cloisters, decorated in the High Gothic style of the finest Imperial architecture. Intricate engravings scrolled across the arches, depicting scenes of glory and honour from the history of Tartarus and displaying the ritual iconography of the Imperial cult itself. Above the largest arch in the north wall was a magnificent icon, carved deeply into the pristine stone. It showed the image of the Golden Throne, ringed by the ineffable presence of the Astronomican, singing the Emperor's grace for all the galaxy to hear – sending out a beacon for the souls of the faithful, no matter where they might be.

But the icons were defaced and vandalised, sprayed with blood and chipped away by the clumsy strikes

of clubs, sticks and fists. Here and there, the stone
was riddled with pits and holes, as though it had
been struck by a barrage of gun shots from close
range. And, in the centre of the courtyard, the once
verdant and beautiful plants had been burnt to
ashes. In their place stood a ring of human cultists,
stripped to their waists, trembling with fear and
excitement. A series of grooves had been etched into
the flagstones, leading from their feet to a small, circular hole in the middle, like the radials of a wheel.
The hole dropped away from the temple, plunging
down into the great subterranean reservoir of blood,
hidden in the vaulted chamber under the city, like an
underground cathedral in its own right.

When Sindri had realised that the temple had been
built directly above the blood-chamber, he had
laughed – there are no coincidences on Tartarus. It
was as though the whole planet had been designed
with this ceremony as its goal.

The sorcerer paced around the ring of cultists, dragging the eldar's curved blade over their backs as they
winced and moaned, concentrating in towards the
hole in the centre of the circle. Thin trickles of blood
seeped out of the cuts in their backs, running down
their bodies and dripping into the blood grooves in
the stone floor. Gradually, the grooves began to fill
with red, and the lines pushed slowly towards the
hole, one droplet at a time.

As they bled, the cultists chanted and swayed to an
erratic, ugly rhythm, and Sindri stepped spasmodically, in time with the broken beat. The spell seemed
to inflate throughout the courtyard, spilling out of the
mouths of the cultists and pushing against the cloisters that surrounded them. A field of scintillating

energy was building gradually, as the chanting grew louder and the blood flowed thicker. The cultists were being bled in body and soul together.

Suddenly, Sindri stopped circling the group, halting behind one of the cultists. In an abrupt movement, the sorcerer lunged forward and grasped the woman's hair, pulling it violently back to expose her neck. Spinning the dagger in his other hand, he brought it smoothly across the cultist's throat, dropping her onto the ground as her life-blood gushed from the mortal wound. She fell forward, along the blood groove, spilling her blood into a river that flooded the channel and rushed towards the hole in the ground.

The other cultists continued to chant and sway, their eyes wild with fear and ecstasy as Sindri started to circle them once again. Guardsman Katrn watched the movements of Sindri with hungry eyes, imploring the sorcerer to give him the honour of being next, impatient to blend his blood with the thousands of other devotees whose essence had drained into the great reservoir over the decades and centuries. He chanted the spell with extra energy each time Sindri passed behind him, as he felt the cold slice of the curved blade cut into his back.

Katrn had already shed the blood of many Tartarans, fighting his way from Magna Bonum, but now it was time to give his own blood to the cause. His mind reeled with disbelief at the thought that so many of his brethren could still not see the truth of their origins; they were still blind to their place in the plans of the daemon prince; they still thought that war had to have a purpose – that shedding blood for the Blood God was not enough in itself. The fools.

Sindri stopped again, yanking back the head of another cultist and slitting his throat without ceremony, dumping the body forward into the circle with a casual push. The sorcerer was moving faster now, driven into a trance by the chanting, the motion, and the pungent scent of the fresh blood. The incandescent field around the courtyard was pulsing with energy, pressing against the stonework and splintering cracks into the Imperial icons.

Finally, the sorcerer stopped behind him, and Katrn's soul rejoiced as his head was pulled back, exposing his neck to Sindri's blade.

'Sindri!' bellowed a voice, shattering the discordant chant and making the energy field flicker.

Please, oh please cut me, begged Katrn in his mind. *Please.*

Sindri stayed his hand and snapped his head round to see who dared to intrude on the ceremony. 'What!' he hissed. 'What, my lord,' he added, struggling with the words.

'The Space Marines have breached the Dannan sector – they are on their way. Your cultists bought us almost no time at all,' said Bale, his voice full of disgust. He was growing sick of the sorcerer's plans collapsing into ruin just on the verge of their success.

Katrn felt the sorcerer release his head and withdraw the knife from his neck, snatching him back from the verge of glory. He cried out in frustration as Sindri walked round the circle towards the Chaos Lord, instructing the cultists to carry on chanting while he was away.

'The circumstances that you mention demonstrate divine providence, Lord Bale,' said Sindri, raising his arm and guiding Bale out of the courtyard. 'Everything is proceeding according to plan. Once I have completed the ceremony, you will have that which we have plotted and schemed to achieve.'

Bale looked at Sindri for a moment, suspicious of his choice of words. 'I do not trust you, sorcerer,' he said frankly. 'What will happen if the Blood Ravens should arrive before this "providence" graces us?'

'Providence has already graced us, my lord – if only you had the eyes to see it. When the Space Marines arrive, then we shall play the good hosts and indulge them in a bloody feast,' answered Sindri, risking a subtle slight. 'But at all costs, Lord Bale, you must keep them from interfering with the ceremony. This is a delicate process, and I cannot afford for it to be interrupted... again.'

Uncertain, Bale nodded and turned to walk away, leaving the sorcerer to do what needed to be done.

'And Bale,' called Sindri after him, using his unadorned name once again, 'might I advise that you throw everything at the cursed Blood Ravens. Everything. Their contribution to our project might prove most useful in the end, especially at this critical juncture.'

'Do not tell me how to fight Space Marines, sorcerer!' retorted Bale, stamping to a halt and looking back over his shoulder.

'My apologies,' said Sindri smoothly. 'I just thought that you would be pleased to finally get your chance to engage the Blood Ravens.'

Bale did not answer, but stormed back into the dark interior of the temple, leaving Sindri to turn back to the cultists in the courtyard. If the truth were known, he was pleased at the prospect of a proper fight at last.

Now, where was I, thought Sindri, as the rhythm of the chanting started to penetrate his soul once again? Ah yes… power demands sacrifice.

Katrn gasped with ecstasy as the sorcerer tugged back his head once again and drew the icy touch of the eldar blade across his throat. As the Guardsman slumped down into the blood groove at his feet, he could feel his life gushing out of him, pouring his soul into the fecund embrace of the Blood God himself.

ANOTHER THUNDERHAWK ROARED overhead as Inquisitor Toth's own vessel blasted into the air to return to the spaceport at Magna Bonum. All of the transports were required to help with the evacuation, but Colonel Brom had released a detachment of his Tartaran Guardsmen to assist the Blood Ravens, and a Thunderhawk was temporarily requisitioned to take them to Lloovre Marr.

The gunship did not even land, it just dropped down above the road and opened its hatch, tipping a couple of squadrons of Imperial Guardsmen out onto the flagstones. Then, with a roar of power, it eased back into the sky and flashed off into the night, heading back towards the evacuation point.

One of the Guardsmen rushed forward to greet Gabriel, stooping into a bow as he approached.

'Captain Angelos, I am Sergeant Ckrius of the Tartarus Planetary Defence Force,' said the young soldier proudly. His uniform was ripped and dirty, and his face was blackened by the smoky report of his weapon. But his sergeant's pips were sparkling and clean, as though he had just finished polishing them. He looked up into the face of Gabriel with fierce determination burning in his eyes. 'I bring two squadrons of storm troopers and the regards of Colonel Brom. He regrets that he cannot spare more.'

'Thank you sergeant, you are most welcome here,' replied Gabriel, nodding to the young Guardsman and wondering how bad things must be at the spaceport for such a youthful soldier to be put in charge of two entire squads. He studied the lad's face and saw how it must have aged over the last couple of days; he was not much more than a boy, but he had survived more than many men, and his sparkling eyes spoke of an undiminished resolve to save his homeworld.

For a moment, Gabriel saw himself in those eyes – he had once been a young Guardsman on Cyrene, before the Blood Trials, before the Blood Ravens had changed his life forever.

'Tell me sergeant, how fares the spaceport?' asked Gabriel.

'The orks have regrouped and are attacking in force, captain. Many civilians have been killed in the crossfire as they struggled to get into the spaceport, but we are holding out as best we can...' Ckrius trailed off, apparently unwilling to go on.

'Is there something else, sergeant?' asked Mordecai, overhearing the conversation and joining the group.

'Yes, there is something,' said Ckrius, puffing out his chest and steadying his voice. 'It seems that some of the Tartarans themselves have turned against the Emperor – a number of squadrons have deserted their positions, including an elite Armoured Fist squad.'

'They are cowards, then,' replied Gabriel, remembering the scene that greeted him when he first set foot on Tartarus.

'It is worse than that, captain,' confessed Ckrius, flinching at the insult on the honour of his regiment, but unable to deny it. 'The squads have not fled, they have turned their guns against us, and some even fight along side the orks.'

'It is as we feared, Gabriel,' said Mordecai, turning to face the Blood Raven. 'The Maledictum is working its dark magic on the people of Tartarus, twisting their wills against themselves. Their bodies were prepared by the taint in the soil itself, and now their souls are lost.'

'More and more turn every hour, captain. Before long, the spaceport will fall – the evacuation must be completed within the next few hours,' added Ckrius.

'It must be completed today in any case, sergeant,' responded Mordecai. 'The warp storm will be here before the day is out, and when it arrives, it is all over for anyone left on the surface.'

'Thank you, sergeant, for bringing us this news and for joining us at this troubled time,' said Gabriel, impressed by the resolve and strength of the young trooper. He bowed slightly to the sergeant in a rare sign of respect for a junior officer. 'Now, we have work to do.

'Sergeant, we are going to launch a two-pronged assault against the Alpha Legionaries in the Temple of Dannan. You and your storm troopers will assist Sergeant Tanthius and the Blood Ravens' Terminators – you will storm the temple doors from the front. You will be supported by a team of Devastator Marines – but most of the heavy weapons batteries are still on the other side of this chasm. The Whirlwinds may be able to provide some covering fire from there, but the other tanks will be of no use.

There is a ceremony being performed in the temple, and it is imperative that we do not allow it to reach completion – do you understand?' explained Gabriel quickly.

'Yes, captain. You may count on us to do our part,' replied Ckrius, saluting crisply, despite his fatigue and the grime that covered him.

'The rest of you,' continued Gabriel, turning to face Mordecai, Matiel and the remains of the Assault squad. 'The rest of you are with me.' He hesitated for a moment, looking for Isador. The Librarian was standing a little way off, talking to a small group of Marines. He nodded briskly to Gabriel as their eyes met, as though indicating some sort of understanding, and then he stalked off towards the temple with the Marines in tow.

A ROCKET ZINGED overhead, crashing into the steps of the temple and exploding into rains of shrapnel. Another fell short, drilling down into the flagstones in the square and excavating a large crater. The cultists who were collected outside the Temple of Dannan did not scatter – they stood their ground and were slaughtered in their dozens with each blast from the distant Whirlwind rocket launchers. In only a few moments, the rockcrete surface of the temple precinct was slick with blood and gore.

As the bombardment ceased, Tanthius stepped forward into the square, flanked on both sides by a short line of Marines with full Terminator honours. The Blood Ravens opened fire, punching a volley of hellfire shells through the square, shredding the cultists with splinters of toxicity.

This is too easy, thought Tanthius as his storm bolter spluttered in his hand. *Where are the Alpha Legionaries?*

The sound of breaking glass made him look up. Great sheets of stained glass were tumbling out of their frames in the upper levels of the temple. Huge monuments to the glory of the Emperor were being desecrated and shattered from within, as sleets of bolter fire flashed down through the early morning darkness. Tanthius could vaguely see the horned helmets of Alpha Legionaries moving in the shadows beyond the window frames.

Angling his bolter fire up towards the wrecked stained glass windows, Tanthius drew his power sword and lashed out with it into the throng of cultists, cutting through a swathe with ease. His brother Terminators echoed his movements, dragging their line of fire up the front of the temple and peppering the window cavities in the upper levels. Their secondary weapons continued to slice into the seething crowd of cultists – a plume of fire jetted out of a flamer on the arm of one, and the hum of power fists sizzled in the air as they pummelled anything that strayed too close.

Meanwhile, Sergeant Ckrius waved some quick signals to the storm troopers, who peeled into two squads. One knelt into a firing line and unleashed their hellguns, spraying a tirade into the throng of cultists at the side of the knot of Terminators. The relentless fire cut a sudden corridor into the crowd, and Ckrius stormed into it, his hellgun bucking with automatic fire as he sprinted towards the temple steps. Behind him came one of the storm trooper squads, pounding over the carpet of corpses, desperate to reach the other side of the square before the corridor closed in on them again.

Ckrius burst out of the crowd on the far side, diving up the steps of the temple and crashing his weight into the heavy doors. He rolled instantly, bringing his hellgun round to bear on the cultists once again. An instant later, and seven more storm troopers flew out of the crowd, launching themselves out of the reach of the grasping hands and turning to riddle them with bullets.

The eighth member of the squad nearly made it, but the corridor collapsed just before he broke through, and the cultists pressed in on him from both sides, swamping him under the sheer weight of numbers. For a moment, his head rose above the throng, thrown back in agony as the cultists bit and clawed into his flesh, trying to bleed him dry.

Without breaking his firing rhythm, Ckrius snapped his pistol from its holster and clicked off a single round, striking the storm trooper directly between the eyes and killing him instantly. The pistol was reholstered immediately, as Ckrius grasped his hellgun back into both hands for better control – he hoped that his men would do the same for him, when his time came.

With a command from Ckrius, the line of storm troopers on the temple steps focussed their fire into a single strip of the square, cutting another corridor in the crowd, leading right up to the feet of the storm troopers on the other side. As soon as the corridor opened, the troopers broke into a run, sprinting across the square with their hellguns blazing before them. Ckrius rose to his feet and braced his gun against his shoulder, picking off cultists one at a time as they threatened to obstruct the storming troopers – he was determined not to lose any more men so early in the day.

As the two squadrons were reunited on the temple steps, the cultists found themselves caught in the crossfire between the storm troopers and the Blood Ravens' Terminators. The whole precinct was instantly transformed into a giant killing zone, with bullets, bolter shells and flames flashing maniacally through the space from both sides. Every shot hit something, and in a matter of seconds the crowd had been reduced into a pummelled, broken and bloody pile of corpses.

Tanthius strode forward into the square, scanning the upper windows of the temple for signs of Chaos Marines, but he could see no movement. His feet squelched horribly as they trod through the gory mess on the ground, but he nodded an acknowledgment to Ckrius on the temple steps.

The clink of grenades hitting the flagstones sounded an ominous note in the morning air. Suddenly, explosions rocked the temple precinct and, with a crack the temple doors burst open – a volley of bolter fire punched out into the square, scattering the storm troopers and peppering the armour of the Terminators.

A phalanx of Alpha Legionaries stormed out of the temple, their guns blazing in all directions at once. Simultaneously, more stained-glass windows shattered and fire hailed down into the square from above.

THE SOUND OF combat outside echoed through the narrow passageway, shaking the stone blocks in the foundations of the temple. Gabriel crouched and rushed the last few steps, emerging into one of the antechambers in the interior of the temple. He snatched his bolter from one side to the other, but the room was empty. He whistled a signal, and the rest of his team stalked out of the service tunnel, immediately spreading out into a firing formation with their weapons primed.

Gabriel held a finger to his lips to silence the others as he strode towards the only doorway, his heavy boots clanking against the stone floors in blatant disregard for his own order. Outside the small stone chamber was one of the low, subsidiary aisles of the majestic nave, cast into deep shadow at this time of the morning. Beyond it, through a series of wide arches that ran the length of the temple, the grand, vaulted nave stretched off in both directions, leading to the main entrance on the left and the altar on the right.

The huge front doors were a frenzy of activity as Alpha Legionaries arrayed themselves around it in a tight firing arc. Others had already rushed outside, and Gabriel could see the report of their bolters in the darkness of the precinct. In the other direction, behind the altar and beyond the apse, a coruscating purple glow spilled into the temple from the cloistered courtyard in the heart of the temple. And high above, in the rafters and ramparts, Gabriel could see other Chaos Marines running to the front of the temple to find vantage points for the battle.

'Sergeant,' whispered Gabriel to Matiel, as he ducked back into the antechamber. 'Take the Assault squad into the shadows of the aisles and wait for my signal. You can provide support for Tanthius and

Sergeant Ckrius from there, catching the cursed Chaos Marines in your crossfire.'

Matiel did not answer, but he nodded briskly, flicking some silent hand signals to his squad. The Assault Marines dropped into crouching positions and darted out of the door, filing along the arched side-aisles, virtually invisible in the deep shadows. Finally, Matiel nodded again to Gabriel. 'May the Emperor guide your blade, Gabriel,' he said as he ducked out to join his squad.

'What about us, captain?' asked Mordecai, swinging his warhammer between his hands.

'We have a ceremony to interrupt,' hissed Gabriel, peering round the doorway and then dashing out into the nave towards the altar.

'SINDRI!' CALLED THE Chaos Lord as he burst into the courtyard, his eyes quickly scanning the scene of carnage. The sorcerer had gone, leaving a ring of dead cultists in the centre of the courtyard, lying in the blood grooves like spokes on a wheel.

'Sindri, you coward!' he bellowed, spinning to search the shadows in the cloisters around the edge of the courtyard. That vile sorcerer, thought Bale, his anger rising. His plans have failed and he has deserted me.

The Chaos Lord kicked his boot against the ribs of one of the sacrificial cultists. It made no noise, except for a moist squelch as a bubble of blood burst out of its slit throat under the sudden pressure.

'SINDRI!' roared Bale, thrusting his scythe into the air and spinning it in a vicious arc, smashing it down into the body of the cultist at his feet. The blade clanged and sparked against the flagstones as it hacked straight through the dehydrated human form. 'You will suffer for this,' he muttered under his breath.

'You will suffer first,' came a voice from behind him.

The Chaos Lord looked back over his shoulder, his scythe still buried in the distended flesh of Katrn. Stepping through the purple energy field that still enveloped the courtyard strode a Blood Ravens' captain, his chainsword drawn. Behind him came the figure of an inquisitor, wielding an ancient-looking warhammer with controlled malice.

Bale laughed, dragging his blade free of the corpse and spinning it round his head, sending a spray of blood splattering across the courtyard as he turned to face the intruders. He dropped into a low fighting stance, the blade of his manreaper scythe held above his shoulder as he shifted his weight onto his back foot. At last, he thought, an opponent worthy of a Chaos Lord of the Alpha Legion.

'Don't worry, we will deal with your sorcerer later,' added Gabriel, holding his chainsword vertically at his side in both hands, and pushing his left leg forward into a long combat stance.

'This one is mine,' he hissed to Mordecai, as he darted forward, lifting his chainsword above his head and driving it down towards the Chaos Lord. Mordecai hesitated, eager to assist but aware of the age-old rivalry between the Blood Ravens and the Alpha Legion – this was an honour duel, and he had no place in it. He switched his warhammer into one hand and retreated into the shadows of the cloisters. As he did so, something caught his eye on the other side of the courtyard – a figure in blue power armour had emerged from one of the transepts. He only saw it for a moment, before it sank back into the shadows. It looked like Isador.

The Chaos Lord was as quick as Gabriel, dropping his scythe into a vertical sweep and smashing his blow aside, lifting his front foot simultaneously and kicking it into the Blood Raven's chest. Gabriel staggered back under the blow, regaining his balance and repositioning his chainsword in a horizontal pose above his head, pointing at the Chaos Lord.

Letting his momentum turn his body, Bale spun his other leg in a low sweep towards Gabriel's front foot, bringing his scythe around at the same time. Gabriel lifted his foot just in time, stamping it down again on Bale's ankle, feeling the joint collapse under the force. Simultaneously, he dipped the point of his chainsword and swept it round to parry the scythe blade as it streaked towards his head.

The Chaos Lord let out a scream, part pain and part fury, as he tugged his broken leg back out of Gabriel's reach. 'Sindri!' he yelled. 'You will pay for this!'

No, I don't think so, Lord Bale, came the smooth tones of the sorcerer, slipping directly into Bale's mind. *I'm afraid that the ceremony failed to break the protective seal guarding the stone – I confess that I had expected that it would not work... yet. We need a larger sacrifice, my lord. We need more blood to fully consecrate the ground.*

All of a sudden, a series of explosions sounded from within the nave of the temple, and then the rattle of bolter fire erupted in their wake. Matiel and the Assault Marines had joined battle against the Alpha Legionaries.

'You have failed, sorcerer!' bellowed the Chaos Lord, bringing his scythe down for another attack. Unbalanced by his broken leg, the strike was more clumsy than the last, and Gabriel stepped comfortably inside it, pushing his chainsword into Bale's midsection.

No, my lord. Power demands sacrifice – and I thank you for yours.

The manreaper fell from Bale's grasp, clattering to the ground as he staggered back, gasping for breath. The morning sun had just crested above the cloisters, sending the first red rays of the day lancing into the courtyard, accompanied by the cacophony of battle in the nave and in the precinct outside.

'This is not the end, Blood Raven,' spat Bale as he slumped to the ground, sliding his weight along the grinding teeth of the chainsword and splashing blood into Gabriel's face. 'No, this dawn is the dawn of a new war...' His voice trailed off as the dark light faded from his eyes and his mouth fell open in a last gasp of horror.

Gabriel pulled his chainsword clear of the dead Chaos Lord, its spluttering teeth spitting droplets of blood and gore across the courtyard. The huge stomach wound was pouring with blood, rapidly forming a wide pool around the fallen Marine. But Gabriel noticed the danger too late, and the blood seeped its way into the blood grooves cut into the flagstones and started to race along towards the hole in the centre of the courtyard.

Intuitively, Gabriel sprinted for the cloisters, launching himself off his feet just as the stream of Bale's blood poured into the hole and cascaded down into the reservoir below like a waterfall. The purple energy field around the courtyard exploded in a brilliant flash of light, and the flagstones on the floor vaporised immediately, sending jets of steam fizzing into the sky. The corpses of the cultists slipped into freefall, tumbling down into the lake of blood below.

As the commotion died down, a pillar started to rise out of the subterranean lake, grinding up towards the gap where the courtyard had once been. It rumbled into place, like a peg filling a round hole, sealing the courtyard once again. The stone of the new floor was stained a deep red, from centuries of submersion beneath a sea of blood. In its centre was a small altar, pristine and white, as though untouched by the hideous taint of its surroundings. And on this altar rested a small gemstone, glowing red with unearthly powers, as though lit by the fires of hell itself.

Drawn by the ungodly noise, Matiel came storming into the cloisters from the nave, accompanied by two Assault Marines. They ran over to Gabriel and Mordecai, pushing the piles of debris and masonry off them and helping them to their feet.

'What happened, captain?' asked Matiel. But Gabriel was staring over the sergeant's shoulder into the courtyard beyond. There, on the other side, just emerged from the shadows of the cloisters, stood Isador. The Librarian appeared to be muttering to himself, staring at the ground, whispering and twitching his head, as though fighting with his own private daemons.

'Old friend,' called Gabriel, pushing Matiel gently aside and stepping out into the courtyard once again.

The Librarian stopped mumbling and raised his eyes, meeting those of Gabriel for a moment. Then, in a sudden movement, Isador raised his arm into the air, and the Maledictum stone flashed across the courtyard into his hand. Gabriel saw his friend's eyes switch from icy blue into a blaze of reds and golds, burning with hellfire. A crackling purple energy field erupted around Isador's armour, as the Librarian slowly lowered his arm, pointing it towards his oldest friend.

Gabriel dived to one side, drawing his bolter as he rolled. Flipping back onto his feet, the captain snatched off three shots. At the same time, shots echoed out from Matiel and Mordecai. The shells punched into Isador, staggering him and making him stumble backwards. But then the force field around him flared with even greater energy, and he pulled himself upright again.

By this time, Gabriel had broken into a run, charging towards his one-time friend, firing a stream of bullets. The shells pummelled into the field around Isador, but then a great explosion erupted under the impacts, throwing Gabriel off his feet and back towards the Blood Ravens in the cloisters.

When he stood up and looked back across the courtyard, Librarian Isador Akios had vanished.

CHAPTER THIRTEEN

THE VOICES ECHOED and rang, as though being chanted in the great vaulted spaces of an ancient cathedral. They were pristine and perfect, like points of silver starlight in the dead of the night, guiding travellers home and keeping them away from danger. And they soared, filling Gabriel's head with spirals of glittering faces as the choir of the Astronomican cycled through his mind, growing louder and louder as though drawing closer with every passing second.

And then the shift: the faces palled into mutation, their flesh running from their skulls as though melted by some immense heat, and their song was transformed into a cacophony of screams. But Gabriel was ready for his vision this time, and held his nerve, letting the abhorrent images spiral and swim, whirling into a cyclone of guilt and doubt. And there, gradually forming from the drips and tears of rendered flesh, swirling into focus in their core, there was the face of his friend. Isador stared back at him from his own consciousness, his face ripped and scarred, with tears of blood cascading down his cheeks.

A gentle pressure landed on his shoulder, and Gabriel flicked open his eyes. Chaplain Prathios stood before him, his hand resting firmly against Gabriel's armour, and his wise eyes staring down at the captain, filled with compassion.

'I am sorry, Gabriel,' said the Chaplain in barely audible tones.

'He was a finer man than I am, Prathios. A more powerful warrior, and a devoted servant of the Emperor,' confessed Gabriel, unable to hold the Chaplain's gaze for long.

'We all admired him, Gabriel,' replied Prathios simply, nodding his head towards the other Blood Ravens.

Kneeling in front of the ruins of the Emperor's altar in the Temple of Dannan, Gabriel looked back over his shoulder. Matiel and Tanthius bowed their heads, each kneeling at the front of their squads, filling the centre of the nave with two brilliant columns of crimson armour, each Marine perched reverently on one knee with their helmets on the ground next to them.

The battle for the temple had not outlasted the death of the Chaos Lord. The Alpha Legionaries in the nave had been rapidly overrun, attacked from the front by the Terminators and Ckrius's storm troopers, and from behind by Matiel's Assault Marines. In the end, it seemed that the Alpha Legion had left only a small force in the temple to defend their lord –

although Mordecai was certain that this was because the bulk of the Chaos Marines had left with the sorcerer, slipping out of the temple through one of the many subterranean tunnels.

Gabriel rose to his feet and turned to face the assembly. Hidden in the shadows of the side aisles, he could see Sergeant Ckrius and his storm troopers – each standing to attention, but with their heads bowed, helmets tucked under their arms. And standing on his own in the opposite aisle was Mordecai, his warhammer slung casually over his shoulder, leaning back against the wall. He was an inquisitor, after all, reflected Gabriel, and not prone to feelings of regret or forgiveness.

'I knew Librarian Akios from the first moments that I donned the sacred armour of the Blood Ravens,' said Gabriel, addressing his men as though his old friend had died in the service of the Emperor. In a manner of speaking, he had died. If only he had died, thought Gabriel. The faces of the assembled Marines looked up to him, waiting for his words. 'I knew him before then – as young warriors on the planet of Cyrene. He was a greater soldier than I ever was, and a wiser man. I have seen the powers of Librarians many times over the long decades of my service, but never have I seen a Blood Raven wield the kind of raw power, ability and will that was possessed by Isador. He saved my life many times, and was a guardian of my soul. He will be missed... I will miss him,' said Gabriel, his voice drifting off as his emotions caught up with him.

'But the Emperor's justice is even – none may escape it. The Adeptus Astartes carry the wrath of the Emperor to all parts of the galaxy, visiting his righteous retribution against all those who turn against him. There can be no exceptions. Not even for a servant as loyal and devoted as Librarian Akios,' and not even for the innocent souls hidden in the midst of a cursed planet, added Gabriel in his mind. 'The Blood Ravens prove their worth only in the face of the enemy, and even more so when this enemy is close to our hearts. Isador, my friend, is dead – and I vow here and now to liberate his body to this realisation.'

Throughout the temple, the Blood Ravens touched their right fists to the flagstones, and Gabriel nodded to them in silence. 'The battle to come will test us all,' he continued, 'and many of us will fall. But we will fall with our blood pure and our souls in the hands of the Emperor. We will die in glory, as the saviours of the burning remains of Tartarus, and as the van-quishers of the cursed Alpha Legion. We will die, but we will kill – and we kill for one reason, and for that reason alone: because we are right.'

There was no cheer from the Blood Ravens, no rousing cries to bring their souls to a frenzy. Rather, the Marines lifted their fists from the ground in silence, clasping them into their other hands, and offering them forward to Gabriel. Without exception, each Blood Raven bowed his head and offered his oath to his captain, vowing to follow him into the very gates of hell – for that was where they were going.

'WHERE TO NEXT, inquisitor?' asked Gabriel, striding down the steps outside the temple, side by side with Mordecai. 'Isador was our best guide to the riddles of this planet. And we have wasted enough time on riddles

– so be frank with me, Mordecai,' he continued, using the inquisitor's personal name for the first time, 'do you know where the Chaos Marines have gone?'

'The battle fought between the eldar and the forces of Chaos three thousand years ago took place on the summit of the twin-peaked mountain. It is not far from here – just a few kilometres to the north,' replied Mordecai. 'But I cannot guarantee that the Alpha Legion will be there, Gabriel. I know nothing of this "Sindri" of whom the Chaos Lord spoke, and… and I do not know how much your Librarian understood.' The inquisitor chose his words carefully, in an uncharacteristic display of compassion towards the Blood Ravens' captain.

'Sindri is not my concern, Isador is. He has fallen… and he will find my blade waiting for him as he hits the ground… You may trust that he understands more than enough, inquisitor – he was a Blood Ravens' Librarian, and well schooled in the arts of the scholar.'

'Then we should head for the mountain,' responded Mordecai, hesitating before going on, unsure how to phrase his thoughts. 'Gabriel – you must understand now the weight of my original concerns here on Tartarus. I am sorry for your Librarian, but his loss is a potent symbol of the power of the Maledictum. I must admit… I was surprised that it was Isador who succumbed.'

'I know, Mordecai,' said Gabriel in a conciliatory tone. 'You suspected me… You were not alone, inquisitor. For a while, I also doubted myself,' continued Gabriel, wincing slightly at the thought of the visions that had plagued him since his arrival on Tartarus.

'It takes either steel or rot to willingly condemn your own homeworld, captain. You must understand my concerns – even a captain of the Adeptus Astartes has a breaking point, and putting your home and family to the torch could have been it. I sensed the burgeoning seed of Chaos in the midst of your company, and you seemed all too eager to shed more blood on Tartarus,' explained Mordecai, relieved to finally make his confession to the Blood Raven. 'I was so certain, in fact, that I failed to notice its true source in the Librarian. I… I was wrong, captain.'

Gabriel nodded simply; he was unsurprised by the inquisitor's revelations. Despite the fact that he could see the way that Mordecai was trying to be compassionate, Gabriel had more important things on his mind than the conscience of this inquisitor.

'We will discuss the matter another time, Mordecai. For now, we have an enemy that demands our ministrations,' said Gabriel as the two men reached the great chasm around the Dannan sector once again. The far side was a blaze of crimson armour, as the rest of the Blood Ravens from throughout the city had made their way to this point. Cut off from their captain after the battles with the eldar and hearing the roar of battle around the temple, the Marines had already rebuilt the bridge over the ravine. Now they stood waiting for the return of their captain, with their armour gleaming, and the turrets of their tanks raised in salute.

Gabriel and Mordecai strode over the bridge, with Tanthius and Matiel leading their squads behind them. Alongside the Blood Ravens marched Sergeant Ckrius and his storm troopers, proudly receiving the honour of the Space Marines as they joined the assembled force on the far bank. As they strode across the bridge, the towering Terminator armour of Tanthius leant down towards Ckrius, placing an immense gauntlet on the sergeant's human shoulders. 'You fought well, Ckrius. I will ensure that the captain is not ignorant of that.'

THE SUN WAS nearly at its apex, piercing between the clouds that always gathered around the high summit of the twin-peaked mountain. Isador clambered up the steep pass, cresting a rocky rise as he broke through the cloud line. For the first time he saw the ruins of the ancient mountain-city, now barely more than rubble. The city had been destroyed long ago, and the people of Tartarus had never bothered to rebuild it. They were not fond of high places, and, in any case, the sides of the mountain were barren and infertile – Lloovre Marr himself had instructed that the cities should be built down in the fecund valleys, on the alluvial plains.

Climbing onto the remains of the old city wall, Isador turned and looked back down the mountain. A few kilometres away, on the rim of the great valley, wherein nestled the city of Lloovre Marr, a cloud of dust barrelled towards the foot of the mountain. As the sun beat down on the movement, Isador could see glints of crimson sparkling through the dust, and he knew immediately that the Blood Ravens were on their way.

Are you looking for me? The familiar whispering voice eased into his head and made him turn away from the vista, turning to look down into the ruins of the old city itself. In the midst of the moss-enshrouded rubble, his dual-pronged staff held

vertically in one hand, stood the acid-green figure
of a Chaos sorcerer. His bladed helmet glinted in
the midday sun, and his visor glowed with a deep
red.

Sindri, whispered Isador, returning the voiceless
conversation. *You are a difficult person to find.*

I have been waiting, not hiding, Librarian, slithered
the thoughts of the sorcerer, as Isador leapt down
from the wall, crunching the uneven ground under
his boots.

'You allowed me to take this stone,' said Isador,
producing the Maledictum and holding it out in
front of him. 'You were true to your word – which
makes you a fool.'

'It remains to be seen whether you will be true to
yours,' replied Sindri, holding out his hand, as
though expecting the Blood Raven to surrender the
stone voluntarily. 'Will you use it to slay me, as you
promised… or will you simply hand it over, like a
good little puppet.'

'I think that I will keep the stone with me, sorcerer.
You are too weak to stomach its gifts, otherwise you
would have taken it yourself,' said Isador, pacing in a
circle around Sindri at a careful distance. 'And now, I
will keep my promise – to you and to the Emperor.
Now, I will destroy you and end your delusional
scheme here on Tartarus.'

Isador took another couple of strides, prowling
around his victim. Stopping abruptly, Isador set his
back foot into the ground and pushed off towards
Sindri, the Maledictum held clasped against his staff,
pushed out like a lance in front of him. As he dived
forward, his force staff burst into life, a field of coruscating energy erupting along its length.

The Chaos sorcerer turned to face the thrust, but made no attempt to evade it. Instead, he held out one gauntleted finger and a tiny thread of purple jetted out of it, striking the Maledictum. With a sudden flare of warp energy, the stone burst into life, magnifying the power of Isador's staff immeasurably, and surrounding the Librarian in a crackling, pulsing field of purple light.

As he lunged towards the sorcerer, Isador felt his feet lift off the ground, but he pushed on, focussing his will and driving forward with sheer determination. But his lunge was never completed. The field of warp energy stopped him in his tracks and lifted him into the air, suspended on a thin thread of power that flowed out of Sindri's forefinger.

A flood of whispers and slices of pain cut into Isador's mind, taunting him and attacking the very fabric of his soul. His body spasmed, racked with agony as the daemonic force of the Maledictum fought against his grip. Chaotic voices cried into his ears, and his body went suddenly rigid, as though shot through with electricity. Then his force staff erupted into flames, burning his hands until the flesh in his gauntlets started to blister and melt. With a sudden explosion, the staff shattered, spraying fragments and shards of the ancient weapon into Isador's face and lacerating his skin.

As suddenly as it had begun, it ended, and Isador collapsed to the ground, broken and bleeding, the Maledictum glowing faintly in his ruined hands.

'Lord Bale was likewise foolish in believing that I was defenceless, Librarian. He also thought that he was in control of his own destiny. Like you, he was wrong,' said Sindri, peering down into the face of

Isador with mock concern as the stone flared again and the Librarian writhed in agony.

'The orks also thought rather more of their own abilities than of mine. And their simple arrogance was very useful to me,' continued Sindri, apparently compelled to share the details of his machinations with his fallen adversary. 'And now it seems that even the great Blood Ravens have played their part, exactly as planned.'

The stone pulsed again, and Isador cried out as its energies riddled his body with pain. He looked up at Sindri and spat. 'You have not seen the last of the Blood Ravens, sorcerer. I am their worst, not their best.'

'Ah, such humility, Librarian,' replied Sindri, his voice dripping with sarcasm. 'I think that you hold much promise – much promise, indeed. And for that I should kill you, in case your abilities prove too great a threat to my plans – your honoured battle-brothers are far too narrow-minded to appreciate them.'

With a slow gesture, Sindri pushed his hand down towards the fallen Librarian, his fist crackling with energy, and Isador braced himself for the death blow. But it never came. Instead, the Maledictum flashed out of his grasp and darted up into the outstretched hand of the sorcerer. Isador slumped back against the ground as the agony left his body.

'But I have already invested so much in you. And, to be honest, even if you had a century to prepare, you would still be too late to prevent me from achieving my glory tonight. Now, I must see to my own preparations, and you… you must attend to your dear captain's demise, if you are capable,' said Sindri, taunting the broken Librarian.

'I will not serve you, sorcerer,' moaned Isador, hardly able to move.

'It does not matter what you want to do, Librarian – you have already ensured that the valiant Captain Angelos will hunt you down. You will either kill him, or you will die. The choice is yours, but it is not much of choice, is it…' said Sindri, turning away from the crumpled figure of Isador and striding away into the ruined city.

As he disappeared behind the remains of a stone building, his thoughts washed back into Isador's mind: *You have already served me, Librarian – I forgot to thank you for delivering the Maledictum.*

IN THE DISTANCE a bolt of lightning flashed out of the sky, striking the forest off to the east of the huge mountain. A brood of dark clouds was gathering on the horizon, and distant thunder rumbled with foreboding. The landscape was cast into two, with half lit under the brilliant afternoon sun and the other half shrouded in the advancing shadow of the storm.

The faint rattle of gunfire and the distant, erratic thud of explosives sent little shockwaves pulsing down the mountain side, but Gabriel could not yet see the site of the battle, as he stood atop the leading Rhino in the column of Blood Ravens.

As the convoy roared up the mountain, grinding over the barren, rocky terrain, Gabriel started to see signs that combat had been joined along that route. It started with the broken body of an Alpha Legionary, riddled with holes and his back broken as he lay slumped backwards over a large boulder. But then, as they made their way higher up the slope, there were more bodies. Not only the shattered, bulky forms of Alpha Legionaries, but also the hacked and mutilated bodies of the graceful eldar. Gabriel took all of this as a sign that he was on the right track. More worrying, however, was the occasional bloodied body of an Imperial Guardsman, perforated by shuriken fire.

'It looks like we are the last to join the party,' said Gabriel, his face taut against the wind as the Rhino rushed up the mountainside.

'No, captain,' replied Mordecai, his mouth cracking into a smile for the first time. 'The party can't start without us.'

Gabriel laughed weakly, straining his eyes against the wind, trying to distinguish individual shapes amongst the flashes and confusion at the summit of the mountain. But they were still too far away, not even the Space Marine's enhanced ocular system could resolve the images. He stamped down on the roof of the Rhino, willing the machine to move faster.

Behind him, the full force of the Third Company was arrayed in a glorious convoy. He had lost too many Marines on Tartarus already, but this was the moment for which they had all fought and died. The remnants of the Assault Bike squadrons bounced along the flanks of the column, and the remaining tanks rumbled along in the middle, interspersed with Rhinos. On either side of Gabriel's Rhino skimmed the Typhoons, and immediately behind came the Razorback, which contained Tanthius's surviving Terminators. Standing on the roof was Tanthius himself and, dwarfed by the immense size of the Blood Raven, Sergeant Ckrius rode along side him – his storm troopers having been loaded into the spaces left by fallen Marines in the various Rhinos.

'Sergeant Ckrius is a fine soldier,' said Mordecai, flicking his head back towards the Razorback.

'Yes, Tanthius has spoken highly of him,' replied Gabriel without looking round. 'But look at his brethren,' he added, casting an arm out to indicate the bodies of the Guardsmen on the mountainside. 'They are cowards and traitors, tainted by Chaos.'

'There are some pure souls on Tartarus, Gabriel,' countered Mordecai. 'Not all of them have succumbed. It is a testament to his character that he has remained so resolute.'

'Perhaps,' said Gabriel, 'but we are not here to recruit new Marines, inquisitor.'

'So many have fallen, captain. You must look to the future – not even the mighty Blood Ravens live forever,' said Mordecai, hesitating as he wondered whether he was overstepping the mark. 'Even Cyrene had some souls worth saving,' he added, aware of the ambiguity of his words.

'And yet we saved none – and some who survived have betrayed the memory of those who should have been saved,' responded Gabriel bitterly, snapping his head round to face Mordecai, his eyes burning with a confusion of pain – Cyrene, Tartarus, and Isador spiralled through his mind. 'I know nothing of the soul of this Ckrius – how can I know that he will not crack under the responsibilities of a Blood Raven?'

'You cannot know, captain. You must have faith,' said Mordecai gently. 'Just as Chaplain Prathios once showed such faith in you.'

Gabriel looked off into the distance, watching the storm gathering on the horizon. Then he nodded, reaching a decision. 'Very well, inquisitor – you are right. If the young sergeant survives this day, he will

take the Blood Trials. The loss of Isador warrants a
new birth in the Blood Ravens.'

A scout bike came bouncing down the mountainside towards the convoy, followed by two more bikes,
struggling to keep pace with their speeding sergeant.
The lead biker hit the brakes as he drew along side
the Rhino and slid his back wheel round 180
degrees, spinning it in the dust as he drew level with
Gabriel. The sergeant tugged at his helmet, casting it
aside, and Gabriel smiled broadly, dropping onto
one knee to talk to the veteran sergeant.

'Corallis! It is good to see you, old friend,' called
Gabriel through the wind.

'Thank you, captain,' he answered, waving his new
arm for his friend to see. 'The Apothecaries on the
Litany of Fury patched me up and packed me off
again – it is good to be back, Gabriel.'

Gabriel just nodded, this was not the time for
reunions, and Corallis knew that he was pleased to
have him back. 'What news?' he said, indicating the
area of the mountain from whence Corallis had
come.

'A ruined city lies around to the west. It appears
deserted. To the east there is a mob of orks lumbering towards the summit. On the summit are the
Alpha Legion and a few eldar – the aliens are badly
outgunned, captain. Their numbers are small,'
reported Corallis.

'Lend me your bike, sergeant,' said Gabriel, reaching his hand down to clasp that of Corallis. 'I have a
feeling that destiny is calling me from that old city –
and I don't want to keep it waiting.'

In a smooth movement, Gabriel lifted Corallis off
the bike and leapt down onto it, taking the sergeant's

place before the bike unbalanced. From the top of the Rhino, Corallis looked down at his captain: 'I hope that you find him, Gabriel.'

'He will be waiting, I know it… Keep the Blood Ravens on course – I will see you on the summit,' said Gabriel, revving the bike's engine into a great growl and spinning the back wheel as he peeled away from the convoy and roared off to the west.

A CLOUD OF dust kicked up off the ground as Gabriel slid the rear of his bike round, bring it parallel to the ruins of the old city wall and killing the engine. He stood onto the bike and then vaulted up onto the crumbling wall. On the other side was a small clearing, strewn with rubble and cracked masonry, some of it overgrown with moss and creeping plants. Once, it must have been a courtyard or a marketplace, but now it was just a mess of stone fragments and wreckage.

On the far side of the clearing, between two ruined buildings, stood the blue-armoured figure of a Space Marine. His back was turned and his arms were outstretched to the sides, his palms pressed against the walls as though he were holding them up.

Gabriel saw Isador at once and stood for a moment, motionless on the top of the city walls, staring at the back of this old friend. He had never thought that it would come to this, and his soul rebelled against the very ethical imperative that gave his life direction – perhaps Isador could be an exception?

No exceptions, Gabriel, came the voice of Isador, slipping into Gabriel's mind as though whispered lovingly in his ear.

The Blood Ravens' captain vaulted off the wall and crunched down into the old marketplace, landing with one knee touched to the ground and his fist driven into the flagstones, while his other hand rested on the hilt of his chainsword.

'No exceptions, old friend,' said Gabriel in a whisper that Isador could not have heard.

As Gabriel rose to his feet, his hand still poised over the hilt on his chainsword, Isador's feet lifted off the ground. The Librarian rose about a metre off the flagstones, with his arms still stretched out by his sides, and then he started to revolve slowly. After a few seconds, his body faced directly towards Gabriel, but his head was bowed to the floor, hiding his face in shadows.

You are a fool, Gabriel, came Isador's thoughts. *You were always short-sighted – your mind closed to the very powers that could make you great. I have seen you struggling with yourself. Why struggle, when the power is there just waiting to be released?*

'Because it is wrong, Isador. Because there are some things more important than power,' said Gabriel, stalking slowly towards the levitating figure.

There was no movement from Isador – he just seemed to hang in the air, as though suspended on an invisible cross. *You are wrong, old friend. There is nothing more important than power: how ridiculous that you, a Space Marine, can still believe that power is not the goal of all our efforts. We crave it – and without it we would be nothing more than primitives. Without it, Cyrene would still be a seething pool of mutation and heresy. Power makes us right, Gabriel. And you are wrong – for you and your faith are no match for me.*

'Of all my brothers, why you? You, out of all of us, you were always the strongest,' said Gabriel, taking another cautious step towards the Librarian, his voice rich with emotion.

That is why, foolish Gabriel. That is why. Can you imagine being forced to serve the weak and the fumbling? Could you be commanded by that nauseating wretch Brom? Strength should command, not some pathetic notion of justice. The thoughts were bitter and dripping with venom, making Gabriel's mind recoil.

'You are not yourself, old friend. I have heard these words before – the cursed Warmaster Horus said as much to the Emperor himself as he unleashed bloody civil war on the galaxy. These sentiments would have found no place in the heart of Isador Akios, Librarian of the Blood Ravens,' said Gabriel, reaching his hand to his head in a reflex response to the pain. 'These are not the words of my friend.'

A crack of lightning arced across the sky and thunder crashed as the storm drew closer to the mountain. Isador finally raised his face from the ground and stared at Gabriel, his eyes ablaze with red and golden flames, and his face a ruined mess of cuts, scars and streams of blood. *Then I am not your friend.*

The words wracked Gabriel with pain, and he slumped to the ground clutching his head. *Isador was weak-willed, but his body is strong. He resisted a little, but I broke him easily. This form will be enough to smite you, captain – an entertainment while I await the coming storm.*

The voice in his head had lost its aura of Isador; it hissed and cackled, burning Gabriel's mind and licking at it with blades, slicing at his soul to the point of submission. Gabriel writhed on the ground, his body spasming as his mind played cruel tricks on his nervous system.

I am stronger than you could ever imagine – the daemons and the gods tremble before me, fearing my wrath, fearing my power, fearing the coming of the storm.

Gabriel staggered back to his feet, swaying uneasily and gripping his head in the gauntlet of one hand.

This could have been you, Gabriel. You showed such promise on Cyrene – slaughtering the innocent with the guilty in one stroke. Such power. Such glory. There was a part of you that thrilled when you ordered the strikes, I know it. Part of you thrilled when you betrayed your own people – because you had the power to do it.

Roaring with the release of pent-up rage, Gabriel lurched forward towards the husk of Isador. 'I betrayed no one!' he cried as his chainsword flashed from its scabbard, spun once in the air, and then plunged deeply into the Librarian's chest. 'Not even you, Isador.'

The fires in his eyes flared suddenly and his mouth fell open in shock, then Isador fell out of the sky and collapsed to the ground. Immediately, the daemonic whisperings in Gabriel's head subsided, and he could hear the faint chorus of the Astonomican echoing around his soul once again, giving direction to his faith.

'Innocents die so that humanity may live, Isador,' said Gabriel, pulling his blade out of his friend's primary heart, 'not because we prove our power by killing them. I ended their suffering and saved their souls – and I will do the same for you... not because I can, but because I must.'

The Librarian's eyes flickered back into blue, and he gazed up at his old friend with his own eyes for the last time. 'I was wrong, Gabriel,' he coughed, trails of blood seeping out of the corner of his mouth. 'I thought that I was strong enough to control it. I thought that I could use its power for the good of the Imperium… you must see that.'

'I believe you, old friend,' said Gabriel, smiling faintly as he saw the familiar light return to Isador's eyes. It flickered weakly, on the point of extinction. 'That is why I bring you redemption myself.'

Gabriel dropped his chainsword to the ground and drew his bolt pistol. He knelt for a moment at the side of the dying Librarian, and reached out his gauntleted hand, grasping Isador's wrist firmly. 'Goodbye, Isador. May the Emperor shelter your soul from the storm.'

Standing slowly, Gabriel fired a single shot from his bolter and turned away. He strode to the ruined city wall without looking back, and vaulted over it, landing smoothly onto his bike on the other side. Kicking the bike's engine into life, Gabriel spun the rear wheel and left the old city in the dust.

CHAPTER FOURTEEN

THE CONVOY OF Blood Ravens had ground to a halt several hundred metres short of the summit. The storm had finally reached the mountain, and great sheets of lightning tore into the mountainside, forming a ring of warp energy and fire around the twin peaks. The mountain itself had cracked open along the line of the barrage from the storm, and the dual summits had been torn into the air, floating like impossible islands of rock in the tumult of energised rain. An archipelago of islets, blasted free of the mountain top, were held in impossible suspension all around them.

Through the purpling curtain of warp lightning, Inquisitor Toth could make out dozens of figures on the two islands, and constant flashes of gunfire. Right on the point of the highest peak, Mordecai could see the silhouette of a Chaos sorcerer in a bladed helmet,

his arms held up into the storm as though calling it
to him. In his hands burned two red flames.

The storm washed down the mountainside, rippling out from the sorcerer's peak and hurling lashes
of hail and spikes of lightning through the gale-force
winds. The tumult roared through the ring of warp
energy and beat against the Blood Ravens as they
waited for the order to advance on the summit.
Mordecai and Corallis stood atop the lead Rhino,
surveying the unnatural scene as the lashes of
another realm streamed into their faces. Against the
roar of the wind, they could not even hear each other
speak.

Corallis stared into the firestorm, his enhanced
vision able to pick out individual figures in the kalei-
doscope. He narrowed his eyes in disgust as he
recognised the shapes of a number of Imperial
Guardsmen in the fray, fighting alongside the hulking figures of the Alpha Legionaries. On the second
island-summit, lower than the one on which Sindri
stood calling to the storm, stood an eldar farseer, her
arms upheld to the heavens as though entreating the
gods for assistance. Around her was a small, dwindling group of eldar warriors and wraithguard. They
were completely outnumbered and outgunned, but
they fought with incredible desperation, discipline
and grace, as though their very souls depended on it.

Dropping his eyes from the scene, Corallis shook
his head – he had never seen a battlefield like it
before. It was as though the forces of nature themselves were at war, and the various races of the galaxy
were simply caught in the fray. He looked along the
line of the sheet of coruscating energy that stood
between the Blood Ravens and the theatre of battle,

and saw that the border was strewn with corpses – some human, some eldar, and some hidden in the huge suits of armour of the Alpha Legion. They had clearly fought all the way up the mountainside.

He turned to look back down the mountain, over the heads of the Blood Ravens and Imperial storm troopers that had spilled out of their transports, realising that the only way onwards would be on foot. Even in the gathering darkness shed by the black clouds of the warp storm, Corallis could see how the route was speckled with death and doused with blood. He did not pretend to understand what was unfolding here, but he knew that it had to be stopped.

Cresting a rise to the west, Corallis saw a burst of red in a cloud of dust. Flashes of lightning reflected brilliantly off the speeding form, making it flash like a beacon. The sergeant gripped Mordecai's shoulder and spun the inquisitor round so that he could see, nodding his head towards the approaching rider. Mordecai squinted his eyes against the wind and rain, but then a crack of lightning lit the mountainside and Gabriel's assault bike shone in the sudden light as he roared across the slope towards the Blood Ravens.

Mordecai nodded firmly to Corallis, but the sergeant was still staring out across the mountain. There was something else over there. As Gabriel drew closer, a great cloud of dust began to emerge over the rise behind him. After a couple of seconds, the cloud of dust turned into a line of ork warbikes, bouncing and roaring in pursuit of the captain. And in the wake of the warbikes came a clutch of wartrukks, battlewagons and the rumbling forms of looted Imperial Chimera transports.

'Orks!' yelled Corallis into his armour's vox unit. 'Orks approaching from the west.'

Mordecai snapped his head back towards the speeding figure of Gabriel, who was already within range of the small vox units built into Blood Ravens' armour. The ramshackle line of orks behind him was clearly in view now.

'Ordnance!' came the crackling voice of Gabriel, as his bike bumped and skidded over the increasingly wet ground.

The turrets of the Predators and Whirlwinds rotated smoothly to the west, and a flurry, of fire erupted from the tanks in the Blood Ravens' convoy, their shells flashing through the air over Gabriel's head. A series of explosions detonated on the mountainside as the rockets and shells punched into the ork line, toppling a gaggle of warbikes and dropping a battlewagon into a sudden crater.

At the same time, Tanthius's Razorback streaked through the driving hail towards the orks, passing Gabriel's bike on its way. Behind it growled one of the Rhinos being used by the storm troopers. Tanthius and Ckrius, standing against the elements on the roof of the Razorback, snapped a crisp salute to Gabriel as they roared past, the vehicle's gun turret lancing parallel streams from its twin-lascannons as it went.

As he reached the rest of the Blood Ravens, Gabriel hit the brakes hard, skidding the bike over the sodden ground and stopping perilously close to the lead Rhino. He vaulted from the bike, straight up onto the roof of the transport, greeting Corallis and Mordecai with abrupt nods.

'We cannot approach the summits, captain,' explained Corallis through the vox-channel. 'The storm hobbles the systems in our vehicles, and… well, the mountain top is unsound, as you can see.'

Gabriel stared forward into the curtain of warp energy for the first time, his mind racing with questions that had no answers. The scene on the other side was simply impossible – with islands of rock floating amidst floods of fire, wracked with bolts of purple lightning and lashed by torrents of rain and hail. The Alpha Legionaries and a knot of damned Imperial Guardsmen were assaulting a sub-summit, held by the eldar witch that had saved Gabriel's life in Lloovre Marr. She was a blaze of blue fire, but her forces were dwindling. And there was Sindri, standing on his own on the top of the highest island, calling to the daemons of the warp, the Maledictum in one hand and the curved dagger in the other.

'We have little time left, Gabriel. The sorcerer must have released the daemon,' said Mordecai, clearly relieved that Gabriel had returned to lead the Space Marines.

'Our course is clear,' said Gabriel resolutely, making his decision instantly. 'We must destroy this Chaos sorcerer and his lackeys… and we must attend to the daemon before it is too late – it will not find our souls as weak as it has those of others,' he added, Isador's face flickering behind his eyes.

'What about the eldar, captain?' asked Corallis, unsure about how to approach the aliens.

'This is a desperate hour, sergeant, and the eldar risk their already meagre forces to confront the evil on Tartarus. They are our allies, at least for today,' replied Gabriel with only a hint of hesitation, speaking such heretical words in front of an inquisitor of the Emperor. But Mordecai simply nodded his agreement, and Corallis leapt down from the Rhino to disseminate the orders.

THE RAZORBACK ROARED through the hail, its lascannons slicing into the greenskins and cutting them down in swathes. Splutters of gunfire rattled back at the charging transports, pinging off their thick armour and grinding gashes out of their bodywork. But the Razorback showed no signs of slowing as it powered onwards, heading directly for the biggest wartrukk in the ork line, pulsing javelins of las-fire into its front armour.

Gretchin and slugga boyz scattered out of its path as the Razorback drove through the vanguard of the ork force, flattening a warbike as it fell under the heavy tracks of the huge vehicle, making the transport bounce and swerve.

'Brace for impact!' yelled Tanthius from the vehicle's roof, preparing the Terminators within for the collision. Sergeant Ckrius linked his arm around a brace in the gun turret just in time; the Razorback crashed straight into the front of the rumbling wartrukk.

The impact sent Tanthius flying over the wreckage of both vehicles. He reached out his arms in front of him and let the powerful servos in his armour absorb his weight as he struck the ground on the other side. His momentum pushed him into a roll, and he was quickly back on his feet, unleashing the might of his storm bolter into the backs of the orks on the wrecked wartrukk.

Ckrius quickly unhooked himself from the Razorback and dashed to the edge of the roof, drawing the officer's sword that he had salvaged from a battlefield corpse as he saw a huge greenskin slam its choppa into the side hatch. Only a couple of days earlier, Ckrius would have had no idea what to do, and would certainly never have dreamt of leaping off a roof onto the back of an enormous, massively muscled green alien. But today he was a seasoned ork-killer. Holding his blade firmly in his right hand, he dropped off the Razorback directly down onto the creature's back, driving his sword cleanly between the beast's collarbone and its shoulder blade, letting his fall push the blade in right up to its hilt. The ork hardly even had time to shriek before the blade pierced straight down through its heart, killing it instantly.

The side hatch of the Razorback burst open and a Marine in Terminator armour sprang out with a massive thunder hammer swinging around its head. The Marine stopped suddenly at the sight of the little human soldier tugging his brittle sword out of the greenskin's shoulder. Then he nodded to Ckrius and leapt forward into the crowd of orks that were pressing towards the wreck, his hammer sweeping in lethal arcs. Three more Terminators stormed out of the Razorback in his wake, each stealing a surprised glance at the solitary storm trooper blasting away with his hellgun, before they opened up with their storm bolters and flamers.

Disciplined volleys of fire riddled the greenskins that charged towards Ckrius, and he flicked a glance to his right. Pounding across the slick battlefield towards their sergeant came the rest of the storm troopers, leaving a couple of Marines to support the heavy guns of the Rhino from which they had spilled.

* * *

BOLTER SHELLS FLASHED past her head, but she ignored them, trusting that the remnants of the Storm squadron and the wraithguard would keep the shots away from her. At her side, the last of the Biel-Tan warlocks sent crackling blasts of warp energy jousting from his fingertips, cooking the flesh of Chaos Marines inside their armour and making their souls cry out in horror. The once pristine white armour of the Storm squadron was now scratched and dull, coated in layers of dirt and blood. But they fought with a passion and determination known only to the eldar race.

Skrekrea had been here before, on this very mountain side with her brother, all those centuries ago – and now her brother, Jaerielle, was gone. These daemons would pay dearly for his soul. She flipped and danced around the rain of bolter fire, rattling off shuriken from her pistol and slicing her power sword with immaculate precision. She plunged her blade straight through the acid-green armour of a Chaos Marine, shrieking a cry into his face as she withdrew it, and watching his head shatter and explode as her rage was funnelled through the Banshee Mask on her own head, transforming it into a psychosonic blast. As her sword withdrew, she flipped it over and drove it blindly behind her, skewering another Alpha Legionary in the back of the neck as he tried to slip past towards the farseer.

Macha held her arms up into the heavens and called down the lightning, forming it into spheres of pure, blue energy that revolved in the air in front of her chest. With a slight contraction of her eyes, she fired the energy balls searing through the dark, moist air towards the Chaos sorcerer on the higher island-peak.

With his arms also raised to greet the storm, Sindri hardly even noticed the fireballs blazing towards him. But at the last second, one of his arms snapped out to his side, punching the blue flames and exploding them into showers of red fire, as the Maledictum stone in his fist flared with power.

Turning his eyes to face Macha, Sindri glared through the hail, wind, and bolts of warp energy, his eyes burning with red and gold fires, daring her to interfere. For a moment, Macha felt like the sorcerer was breathing into her face, as his eyes seemed to fill her entire field of vision. But then he turned away from her again, raising his face and hands back to the storm, crying into its heart.

A phalanx of Alpha Legionaries strode around Sindri, repositioning themselves between the sorcerer and the farseer, as the islands of rock bobbed and swirled on the flood of fire around the mountain top. They braced their bolters, checking their aim against the motion of the ground beneath their feet, and then loosed a volley of fire down towards the eldar. Macha, with nowhere to go, raised her hand and a jolt of blue flame seared out to meet the bolter fire, detonating the shells in mid air. The Marines fired again and again, and Macha was forced to contend with them rather than Sindri, despite the fact that he was so close. If only more eldar had survived. Then she realised that the eldar had failed: *Gabriel…* *Gabriel…*

'Almost! Almost!' cried Sindri into the storm, his face convulsing with power and pain as tendrils of daemonic energy started to lash down at his skin. But he could not wait any longer; he had waited so long and been so patient all these years, even putting up with the humiliations of service to that cretin, Lord Bale.

Raging with impatience, Sindri pointed the Maledictum towards a knot of Alpha Legionaries and Imperial Guardsmen on a floating mass of rock nearby. The stone blazed with power and a lance of red light flashed into the soldiers, exploding them into a rain of blood and disintegrating the rock beneath their feet.

'Yes!' he cried as he felt the currents of power shift in the storm above him. 'Yes! It is upon us!' he screamed, crashing the Maledictum into the hilt of the curved dagger, where it burst into flames as the stone found an empty socket. Streaks of purple lightning and tendrils of warp power whipped down out of the storm, lashing themselves around the body of the sorcerer and lifting him into the air. He screamed and wailed in ecstasies of agony, feeling the daemon prince tugging at the tendons of his soul from the other side of the breach in the immaterium, clawing at his mind, desperately trying to make the leap into the material realm and into the solid body of this devoted sorcerer.

'Bear witness to my ascension!' bellowed the voice of Sindri, echoing with power into the ears of everyone on the mountain, resounding through the storm itself. For a moment, it seemed as though the entire battle ceased as all heads turned towards the levitating form of the Chaos sorcerer.

GABRIEL STOOD IN the centre of a resplendent line of Blood Ravens, their crimson armour shimmering in the lightning flashes, their resolve unshaken by the daemonic fury that stormed around the mountain top. They were poised, ready to advance through the ring of warp energy that held a column of liquid fire on which floated islands of battle and damnation. They were unflinching in the face of a Chaos sorcerer, ascending to daemonhood before their very eyes. They were the Adeptus Astartes, and this was their purpose: to defend the Emperor's realm against the unholy. In the fires of battle, they would test their resolve and prove themselves worthy of a place at the Emperor's side.

Bowing his head for a moment of silent prayer, Gabriel heard a delicate voice calling his name: *Gabriel… Gabriel…* It repeated over and over, gradually shifting into a beautiful rhythm and then, slowly, a chorus of other voices started up underneath it. The pristine, clear, silvery tones of the Astronomican soared into his soul, pressing the strength of the Emperor himself into his heart.

He lifted his head, and raised Mordecai's daemon-hammer – the god-splitter – the air: 'For the Great Father and the Emperor!' he yelled, his voice carrying against the vicious wind. A tremendous call came back, thundering from the lungs of every Blood Raven, shaking the ground itself: 'The Great Father and the Emperor!'

With that, Gabriel strode forward through the curtain of energy, vaulting up onto the first island of rock and swinging the god-splitter for the first time. It erupted with power even before its arc was complete, spitting unearthly energy from its head as it approached the body of the first Alpha Legionary, before erupting into an immense explosion as it impacted, blasting the Chaos Marine off his feet and casting him into the sea of fire.

Gabriel swung the hammer again, crashing it into the side of the next Chaos Marine's head and knocking it clean off his shoulders. He let the arc continue, sweeping it lower as he spun his own body, pushing the hammer through the stomachs of two more Marines before hoisting it up into the air and screaming in a defiant cry: 'I come for you, sorcerer!'

Mordecai had said that this daemonhammer was constructed from a fragment of the weapon of an eldar avatar – the very weapon used by the eldar to defeat the daemon prince three thousand years before. He had entrusted the ancient artefact to Gabriel, pushing it into his hands before they had jumped down off the Rhino to take their positions in the line of Blood Ravens. 'Call it a premonition,' Mordecai had said, 'and damn my unsanctioned soul, but I believe that you will end this fight, Gabriel, not me. You are the Emperor's champion, and I am a mere servant. You, like your Captain Trythos before you… you must wield the daemonhammer on Tartarus and save us all from this daemon.' Gabriel had just nodded and taken the weapon, appreciating the inquisitor's confidence, and knowing that he was right.

The little platform of rock was swimming in the blood of Chaos Marines and strewn with their corpses; Gabriel stood alone. Looking around, he saw his Blood Ravens leaping from one island to another, hacking into the Alpha Legion with chainswords and power fists. Lines of Devastator Marines were punching out volleys of bolter fire, shredding those Imperial Guardsmen who had turned against the Emperor. And Matiel's Assault squad roared above the flaming ocean with their jump packs spilling fire, raining frag-grenades onto Chaos positions and spraying them with bolter shells.

Gabriel vaulted up onto the next rocky island, heading towards the highest summit where Sindri was still held in the heart of the storm by the wild tendrils of energy. Beneath him, a phalanx of Chaos Marines was bunched into a firing line, loosing bolter fire across a chasm towards the eldar farseer, whose bursts of defensive flame seemed to be growing weaker.

Crunching down into a crouch as he landed, Gabriel saw that this platform contained a knot of Imperial Guardsmen, each mutated and contorted into inhuman shapes. They were concentrating their fire against a squadron of Gabriel's Devastator Marines, ensconced on a nearby islet, who ceased fire when they saw their captain suddenly appear amongst their targets. For a moment, the Guardsmen were confused by the unexpected turn of events, but then one of them caught on and turned. He yelled something to the other men, and they all turned at once, lumbering towards the Blood Raven with their shotguns barking, brandishing blades in the air.

With a swift movement, Gabriel swung his hammer in a horizontal arc, scattering Guardsmen into the seething fires around the platform – he didn't have time to waste on these heretics. But something made him pause before he struck the one who had told the others to turn. He stopped the hammer just next to the Guardsman's head, and then dropped it to his side, staring at the officer while his brain rushed to put a name to the face.

Then it hit him: Brom. It was Colonel Brom. His face was bright red, burnt, and covered with lacerations. His uniform was ripped and dirty, and parts of it were clearly soaked with blood. But it was definitely him.

'Brom?' asked Gabriel, still unwilling to believe what he was seeing. 'Brom? Is that really you?'

'Ah, the heroic Captain Angelos – how good of you to notice me, at last,' hissed Brom, his voice distorted and barely recognisable. 'I thought that this might get your attention,' he added, stabbing forward with his power sword.

Gabriel parried the clumsy lunge with his gauntlet, catching the blade in his fist and pulling the weapon out of the colonel's hand. 'What are you blathering about, Brom?' he asked, casting the sword into the flames.

'Do you know how long I have been on this planet?' asked Brom, apparently rhetorically. 'My whole life – that's how long. And then you arrive and it is as though I wasn't here at all. You and that inquisitor–'

A tickle of blood suddenly appeared out of a hole in the centre of Brom's forehead, and he slumped to the ground, dead. His mouth was still open, ready to continue his list of grievances, and Gabriel was grateful that he had not had to listen to any more drivel from the colonel. He strode to the edge of the platform and looked down, seeing Matiel hovering between two islets on his jump pack, squeezing off bolter shells in all directions. Nodding his gratitude to the sergeant, he turned and jumped towards the base of the summit.

* * *

SOMETHING HAD SHIFTED within the warp field, and Macha cast her eyes around the fiery landscape searching for the source of the movement. She felt a familiar presence, one she had not felt for thousands of years. And then she saw it, flashing through the hail and pounding into the forces of Chaos like the tool of a deity. It swept and spun, crashing into Alpha Legionaries and fallen Guardsmen, as though guided to them by some ineffable power. It was majestic and effortless, wielding its wielder and gifting him with the illusion of control.

The Blood Raven has a fragment of the Wailing Doom – all is not yet lost. We must help him, said Macha, reaching out with her mind to the best of her warriors.

Understood, replied Skrekrea as she somersaulted over the collapsing form of a dying Chaos Marine and brought her blade round into a vicious vertical arc in her wake, driving it down between the neck and shoulder plates of another. She turned to face the farseer, and sprinted up the slope towards her, pushing her foot hard into the ground as she reached the summit, next to Macha, and leaping out into the fiery space between their islet and the one above where Sindri levitated. She flew through the flames, her legs cycling and her back arched with the effort of the long jump.

Macha sent out bursts of blue energy from her fingertips, incinerating the sleet of bolter shells that flashed out towards Skrekrea as she leapt towards the Chaos Marines. The warlock, just down the slope from Macha, power coruscating around his hands as he unleashed bolts of raw energy against the forces of Chaos that besieged their own island-summit,

turned to assist the farseer, throwing blue flames
across the chasm in support of Skrekrea. Macha nodded her thanks to the warlock and started to redirect
her own assault against Sindri himself once again,
forming revolving balls of blue energy and hurling
them across the void towards the Chaos sorcerer.

But the loss of Skrekrea and the warlock from her
own defences left Macha vulnerable to the pressing
forces of Chaos behind her. Bolter shells zipped past
her head, and she could hear the wails of her diminishing Storm squad as they fought to keep the Alpha
Legionaries and fallen Guardsmen off her back.

The emerald-green wraithguard reorganised their
positions behind the Storm squad, forming a solid
shielding line between the enemy and the farseer,
standing implacably with their wraithcannons a constant blaze. Aggressive fire zinged out of the Chaos
forces, zipping into the wraithguard, and punching
out great chunks of their psycho-plastic armour. But
the un-living eldar warriors held their ground,
unafraid of death, afraid only of failure.

Without their leader, the Storm squadron began to
falter, pinned down under the relentless fire of the
Alpha Legionaries, and engaged on all sides by lunging blades and hacking axes. The squad leapt and
spun, their own blades blurring into torrents of violence, but they were outnumbered, and their own
numbers were falling all the time. It would not be
long before the eldar were overrun and the Alpha
Legion would have a clear line to the farseer.

*You must hold the line – Kaela Mensha Khaine is with
us,* came the thoughts of Macha, filling the souls of
the eldar with hope. *The spirit of our avatar is with us
in the mon-keigh's daemonhammer.*

The Storm squadron seemed to lurch with new energy, leaping and striking with inhuman speed, cutting a swathe through the Chaos forces, and an eerie chant flowed out of their diminishing numbers, filling the storm with a chorus of eldar magic: 'Kaela Mensha Khaine!'

THE DAEMONHAMMER SEEMED to erupt into flames as Gabriel crashed down onto the rocky platform, and the strange alien music flooded through the hail and wind. The hammer pulsed with power, radiating energy into his body as he brandished it above his head and charged towards the phalanx of Chaos Marines that stood guard around the very peak of the dismembered mountaintop.

As he closed, a group of Marines snapped round to face him, their bolters coughing with fire, while their brother-Legionaries continued to focus their shots elsewhere, to the other side of the pyramidal rock, where Gabriel could not see. The bolter shells flashed through the dark air, heading straight for Gabriel in a lethal horizontal sheet than threatened to cut him in two. But suddenly, the shots seemed to reduce into slow motion as the eldar chants rose into a deafening chorus, mixing with the silver tones of the symphony that still played in his mind. The daemonhammer glowed with power. With consummate and casual ease, Gabriel brought the daemonhammer round in a horizontal arc, sweeping it through the oncoming fire and detonating each shell as the hammerhead crunched into it. He didn't even break his stride as he pounded onwards towards the shocked Alpha Legionaries, bursting out of the line of explosions unscathed by their vicious tirade.

As he ran, Gabriel saw one of the Chaos Marines suddenly throw up his arms, casting his bolter to the ground, and then slump forward onto his face. Standing in his place, her curving blade dripping with blood as lightning flashed behind her, an eldar warrior paused for a moment, throwing back her head and letting out a cry of victory. The cry rose shrilly, gathering volume and power until it drowned out even the sound of the storm and the chanting of her brethren.

The Chaos Marines on either side of the eldar warrior collapsed to the ground, clutching their hands to the sides of their helmets, shaking their heads in insane agony. As they fell to their knees, the eldar snapped back into motion, spinning into a pirouette with her blade outstretched, taking the heads of both Marines in a single fluid movement.

Gabriel was closing now, swinging the hammer above his head in preparation for the combat to come as he stormed over the uneven terrain. The Chaos Marines were in disarray, trying to deal with the slippery eldar in their midst and with the charging Blood Raven all at once – they snatched bolter fire in all directions, snapping their weapons from side to side whilst drawing their chainswords ready for close-range combat.

Diving forward into a roll, Gabriel cleared the last few strides in an instant as bolter fire zinged off his armour and flew over his head. He flipped back onto his feet, bringing the hammer down vertically on the head of one of the Chaos Marines, shattering his spine as the hammer flared with power. To his left, the eldar warrior was dancing and springing between Marines, slicing into their armour with her blade and spraying out shuriken from her pistol. For a brief moment, the eldar and Blood Raven came to rest, back to back in the midst of a ring of Alpha Legionaries.

Looking up, Gabriel could see the figure of Sindri, suspended above the floating mountaintop, hanging by tendrils of power that seemed to pulse, feeding him with the energy of the storm. Time was running out, and he leapt forward towards the Marines that blocked his path up the summit, sweeping the daemonhammer in front of him and clattering through their outstretched chainswords. He felt a movement breeze past his shoulder as he started to run forward, and then the eldar warrior landed lightly in front of him, having somersaulted over the Blood Raven's head.

Skrekrea bounced into a spin, flashing her blade out in every direction, slicing into the Chaos Marines all around, but leaving Gabriel completely unscathed. As she danced through the combat, she opened a gap in the line of Marines, and Gabriel barged through it, dropping his shoulder and pulling the weight of the daemonhammer behind him. He knocked two Alpha Legionaries off their feet as he crashed through them, and then leapt up the slope towards the peak, the way ahead clear.

A wail of agony from behind him made Gabriel pause. He looked back over his shoulder and saw the eldar warrior skewered on the blades of three Chaos Marines. Her head was thrown back and a death cry was gurgling unevenly from her throat as the Marines twisted their blades. Gabriel turned to face them, his blood boiling and rage flooding into his head, and he brought the daemonhammer crashing down against the rock at his feet. The hammerhead exploded with power as it pounded into the rock, ripping a crack into the islet and rendering it asunder, breaking the platform under the Chaos Marines free of the mountain summit and sending it tumbling down into the sea of flames below. The Alpha Legionaries scrambled to keep their footing on the plummeting platform, but the rock flipped end over end, throwing the traitorous Marines screaming into the daemonic firestorm.

Gabriel watched them fall, and then turned back to the mountaintop, looking up as Sindri started to glow with power, radiating purple light from his body as the blood of the dead Marines blended with the swirling ocean that consecrated the tainted ground of Tartarus. The Blood Ravens' captain swung the hammer over his shoulder and started to climb up towards the emergent daemon prince.

'YES!' CRIED THE bellowing voice of Sindri as the storm pulsed through his veins, filling his body with the oscillating energies of the warp. A great ring of purple flame blew out from his position, rippling across the fragmented mountaintop in concentric circles, dousing the combatants in warp energy. The Alpha Legionaries roared with renewed passion as the power washed over them, and the Blood Ravens staggered under the tidal onslaught. But Matiel blasted over the waves with his jump pack spilling orange flames into the sea of fire. He roared towards the Chaos sorcerer, determined that his Assault Marines would not meet their end at the hands of such a foul creature. His bolter coughed and spat shells, and his chainsword spluttered in readiness as he barrelled through the hail and wind, yelling his determination into the storm: 'For the Great Father and the Emperor!'

Gabriel pulled himself up onto the summit just in time to see Sindri turn his head towards the sergeant, as he seared through the air towards him. A sudden javelin of purple flashed out of the daemon's eyes, punching into the jetting form of the Blood Raven and halting him in midair. Sindri shrieked with pleasure, immersing himself in the daemonic energies that flowed through him as a conduit into the material realm.

Matiel was held for a moment, suspended in the onrush of warp fire, held high above the frantic battle that raged on the sundered mountaintop. His arms snapped out to his sides, and his weapons fell away from his hands, as he was held in a blaze of agony for all the warriors to see.

'No!' yelled Gabriel, hefting the daemonhammer onto his shoulder and crouching, ready to pounce. 'Matiel!'

Suddenly, a blue fireball hissed through the sleeting rain and punched into the levitating form of the Chaos sorcerer, knocking him back. Sindri, the emergent daemon prince, snapped his gaze back round to face the eldar farseer, raking his flaming eyes in a great arc of destruction across the islets of the mountaintop, exploding rock and incinerating Marines as his stare touched them. The purple river crashed against the figure of the farseer, splitting into a series of streams that ran around her, as she stood defiantly against the current.

Meanwhile, released from the daemon prince's thrall, Matiel tumbled out of the sky, crashing down against a rocky outcrop far below.

'No!' yelled Gabriel, as he launched himself into the air, swinging the daemonhammer up in a vertical arc and throwing himself towards the pulsating form of Sindri. He jumped three metres into the sky, carried upwards on the back of the eldar chants, the chorus of the Astronomican, and the righteous will of the Blood Ravens themselves. The daemonhammer seemed to drag him higher and higher, pulling him into the eye of the storm as though it were a guided missile, as though it had a will of its own.

Sindri narrowed his eyes, concentrating the river of fire into a torrent that crashed into the farseer as she staggered back under the daemonic onslaught. But she would not fall, and the daemon prince roared his rage into the storm, bringing down forks of purple lightning and ravaging the mountain with hurricane force winds. Just at the last minute, he saw Gabriel out of the corner of his eye. But it was too late.

The daemonhammer swept up and around in a spiralling blur, dragging Gabriel in a loop around the daemon until he was suspended in the eye of the storm alongside the husk of Sindri. Without even a moment's hesitation, Gabriel shouldered the hammer and spun his whole body, bringing the daemonhammer around with all his strength. The ornate, rune-encrusted hammerhead flared with blinding light as it punched into the chest of the emergent daemon, driving straight through its body in an explosion of warp fire and gore. Sindri's body was rent in two, as his chest crumpled into nothing and then exploded out of his back, leaving his head hanging momentarily in the air above his stomach.

The storm itself seemed to reel in agony as its eye was shattered by the captain of the Blood Ravens. The clouds whipped into a giant whirlpool, pulling the lightning into spiralling streams that seemed to be sucked back in towards the core, dragging the energy of the immaterium back through the Chaos forces in an immense backwash that left the Alpha Legionaries boiling within their armour. The storm was collapsing back on itself, as Gabriel tumbled down towards the rocky summit of the mountain, and the floating islets of rock themselves started to fall back into place on the mountaintop.

As Gabriel crashed into solid ground, he pulled himself to his feet and watched the maelstrom raging all around him. The remaining Blood Ravens were struggling to maintain their balance as the mountain shifted and rocked, spilling the boiled Alpha Legionaries and the treacherous Guardsmen into fiery chasms that were quickly sealed as the mountaintop reformed. Further down the mountainside, Gabriel could see the remnants of the orks turning tail and fleeing down into the valley. Then, with an earth-shattering crack, the Maledictum dagger thudded into the stone at his feet, its curved blade biting into the rock with the hilt holding the stone itself.

He hoisted the daemonhammer for one last strike, but a thought stayed his hand, pressing into his mind.

Human! Do not destroy the stone… you will doom us all!

Gabriel paused with the hammer held aloft, poised, ready to crash down on the Maledictum. He could see the eldar farseer, shining like an angel in the spiralling maelstrom of the collapsing storm. She was staring at him, willing him not to crush the stone. There were a few eldar warriors standing beside her, a couple of wraithguard and a warlock. The eldar had paid a heavy price for the souls of the Tartarans.

'Captain!' came a shouted voice from behind him. 'Destroy the stone before it leads others to ruin – it lies at the root of the damnation of Tartarus!' cried Mordecai, straining his voice against the torrential storm, standing on the edge of a nearby islet.

Gabriel shook his head and closed his eyes, trying to find some calm in the eye of the storm, searching his soul for the guidance of the Astronomican. But there was nothing but fire and darkness swirling behind his eyelids.

You know not what you do… came the thoughts of Macha once again, but this time they were accompanied by a rain of shuriken and blasts of wraithcannon. *I cannot let you destroy it.*

The fire zinged against Gabriel's armour, ricocheting in sparks, but he did not move. He stayed silent and still, waiting for calm, waiting for certainty. The hammer hummed in his hands, hungry for destruction. His mind was congealing with disparate images: he saw flickers of the silver choir transforming into the tortured faces of the people of Cyrene; he saw Isador's eyes burning with fury and hatred; and he saw the disfigured form of Brom, a bullet hole fresh in his forehead.

Opening his eyes, not even wincing at the sleet of shuriken that peppered his armour and sunk into his flesh, he looked down into the Maledictum. Something dark and shadowy moved within, and inchoate whispers reached for his mind.

'No!' he cried, bringing the daemonhammer crashing down on the stone, driving the dagger down into the rock below but shattering the Maledictum into a rain of tiny shards. A immense explosion detonated as the hammer struck the daemonic stone, sending concentric shockwaves of warp energy radiating out from the mountaintop. The explosions knocked everything flat, rippling down the mountainside after the fleeing orks. Then, with a sudden reversal, the shockwaves were sucked back up the mountain, gathering in the storms, the hail and the lightning, dragging the darkness back to the hilt of the curved dagger, and sucking them into the abrupt implosion.

The twin-peaked mountain was thrown into sudden silence, leaving the motionless, prostrate forms of Blood Ravens and Biel-Tan eldar lying on the rocky summit. The clouds parted, and the dusky red sun shone warmly through the cold, still air.

EPILOGUE

'THE THUNDERHAWKS ARE on their way, captain,' reported Corallis, finding Gabriel bent over the body of Sergeant Matiel. 'Matiel was a fine Marine, Gabriel. He will be missed,' he added, kneeling at Gabriel's side.

'Yes, sergeant. We have lost many fine Marines on Tartarus. The Blood Ravens have suffered greatly for their part in this debacle,' said Gabriel gently.

'It is our role to suffer, so that others will live,' replied Corallis. 'This has always been the way of the Adeptus Astartes. It is what makes us better than our foes.'

'But even the Blood Ravens must survive, sergeant,' said Gabriel, rising to his feet. 'We must collect the gene-seed of our fallen battle-brothers, ready for transportation back to the *Litany of Fury*. We will burn the bodies in a pyre on the mountain top, so that the evacuated civilians in orbit will see the flames of those who sacrificed themselves to save their planet. Their legends will live on, even as their souls ascend to the side of the Golden Throne itself.'

'Yes, captain. It will be done,' said Corallis, nodding a slight bow.

'Did the young Sergeant Ckrius survive the fight against the orks?' asked Gabriel, slightly preoccupied with other things.

'Yes, captain. He was badly injured, but Tanthius has recommended him for battle honours,' replied Corallis. Like many of the other Blood Ravens who had seen the young trooper fight, Corallis was impressed and proud of the boy's achievements.

'Good. Make sure that he doesn't die, and see to it that he receives medical care aboard the *Fury*. We have to look after the future of our Chapter, Corallis,' said Gabriel, smiling faintly.

'Yes, captain,' nodded Corallis, returning Gabriel's smile. 'I will inform Tanthius at once – he will be keen to see to these arrangements himself.'

'Very good, sergeant,' said Gabriel, turning away and scanning the desolate scene in the dying light. The mountaintop was littered with the bodies of Alpha Legionaries and the mutated corpses of treacherous Guardsmen. Interspersed with them were the red-armoured forms of fallen Blood Ravens, and Gabriel shook his head painfully.

'Well done, captain,' said Mordecai, striding through the killing field towards Gabriel. 'I knew that I was right about you.'

Gabriel looked at the inquisitor, unable to return his familiar tone. Something still did not feel right about this episode, and he was certain that Mordecai had more to answer for than he was letting on. The Inquisition never released more information than they needed to – and knowledge is power, as the Blood Ravens knew well.

'What happened to the eldar?' asked Gabriel, keen to fill in some of the missing pieces.

'They disappeared after you destroyed the stone. They simply vanished,' he said, holding out his hand.

Gabriel stared at the hand for a moment, uncomprehending. Then he realised what the inquisitor was waiting for, and he slapped the shaft of the daemon-hammer into Mordecai's gauntlet. He snorted inwardly, utterly unsurprised by the actions of the inquisitor.

'And the orks?' he asked.

'As you know, most of them were drawn to the mountain by the commotion of battle. And those that were not dispatched by your Terminators were seen to by the explosion. The Tartarans from Magna Bonum are mopping up the few survivors,' replied Mordecai, almost gleefully, feeling the weight of the daemonhammer in his hands.

'Good,' said Gabriel uneasily, nodding a quick bow to the inquisitor before turning away from him. 'I must find Chaplain Prathios,' he added as an explanation, striding away.

HUGE FLAMES LAPPED out of the massive funeral pyre on the summit of the mountain, filling the night sky with dancing fire and shadows. The bodies of each Blood Raven had been removed from their ancient armour, with their gene-seed carefully extracted, and then laid onto the pyre with every dignity. Gabriel had stood before the bodies with a torch burning in his hand, the surviving Marines and troopers arrayed behind him, each kneeling respectfully. Then he had thrown the torch in a spinning parabola, flipping over and over through the darkness until it landed in the heart of the pyre, which erupted into blossoms of flame immediately. Plumes of dark smoke wafted up into the night, blotting out the stars in an otherwise clear sky.

Gabriel watched the smoke rising slowly, feeling the heat of the flames against the skin on his face. The smoke swirled and eddied in the breeze, gyrating into transient shapes before dissipating.

He hung his head slowly, his heart aching with the amount of blood that had been shed over the last few days.

Kneeling in prayer, Gabriel closed his eyes and calmed his breathing, knowing that the rest of the Blood Ravens would be doing exactly the same thing behind him. Over to the side of the funeral pyre, standing on his own, Gabriel knew that Mordecai was watching the ritual with disapproval – there were some aspects of the Adeptus Astartes that the Inquisition simply had to tolerate, and ritualised cremations of Marines were one of them.

From the silence in his mind came a single, solitary voice. It was a soprano, soaring quietly into the heights. One voice became two, the second low and rumbling, plunging into the ancient depths of his soul. Then another voice joined the harmony, and soon the silvery chorus filled his head once again. It was pure and clear – the majestic music of the Emperor himself, guiding Gabriel's soul and purging his sins. At last, it seemed that Gabriel was at peace.

Then, one of the voices faltered, and the soprano shifted into a piercing scream. The silver lights started to tinge with red, and Gabriel screwed his eyes closed tightly, trying to shut out the invading images. But the silver ran with blood, and the faces of the angelic choir started to melt and ooze, rendering themselves into perversions of Imperial grace.

He twitched his head from side to side, trying to shake himself free of the vision, but something held him there, trapped inside his own head. Isador's face flashed past his eyes, whispering to him that he should not falter. Myriad faces exploded into sight, speckling his consciousness with the visages of Cyrene and Tartarus. The faces started to merge and swirl, spiralling together as though stirred into an emulsion. And then, peering out of the curdling mess came a familiar voice, laughing and cackling with amused triumph.

I am free, Gabriel – you have my thanks.

Show yourself, daemon! yelled Gabriel into his own mind.

You will see my form soon enough – you who are my herald!

I am not your herald, warp-spawn – I am your vanquisher. It was I who destroyed the Maledictum, said Gabriel, shaking his head invisibly.

Yes, it was you who released me from that prison, liberating me with your every sacrifice…

Gabriel's soul rebelled, struggling to keep its distance from the vile rape of his consciousness. He refused to believe. *My sacrifices were not in your name, daemon. We fought to destroy you.*

And yet it was you who spilt the blood of the orks. It was you who mixed the blood of the Chaos Lord and his sorcerer into the giant altar that is Tartarus. And it was you who thwarted the attempts of the eldar witch to prevent my coming…

'No!' Gabriel let out a scream of defiance, throwing himself forwards into the flames of the pyre and burning his body out of its vision. A strong hand gripped his shoulder and dragged him out of the fire.

'They are gone, Gabriel,' said Prathios in soft, low tones. 'You must think about the future now.'

Gabriel shrugged the hand from his shoulders and jumped to his feet, realising at last whose voice he had heard curdling around in his head. He strained his eyes against the firelight, staring over to the side of the funeral pyre, but there was nobody there. He spun on his heel, scanning the darkness around the assembly of kneeling Blood Ravens – nothing.

I knew that I was right about you, Captain Angelos, came the voice again, slipping into his mind and taunting him. *The righteous are always the easiest to lead, especially the ignorant and the righteous.*

'I know you now!' cried Gabriel, spinning on the spot and yelling into the night, as the smoke from the funeral pyre started to squirm and coil. The eddies began to curdle and mould into swimming shapes, hinting at a face in the firelight. Standing on top of the pyre was the immolated figure of man, his flesh blazing with flames and dripping down into the inferno below.

The face in the smoke resolved for an instant, and a low, cackling laugh echoed down the mountainside. It was the face of Mordecai Toth, frozen for a moment, but then whirled into a blur by a sudden gust of wind. Then it was gone, leaving only the distant echoes of laughter in the valley below.

'Knowledge is power, daemon! I know you now! I know your name and your form! You may have escaped the confines of Tartarus, but you will never escape me. With your freedom, you have guaranteed your annihilation,' yelled Gabriel, his voice dropping from a cry to a whisper as he muttered his silent vow.

ABOUT THE AUTHOR

C S Goto has published short fiction in *Inferno!* and elsewhere, including Japan. In real life he is a university lecturer, with a PhD in philosophy. But real life isn't all that it's cracked up to be. He lives in Nottingham with a wife and three cats, where he remains very anxious about being a writer, since he is also a fiction himself. In his spare time he dreams about what he would do if he had more of it.

WARHAMMER
40,000

'Hardcore military sci-fi.'
– RPG United

BLOOD ANGELS
DEUS ENCARMINE

The explosive first instalment in
the Blood Angels series

James Swallow

Coming soon from the Black Library

BLOOD ANGELS: DEUS ENCARMINE

A Warhammer 40,000 novel
by James Swallow

AMID THE GRAVES, it was difficult for Rafen to tell exactly where the sky ended and the land began. He became still for a moment, halting in the shadow of a large tombstone in the shape of a chalice, the muzzle of his bolter calm and silent at his side. The wind never ceased on Cybele; on it came over the low hills and shallow mountains that characterised the planet, moaning mournfully through the thin stands of trees, rippling the grey-blue grass into waves. The gently rolling landscape flowed away from him toward an endless, unreachable vanishing point, an invisible horizon where grey land met grey sky. The distance was lost in the low clouds of stone dust that hovered overhead, stained like a great shroud of oil-soaked wool. The haze was made up of tiny particles of rock, churned into the sky by the torrent of artillery fire that had etched itself across the planet hours earlier.

Cybele wailed quietly around Rafen. The wind sang through the uncountable numbers of head-stones that ranged away in every direction as far as his visor's optics could see. He stood atop the graves of a billion-fold war dead and listened to the breeze as it wept for them, the familiar hot battle-urge of caged frenzy boiling away beneath the veneer of his iron self-control.

Steady and unmoving, an observer might have mistaken Rafen for a tomb marker. Indeed there were places on Cybele where stone-carved likenesses of Space Marines topped great towers of granite. In those hallowed grounds, men bred from Brother Rafen's own bloodline were buried as a measure of respect for the planet and the great memorial that it represented to the Imperium. The moon of a vast gas giant, Cybele was a war-grave world, one of hun-dreds of planets declared Mausoleum Valorum throughout the Ultima Segmentum. Rafen kept his statue-like aspect as a flicker of movement danced on the edge of his auspex's sensors.

Presently, a figure emerged from behind an oval sepulchre carved in pink vestan stone, and it nod-ded toward Rafen before making a series of sign-gestures with a gauntleted hand. The two of them were almost identical: their man-shapes broad and hulking in red ceramite sheaths, the colour glis-tening from the soft, reverent rain.

Rafen returned the nod and emerged from his cover, low to the ground and swift. He did not pause to check if Brother Alactus was following him; there was no need. As Alactus followed Rafen, so Brother Turcio followed Alactus, and Brother Bennek followed him. The team of Space Marines had drilled and fought alongside each other for so many decades that they functioned as pieces of the same machine, each a finely-tooled cog linked to the other, operating in perfect unison. To move now in silence, without a single spoken word between them, was child's play for soldiers who had trained to fight under the most testing conditions. He could sense their eagerness to meet the foe; it was like a palpable scent in the air, thick and coppery on his tongue.

Rafen slipped around a smashed obelisk that rose like a broken bone from the cemetery grass, an accusing finger pointing upward and decrying the foul clouds. He dropped down into a shallow valley. A day earlier, this sheltered place had been a devotional garden dedicated to naval pilots lost in the war for Rocene, but now it was a ruined bowl of broken earth. A stray round from the enemy's opening sub-orbital bombardment had landed here and carved out a hemisphere of ground, fusing the dirt into patches of glassy fulgurites. Brown puddles gathered where ornate caskets were torn open and their contents scattered around Rafen's metal-shod feet: bones and decayed, aged medals crunched into the dirt where he walked. The Space Marine picked his way through the skeletons and traversed the opposite lip of the crater, pausing to check his bearings.

He glanced up to see the shape of an angelic statue curving away above him, arms and wings spread as if about to take flight. The statue's face was unblemished and perfect; its eyes were raised to stare at some exquisite heaven that was an infinity away from the crude reality of this earthly realm. For one serene moment, Rafen was convinced that the stone seraph was about to turn its countenance to him, to display the face of Lord Sanguinius, the hallowed founder and primogenitor of his Chapter. But the instant fled, and Rafen was alone with the dead once more, stone angel and Blood Angel alike both wreathed in the mist and rain. He looked away and allowed himself to listen to the wind once more.

Rafen felt a churn of revulsion in the pit of his gut. A fresh sound was being carried to his helmet's auto-sense array, buoyed along with the ceaseless moans of the breeze: screaming, thin and horrific. It was a noise torn from the very darkest places in a man's heart, an utterance that could only have issued from the lips of one truly damned. The Marine surmised the Traitors were preparing to make an augury from the entrails of one of their slaves before they began another sortie.

Rafen considered this for a moment. If the archenemy were getting ready for another attack, then it made his mission all the more urgent. He moved off, a frown forming behind the formidable mask of his breather grille. A troop of lightly armoured, fast-moving scouts would have been able to accomplish the same task in half the time. But every single one of the pathfinder squad in Rafen's detachment had been killed in the first assault, when a fusillade of krak shells had torn through their ranks. He had been standing in the lee of a Rhino's hull when the shriek of superheated air signalled the incoming salvo, and in his mind's eye Rafen recalled the moment when a scout bike had spun up and over his head, as if it were nothing but a plaything discarded by a bored, petulant child. All that remained of the young Marines were some torn rags and flecks of burnt ceramite.

He buried the dark ember of his anger deep and pressed on, shuttering away his recriminations. It mattered little now what they had been told before arriving on Cybele, that the posting here was purely a ceremonial one, that it was a matter of honour rather than a battle to be fought. Perhaps he and his battle-brothers had been lax to believe that the corrupted would have no interest in a cemetery world; now they would repay that mistake with the blood of their foes.

Rafen slowed to a steady walk as they closed in on the grove the enemy had chosen for their staging area. The pristine, manicured lawns of the graveyards elsewhere were no longer evident here – around the perimeter of the Traitor camp, great dark tendrils of decay were trailing out through the grasses, emerging through an expanding ring of soiled plants and toxic slurry. In some places, the ground had broken open like an old wound and disgorged the dead from beneath it. Grave markers lay slumped and disfigured next to black twists of bone vomited from the newly putrid earth. Rafen's finger twitched near the trigger of his bolter, his knuckles whitening inside his gauntlet. The rush of righteous fury was tingling at bay within him, the longing for combat singing in his veins. He gestured for the other Blood Angels to stand back and hold their positions. He found a vantage point at the corner of a ruined vault and for the first time that day Rafen laid eyes on the enemy. It was all he could do to resist the urge to riddle them with gunfire.

Word Bearers. Once they had been an Adeptus Astartes Chapter of the most pious nature, but those days had long since turned to dust. Rafen's lips drew back from his teeth in a sneer of disgust as he watched the Traitor Marines move to and fro, marching arrogantly between tents of flayed ork-hide and the still steaming orbs of grounded dreadclaw landers. He closed his ears to the pestilent shouts of the enemy demagogues as they wandered about the edges of the encampment, spitting their vile prayers and chants over the cries of the slave-servitors, and the incessant cracks of neuro-whips against the backs of the helots.

The Word Bearers were a dark mirror of Rafen and his brethren. Their battle gear was doused in a livid scar-red the shade of fresh gore, their armour dominated by a single sigil – the face of a screaming horned demon against an eight-pointed star. Many of the Chaos Marines sported horned helms with filigree and fine workings cored from children's bones, or pages of blasphemous text drawn on skin-parchment and fastened into the ceramite with obsidian screws. Others went about bareheaded, and these ones displayed faces rippled with ritual wheals, tusks or hooks of warped cartilage.

It was one such Traitor Marine who was carefully ministering to the torture of the slave whose screams had carried so far on the wind. One of his arms ended in a writhing cluster of metallic tentacles that flicked and whipped at the air as if they had a mind of their own. In his other hand, the torturer held a vibra-stave that he used like a sculptor, lopping off slips of flesh with infinite care. The victim's cries wavered up and down the octaves and Rafen abruptly realised that the enemy soldier was playing the man like an instrument, amusing himself by composing a symphony of pain. Rafen looked away, concentrating on the mission at hand. His squad leader, Brother-Sergeant Koris, had made the orders quite clear – Rafen and his team were to merely locate the enemy camp and determine the strength and disposition of the foe. They were not to engage. Training his auspex on the assembled force, he picked out assault units and the massive bulks of Terminators, but only a handful of vehicles. He considered the options: this might be a testing force, perhaps, maybe a blunt brigade of heavily armed troops sent in to probe the defences of the planet before a larger attack could begin. For a moment, Rafen wondered about the fate of the ship his company had left in orbit; it was a forgone conclusion that if so large a Traitor force had made planetfall, the skies already belonged to the enemy. He did not dwell on the prospects of what that would mean for them. With a full half of their force dead or crippled in the initial surprise bombardment, the Space Marines were reeling and on the defensive; the momentum of battle was on the side of the foe.

But in the next instant, Rafen's grim train of thought was abruptly stalled. From out of the open hatch of a deformed Razorback transport strode a figure that came a full two heads higher than every other man in the Traitor camp. His armour was chased around its edges with sullen gold plating and traceries of infernal runes that smudged and merged as Rafen's auspex struggled to read them. Wrappings of steel chain ending in flaming, skull-shaped braziers dangled from his arms and waist, while his shoulder plates mounted a fan of necrotic spines that appeared to be venting thin streams of venom into the air. Rafen had seen the champions of the archenemy before and so he was in no doubt that the being he looked upon was the master of the war force at Cybele.

A fragment of memory drifted to the front of Rafen's mind as he watched the tall Word Bearer approach and converse with the torturer. He recalled a snatch of description from the indoctrination lectures of his training, the words of old Koris back when the grizzled veteran was serving as a mentor. The Word Bearers, who forever bore the aberrant mark of Chaos undivided, practised their foul religions under the stewardship of the highest ranked Traitors among their number – and Rafen was sure that the tall one was just such a being. A Dark Apostle, and here, in his sights! The hand around the bolter twitched again and he allowed himself to entertain the idea of killing this bestial adversary, despite the sergeant's orders ringing in his head. Bloodlust rumbled distantly in his ears, the familiar tension of pre-battle humming in his very marrow. With a single shot, he might be able to send the enemy into instant disarray; but were he to fail, their survey would be compromised and his brethren back at the Necropolita would be lost. Reluctantly, he relaxed his grip a little.

In that moment of choice, Rafen's life was almost forfeit. A fierce rune blinked into being on the Space Marine's visor, warning him too late of movement to his flank. With speed that belied the huge weight of his battle armour, Rafen spun on his heel, reversing his grip on the bolter as he did. He came face to face with a Word Bearer, the Chaos Marine's hideous countenance a series of ruined holes and jagged teeth.

'Blood Angel!' it spat, declaring the name like a venomous malediction.

Rafen answered by slamming the butt of his bolter into the Word Bearer's face with savage ferocity, forcing the enemy warrior to stagger back on his heels and into the cover of the vault. He dare not fire the weapon, for the report of a bolt shell would surely bring every Traitor in the camp running, and he knew that none of his other battle-brothers could come to his aid lest they expose themselves. It was of little import, however, Rafen had killed enough warp-spawned filth to be sure that he could murder this heretic with tooth and nail alone if need be. Caught by surprise, he had only heartbeats in which to press his advantage and terminate this abomination – this thing that had polluted the universe since before he was born.

The Word Bearer's hand snapped toward the gun on its waist. Fingers with far too many joints skittered across the scarlet armour. Rafen brought the bolter down again and smashed the hand flat like a pinned spider. The Traitor recovered and swung a mailed, spike-laden fist at Rafen's head; the blow connected with a hollow ring and Rafen heard his ceramite helm crack as fractures appeared on his visor. Letting the gun drop into the oily mud at his feet, the Blood Angel surged forward and locked his gloved hands around the Word Bearer's throat. Had his enemy been helmeted too, Rafen would never have been able to strike back at him this way, but the corrupted fool had thought this place secure enough to show his face to the air. Rafen pressed his fingers into the tough, leathery hide of the Word Bearer's neck, intent on showing him the cost of his folly. Gouts of thick, greasy fluid began to stream from the Traitor's wounds, and it tried in vain to suck air through its windpipe, desperate to scream for help from its brethren.

The spiked glove returned, crashing into his head again and again. Warm blood filled Rafen's mouth as his teeth rattled in his jaw. The Traitor butted him, but the Blood Angel stood firm, the joyous lust of his hate-rage flattening the pain. Rafen's vision fogged with the sweet anticipatory surge of a hand-to-hand kill, as the Traitor's black snake-tongue twitched madly, lapping at breaths it could not draw in. He was dimly aware of the Word Bearer punching and striking at his torso, flailing to inflict some sort of damage on him before he ended its repellent life.

Rafen registered a flashing bone dagger at the edges of his vision, then the sudden bloom of pain on his left thigh; he ignored it and squeezed tighter, compacting the Word Bearer's throat into a ruined tube of bloody meat and broken cartilage. Voiceless and empty, the Traitor Marine died and slipped from his ichor-stained fingers to the ground. Rafen staggered back a step, the thunder of adrenaline making him giddy. As his foot came down, fresh streams of agony surged out of his leg and he saw where the Traitor's tusk blade had cleanly pierced his armour. Shock gel and coagulants bubbled up around the wound, and turned dark as they struggled to combat the after-effects of the cut. Rafen grimaced; the daemon knives of the adversary always carried venom and he did not wish to be cut down by the dying blow of such an unworthy foe.

The Blood Angel gripped the haft of the Chaos blade and he felt it writhe and flex in his grip, quivering like a creature seeking escape. He could feel the movement of bladders inside it, fleshy organs pulsing as they sucked in his blood like a parasite. With a snarl, Rafen tore the serrated weapon from his thigh and held it up before his eyes. The blade was a living thing, each ridge of its saw-tooth edge a yellowed chevron of enamel crested by a tiny black eye spot. It hissed and chattered at Rafen with impotent hate, contorting in on itself. Before the Space Marine could react, the blade puffed up its air sacs and spat out a cloud of his siphoned blood, scattering it in a fine pink vapour.

Rafen broken the thing in two but it was too late: in the enemy encampment, the Word Bearers had stopped what they were doing and were glancing upward, nostrils and tongues taking in the thin stream of scent-taste.

He swore a blistering curse and tossed the dead creature aside, breaking vox silence for the first time in hours. 'Fall back!'

The four Blood Angels erupted from cover, moving as fast as their augmented limbs and power armour would let them; ten times that number of Word Bearers crested the lip of the grove and gave chase, bolters crashing wildly and voices raised in debased exaltation.

IN THE ENCAMPMENT below, Tancred hesitated, the vibra-stave wavering in his hand as he shifted forward to join the pursuit; but then he realised that his master had not moved an inch, and with careful deliberation he relaxed and cocked his head.

Iskavan the Hated, Dark Apostle of the Ninth Host of Garand, let his bloodless lips split in a smile wider than any human orifice was capable of. One of his tube-tongues flickered in and out, sampling the damp air. 'A mewling whelp,' he pronounced at last, rolling the faint flavour of Rafen's spilt blood around his mouth. 'A little over a hundred years, by the taste of him.' He eyed Tancred. 'Perhaps I should be insulted that these mongrels saw fit to send children to spy on us.'

The torturer glanced back at the twisted ruin of flesh that was his handiwork. 'A handful of scouts are hardly worth the effort, magnificence.'

Tancred saw Iskavan nod in agreement from the corner of his eye, and he suppressed a smile. The Word Bearer had risen to the rank of second to the Dark Apostle through a mixture of guile and outright ruthlessness, but much of his skill stemmed from his ability to predict Iskavan's moods and to know exactly what his commander wanted to hear. In four and a half centuries of service, Tancred had only earned his master's displeasure on three occasions, and the most severe of those was marked forever on him where his organic arm had been severed by Iskavan's dagger-toothed bite. The torturer gave his tentacle replacement an absent flex.

'Let the hungry ones hound them back to their verminous hiding place,' said Iskavan, as much to Tancred as it was to the rest of the Word Bearer camp. 'We will join them momentarily.' The Dark Apostle turned the full force of his baleful gaze on the torturer and toyed casually with a barbed horn on his chin. 'I shall not be interrupted before I have completed my sacrament.'

Tancred took this as a cue to continue and beckoned a pair of machine-bound helots forward. Each of the once-men picked up an end of the rack on which Tancred's victim lay. The homunculae moved into the centre of the camp on legs of burping gas pistons, their arms raw iron girders ending in rusty blocks and tackle, rather than flesh and bone. Their burden was moaning weakly but still clinging to the ragged edge of life, thanks to the consummate skill of Tancred's art.

The Word Bearer bent close to the dying slave's head and whispered to him. 'Give,' he husked. 'Give up your love.'

'I do,' the helot managed, between blood-laden gurgles, 'I give my heart and flesh and soul to you, great one.' His teeth appeared in a broken grin, the beatific glaze in his eyes locked on the heavy, dolorous clouds overhead. 'Please, I crave the agony of the boon. Please!' The slave began to weep, and Tancred ran his clawed hand over the man's scarred forehead. The poor wretch was afraid that he would be allowed to die without the exquisite pain of Iskavan's blessing.

'Do not fear,' Tancred cooed. 'You will know torment such as that which Lorgar himself endured.'

'Thank you! Oh, thank you!' The helot coughed and a fat globule of heavy, arterial crimson rolled from his mouth. Tancred resisted the urge to lick at it and turned to bow before his master.

'With your permission, lord Apostle?'

Iskavan wet his lips. 'Bring me my crozius.'

THE BLOOD ANGELS had reinforced the edifice of the Necropólita even as the dust was still settling from the bombardment, toppling stone needles and broad obelisks to serve as makeshift cover. The building had been an ornate combination of Imperial chapel and outpost facility, but now it was in ruins. Its sole occupants, the priest-governor of the planet and his small cohort of caretakers, were among the first to perish when the building's central minaret had been struck. Now for good or ill Cybele was under the complete command of Brother-Captain Simeon, the ranking Marine officer. Crouching atop the corner of the Necropolita that still stood, Simeon was the first to see the enemy approach through the tombstones, and he drew his chainsword with a flourish.

'Sons of Sanguinius!' His voice cut the air like the peal of a cloister bell. 'To arms!'

Below him, where the marble plaza ended and the graveyards began, Brother-Sergeant Koris dug one armoured hand into the fallen stone pillar and pushed himself up to sight toward the foe. He saw Rafen's unit charging and firing, sending controlled bursts of bolter-fire over their shoulders as they closed; behind them was a seething wall of Chaos Marines, a cackling, screaming horde that moved like a swarm of red locusts.

'Brothers on the field! Pick your targets!' he ordered, and to illustrate his point, the seasoned soldier shot the head from a Word Bearer just handspans away from Turcio's back.

Bennek was less fortunate, and Koris growled in anger as the Marine lost his leg from the near miss of a plasma gun. Bennek's armoured form tumbled and dropped, and the Word Bearers rolled over him without stopping.

With a yell of effort, the crimson flash of a Marine leapt over Koris's head and twisted in mid-air, landing perfectly behind the stone barricade. The sergeant turned as Rafen, panting hard, brought up his bolter and laced the air above him with shot; a Traitor who had been snapping at his heels made it halfway over the obelisk before Rafen's shells sent him screaming backward. The air sang with energy and explosion around them as the two sides clashed.

'Damn them, these fiends are on us like desert ticks!'

Koris gave Rafen a brief, sharp grin. 'You brought some company back with you then, eh lad?'

Rafen hesitated. 'I…' Salvos of Traitor gunfire chopped at the dirt near their feet.

'Brother Rafen!' Simeon loped over the pock-marked ground toward them, weaving around the flashes of new impact craters and the keening of lethal ricochets. 'When I told you we needed to study the enemy closely, I did not expect you to take me so literally.' The captain let off a ripping discharge from his bolt pistol, right into the enemy line. 'No matter.'

Koris drew back from the skirmish and let Turcio take his place. 'Speak, lad. What do these warp-spawn have for us out there?' His voice was urgent, carrying over the constant fire.

Rafen gestured to the south. 'An assault group, most likely a reconnaissance in force,' he replied, calmly relaying his report with the same dispassion he would have showed in a training exercise. 'A squad of Terminators and armour, at least three Razorbacks.'

Simeon grimaced. His few tactical Marines with little or no heavy weapons would be hard pressed to hold the line against such a detachment. 'There's more,' he added – a statement, not a question.

Rafen ignored the low hum of a bolt that lanced past his head. 'Indeed. Terra protect me, but I looked upon one of their foul ceremonies, a sacrificial augury. There was a Dark Apostle in the camp to observe it.'

'You're sure?' Koris pressed, the crack of rounds flicking off the tiles around them.

'As the God-Emperor is my witness,' Rafen replied.

Simeon and Koris exchanged glances; this made matters more complicated. 'If one of those arch-traitors has befouled the graves here, then his plans for Cybele are clear.' Simeon loaded a fresh clip into his gun, eyeing the torrid battle line as blood-red and gore-red armour clashed and fought. 'He will seek to erect one of their own blasphemous monuments here and salt the earth with their profane benedictions.'

'It shall not be,' Rafen grated. A heat of fury flooded into him.

'No, it shall not,' Simeon agreed, bearing his fangs. With a roar, he dived into the fray, his chainsword braying as it cored a Word Bearer sending it skittering over the marble. Rafen and Koris waded through the fight with him, weapons flaring.

'Hear me, Blood Angels!' Simeon's voice called. 'In the name of the red grail, turn back this tide–'

The captain's words were cut short as a tiny supernova engulfed him, and wreaths of hot plasma turned the stone to slag around his feet. Rafen had a single, momentary vision of brilliant white, then Simeon's ammunition packs detonated all at once and threw him aside in the shock wave.

ISKAVAN GATHERED UP his most impious symbol of office and cradled it as a parent would a beloved child. The crozius in his hand gave off an actinic glow that surged as his fingers wrapped around it. The weapon sighed, pleased that its master was near, excited by the prospect of what was to come next. Murmuring a litany of un-blessing beneath his breath, the Dark Apostle dipped the disk of blades at the staff's head into the catch-bucket beneath Tancred's torture rack. He stirred the thick, fresh blood. The liquid flashed into steam, boiling around the accursed weapon.

'From the fires of betrayal,' Iskavan droned. 'Unto the blood of revenge.'

Tancred raised the vibra-stave over the helot's body, so he could see that death was upon him. 'By the bearer of the word, the favoured son of Chaos.' The torturer plunged the stave into the slave's stomach and tore it open, savouring the screams.

The Word Bearers standing watch around them spoke as one voice. 'All praise be given unto him.'

Iskavan held up his soaked crozius to the grey sky, the ritual of desecration repeated once again as it had been on countless worlds, before countless victories. He glanced at Tancred, who hunched over the spilt innards of the sacrifice. 'What do you see?'

It took the most supreme effort of Tancred's life to lie to his master. 'Death comes. Lorgar's sight is upon us.' The words were almost choking him. 'We shall feed the hunger of the gods.'

His black heart shrinking in his chest, Tancred stared at the entrails before him in fear and dismay. The loops of fallen intestine, the spatters of blood, the placing of the organs – the configuration was terrible and ominous. There, he saw the signs of something impossibly powerful rising into life, a coming force so strong that it dwarfed Tancred and his master. The play of light and shadow was confused, and so the torturer could not be sure from where this energy would emerge, but he could see clearly that it would bring ruin and destruction in its wake. At last, he managed to tear himself away from the sight, his final reading bringing a disturbing prediction to bear. Both he and Iskavan would not live to see the end of the events they would set in motion on this day.

The Dark Apostle met his gaze and something like suspicion danced there. 'Is that *all* you see, Tancred?'

The words pushed at the torturer's decaying lips, fighting to be heard, but he knew with blind certainty that such a fatalist divination would enrage Iskavan, to the degree that Tancred would be first to taste the freshly-blooded crozius's power. He looked down in what he hoped would seem like reverence, praying to the gods that he be spared his master's displeasure. 'I see death, lord.'

'Good.' Iskavan chained his twitching, eager weapon to his wrist. 'Let us take the word to our adversary, and see them heed it… Or perish.'

The Chaos Marines whooped and yelled black hymnals and mantras as the battle force rolled forward and amid them all, Tancred picked at his newborn fears like a scabbed wound.

SIMEON'S VIOLENT END tolled around the perimeter like a death knell; it was felt almost as a physical shock by the Blood Angels ranged about the Necropolita's edge. The hero of Virgon VII, victor at the Thaxted Insurrection and decorated warrior of the Alchonis Campaign, was gone, swept away. The brother-captain was honoured and respected by every Marine in the Chapter, and in the centuries they had fought alongside him, each one of them could trace a debt of life to the bold officer. Rafen himself had almost been killed on Ixion by a mole-mine that Simeon had spotted a moment before it emerged. And now, as the Blood Angel considered the patch of scorched ground that marked the spot where the captain had died, he found the memory of that moment slipping away from him, as if it too had been lost in the plasma burst.

Koris was the ranking officer now, and the craggy old warhound seemed determined to cut a blood cost for the captain's death from each and every Word Bearer. But Rafen knew the veteran better than most of the Marines there, and he saw the signs of distress on his former teacher that others did not.

For all of Koris's encouragement and rousing, Simeon's sudden killing had dealt their morale a fatal blow, and the will of the remaining men lay wounded, bleeding out into the grass.

Rafen saw the surge in the enemy line as the rest of the Word Bearers' force joined the fight, and in that moment, he was certain they would die here. Unhallowed lighting flashed in the distance from a blazing force weapon, and the Traitors roared with approval. They drew back, a ruby tide retreating from the land's edge before returning as a flood. And then on they came, killing and ripping Rafen's comrades into fleshy shreds. His gun clattered, the barrel spitting hot as rounds big as fists tore into the foe – but then a sound, a heart-stopping shriek of sundered air, fell across the battlefield.

Rafen instinctively looked up, and felt ice in the pit of his stomachs. Swooping in through the low cloud by the dozen were bright red Thunderhawk drop-ships, each one bristling with missile and cannon, each one heavy with more Marines to feed the fray. Half-glimpsed in the contrails and gunsmoke, the flyers looped over the enemy and turned.

'We are lost,' said Turcio, as if the words were his dying breath. 'With such reinforcements, we will be drowned in a sea of corrupted ones.'

'Then we'll litter this place with their dead before we do…' Rafen's voice tailed off as the Thunderhawks opened fire as one, and bright spears of light lanced from their lascannon. But the shots never reached them. The beams fell short of the Marines and struck the middle of the Word Bearers' force with devastating effect, killing a unit of Chaos Terminators in one blaze of fire. Now the other flyers released packs of hellstreak warheads, which tore into the Traitors with furious abandon.

Rafen's eyes widened as the leading drop-ship cut the sky above him, and in a blink of crimson he saw the sigils painted on the aircraft: a pair of silver angel's wings, adorned with a shimmering teardrop of blood. As the Emperor willed it, so the Blood Angels had been delivered from the jaws of oblivion by their battle-brothers.

The story continues in
BLOOD ANGELS:
DEUS ENCARMINE
by James Swallow

Available from the Black Library
www.blacklibrary.com

READ TILL YOU BLEED
DO YOU HAVE THEM ALL?

WWW.BLACKLIBRARY.COM

Coming Soon!

INFERNO!™

Inferno! is the Black Library's high-octane fiction magazine, which throws you headlong into the worlds of Warhammer. From the dark, orc-infested forests of the Old World to the grim battlefields of the war-torn far future, Inferno! magazine is packed with storming tales of heroism and carnage.

Featuring work by awesome writers such as:

- **DAN ABNETT**
- **BEN COUNTER**
- **WILLIAM KING**
- **GRAHAM MCNEILL**
- **C S GOTO**

and lots more!

Published every two months, Inferno! magazine brings the grim worlds of Warhammer to life.